The One Forever Promise

THE CALIFORNIANS

The One Forever Promise

SEAN DONOVAN

DONOVAN'S DAUGHTER

TWO BESTSELLING NOVELS COMPLETE IN ONE VOLUME

LORI WICK

First Inspirational Press edition published in 1999.

Inspirational Press
A division of BBS Publishing Corporation
386 Park Avenue South
New York, NY 10016

Inspirational Press is a registered trademark of BBS Publishing Corporation.

Published by arrangement with Harvest House Publishers.

Library of Congress Catalog Card Number: 99-71866

ISBN: 0-88486-247-X

Printed in the United States of America.

Contents

Book I

Sean Donovan

This book is dedicated to my nephews,
Derek Kolstad, Angus Wick, Bob Kolstad,
Billy Wick, and John Wm. Wick.
I pray that you will know God intimately,
and serve Him with your whole heart.

Visalia Families–1876

Sean Donovan

Charlotte Cooper (Charlie)
Sadie Cox (Charlie's Aunt)

Sheriff Lucas Duncan
Wife—Lora

Santa Rosa Families–1876

The Marshall Riggs Family
Wife—Kaitlin Donovan Riggs
Children—Gretchen
Molly
Extended Family—Marcail Donovan

The William Taylor Family
Wife—Mable (May)
Children—Gilbert

The Jeffrey Taylor Family
Wife—Roberta (Bobbie)
Children—Cleo
Sutton

The Nathan Taylor Family
Wife—Brenda
Children—William (Willy)

One

Santa Rosa, California— May 1874

"THAT'LL BE IT for the night, Sean. Close up the back and head home."

The brooding young man nodded but did not speak. It was on the tip of his tongue to tell the livery owner that he would go home if and when he felt like it, but that remark would probably cost him his job, and that was something he could not afford if he was ever going to get out of this town.

Carefully hiding his anger, Sean Donovan closed the rear doors of the livery with little more than a glance in the direction of his employer. He didn't speak or bid his boss goodnight, even as he made his way to the front door and out into the street. Dozens of other Santa Rosa residents were closing up shop and heading home. Many knew Sean by sight if not by name, but he chose to meet no one's gaze nor even return their greetings.

His sister's house loomed before him long before he was ready to face his family. He hesitated in the street for several minutes, hoping he could get upstairs to his bedroom without being noticed.

"Sean?" His sister called as soon as the front door opened, and Sean worked to conceal the anger he felt.

"Hi, Sean." A very pregnant Kaitlin Riggs came from the direction of the kitchen, her voice as sweet and kind as her spirit, but it was totally lost on Sean. "How was work?"

"Fine," he replied sullenly, and Katie found herself fighting to keep her own feelings from showing. All they did lately was quar-

13

rel, and Kate did not feel up to an argument tonight. She couldn't help asking herself, however, how long was he going to stay angry? How long were she and the family going to be made to suffer for something their father had done?

"Supper is nearly ready. Why don't you wash up?"

Sean turned to the stairs without answering her, walking straight past his younger sister, Marcail, without even acknowledging her.

Marcail and Kaitlin exchanged a look, but knew that more words wouldn't change anything. When they entered the kitchen together a moment later, Kate's husband was coming in the back door. Marshall Riggs, "Rigg" to everyone, pulled his wife close and kissed her. He then went to his sister-in-law to embrace her and kiss the top of her dark head.

"Where's Gretchen?" Rigg asked after his daughter, who was not quite two years old.

"She's playing on our bed," Katie answered him.

Rigg went in the direction of the bedroom, tossing the question over his shoulder as he went, "Did Sean get home?"

Kate answered softly, "He's here, Rigg. I can tell he doesn't want to be, but he's here."

Sean lay on his bed waiting for his sister's call to supper. He didn't care to join the family any earlier than necessary. In fact, if Kate would let him, he'd eat alone in his room. No one in this house understood him. He hated school and he hated work. Their answer for everything was "trust in God." Well, he'd tried trusting in God, at least trusting Him to give the things he wanted most, but it never brought him anything more than pain and confusion.

With these restless thoughts, Sean stayed on the bed for only a few moments. Rolling to the edge of the mattress and standing in one move, he went straight to the dresser, opened the top drawer, and removed a wooden box. He counted the money within, knowing the exact amount but somehow hoping it had increased from when he had counted it the night before.

"Still not enough," Sean whispered, rage boiling within him as he replaced the box. "Still not enough to get away from here." Again his voice was whisper soft, but this time it held a hint of desperation.

He stood for some time trying to calm down, knowing that if Kate called now he would be too angry to join the family for supper and they would want to know why. Suddenly the door opened. Sean turned with a furious word for the intruder, but what he was going to say died in his throat at the sight of his niece Gretchen. She stood on the threshold, an adorable smile lighting her face.

For the first time that day, some of Sean's fury drained away. He held his arms out toward the beloved little girl and smiled as she threw herself at him. With her small arms circling his neck, she chatted up into his face. Sean, very much enamored with this child, gave her his full attention. They were still talking when Rigg's voice sounded from the bottom of the stairs.

"Gretchen, did you tell Uncle Sean that supper is ready?"

Gretchen, with a little hand to her surprised mouth, delivered the forgotten message, and the two of them made their way downstairs. Sean's face, all smiles for Gretchen, was now shuttered as the family gathered around the table. He did not close his eyes or even bow his head for the prayer.

Everyone save Sean talked with familiar ease throughout the meal. In the past Sean's silence had been oppressive and even intimidated the family, but now they had learned to live around it. Rigg, never intimidated by anyone, talked to his young brother-in-law as though nothing was out of the ordinary, including telling him to help with the dishes at the end of the meal. Rigg ignored the black scowl Sean sent in his direction.

"Do you want to wash or dry?" Rigg asked casually when the girls had emptied out of the room.

"I don't want to do either. Why can't Marc do—"

"That's enough, Sean," Rigg said easily. "She takes your turn more often than she should. And," Rigg spoke quickly when Sean opened his mouth yet again, "if you dare suggest that Kate come back in here, I'll flatten you. She could have the baby any time now and I don't—"

"Any time?" Sean's voice was incredulous. "I thought she was due in June."

"Sean," Rigg's voice was long-suffering. "There are only three days left in May. The doctor told Katie yesterday that it could be any time." Rigg wanted to add that if Sean would get his head out of his angry cloud and think about someone else for a change, he might have noticed how large and uncomfortable his sister had become.

Rigg would have been surprised to know that such words were unnecessary. Sean was giving himself the same speech. Unfortunately, he didn't believe his attitude to be his own fault; his father was to blame. If his father had kept just one of his promises, Sean believed he'd feel differently, but it was easier to blame his father than himself, and easier still to hide his pain behind a mask of fury.

The next evening, just after supper, Kate announced that they had received a letter from Father. Patrick Donovan, father to Kaitlin, Sean, and Marcail, was a missionary in the Hawaiian Islands. He'd been away and promising to come and see them for several years. Katie and Marcail had both suffered with his absence, but not to the same degree as Sean. When their mother had died just before Patrick left, Marcail and Kaitlin had clung to each other. But Sean, try as he might to fit in, had felt completely on his own.

"He says," Katie began, "that it looks like he'll be getting away in a few months. I'll read that part. 'I know I've said this before, but I'm sure I'll be able to break away from here and be with you by midsummer.'"

Kate fell silent then, praying that this time it would be true. So often he'd tried to come, but something always interfered. They were all beginning to believe that they would never see this man again; Sean was *hoping* he would never see his father again. Rigg, closely watching Sean's face, realized with a start that Sean actually wanted to avoid his father. That night in bed, the house quiet, Rigg said as much to Katie.

"I can't believe that, Rigg," Kate spoke in protest. "Sean has missed Father more than any of us. Seeing him again has been all he's living for."

"I understand what you're saying, Kate, but think about how betrayed he feels. You can feel his anger the moment he steps into the room. I don't want to upset you, but I thought you should be warned."

In the dim lantern light, Kate studied Rigg's face. "What are you *not* telling me," she finally asked.

"You might disagree with me, Kate, but I think he's trying to gain the courage to leave here. I think if he had the money, he'd walk away from Santa Rosa right now."

Kate's eyes grew to the size of saucers. "He has a box of money in the top drawer of his dresser," she whispered, as though afraid of being overheard. "I came across it by mistake just yesterday when I was putting his clothes away. The lid flipped up, and I saw what was inside. I closed the drawer right away, so I don't know how much there was, but—"

"Shhh," Rigg hushed her as she began to cry, his arms moving to surround her swollen frame. "It's all right, Kate. You didn't intrude. As hard as it seems, it just might need to be this way."

"Rigg, he's not ready to be out on his own," she sobbed.

"I realize that, but as you've said many times, he might need to go through more pain before he sees that God has been in control from the very start."

Kate was out of words then, as she cried and prayed into her husband's chest. Rigg held her until he fell asleep, only to be awakened once again, several hours later, with Kate telling him that he should probably go for the doctor.

Two

THE NEXT AFTERNOON Sean sat in his sister's room and held his niece Molly. She was a tiny dark-haired bundle, ten hours old and looking just like Gretchen had at that age. His sister was resting in the bed, and Sean was unaware of her scrutiny.

Help him turn to you, Heavenly Father, Kate prayed silently. *Help him see that running will do no good. If it be Your will, use this precious baby to soften him, to show him that you are a God of love and tenderness, especially when we hurt.*

Rigg entered the room then, and Sean's attention was drawn away from the sleeping infant. He surprised both parents with a compliment, something he hadn't given in ages.

"I don't know how you do it, Katie, being married to a great hairy beast like Rigg, but Molly is a beauty."

"Beauty runs in my family," Rigg told him, his voice amused.

Sean snorted in disgust and startled the babe in his arms. Kate watched in fascination as he spoke to Molly in soothing tones and held her even closer to his chest. Husband and wife exchanged a glance after witnessing this tender act, their hearts praying for the same thing.

The next two weeks were nearly idyllic in Kate's estimation. Molly was a good baby, and Sean was as civil as she'd seen him in months. He was also very helpful and unashamedly in love with his new niece. He played with Gretchen every spare minute and appeared to be making an effort to once again join the family. All of

18

this changed abruptly, however, when a letter came from Aunt Maureen in San Francisco.

She was bubbling over with excitement over Patrick's promised arrival, really believing that this time he would come. Kate read the letter to everyone after supper, and both she and Rigg took note of how tense Sean became, how shuttered his features.

They talked that night and decided not to confront Sean, but to keep their eyes open for a while and pray for an opportunity to speak with him.

But no such opportunity arose. Rigg was at work, Marcail was at school, and Kate was with the girls at Grandma Taylor's house the day Sean wrote a brief note, left it in his room, and walked to the other side of town to catch a stage headed south. What never occurred to Sean was that his actions were exactly like those of the man he told his heart he most hated.

Maureen Lawton Kent, sister to Patrick Donovan, stood in her library trying to calm the frantic beating of her heart. Her nephew Sean was upstairs in one of the bedrooms, and she knew he would be coming back down for supper at any moment. She wondered how swiftly she could get word to Kaitlin and the family, somehow certain that none of them knew where Sean was. The thought had barely formulated when the subject of Maureen's thoughts appeared in the door.

Sean's appearance surprised her. He'd filled out even more from when she had seen him at Christmas, losing almost all of his boyish looks in the process. His brows were low over his unsmiling eyes, and his mouth, even when he spoke, was set in a grim line.

"Oh there you are." Maureen hated how breathless she sounded. "Are you ready for supper?"

Sean nodded and followed his aunt to the table. For the most part, the meal was silent and tense. Sean was starting to regret his decision to come here; in fact, he was starting to regret his decision to leave Santa Rosa. He knew he would have to force his family's faces from his mind or there would be more tears. Sean's anger rushed in and rescued him. There had been tears on the stage and then again in the room upstairs, but no more, he told himself.

Maureen, who was watching some of the emotions cross her nephew's face, quite frankly did not know what to say. He'd become a stranger since they were last together. By the time coffee was served she had gained some courage, telling herself that if he felt free enough to come here and live, then she was within her rights to ask a few questions.

"Sean," she began tentatively, "does your family know you're here?"

"No." He answered without looking at her.

"Won't they be worried?"

Sean shrugged. "I left a note saying I was leaving town. They'll have to be satisfied with that." It caused Sean more pain to say that than he let on, but Maureen was so surprised at his anger that she did not notice. In the face of that ire, some of her courage deserted her. A moment passed before she summoned a falsely cheerful voice and went on.

"Are you going to be looking for work?" Maureen's grown son, Percy, had lived off her income for years, so she did not take for granted that Sean would look for work.

"Not here. I don't like the weather." Sean said the first thing that came to mind, not wanting to admit that San Francisco was too close to Santa Rosa.

Maureen nearly panicked over his words. It never once occurred to her that he was just stopping off on his way through; in fact, she had a faint hope that he had come here because this was where his father's ship would be docking.

"Aren't you worried about missing your father's visit?"

Her question was met with a cold stare, and Maureen, so surprised at how far off her guesses had been, subsided into silence. Not many minutes passed before Sean took himself off to bed. In the hours before she went to bed herself, Maureen had a one-sided conversation with her absent brother. She told him in no uncertain terms that he should have come home ages ago, that letters had not been enough, and that his family needed him.

Maureen was utterly drained by the time she retired. Knowing how hard it would be to get to sleep, she tried to put her worries aside by telling herself that Sean might be more congenial in the morning. This was her last thought as sleep crowded in to claim her, but her hope was not to be realized. In the morning, Sean Donovan was gone.

Three

SEAN HAD LIED about not liking San Francisco's cool temperatures in order to get away, but as he bent over another row of cotton in the hot Fresno sun, he found himself wishing he'd stayed a little longer. Never had he lived and worked in such high temperatures. Most of the other workers around him were shorter and for the first time, Sean envied them their small size. He had been picking crops for two weeks, and his back was still screaming at him.

He paused to wipe the sweat from his face and saw the very pregnant woman working next to him bending over the row with difficulty. She lost her balance, and Sean reached for her, taking her arm until she was once again steady on her feet. The smile she gave him was tired and sweet, and Sean hurriedly bent his head.

The sight of her and that fatigued smile caused him to think of Kaitlin just months before he left, and then of Molly just an infant when his stage left town. Sean suddenly felt like his emotions would choke him.

You've left, Sean, he said to himself, *and by now, they don't want you back. Even if they did, you don't want to go.* Convinced of this, he pushed the sight of Gretchen and Molly from his mind. They were the last things he needed to be dwelling on right now.

"I wonder if *Father* made it home," Sean muttered to himself, bringing his anger to a head as he again bent his back.

Routine began to develop, and by the time Sean had been on the job for two months, he had made a few friends. Most of his co-

21

workers were family men, but a few were single, and these were the men who took their pay to the bar as soon as it was placed in their hands.

Sean had never been in a bar, but he found the one in Fresno to be a place where he fit in. He never drank enough to become drunk, but the way he was left alone to sit in peace with his friends was just what he needed, or so he told himself. It was on one of these occasions that his co-workers told him he was in the wrong business.

"What are you talking about?" Sean frowned at them. He had been something of a mystery to them, but one night they'd coaxed his age out of him and realized he was just a kid with a chip on his shoulder. They grinned in his direction as they answered.

"Do you think we would be out picking crops if we were your size? Look at that guy at the end of the bar. You're bigger than he is, yet you're out there sweating in the sun with us."

"And probably getting paid a whole lot less for your effort," another man contributed, and the group roared with laughter. Sean didn't laugh; he was already moving down the long counter toward the end of the bar.

"What'll it be?" The bartender spoke without preamble.

"A job," Sean flicked his head in the direction of the strong-arm. "Any chance you're thinking of a change?"

The bartender was quick on the upswing, his eyes taking in the breadth of Sean's chest. He only smiled and shook his head no.

"I like Bear. He's not very bright, but he's reliable." Sean frowned and the man went on. "I'll tell you what I'll do, though. My brother owns a place in Selma, bigger than this, with a stage and girls and all. How old are you?"

"Old enough," was Sean's answer, and the smaller man behind the counter didn't press him.

"I'm sure you'll do. Head south a bit, downtown Selma. The place is called Buck's. Ask for either Buck, that's my brother, or his partner, Sal. They'll do right by you."

Sean's co-workers were ecstatic when he relayed the conversation, and for once Sean's face was not void of expression. He stayed long in the bar that night, laughing and talking with his friends in a kind of farewell celebration. Leaving just a few hours before dawn to return to the shabbiest hotel in town, he packed his few things and lay on the bed waiting for the sun to rise. When it did, Sean was up, shaved, and waiting for the stage that would yet again take him south.

Four months later Sean, now eighteen years old and dressed in immaculate dark slacks, a snow white shirt, and dark tie, kept his eyes on his boss's profile. The men at the corner table were quickly growing out of hand, and Sean knew that any moment he would be called in. A woman came by, heavily made up, and seductively ran her hand across Sean's chest. As usual, he barely took notice of her.

Buck's head turned a moment later, and Sean went into action. He was only one of three bouncers in this posh establishment, and their movements were never to be hurried or ungainly. With natural grace Sean and one other man moved toward the rear. And with far less noise or action than one would have dreamed possible, the two troublemakers were extracted from the game and *shown* into the alley.

The show started moments later. Sean stood at one corner of the stage, his eyes constantly scanning the room for trouble. Tonight's crowd was raucous, but no one was out of control. At closing Sean made his way upstairs to his room with only the faintest feeling of dissatisfaction. He realized as he climbed into bed that he'd been spoiling for more of a fight. The men they'd taken into the alley had gone much too willingly.

He lay in the beautiful room he called his own and listened to the hotel bar grow quiet. Someone knocked on his door, but Sean didn't answer. It would only be one of the girls, asking if he'd changed his mind about joining her in her room. The answer was always no, and Sean had started ignoring the questions altogether.

They believed he thought himself too good for them, but that wasn't the case. In truth, Sean wasn't sure what held him back. He never hesitated to gamble or drink in the worldly environment in which he lived. His hesitance might have had to do with the fact that every time he was tempted, he saw his mother's face. She died when he was 14, but he could still hear her voice telling him when he was just 12 that saving himself for marriage must be a priority. "You'll never regret it, Sean, but if you don't wait, I can make you no such promise."

As usual, Sean didn't care for the direction of his own thoughts. Determined to sleep, he rolled to his side, shifting his thoughts to the stage downstairs with its heavy gold curtain and velvet trim. The name "Buck's" had given Sean an image of a rough-and-tumble bar, but Buck's was more than a bar; it was a hotel, and a classy one at that.

Sean fell asleep telling himself that for the past three years he had been working too hard. This was the life he was meant to lead. This was where he belonged.

"I'm telling you, I don't like him," Sal told his partner

"He's a good worker," Buck reasoned.

"He's too sure of himself," Sal went on. "I don't trust him."

Buck only sighed. He liked Sean Donovan, but Sal had never been comfortable with their new bouncer. Sal had wanted to fire him on several occasions when there was really no reason, but Buck had always forestalled him Sean was the first strong-arm they hadn't had to teach to use a fork. Sean had class. Where he came from, and how he came to be working in a bar, Buck didn't care. All he knew was that Sean worked hard and made the place look good with his broad build, black curly hair, and dark compelling eyes. He didn't smile much, but he was always polite to the patrons, and Buck's clientele was his main concern.

"He stays," Buck said with finality. Sal, knowing he was needed on the floor, let the matter drop. He hoped though, that something would happen to give him a reason to sack Sean Donovan, one that not even Buck could dispute.

Two months later, Sean was once again in the mood for trouble. These feelings did not come on very often, but when thoughts of his past plagued him, he felt mean. On this particular day, he had thought of nothing but Marcail. She would be 13 by now and, with her dark hair and large expressive eyes, probably leading the boys on a merry chase.

"Rigg better be taking care of her," Sean said into the mirror as he tied his tie. He suddenly shook his head. All of this because one of the new show girls had smiled at him, a smile so sweet and young that Sean had been stunned. Marcail's face had immediately swum into view, invading his thoughts to a ridiculous degree so that by the time he went on duty, his temper was at its worst.

Early in the evening, a fight broke out. It seemed completely routine to all involved, but in his present mood, Sean was a bit too rough. Before anyone could guess what was about to happen, the man Sean had by the arm, threw a punch, and missed. Sean, trained to ignore such things, flattened the man. Within seconds several tables full of men were in a fight, and before a minute had passed, half the place was in an uproar.

Sal was thrilled with everything but the damage. Buck could see it was a losing battle this time: Sean would have to go. What neither Buck nor Sal understood at first was that it would have happened anyway. The first man Sean hit had been the sheriff's brother. Within the space of 12 hours, Sean was on yet another stage headed out of town.

Four

SEAN HAD NOT liked the look of the livery owner from the day they met, but he'd given him work and at the time that was all he wanted. The repairs at Buck's had nearly cleaned him out, and Sean knew that his money was not going to last long.

Sean came to Tulare thinking to find more work in a bar, but the owner of the place he tried had not been interested. It went against Sean's grain to be doing manual labor once again, but the future need for food and lodging had been at the back of his mind, and he had relented. That had been over two weeks ago, and Sean had yet to see a dime of his earnings.

In truth Sean enjoyed livery work, but he was still angry over the way he'd been treated at Buck's, and wouldn't have admitted this to anyone. Right now he was down to his last few coins and decided that today he would collect his pay. He dropped what he was doing, a sudden premonition coming on him, and went right then to seek out his boss.

"Get back to work." The obese, bald man spoke from a chair by the door.

"When do I get paid?"

"You haven't worked here long enough."

"I've been here two weeks," Sean's voice dropped to a dangerous note, but the fat man took no notice.

The big man laughed. "Come back when it's been a month."

25

"I'll take my pay now."

The man only laughed harder, now looking at Sean's flushed face. "You're a fool," the man chortled. "It wouldn't matter when you came, I don't have the money. The wife takes every dime." The man found this highly amusing and laughed as though he hadn't a care in the world.

Sean was furious. He started toward the man, intending to beat the money out of him, but a gun appeared in the livery owner's hand. Sean kept coming. It took a moment for the fat man to see that this time his scheme was not going to work. He scrambled to his feet, fear making him clumsy. Sean had the man backed into a stall when a voice interrupted him.

"Is there some problem?"

The voice stopped Sean's movement, but he didn't turn to see the man standing just inside the door.

"We're closed," Sean barked over one shoulder.

"Put the gun down, Pinky." The voice spoke again, not at all intimidated by Sean's anger. "Have you been cheating someone again, Pinky?"

This time the voice captured Sean's attention. He turned to find a small man dressed in a well-cut suit regarding him with an almost gentle smile. At the same time, the fat man, now behind Sean, began to babble.

"It's not my fault, Hartley. You know what she's like. I should send this guy over there and let him beat it out of her." The man sounded on the verge of tears, and Sean's face showed his disgust.

Without a word to either man, he strode to the back, picked up his jacket, and went out the door. In his anger it took some minutes for him to realize that someone was calling his name. He stopped and turned. Once again the small man, Hartley had been his name, was smiling at him and approaching with bold confidence.

"I'm sorry about what happened in there. Pinky is a disreputable worm, but compared to his wife he's an angel."

Sean had stayed silent through this recital, and Hartley spoke as though he'd suddenly remembered his manners.

"Where is my head," he said when he saw no answering smile in the younger man's eyes. "I'm Hartley. Pinky told me your name is Sean."

Sean stared for a moment at the offered hand but finally gave his own. "Sean Donovan."

He turned in the direction of his lodgings, and Hartley, with practiced ease, fell in step beside him.

"I'm not sure what your plans are for the rest of the day, Sean, but if you haven't a previous engagement, I'd like to take you to supper."

"Why?" Sean answered, stopping again and scrutinizing Hartley with eyes hard as flint.

"I have a business proposition for you."

Sean weighed this carefully, trying to gauge the man's honesty. His first thought was that the man was not the least bit honest, but there was something fascinating about him, and in a moment Sean found himself agreeing.

In an hour he had cleaned up and was walking through the door of the best hotel in town. Sean and Hartley were shown to a table as though they were royalty, and after Hartley ordered for them, he turned to Sean, again sporting that gentle smile.

"I will admit to you straight away, Sean, that I sought you out because of your size. You see, I'm in need of a personal bodyguard, and I think you might be the man."

Sean was quiet, and Hartley was relieved that he didn't ask what became of his last one. Hartley knew it would do nothing for his position if he had to admit that his last "bodyguard" died while they'd been robbing a bank. He was quite certain that Sean would eventually join him in his robberies, but now was not the time to go into that.

"What do you do for a living?"

"I'm in finance," Hartley told him smoothly. "There are times when I'm required to carry large sums of cash. I'm certain that having a man of presence with me will deter even the most persistent pursuers. Tell me, Sean, can you fire a gun?"

"No." Sean hated to answer because he suddenly wanted this job. This man, the way he was dressed, and the way he carried himself reminded him of Buck's, and Sean missed the class and excitement of that place.

"Well, no matter," Hartley assured him. "I can teach you."

Long before the meal ended, Sean's head was swimming with all that Hartley promised. For the last several weeks it seemed his luck had been bad, but now as he crossed the street with Hartley to a fancy bar, not as a worker but as a patron, Sean believed his luck had finally turned around.

A sudden noise outside the door had Sean on his feet. Listening intently, he reached silently for his gun and made his way out to the living room. Not having bothered to dress, he eased the door open to the hall, but found the passageway outside their suite of rooms empty. He closed the door again, and went back to bed, telling himself he was taking his job too seriously.

It had been six weeks now since he had met Hartley, and never had he lived in such luxury. A niggling irritation that he wasn't doing much to earn his keep popped up in the back of his mind, but Sean effectively pushed it away. He now knew what Hartley was, and had to force himself to push that thought away as well.

He had always hated stealing, and even though he'd been well on the way to getting drunk, Hartley's news about being a professional thief had come very close to sobering him. That had been just two weeks ago, and Sean could see now how very carefully he'd been maneuvered. At first he'd been furious, but Hartley was as smooth as they came, and Sean had never lived as he was living now.

Meals were delivered, beds were made, his clothes, finer than those at Buck's, were always kept washed and pressed—he had everything but the red carpet. It didn't even seem to matter that Sean was a bodyguard and not the man with the money; he was treated like a king.

The job had very few drawbacks—none at all, if Sean could keep his conscience silenced. It wasn't the easiest thing when Hartley would get roaring drunk and pass out, leaving Sean to put him to bed. And it was harder still when Hartley brought girls up to his room, only to have them wait until Hartley was asleep before they paid a visit to Sean. He never let them stay, but there were times when he wondered why.

Sean convinced himself that on the whole, it was a good life. It even included travel. Hartley had informed him just the day before that they would be leaving Tulare today. He hadn't said exactly where they were going, and almost before Sean could question him, he found himself on horseback, following his employer out of town.

The weeks to follow were spent in a dusty haze. Gone were the fancy hotel rooms and room service.

When Sean finally questioned his employer, Hartley responded, "It's time to go back to work."

Sean wondered at his own stupidity in thinking the luxury would last forever. They could only live high until the money ran out, and then Hartley was back at his thieving game. He didn't care from whom he stole, just so long as the victim was outside of Tulare. They rode into some towns in the dead of night, and Sean knew if he'd been questioned he would not have been able to tell anyone where he had been.

He also realized with sobering clarity that even though he was not a part of the robberies, his presence made him an accessory. There were times when he asked himself why he stayed, especially when he stood waiting in dark alleys and back streets for Hartley to appear. It never took more than a few minutes to remind himself, however, that he had been the one to walk away from Santa Rosa and his family. With that in mind and convincing himself they wanted nothing more to do with him, he knew he had no place else to go. He stayed on.

Weeks passed. Thanksgiving came and went and still they were on the road. Christmas passed, as did Sean's nineteenth birthday, with little or no notice. Finally, after an especially profitable night, Hartley stole some supplies, loaded them on Sean's horse, sat a comely barmaid he'd been taken with onto his own mount and headed them up into the foothills outside of Visalia.

When Sean woke, fully dressed and in an unmade bed, he realized how long and exhausting their mid-night ride had been. Once again he had no idea where he was. He emerged from his bedroom to a spacious, if rundown cabin. The view out the dirty windows was glorious, and not bothering to close the door behind him, Sean went outside. Beauty notwithstanding, Sean was already feeling restless, and was glad when Hartley joined him.

"You're up early," the smaller man commented as he rolled and lit a cigarette.

"What are we doing here?" Sean came directly to the point.

"It is necessary, Sean, to lay low for a time. I have a few more jobs to do, but they will take some planning."

"I don't care to be stuck up here with nothing to do."

"But there is plenty to do. There is money to count, food to eat, beds to sleep in, and of course, there is Anita."

Sean gave him a blank look. "No, thank you."

Hartley had been looking forward to a rest, but he could see that Sean was not going to stand for it. He was a little surprised to find that he liked Sean enough to alter his plans. Sean was one of the best men he'd ever ridden with; his sharp eyes and usually calm ways were a valuable asset. There was much about him that remained a mystery, but Hartley was sure they'd be together for a long time, plenty of time to someday learn it all.

Hartley returned to the cabin without a word, and told Anita to start breakfast. Sean, telling himself to relax, let the matter drop for the time. Just 24 hours later he was calling himself a fool for doing so. He woke and found that Hartley had ridden out, leaving him and Anita alone.

Five

SEAN WAS IN a tower rage as he packed his saddlebags and gear. He hoped to never see Hartley again, because if he did, he was going to strangle him. The woman at the house watched in surprise as he took supplies from the kitchen, leaving disaster in his wake. She then watched from the front door as he rode away from the cabin without a word. Had Sean cared to put his emotions aside, he'd have noticed her calm, and understood that Hartley hadn't left for good, and was, in fact, planning to return as soon as possible.

As it was, Sean returned also. Try as he might, he could not find his way out of the hills. It seemed that each trail he found became impassable within several miles of the cabin. Angry and frustrated, he returned late at night, now wishing Hartley was on hand so he could choke the life out of the man. He dropped on his bed, fully clothed and asking himself how he'd come to be in this place. At last he fell into a restless sleep.

In the morning Sean's mood had not improved. Anita had put some breakfast on the table, but was nowhere to be found. This was fine with Sean, who sat down and ate like he'd not had a meal in weeks, still asking himself why he'd let himself be suckered in by Hartley.

Having lost his razor, he hadn't shaved since they'd left Tulare, but that didn't stop him from wanting to be clean. "I can hardly stand myself," he grumbled as he stripped to the waist after his meal and scrubbed up at the basin that stood next to the cabin's only door.

He was just finishing his wash, changing into the last of his clean clothes, when two riders came into the yard, Hartley and another man. Sean was out the door and reaching for Hartley before he cold dismount. He yanked the smaller man from the saddle and held him in the air by the front of his vest.

"I will not be toyed with," his voice sent a chill down Hartley's spine, and he actually smelled fear, thinking Sean was about to kill him. "I am not your slave. Now you can get back in that saddle and lead me out of these hills, or I'm going to put a bullet through you."

Sean dropped a gasping Hartley in a heap at his feet and strode back into the house to collect his gear. Hartley followed, and for the first time Sean saw him lose his perfect composure.

"I'm sorry, Sean. Listen to me," the older man begged. "I never dreamed you wouldn't know I was coming back. I left Anita. Didn't she tell you we needed another man? I didn't think you'd want to come. Honestly, Sean, I was just thinking of you. You're my partner, Sean—I wouldn't do anything to hurt you."

This last sentence was the only one to arrest Sean's attention. Hartley had never called him a partner before, and for some reason the word had a claming effect on him. Hartley, smooth as a snake-oil salesman, saw that he'd penetrated Sean's anger. In the blink of an eye he had everyone gathered around the table, talking to them and including them in his plans as though they'd been friends for years.

It took Sean the better part of the next 15 minutes to fully understand that Hartley was planning something bigger this time. The man who had come with him, Rico by name, was a bit dim, but seemed all for the plan.

"You're going to rob a bank." Anita too, had been slow on the uptake, and Hartley patted her cheek when she understood.

"I thought we were going to break into someone's house," Rico admitted, sounding just a bit unsure.

"How about you, Sean, did you understand?"

"Only just. Have you done this before—robbed a bank?

"Never in Visalia, but elsewhere." Hartley spoke with casual ease. "There's nothing to it, Sean; you'll see. And if there is some danger, we're talking about thousands of dollars here—well worth the risk."

"Who gets the money?" Anita wanted to know, catching Hartley's excitement.

"We all do," Hartley told her with a smile.

Sean knew that this was a now-or-never point in his life. His father's face suddenly sprang into his head, and Sean wondered where he was. *It doesn't matter,* he thought after just a moment. *He doesn't want to see me anyway.*

In an effort to hide the pain Sean bent low over the bank plan now laid out on the table. "Count me in" was all he said before everyone fell quiet and allowed Hartley to explain.

Six

Santa Rosa, California

RIGG WAS EXHAUSTED, but sleep would not come. He was sure this stemmed from the fact that his wife was not in bed with him. He rolled onto his side to better see the woman who sat in the rocking chair, her silhouette illuminated by the moonlight flooding through the window.

Katie had been sitting motionless for more than an hour. She knew she would never be able to get out of bed in the morning if she didn't lie down and get some rest soon, but her heart was so heavy with thoughts of her brother, Sean, that sleep seemed hours away.

How long had it been since they had seen him? Nearly two years—Molly had been an infant. Nearly two years since Aunt Maureen had written, beside herself that he had gone off on his own. They had been forced to accept Sean's decision, but there had been times when it had been close to torture to sit and wonder where he might be.

So why, tonight of all nights, was he so heavy on her heart? Every day she thought of him, and prayed that God would guide his path and someday bring him home, but tonight was different; tonight there was an urgency in her thoughts. Something was happening this night, and Kaitlin knew she had to pray.

She also knew that if Sean had been in the room, she would have held onto him with all her strength to keep him from . . . to keep him from what, she was not sure. But somehow Kate was

33

certain that Sean needed protection of some type at that very moment. Not that he would have welcomed her interference in his life. He had wanted as little to do with her at 16 and 17 as any teen could. He hadn't wanted advice or even affection, from her or anyone else.

Nineteen and a half now, Kate thought to herself. Surely he would feel some different.

Rigg stirred in the bed when someone knocked on the bedroom door. Kate, not wanting him to be disturbed, started to rise, but Rigg was already to the door. He opened it and found Marcail, now 14, waiting outside in her gown and robe. Rigg, not understanding why Kate was awake, also wondered at the fact Marcail wasn't sound asleep.

Rigg stepped back and allowed her to see Kate at the window. She moved forward and stopped beside the rocking chair, letting Kate see her face in the moonlight.

"I can't sleep."

"No," Kaitlin spoke softly, "I can't either. Are you worried about Sean?"

Marcail nodded, misery written all over her young face. "Where is he, Katie?"

"I wish I knew."

"I can't get him out of my mind."

"I can't either."

"Do you think he's in trouble?"

This time it was Katie's turn to nod. "We've got to pray, Marc. God knows all about this, and we're going to give it to Him right now."

Both girls bowed their heads. As sisters, each in her own way, they petitioned God on behalf of their brother.

Marcail, really still just a girl, asked God to keep Sean safe, and to bring him back to Santa Rosa right away so they would know he was all right.

Kaitlin, a mother, prayed differently. She prayed that Sean would make wise choices and seek God's will above his own. She also prayed that God would be glorified in Sean's life, even if it meant her beloved brother would have to know a season of pain.

Seven

Visalia, California

WE ALL EXPERIENCE seasons, Sean. They're not the predictable seasons, such as winter and summer, but the unpredictable seasons that come into our lives. I'm talking about times of loneliness or grief, or seasons of joy and peacefulness. But no matter what the weather in our hearts, Sean, we've got to keep our eyes on God.

Why Katie's words of long ago would come to Sean so strongly at that instant was beyond him. He felt another trickle of sweat run from his temple down into his beard, but still he didn't move. How he had gotten himself into such a mess, he couldn't for the moment remember. But then he heard the low whistle—the signal—and there was no more time for thought.

As Sean rushed through the rear doorway of the bank, he nearly stumbled over a body. Stopping dead in his tracks, he felt a sudden jolt as Rico, the man behind, ran into him.

"What are you doing?" Rico sounded as breathless as Sean felt, and Sean turned to find his features in the darkness.

"Nobody said anything about killing."

"He's not dead you idiot, now get over here with those sacks!"

These words were ground out by Hartley from his place by the safe, and the two young bank robbers rushed forward to comply. Sean had never heard Hartley sound so tense. Suddenly the enormity of what they were about to do froze Sean in his tracks.

"Get behind something, it's almost ready to blow."

35

These words were enough to propel Sean into action. He dove for cover just as the entire world seemed to explode. The next minutes were a blur to Sean as he choked on the smoke and tried to be in all six of the places he was being commanded.

He froze again when he heard shots outside, and felt completely rattled as a vision of being shot raced through his mind. Still stunned, he watched in fascination as his companions ran out the back, their arms full of sacks hastily stuffed with United States currency.

"Donovan!"

Not even the furious shouting of his name could compel his feet forward; by the time Sean reacted, it was too late. He spun around as men with guns came pouring in the front door. He turned and moved after Hartley and Rico, but he hadn't gone two steps when another man came through the back door with a gun. Sean listened in stunned disbelief as the men yelled that Sean's partners had escaped.

Sean felt numb. He was barely aware of the man who laid hands on him until he gave a cruel yank to Sean's arms. Now painfully alert as his hands were being cuffed behind his back, Sean started as a face suddenly pressed close to his own and snarled in a voice full of hate, "If he's dead, you'll hang."

"He'll hang either way if I have anything to say about it."

Sean's confused mind barely registered this last comment as he was *escorted* to the door. He was surprised at the number of people on the streets, but then remembered the deafening sound of the explosion and wondered how in the world they had believed they could get away with such a robbery.

The back wall of the jail cell was the only obstacle that kept Sean from hitting the floor as he was pushed violently past the bars. The clanging of the door was like the sound of a death knell in his ears.

Squinting through the gloom of the small cell, Sean saw a cot. He sat down with his hands still tied and leaned slowly back against the wall. If they left his hands tied until morning he was certain to be disgraced as the need to relieve himself was pressing in stronger with every passing moment. That, along with the receding fear, caused Sean's anger to return. He was working himself into a fine rage, telling himself he was going to kill Hartley as soon as he was released, when he heard voices in the outer room.

"It's what he deserves I tell you! This waiting is utter foolishness."

"Yet we will wait for Judge Harrison, and I'm telling *you*, you'll have to go past me to get to the prisoner."

"Be reasonable, Duncan. Why wait two whole days and have the trouble of feeding and watching him?"

There was no reply to that question, and Sean realized that every muscle in his body was as taut as a well-strung bow. He waited in the dark silence, and after a few more minutes he thought he heard people leaving.

He must have been right because his jailer returned to the cell holding a lamp and a shotgun. He was with another man, and this man let himself into the cell to remove Sean's bonds. Sean was more than a little aware of the way the barrel of the shotgun never wavered from his chest. If he could have spoken, he would have told the men he couldn't run. His legs would never hold him.

They didn't speak to Sean or to each other, but before the men left the cell they stared at Sean for a few intense seconds. His fear returned fullscale at having these two men staring at him. Knowing he was completely at their mercy was even more frightening than when the safe blew.

If the light had been better, Sean might have noticed that the older man's look was regretful, not cruel.

"He's nothing but a kid." The deep voice was soft, contemplative.

"How could you tell under all that hair?"

"His eyes. Clear as glass and angry, but scared out of his wits."

The deputy only nodded, sure that Sheriff Lucas Duncan, "Duncan" to all, was right. He usually was.

"Want me to stay the night?"

"No. I'm restless as it is, but stop and let Lora know that I'm all right and ask her to bring breakfast for two."

"Right. I'm off."

An hour passed before Duncan moved again. He'd been deep in thought and knew that his hunch had been right: There would be little if any sleep for him tonight. Had he gone home, he'd have tossed and turned for hours, disturbing Lora.

Duncan pushed away from his desk then, the chair creaking in protest. He had planned to question the boy at daybreak, but if he was as restless as the sheriff, now was as good a time as any.

Duncan was surprised to find his prisoner asleep. He was stretched out on his back, one arm thrown over his eyes. Duncan let his eyes run the length of him. He was big. He covered the cot and then some. It was easy to see why Hartley picked him; his size alone could be intimidating.

But Duncan wasn't fooled. He guessed him to be somewhere around 20 and as wet behind the ears as they came. And at 54, Duncan had seen more than a few prisoners come and go.

He walked back to his desk, sat down, and propped his feet on the flat surface. After laying his gun across his stomach, he tipped his hat forward and his chair back. He caught about an hour's sleep before his wife came in with breakfast and a smile.

Eight

LORA DUNCAN SET her tray on the desk and went immediately to kiss her husband. His arms came around her plump figure as Lora looked anxiously into his eyes. He was exhausted.

"Hartley?"

"He was behind it, but he's not in the cell."

Lora nodded and moved to unload her husband's breakfast. She left the prisoner's food on the tray and followed Duncan to the cell. She hung back slightly until he signaled her forward, and then entered the cell and put the tray on the floor. She didn't linger within, but once outside took a moment to look at the man sitting silently on the cot. He was watching her, and Lora was immediately struck by his youth.

"I'll be coming back to talk to you as soon as I eat."

Lora barely heard her husband's words to the man before she was gently ushered back to the desk.

"He's young and trying to hide it behind his anger," she whispered with tears in her eyes.

"Yes, he is young, and I think I'd better warn you, they plan to make an example out of him."

Duncan's voice was equally soft, and he watched with pain as a shudder ran over his wife's frame. He hated to see her upset, but it was better that she know now than on the day the kid swung from a rope.

Lora had brought along a pot of coffee and joined Duncan as he ate. They talked of nothing in particular, and as soon as Duncan was finished he urged her to go home.

"What if he didn't like the food? I could always fix him something else."

Duncan looked at her with tender eyes, but the set of his mouth told her that no one was going to baby this prisoner. Lora realized he needed to be as stern with himself as he was with her. She left without an argument.

Sean told himself that he wouldn't be able to eat a thing, but one taste of the eggs and bacon on the plate, and the food disappeared like magic. He was sitting back on the cot, the tray still beside him, when Duncan came back.

He unlocked the cell door and signaled Sean out with his gun. Once by the desk Duncan handcuffed one of Sean's wrists and closed the other cuff around a ring on the wall.

"Have a seat." The older man directed him to the chair that sat beneath the ring. It wasn't the most comfortable position, but Sean took little notice.

He watched the sheriff take a seat behind the desk and draw some papers out of a drawer.

"What's your name?"

It was the first of many questions, including everything Sean knew about the robbery and those involved It occurred to Sean that this man might be his ticket out of here, so he didn't lie or try to protect his accomplices He was quiet and somewhat respectful, but his anger at Hartley made him feel like a kettle on the verge of a boilover.

After an hour's worth of questioning about Hartley, the cabin, and the robbery, Duncan asked where Sean was from.

"Santa Rosa."

"North of San Francisco, right?"

"Yes, sir."

The men stared at each other for the space of a few heartbeats.

"Where are your folks, son?"

Not even his anger could hide the pain in the younger man's eyes as he answered. "My mother is dead and last I knew, my father," Sean's jaw tightened on the word, "was in Hawaii."

Duncan didn't reply to this right away. Sean was unaware of how swiftly the other man's mind was moving. *Angry or not, this kid knows he's done wrong, regrets it, and knows he's going to have to be punished.* The thought startled Duncan.

"How'd you meet Hartley?"

"We met in Tulare. He sort of appeared out of nowhere and offered me a job. I was tired and broke and he bought me supper. Then we just sort of struck out together. How did you know it was Hartley?"

"His style never varies. Middle of the night, dynamite, young men as accomplices."

"He's robbed this bank before?" Sean was shocked.

"Three times," the sheriff replied dryly.

What a fool he'd been to think that Hartley had been honest with him about anything. He'd certainly left him fast enough when the bullets started to fly.

"This is a reasonable time to warn you that you probably don't have a chance."

"What do you mean?"

"Only that the owner of the bank is tired of the robberies and believes that if they make an example of you, Hartley will never be back. You see, he waits long enough between robberies to make everyone relax. Just about the time Witt pulls his night guards off duty, or has just one, Hartley hits again."

Sean assumed that Witt was the banker. He also figured out that he had been the man who had not wanted to wait last night. *Wait for what?* Sean had asked himself. Now he knew they had been speaking of his hanging. Suddenly Sean wished he hadn't eaten any breakfast.

Duncan had been correct in assuming that Sean had resigned himself to spending some time in jail, but Sean had never considered being hanged. His calmness abruptly disappeared, and the faces of his sisters sprang into his mind. What would Kate and Marcail say? Would they ever even know?

Sean stood, his panicked heart hammering the walls of his chest before he looked down at his cuffed wrist. Duncan's heart turned over at the look of terror that passed over his prisoner's eyes. He then watched in fascination as the young man visibly worked at calming himself. Sean sat back down and swallowed with difficulty, but when he spoke, his voice was even.

"I have a sister in Santa Rosa. If I give you her address will you contact her after—"

"Let's not rush things," Duncan told him softly. "I just wanted to warn you. If and when I need to contact your family, I'll get the address then."

Sean nodded and realized he had an awful headache. Duncan returned him to the cell, removed the breakfast tray, and left him alone.

A dog barked outside the window, and an old woman was screeching at some kids in the street. Sean heard none of it. He fell asleep trying to pray—something he hadn't done for well over two years.

When Sean woke it was midmorning. He immediately remembered Duncan's words and thought of his own hanging. He realized that his head felt better, and his anger was gone, but his heart still thundered within him like that of a trapped bird. *Trapped.* A very fitting word for a man in a cell, and even though he wanted to blame Hartley, he couldn't. It was time to face the fact that he had no one to blame but himself.

Suddenly Hartley's words from the cabin as they bent over the plan of the bank came rushing back to Sean. "Nothing to it, Sean, you'll see." Sean's throat emitted a hoarse, humorless laugh.

"You've been a fool, Sean Donovan," he whispered. "And you're going to pay for that foolishness with your life."

Sean rolled over to his stomach on the narrow cot and let the tears flow. At the same time he wept, Sean once again began to pray. He surrendered his heart to God, with all its anger and bitterness, for the first time since his mother died.

Nine

Two DAYS LATER Sean was handcuffed and led to the courthouse. The small building was packed and stifling. Sean's mouth had never been so dry, and he longingly eyed the pitcher of water sitting on the judge's table.

Judge Thomas Harrison entered, going straight to his chair. Sean was surprised by his appearance, for he was very small in stature, not even up to Sean's shoulder. The most remarkable feature about him was his full beard; it nearly obscured his face.

The next two hours would forever live in Sean's mind. The sheriff gave a full report on all Sean had told him, including his behavior as a prisoner, his background, and the way Hartley had used naive young men in the past to rob banks with him.

Franklin Witt was not so benevolent. He proclaimed that Sean was no better than a two-bit thief, and that the country was better off without such vermin. He reminded the court that one of his guards had been hit on the head and could have been killed. After this he announced, in a voice heard by all, that Sean Donovan should die.

"Might I remind you," Witt nearly shouted, "that this will continue to happen? And when Hartley and his gang are done with the bank, they'll start on our homes. Are you going to set this man free to rob again?" Witt was in his element, and he was determined to convince the judge that Sean needed to hang.

43

Franklin Witt was a man in his forties with a full head of gray hair and a distinguished air of authority about him that captured everyone's attention. He took great pride in his position as town banker, and even greater pride at the amount of property he owned.

When it came to his business dealings, some said there was a demon behind his smile. He was more than willing to loan money, but if a mortgage or rent payment was overdue, he was merciless. It was said that he had a special book in his pocket where he kept track of how many homes and properties he had repossessed since coming to town five years ago. The joke around town was that whenever Franklin Witt was smiling, he must have been reading in his little black book.

"All right, Witt, I've heard enough. Do you have anything else, Duncan?"

"He's already had his say!"

The judge stared Witt back down into his chair and Duncan stood.

"Only this, judge. Sean needs to pay for the crime he's committed, but not with his life."

Witt came out of his chair once again, but one look from the judge and he kept his mouth shut. Judge Harrison's eyes swung from Witt to Duncan, and finally to Sean. The regret Sean saw in those eyes made his heart pound.

"The prisoner will stand."

Sean complied.

"You're a man, Sean Donovan," the judge began. "No one forced you to rob that bank. As much as I grieve this course of action, this court sentences you to death."

The noise of the court was deafening with protests and cheers alike. *It really is a shame,* the judge thought to himself, *that this young man has to be the example. But Witt is right, it'll continue to happen unless I step in and put a stop to it.* None of the judge's feelings showed on his face as he held Sean's eyes with his own. He spoke when the room quieted.

"The building of the gallows will commence immediately and tomorrow afternoon, at 4:30, Sean Donovan will be hanged by the neck until dead. This court is adjourned."

Duncan caught Sean as his legs began to buckle beneath him. "Steady, son." The softly whispered words were just enough to keep Sean upright. Knowing that someone in this room cared for him was all he needed. The Lord had given him that much, and for that he was thankful.

"Thomas is coming for supper," Duncan told his wife as he came in the kitchen door.

"Good. I made extra, hoping you would ask him." Lora paused and studied her husband's face. She didn't need to ask what the verdict had been for his young prisoner; it was written all over his face.

The ladies from the church had been over that day, and they'd all taken time from their quilting to pray. Most had prayed for the prisoner and the judge's decision, but Lora had remembered her husband. She had prayed for his peace of mind, as well as strength to do his job, even if the worst happened and Duncan would be called upon to hang a man.

"Are you all right?" She asked softly when Duncan sat at the table.

"Yeah. It's going to be rough, but I'm trusting the Lord."

Lora moved away from the stove and put her arms around him. Duncan's eyes slid shut at the feel and smell of her. She was stability when his world felt shattered. She was logical when his emotional strength was at an end. Without a doubt, she was God's most precious gift to him.

He told her as much, and then they took time to pray before supper. Duncan asked God to sustain Sean in the hours to come. Lora asked the same for Duncan, wishing all the while that her husband could be spared from such a task but never dreaming that it could really happen.

"You've done it again haven't you, Lucas?"

The sheriff didn't answer the judge. He took the bowl of potatoes Lora was passing him and served himself. The judge was right—he had done it again. He had grown overly compassionate in his job. It had never made him err in judgment, but it made the inevitable, such as Sean's hanging, feel like a knife in his side.

"I'm staying for the hanging."

Duncan looked at him in surprise. The implication was clear, and he resented it.

"I can handle it."

"I know you can, but I've decided to stay and spare you."

Duncan felt badly for his presumption. Praising God that Duncan would not have to pull that handle, Lora swallowed hard against a sudden rush of tears.

"Thanks, Tom." Duncan said the words aloud; Lora said them in her heart.

Nothing more was said on the subject, and when the meal was finished the men left. Duncan told Lora that he would be home around midmorning. Judge Harrison walked with Duncan as far as the hotel where the men bid each other goodnight.

Duncan's deputy had been expecting him, and other than Sean's not eating his supper, he had nothing to report. Duncan knew how easy it would be to try to coax Sean into eating, but given the same circumstances, he knew he himself would not want to be patronized.

He picked up an extra chair and carried it down to the front of Sean's cell. After turning it around, he sat astride it and looked at his prisoner where he sat on the cot.

"I'm sorry about today, Sean. I prayed it would be different." These words and the actions of the past two days told Sean that the man across from him was a fellow believer in Christ.

"I did too, but I know that since it wasn't, that's the way it's supposed to be."

All of Duncan's suspicions were confirmed. "How did you get this far from God, Sean?"

"It didn't happen overnight," Sean admitted quietly. "I fought Him every step of the way; in fact I fought Him so much that I was certain He had given up on me. I found out today that He hadn't given up at all." Considering that Sean had been sentenced to hang, most people wouldn't have been able to make any sense of his statement, but Duncan understood.

"Want to tell me about it?" Duncan asked quietly.

"It's a long story."

"I've got all night."

Sean stared at the older man for just a moment, and then began to speak in a reminiscent voice, not about all he'd been thinking on that day, but further back, back to his childhood in Hawaii.

"I was born in Hawaii where my parents were missionaries. I went to school there and of course church, and I really believed I'd live there forever. It was my world.

"Then on my sister's twentieth birthday, when I was 14, my father announced that we would be sailing to California for a rest and family vacation. I'd never known such a mixture of fear and happiness. I'd also never really known the definition of the word seasick.

"I prayed for death on that trip. My stomach heaved until it was empty and then heaved some more." Sean's whole body shuddered with the memory. "I was certain I would be dead by the time we arrived in San Francisco. That's where my aunt lives. We moved in with her, and then my parents revealed the real reason we'd left Hawaii. My mother was ill. She was diagnosed with tuberculosis. It was only a matter of weeks and she was gone.

"Father felt burdened to return to the islands and gather our things." A slight tone of anger entered Sean's voice. "We were to stay with Aunt Maureen, and we did, but then my cousin Percy came home."

Questions came to Duncan's mind as Sean talked, but now that Sean had begun, he stayed silent and sensitive to the young man's need to tell his story.

"I swear I could have killed him when I walked in and saw him with his arms around my sister. Kaitlin had tried to warn me, but I thought she was overreacting." Sean took a deep breath as he remembered the pain he felt over Percy's actions and his father's absence. But then Rigg's face came to mind.

"She has a good husband now. He loves her and their little girls. Oh," Sean realized he hadn't explained. "It was after we moved to Santa Rosa that she met Rigg. When Kate felt that we couldn't stay in San Francisco any longer because of Percy's advances, we took the stage north and she got a job teaching school.

"Moving without being able to talk it over with Father was the hardest thing we'd ever done. We were all right though, and I believed my father would come any time but he didn't. Weeks went by before we heard from him, and then his letter said he was needed in the islands and wanted to stay.

"It was worse in some ways than when Mother died, because we waited in anticipation of each letter, only to be disappointed. My heart grew more bitter with each passing month. When he'd been gone for two Christmases in a row, I felt so full of pent-up anger I thought I would explode.

"I finally left Santa Rosa the summer I was 17. It wasn't long before I started telling myself I would never go back. I'd also been telling myself for two years that if my father could desert me then my God probably could as well. So I stopped trying to pray, certain there was no one listening.

"And then today, when you cared enough to hold me on my feet, I knew I'd been wrong. He'd been there all along, waiting to help me with the pain of loss and separation. It's easy to say this now that I know how close my death is," Sean hesitated and tears filled his dark eyes, "but I would serve God with my whole heart if I had another chance."

Duncan wanted to say something but couldn't swallow around the lump in his throat.

"Thanks for coming back and talking to me. It makes things a little easier. Will you take that address now?"

Duncan nodded and went for some paper. When he returned, Sean's voice shook as he gave Kaitlin's full name and address.

"Try to get some sleep, Sean."

"I will, and please tell my sisters that I love them and that I love Father too."

Duncan's throat closed again, and he waited until the younger man lay down before taking the piece of paper to his desk. He sat unseeing for a long time, the paper clutched in his fingers.

When he did open a bottom drawer in the desk to file the paper, he hesitated. It was a mess inside. His file system left much to be desired.

He put the address in his breast pocket for safekeeping and reached again to shut the drawer. Something stopped him, however, something he hadn't thought about in years.

Like a man in a dream he reached into the drawer time and again until the contents were emptied onto his desk. The document was hazy in his mind, but he was sure it must be there. Duncan looked at the mass of papers on the desktop and wondered where to start.

His hesitation lasted only a moment before he remembered that 4:30 the next afternoon was less than 17 hours away. With that thought in mind, he began to read.

Ten

"WHERE DID YOU find this?"

"I've been searching my papers all night. Is it any good?"

Judge Harrison didn't answer, but continued to study the document in his hand. Finally he said, "I'd forgotten all about this law."

"I had too. Is it still legal?"

"Oh, yes," the petite man assured him calmly.

"Will you read it?"

"I'll read it, Lucas," he said as he looked the taller man in the eye, "but you must know that the possibility of a response—"

"I don't know anything, Tom, except that you've *got* to read that proclamation," Duncan cut him off. "I know it's a shot in the dark, but I'm trusting God in that darkness. I don't know how and I don't know who—I just know you've got to read that paper."

The judge studied the sheriff's face for a long moment. He had always respected Duncan's faith in God. "I'll read it Duncan; for what it's worth, I'll read it."

It was a sobering experience for Sean to hear the hammers pounding nails to form the gallows where he would meet his death. Sean's window did not look out onto the building site, but as the sun passed its midpoint in the sky, a shadow was cast across the ground, giving a perfect outline of the tall structure that would see his execution.

49

Sean's hand rose involuntarily to his throat as he lay down on the cot. "I know Your arms are waiting to hold me on the other side, Lord, but the thought of that rope around my neck terrifies me."

The words were whispered, and tears stung Sean's eyes. "Please help me to be strong. I don't know if I've ever given You the glory for anything, but I want to now."

And such were Sean's prayers through the long afternoon. Since he knew his system would hold nothing, he hadn't eaten a thing since before the trial. He was, in a sense, fasting and praying, and God's immeasurable peace had settled upon him. Duncan had come and talked to him again that morning and then prayed aloud, thanking God for the opportunity to know Sean. It had almost been the younger man's undoing.

Knowing that Duncan would write a kind letter to his family, Sean praised God. He tried to push the faces of his sisters and his nieces from his mind, but it did no good. He adored his nieces, and the thought of never seeing them again brought a torrent of tears.

Having dozed off before Duncan came to get him, Sean shook his head to clear his mind and held his wrists behind his back for cuffing.

Sean's heart, which had been beating at normal speed, began to pound when he saw the crowd around the scaffolding. It had never occurred to him that people would care to witness such a gruesome spectacle, but there was indeed quite a crowd gathered, and it was painful to have to walk through the midst of them to his death.

The walk up the steps of the scaffold was the longest of Sean's life. He was momentarily surprised to see the judge waiting for him on the platform, but a second later he stepped onto the trapdoor and felt the rope tighten around his neck and all other thoughts vanished.

The sun was in Sean's face, and not wishing to see the faces in the crowd, he welcomed the excuse to close his eyes. The noises around him and the feel of the rope as it scraped the tender skin of his neck were all he could take.

"It's been recently brought to my attention that a document needs to be read at this hanging. For some of you it will be new. For others, it'll jog your memory from many years ago. But either way I assure you, it is legal and I will hear no discussion to the contrary."

The judge cleared his throat and began to read. "As official of this legal hanging in the State of California, in the County of Tulare, I hereby proclaim that for the offense of bank robbery, Sean Donovan will be hanged by the neck until dead. *Unless*, in said case, a woman of good standing in the community, that is, not being a woman of ill repute, a child beater, or an adulteress, will hereby step forward and claim said prisoner to be her lawfully wedded spouse from this day forward."

The announcement was met with gasps of shock and outrage from the throng. An ominous silence followed.

"Now, I should explain a little further, without having to read the whole thing, that this would not apply to the offense of murder. And since I know I've taken you all by surprise, I'll read it one more time."

The judge did as he said without looking anywhere but at the paper. If he had he would have seen the condemned man staring at him, his eyes nearly popping out of his head.

Sean would have sworn that nothing but the sight of his Savior would have been able to pry open his eyes, but when the judge began reading the document, his eyes flew open and he swiveled his head as best he could to look at the man next to him.

The judge finished reading a second later, and Sean was still so busy staring at him that he didn't hear a woman calling from the crowd. Murmurs of "Charlie" came to his ears, but the name didn't really register.

Sean watched Duncan's face in disbelief as the sheriff loosened the knot and lifted the rope from his neck. Spots danced before his eyes.

"Don't pass out now, Sean. Charlie has just agreed to marry you."

Sean's eyes went from the grinning sheriff to the judge, who was staring down the steps of the scaffold to a woman standing below. Sean followed his gaze and saw black spots again. With Duncan's hand gripping his arm, he was brought back to his senses just as the judge addressed him.

"Well, son, it seems there's been a change in the plans. Can you stay on your feet long enough to be married?"

Eleven

DUNCAN STARED DOWN at the redheaded woman in front of him and tried not to smile. Charlotte Cooper, "Charlie" to the entire town, was the hardest working woman in the area. Deceptively attractive under her dusty clothes, Charlie did a good job of hiding her beauty beneath the hat she wore, the brim of which was always stubbornly pulled down to her brows.

Charlie and Duncan were alone in the judge's chambers where she had just become Mrs. Patrick Sean Donovan III. She didn't appear overjoyed, and Duncan was thankful that they had tied the knot before she could change her mind. He didn't by any means believe this was a match made in heaven, but he *did* believe that if God had brought Sean this far, He would see him the rest of the way.

"I think he'll be just fine, Charlie," Duncan told her after Sean went to her wagon with his deputy.

"He'd better be, Duncan," she told him seriously, wondering again at the impulse that now had her married. "Because if he makes one move out of line, I'll bring him back here and you can just go right ahead and hang him higher than Haman."

Duncan did smile then, not believing for a second that she was as indifferent as she sounded. His smile only caused Charlie to frown.

"What are you grinning about?" she growled at him.

Duncan didn't answer, and Charlie shook her head and exited the courthouse.

Sean was waiting patiently where he had been directed. He watched his wife approach and felt a state of shock settle over him. His wife. He was married! And to an absolute stranger!

Charlie stopped in front of him and looked out under the battered hat. Her eyes were serious, and Sean wondered what she was thinking.

"I hope you're not afraid of hard work," she muttered as she hitched her skirt enough to climb into the wagon unassisted. "You can sit in the back."

Sean did as he was told, careful not to sit on the supplies neatly stacked in the rear of the wagon. Duncan stepped to the sideboard and spoke softly.

"I wanted to warn you about the paper I'd found, Sean, but I was afraid of getting your hopes up. Charlie will do right by you. Just follow the rules and you'll be fine." They shook hands, and Duncan told the still-speechless Sean that the door to his office was always open.

A moment later the wagon was moving down the street. Sean sat still as they went into the next block. No more than 30 seconds had passed before the wagon pulled straight into the livery. The sign above the door read "COOPER'S LIVERY" in large, faded letters.

The horse and wagon stopped inside the sturdy-looking building. Sean jumped out of the back as soon as the wagon halted and without forethought, moved to help his wife. Charlie stared at the hand extended to her and then at the owner. Sean's hand dropped, and he stepped back and watched as she jumped to the ground.

Her manner was plainly suspicious, and Sean told himself he was going to have to watch his step. Feeling rather helpless, he stood back as Charlie stabled her horse and began to rub him down.

"You don't need to unload that wagon until tomorrow, so just push it into the big stall on the end." It was a command and Sean was swift to do her bidding. He stood just outside the stall once the wagon was in place, waiting for his next orders. The livery in which he stood was clean, spacious, and well supplied. There were horses in five other stalls, and from where he stood, Sean thought he could see another wagon and two buggies.

When Charlie finished with the horse, she walked to the front of the livery and pulled the double doors shut. There were double doors at the back also, but they were already closed and Sean watched as she headed toward another small door. She hesitated on the threshold.

"I don't suppose you know an anvil from a saddle, but my blacksmith just walked out on me. I'm finished here for the night, and my supper will be coming. You can start work in the morning." Sean stood still as he listened to his wife, unsure if he should tell her he was an experienced blacksmith. While he was still debating whether or not to speak, Charlie left without another word.

She walked with swift purpose to the door of her house, not turning to look behind her until her hand was reaching for the handle.

"Now where in the world is he?" Charlie muttered to herself when she saw that Sean had not followed her. She stood still and gave a small sigh, wondering once again why she had married him. Charlie told herself quickly it was because of his size. A man that big would be worth hours of work in a livery, as soon as she taught him how to smith.

She waited a second longer, hoping he would appear in the livery doorway, but it was not to be. Suddenly she felt very suspicious. With a mixture of fear and anger, Charlie moved back toward the livery.

Sean glanced around at his new home and wondered in which stall he should bed down. It was early yet, but if he slept he might not notice how empty his stomach was. He stood for a moment, his hand on the tender area of his throat. His eyes slid shut as he once again felt the rope.

"Thank you, Lord," Sean whispered, still staggered by the fact that he was alive. He felt down his own arms and then to his legs before the vision of himself hanging from a rope sprang into his mind. His palms became damp, and he shook his head to dispel the image before beginning to walk along the stalls, desperate for something to distract his mind.

The tack wall caught and held his interest. He was immediately impressed with the quality of halters, bridles, and saddles. He stood looking them over when his wife's suspicious voice made him snatch his cap off and turn to face her.

"Is there some problem?"

"No ma'am." Sean noticed she was frowning as she had been when she exited the courthouse.

"Then why didn't you follow me?"

"I assumed you wanted me to bunk out here."

Something in his voice, as well as the way he held his cap in both hands, tempered Charlie's voice as she replied.

"Your room is in the house." She watched him replace his cap and move carefully toward her. Her anger evaporated, and she suddenly felt a little sorry for him. After all, he was to have been executed today. But by the time Sean was close enough to see her face, she'd carefully hidden this emotion.

"Come on," she said and once again headed outside. Sean followed her this time and saw that she was leading him to a small house some 50 feet behind the livery.

Stepping through the front doorway Sean found himself in the kitchen, but he wasn't given any time to inspect his new home. "This way's your room."

Charlie led him down a short hallway where Sean saw two doors. One door was straight in front of him and one was on the left side of the hall. Charlie opened the door on the left.

"You can have this room. Oh! The bed isn't made. I'll get some sheets." Charlie darted out of the room, and Sean was left alone.

The room was not overly large, but it was more than sufficient. The bed was small, but it definitely outsized the cot in his jail cell, and for that he was thankful. Sean moved to the window. He pulled the curtains back and one of them tore. He knew a moment of panic and then noticed that they were very faded, almost transparent.

"These are clean."

"The curtain tore. I'm sorry." Sean's voice was humble.

Charlie's eyes darted to the window. It was on the tip of her tongue to ask if he was usually so rough with things, but then she remembered how old the curtains were. They had been hanging there since her grandfather was alive.

"It doesn't matter. Here." She threw the sheets onto the bed. "Supper's in half an hour." On those words she exited, closing the door behind her.

Twelve

SEAN CONTINUED TO stand next to the window, the events of the day going once again through his mind until a hunger pain tore at his stomach. The pain was impetus enough to cause him to move. Not wanting to dwell on the hours he had just lived through, he decided to make the bed.

He found himself mentally thanking his brother-in-law, Rigg, for the months he had lived with him. Rigg had taught him to take care of himself. Prior to that, his mother, and then his aunt, had seen to everything.

No water had been offered to Sean in jail beyond that which he'd been given to drink. So when the bed was finally made, and he noticed a pitcher and bowl on the dresser, he decided to find some water and have a quick wash. It couldn't really compare with a bath, but it would have to suffice and would certainly make him more presentable at supper.

Sean's door squeaked as it opened. Carrying the pitcher, he stepped tentatively into the hallway and walked softly out to the main room of the house where he stood looking around. There was no sign of his wife.

He noticed for the first time a large stove in the corner with wood stacked nearby. The kitchen table, appearing to be about four feet square, was made of oak and had four matching chairs.

Sean discovered that a doorway off the kitchen led to the living room. It had a long sofa and one overstuffed chair. There was a small table stacked with a few old newspapers, and all the furniture sat on an old, braided rug.

After a superficial inspection of both rooms, Sean looked more closely in the kitchen for a container of water. He had circled the room twice and figured he'd have to ask his wife or go without.

He turned to head down the hall and nearly dropped the pitcher he was carrying when he found Charlie standing just inside the room watching him.

"Is there a problem?"

"I was looking for some water." Sean gestured with the pitcher before noticing the shotgun in her hand and changing his mind about needing water. "I was going to have a quick wash, but it can wait."

His voice dropped on these last words; his whole body tensed. He wanted to move past her, but she was blocking his path and he wasn't about to do anything to make her use that gun. He stood still and waited.

"There's a well outside at the back of the house. I'll show you."

Sean watched in some surprise as she leaned her gun against a wall and preceded him to the door. Sean noticed as they walked that she was finally without her hat, and had even removed the oversized jacket she'd been wearing. There wasn't much to her; in fact, her frame was rather slight. She had the brightest red hair he'd ever seen.

There was no conversation as Sean filled his pitcher. Not until they were ready to go back to the house did Sean notice a bucket sitting beside the well.

"Charlotte," Sean used her name for the first time. "Do you want me to fill this for the house?"

Charlie's head had whipped around at the sound of her name, but there was no teasing in Sean's eyes. *No one* called her Charlotte, except in wisecracking, and Charlie just assumed that he was getting smart with her. She couldn't have been more wrong. His eyes were as respectful and hesitant as they had been since the two of them had stood in the courthouse and become man and wife.

"Yeah, we'll need it in the morning."

Sean proceeded to fill the bucket. Charlie stayed to watch him, although she wasn't sure why. For a moment in the kitchen she had thought he was out there to make a run for it, but that thought was swiftly put to rest when she had looked into his eyes.

Charlie was finally admitting to herself that his size had little to do with why she had married him. It had been his eyes. How many times were they going to get her into trouble? She had spoken up at the hanging because of those eyes and the way he'd kept them closed. Then in the kitchen, when she confronted him with the gun, it was the fear she saw in them that caused her to put the weapon down and escort him to the well.

Charlie had been amazed to see that he was afraid of her. She found she didn't care for that at all. She didn't plan to get close to this man in any way. They might be married, but in her mind he was nothing more than hired help. Yet to see a man of his size and obvious strength showing fear tugged at her heart.

Sean set down the bucket in the kitchen and took the pitcher to his room. While they had been at the well, a young girl named Ruth had delivered a plateful of food from the hotel to Charlie's kitchen table. By the time Sean returned to eat, Charlie had carefully divided the food. He sat down in the chair across from her.

Sean, believing he could consume five times the amount on his plate, found himself suddenly queasy. He ate slowly of the beef stew before him, and when Charlie tried to pass him half of her biscuit, he declined. Though he found himself hoping there would be more food in the future, for now he was thankful that he had no more to tackle.

The meal was eaten in silence. By the time Charlie rose, Sean was also finished, and he watched as she put their plates in a large pan. She turned and spoke her last words of the evening.

"We start work at 6:00, so you'd better get some rest."

"I'll do that. Thank you for supper," Sean said softly. "Goodnight, Charlotte."

Charlie frowned again at the use of her name before watching him leave. The frown caused Sean to wonder what he had done this time.

Sean's body was trembling with fatigue and something else he couldn't name by the time he crawled beneath the blanket on his bed. Even though the bed was too small, it felt wonderful to relax his tense muscles.

In a state of physical exhaustion, Sean thought he would fall right to sleep, but again the day's events began to play through his mind. One moment he was about to be hanged, and the next he was married. In quick succession the faces of Father, Rigg, Kaitlin, Marcail, Gretchen, and Molly all floated through his mind. Someday he might see them again. The thought was too much for him.

His hand came to the tender line on his neck where the rope had rubbed. This time he let the fear and helplessness come fully to

mind. Tears flooded his eyes. He had cried in the jail cell right before the hanging, but these tears, in the house of a stranger who
now happened to be his wife, made the earlier tears seem minor in
comparison.

Sean's entire body shook with sobs, and he was unaware of the
hoarse cries that issued from his throat. He thought he would never
gain control, and in fact, didn't even try. He wept and thanked God
he was alive, allowing himself for the first time to really believe it.

Unknown to Sean, Charlie stood in the middle of her bedroom
and listened to his cries. Her face was a mask of shock and confusion. Before this time she would have said that the sound of a man's
tears would disgust her, but not now, not this man's.

Charlie's heart was hard, but something was beginning to tear
inside of her. She told herself that if he didn't stop soon, he was
going to make her cry. And that was something she was sure
couldn't happen, since she hadn't cried in years.

She listened until the tears stopped, and wondered what type of
man her husband really was.

"My husband," Charlie said out loud, as if she had just realized
this fact. She whispered, "What have I done?"

Franklin Witt stood in the sheriff's living room, where he had
tracked down Judge Harrison. The banker was fraught with frustration, since the judge would not listen to reason.

"Doesn't anyone recognize that we've let a bank robber loose?
He has probably murdered Charlie and is halfway to Hartley's hide-
out by now."

"I think you've got him all wrong, Witt. For one thing, Charlie
can usually take care of herself, and for another, Sean is not violent.
He's also not really loose, at least, not the way you're talking
about," Duncan assured him. "I'll be keeping an eye on him, you
can count on that."

Witt ran a distracted hand through his hair, and the judge took
pity on him.

"Go home now, Witt. The document was legal, and there's
nothing you can do. Maybe things will look better in the morning."

Seeing that he had no choice, Franklin bid the men goodnight.
Once outside, he stood for a moment on the porch and drew the
night air into his lungs.

"Things might look better in the morning," he said to himself as
determination overtook him, "but I'm not through with Sean Donovan. I'm sure he can tell me more."

Thirteen

SEAN FOUND HIMSELF wishing for a Bible as he dressed for the day. It had been a long time coming, but now with all his heart he'd love to read a few verses in God's Word. Some verses from Proverbs 3 came to mind, and Sean repeated these to himself as he dressed.

They were verses about trusting in the Lord for everything, instead of following your own heart. Even as Sean committed his future to doing just that, he couldn't help but wonder how different things might be if he'd done it five years ago. But no matter how he looked at the past, he was in Visalia now and married, and he'd best determine to follow God no matter what the future might bring.

He moved to the mirror and frowned at his reflection—he had no brush or comb. Before exiting his bedroom for breakfast, he finger-combed his hair and smoothed his beard, knowing it would have to do.

As he had expected, Charlie was already in the kitchen, and Sean approached slowly.

"Good morning."

"Morning," Charlie greeted him without turning from the stove. "You can sit down. I've got some pancakes near ready."

Sean did as he was told and thought the breakfast smelled wonderful. His mouth began to water.

Charlie came to the table a moment later bearing two plates. There were two large pancakes with a drop of applesauce on the side of each plate. The moment Charlie's body hit the chair she

60

began to eat. She didn't rush, but she didn't take time for social amenities such as conversation or giving thanks for the food either.

Sean thanked God silently and began to eat. Since there didn't appear to be any other food, he told himself to go slowly. But Charlie was a good cook, and the first bite was too much for him. Within the space of a few seconds, Sean's plate was clean.

The pancakes did nothing toward appeasing Sean's hunger; in fact, they had only whet his appetite. He was reaching for his coffee when his stomach growled so loudly that he thought it might have been heard on the street.

"Didn't they feed you in jail?" Charlie asked softly.

"Yes."

Sean was careful not to look at his wife as he answered. He could feel the heat in his cheeks and lifted his cup to his lips hoping she wouldn't notice. He had been entertaining thoughts of shaving his beard if the opportunity presented itself, but if he was going to blush every time his wife looked at him, he just might reconsider.

Sean didn't know that neither his beard nor his cup did anything to hide the heating of his face, and Charlie watched in fascination as he flushed. She could hardly believe what she was seeing.

Charlie simply did not know what to think of this man. He was certainly unlike any bank robber she'd ever envisioned. He removed his hat when he spoke to her or entered a room. And he had actually attempted to help her from the wagon. He also blushed like a schoolboy in a roomful of little girls.

"There's more applesauce over there if you want it."

Charlie didn't know why she offered it to him, except that it felt funny to still be eating when the plate across the table was empty and the man behind the plate still hungry.

"Thank you," Sean spoke softly and carried his plate to the stove. The jar was almost empty, but Sean scraped out what he could and returned to the table. He was almost seated when he noticed that Charlie's coffee cup was empty, as was his own.

He didn't see the way Charlie was staring at him as he filled both cups until he'd again taken his seat at the table.

"I'm sorry," he said, gently contrite. "I saw your cup was empty and assumed you would want more."

"How'd you get to be a bank robber? You sure don't act like one."

The question surprised Sean speechless, and then he realized that everything about him, except possibly his looks, belied the situation in which they had first met.

"It's a long story," Sean finally answered after a few awkward moments.

Charlie shrugged. "I don't suppose it's any of my business anyway. And speaking of business," she stood abruptly, "we've got to get to work. Are you ready?"

"Sure," Sean answered, trying to ignore the hollow feeling in his stomach.

Charlie picked up her gun and led the way to the livery. Once inside she threw both sets of double doors wide open. Sean stood and watched her, wondering again when he should mention his experience.

"You ever feed stock?" Charlie asked abruptly.

"Yes, I have," Sean answered with relief, honestly wanting to help. "I've worked in a livery before."

Charlie's stance changed. "With a smithy?"

Sean nodded, and Charlie wanted to laugh at her good luck. She had been certain she was going to have to show this man everything.

"Good," she said simply, looking pleased without smiling. "There are three horses that need shoes. Head on into the forge and get started. I'll do the feeding."

Sean stood for a moment inside the forge and let his eyes caress the familiar tools of the trade. A smithy's job was long, backbreaking labor, but he had genuinely enjoyed the work and remembered it fondly as his gaze took in the anvil, forge, large bellows, drill bits, stocks and dies, and various hammers.

In the two years he had worked for the livery in Santa Rosa, he'd worked almost every aspect of the job from horse shoeing to wagon and halter repair. But never had the full weight of the job fallen on him before. Strangely enough, or perhaps not so strangely, he saw it as a challenge.

Hours later, Sean's shirt was soaked beneath his leather apron and the sound of pounding metal could be heard through the building. Charlie had been in to check on him from time to time, but satisfied with what she saw, she said nothing.

It was nearing 1:00 when Sean felt he needed food to finish the day. He went in search of his wife. He found her talking to a customer, and stood back as she finished.

The breeze was heavenly on his heated skin, and Sean had leaned back against the building and let his eyes slide shut. Charlie stabled a beautiful mare, and then joined Sean by the rear doors. It took him a moment to realize that she had drawn near and stood watching him.

In a move as automatic as breathing, Sean straightened and re-moved his cap. "I know there is a lot of work to be done, Charlotte, but if I'm going to finish the day I need something more to eat." Sean watched her brow lower, not understanding it was self-di-rected.

"You don't have to fix it," he quickly assured her, thinking she was angry. "I can get my own."

Charlie's last two smithies had never done anything but com-plain. When they weren't whining about something, they were talking with the customers and not getting any work done. Sean had achieved more in one morning than her last man could do in a week. He was obviously a hard worker and Charlie felt badly about not stopping him at lunchtime.

"The hotel delivers lunch and supper. I've told them to make it two plates from now on. Go on to the house and eat." None of this was spoken gently because Charlie was attempting to hide her dis-may, but Sean didn't try to understand. He only nodded gratefully and walked away. Maybe he'd been wrong to ask about food, but his limbs were trembling so violently that all he cared about was making the front door and staying on his feet.

Fourteen

"THAT'LL BE THE regular price, Murphy."

"Put it on my bill."

"You don't have a bill, and last time you left without paying. Now I'll have my money this time, or I'll keep your horse."

"Is that right?" came the belligerent reply. "Well, I'm leaving darlin' and you're welcome to try and stop me."

Not about to let this man walk out for the second time without paying, Charlie jumped forward and tried to grab the horse's bridle. Murphy shoved her away with ease. Sean, having finished his lunch, came through the back door just as she righted herself.

He watched in surprise as his wife moved forward to kick the tall man in the leg. Unfortunately, Sean was too far away to stop what happened next. Murphy turned back, and with one backward sweep of his hand, sent Charlie to the floor.

Murphy never heard Sean move, but he suddenly found himself spun around in time to see a fist flying with full force into his face. Sean didn't watch to see if Murphy got up before he went to his wife.

Charlie awoke to the feeling of straw at her back and the sight of a blurry man bending over her. Even before her eyes focused, the beard and hat told her it was Sean. She had no idea why he was bending over her and blinked to try to clear her vision.

"Charlotte?" Sean's voice was soft.

"Yeah," she answered as she lifted a hand toward her face, but Sean beat her to it. With tender care his fingers probed her jaw before gently sliding over her cheek. The left side of her face felt as though it was on fire.

They were both aware of voices and shouting on the street, but Sean didn't move away until Charlie was sitting up in the stall where he had laid her, and only then when he heard the sound of Duncan's voice.

"What's the problem?"

"I'll tell you what the problem is," a man Sean had never seen before said as he entered the livery. "I was walking by when our bank robber here decided to punch ol' Murphy in the face. I say he should've hung."

Murphy came to his feet, and started in with a string of curses and accusations that surprised no one. Duncan looked with regret at Sean, whose large frame blocked his view of Charlie. The sheriff was certain he had been right about this man, and even though Murphy was a trial to everyone in town, Duncan wasn't about to put one of Visalia's residents in danger. Having grown to like Sean made his job all the harder.

"It looks like I'll have to take you back to the jail, Sean, but I would like to hear your story."

Sean was livid with the loudmouthed man named Murphy, but for the moment his anger was directed at Duncan. "If the conditions on that paper state that I have to stand back while some man hits my wife, then you can go ahead and hang me!"

Duncan spun so fast on the foul-mouthed livery patron that Murphy took a hasty step backward into a pile of horse manure. "What is this, Murphy?" Duncan ground out the question, but he didn't wait for an answer.

"Charlie," he called, having just realized she was behind Sean. The young man stood his ground as the sheriff approached, his manner telling Duncan he had been right all along.

Duncan's hand briefly touched Sean's shoulder as he stepped around him and bent over the small livery owner. They spoke softly for some minutes while Charlie explained. Duncan saw red over the bruise on her face; her cheek was already beginning to swell.

Sheriff Duncan turned from Charlie to see that his deputy had come on the scene. In a quiet voice he ordered the deputy to take Murphy to the jailhouse and to keep him there until he arrived.

"He owes me money," Charlie called as Murphy started away.

"He can pay it too," a voice shouted out of the crowd. "He just cleaned me out in a game of poker."

There was laughter all around, and even though Charlie's head felt like it was going to fall off, she looked on with satisfaction as Murphy fished the coins from his pocket.

"Break it up now," Duncan shouted to the crowd that had gathered. Sean and Charlie stood quietly until the townspeople dispersed.

"You should put a cold cloth on that." Sean spoke quietly, watching his wife with very real concern and wishing he had a handkerchief or something to offer her.

"I'll be all right," she said, wanting to say more but afraid he would see the fierce emotions pouring through her. Besides, her face hurt too much to talk.

"I'll get back to work," Sean said.

"And I'll walk you to your house," Duncan told Charlie as he took her arm and headed for the rear door.

"Get your feathers down, Charlie. I'm not offering you charity."

"I've got money."

"I know you do, probably more than most of us realize, but that man who has come to be your husband arrived with only the clothes on his back. If you don't need my money, then take some of your own and buy him an extra set of clothes and a haircut if he's so inclined. Honestly, Charlie, he can't even take those clothes off to wash them without having to go naked!"

Charlie nodded, realizing Duncan was right. The job of smith was very hard on clothing, and Charlie again felt badly at not noticing Sean's lack.

"How's the face?"

"What?" Charlie had completely forgotten that Duncan was sitting there, so intent was she on Sean's clothing.

"Are you sure you're all right?"

The tiny redhead shook her head. "I'm fine, Duncan," Charlie told him with a sigh.

"I think you should press charges."

"Oh, Duncan!" Charlie was now exasperated. "The way you carry on you'd think I'd never been hit before."

Now it was Duncan's turn to frown. He knew she spoke the truth, but it was her resignation to the fact that bothered him. A few minutes later Duncan excused himself, but his mind was still centered on Charlie Donovan, and he prayed with all his heart that Sean would make a difference in her life.

Sean had to force back the groan he felt rising in his throat as he made his body sit down to supper. Every muscle in his arms and back was screaming. He couldn't remember the last time he had put in such a long, hard day.

Sean ate his chicken and corn, unaware of the way his wife watched him. She thought he looked ready to fall asleep in his plate. He was also filthy.

"If the conditions on that paper state that I have to stand back while some man hits my wife, then you can go ahead and hang me." Charlie believed that if she lived to be a hundred, she would never forget those words, uttered so protectively. They made her want to do something for him in return.

"My aunt runs the boardinghouse at the end of the block."

Sean looked up from his plate, wondering how he should reply to this, but Charlie went on.

"I don't have a tub, and she fixes me a bath anytime I want one." Sean continued to stare at her, and Charlie frowned a bit. "If you want, we can head over so you can have a bath tonight."

Sean wanted to weep with relief. He could barely tolerate his own stench. Instead he replied simply, "I would appreciate that."

Nothing more was said on the matter. When they were both finished with supper, Charlie led the way to a boxy, three-story house and without knocking, let them in the rear door.

Fifteen

"IS THAT YOU, Charlie?" The voice came from somewhere in the bowels of the large house. Sean stood still while Charlie moved through the kitchen and beyond.

"It's me, Sadie," Charlie spoke as she found her aunt, down the hall and around the corner, in her tiny sewing room. She had a quilt on her lap and was stitching meticulously, near the window where the remaining sunlight poured through in an orange-red glow.

"Hi, honey," Sadie greeted her warmly.

"I came by for a bath."

Sadie immediately laid aside her sewing. "All right, I'll get it for you right now."

"It's not really for me."

Sadie's brows rose. Sitting back down, she eyed her niece speculatively. "I'd almost forgotten that congratulations are in order."

Charlie didn't look at her aunt. Her gaze was focused on the quilt as though it was the most beautiful piece of work she had ever seen.

"What were you doing at that hanging, girl?" Sadie spoke softly.

Charlie shrugged. "I had to pick up supplies so I was in the area, and I'd heard he was young, and I just—"

"Where is he now?"

"In the kitchen."

Sadie looked stern for a moment and then rose with resignation. "Come on then, introduce me to your husband and I'll get his—" Sadie stopped suddenly as the light fell at just the right angle on Charlie's bruised face.

"That skunk oughta be shot," the older woman spat with fury and disgust. "Where was your *husband* when Murphy was plowing his fist into your face?"

"He came in right after." Charlie tried to defend him, but Sadie only shook her head and led the way to the kitchen. She didn't ask how Sadie knew about the incident; Sadie seemed to know most everything.

Sean stood at the rear door, hat in hand, just where Charlie had left him. The kitchen was spacious, and the odors from supper lingered in the air; he guessed it might have been roast beef and potatoes.

The feeling of unreality was stealing back over him. Twenty-four hours ago he was about to be hanged. Suddenly he was married, working all day as a smithy, and now waiting for a bath in the home of his wife's aunt.

His wife. When was it going to sink in? Sean's mind went to the mixture of hostile and curious stares at the doors of the livery after he had flattened Murphy. His hand clenched in remembrance, and he knew he would do it again in a moment. No one was going to hurt Charlotte if he was around, and considering the terms of the document that Judge Harrison had explained before he'd married them, Sean was going to be around for at least the next five years.

Sean heard the voices of the women before they entered the room. He stood still, waiting for what he was sure would be a scene. He could just imagine what his wife's family must think of her marriage to a condemned man.

Sean watched as a woman of medium height and narrow frame walked into the room. Her hair was dark, with just a touch of gray, and was pulled into a fat bun on the top of her head.

"You can introduce me now, Charlie," Sadie instructed after she'd lit a lantern and inspected Sean from the top of his shaggy head to the tips of his grimy boots.

Charlie cleared her throat uncomfortably. "Sadie, this is my husband, Patrick Dono—"

"Sean," Sean interrupted softly, never taking his eyes from his wife's face. "I go by my middle name, Sean."

Charlie returned his look for the space of a second, and then introduced him as Sean Donovan. Upon the correct introduction,

Sean's gaze swung to Sadie, whose face seemed to have softened from when she had first entered the room.

"Charlie tells me you want a bath."

"Only if it's no trouble," Sean said, his voice still soft.

Sadie couldn't believe her ears. She looked at Charlie, only to see that she was not the least bit surprised by her husband's considerate attitude.

"You don't act like a bank robber," Sadie blurted unthinkingly.

Sean glanced at Charlie. "So I've been told."

"Well, enough small talk." All at once Sadie became very brisk. "The big tub is in the pantry. You can drag it out here and I'll fill it for you."

"Do you suppose I could get something of Uncle Harry's from upstairs?"

"Sure, look in that trunk at the end of my bed." Sadie's gaze traveled over Sean's back as he hefted the tub in his arms. "There won't be anything to fit him, but at least he'll be covered while his clothes get washed."

Sean let his body sink as far down into the tub as the sides would allow. The water had been almost too hot to touch when he'd first lowered himself in, but now it was just right, and Sean wished he could lay there all night.

He'd lathered up already and now his head rested on the rim of the tub. His knees were in the air. He let his eyes slide shut. It was then he heard the voices.

"I can't do that."

"Sure you can," came Sadie's kind voice. "I know things aren't like that between you, but he *is* your husband. Now just take these clothes to him and get his dirty ones."

"Can't you do it?"

Sean didn't hear the reply, but it must have been negative, for a few seconds later his wife entered the room. Sean had to force himself not to cover up, since he believed it would only make an embarrassing situation worse. Charlie, he noticed, was careful not to look anywhere but the floor, even when she addressed him.

"Here's a shirt and some pants that belonged to Sadie's late husband. I'll wash your other stuff when we get home."

"Thank you."

The soft, deep voice was enough to finally raise Charlie's eyes to her husband's, and she stared for a moment in fascination at the blush that covered his cheeks.

"When you're done, we'll go." The words were nearly stuttered in her haste, and Charlie exited the room just as swiftly.

Sean immediately reached for the length of toweling that Sadie had left, and then forced himself into the pants Charlie had brought him.

He emptied the tub outside. The opening and closing of the back door must have signaled the two women, for just as soon as Sean had his shoes on, Sadie and Charlie returned.

They both came to a complete stop just inside the kitchen door and stared at Sean. The borrowed pants were too tight and stopped two inches above his ankles. He hadn't buttoned the front of the shirt because the fabric wouldn't meet over his chest. The seams on the arms and shoulders were stretched to capacity. The women could only stare.

"Thank you for the bath," Sean finally said, breaking the uncomfortable silence. "And for the loan of the clothes."

Again Sadie looked at her niece. Her eyes seemed to be asking if this man was real or merely imagined.

Sean was relieved when Charlie moved toward the door. "Goodnight, Sadie, and thanks."

Sean nodded to the older woman and followed his wife. As soon as they reached the house, Charlie set to work washing her husband's clothes. He stood for a moment in indecision and Charlie, who read the fatigue in his eyes, sent him to bed.

"It'll be a while before you're accustomed to the work, so you'd better get all the rest you can."

"Thank you, Charlotte, and goodnight."

Charlie didn't reply, but she did move away from the wash basin to watch him as he moved down the hall and closed his bedroom door behind him.

$\mathcal{S}$ixteen

SEAN WRAPPED A sheet around his waist the next morning and went in search of his clothes. The kitchen was empty, and there was no sign of his few belongings.

He had just headed back down the hall and knocked on Charlie's bedroom door when he heard her come in from outside. He retraced his steps to the kitchen and saw that she held his clothes in her arms.

"They dried on the line overnight," Charlie explained as she handed the clothes to Sean and tried not to look at his bare chest. It wasn't that she hadn't seen well-built men without their shirts; after all a livery had to have a blacksmith, but Sean was different.

Breakfast was plentiful on this morning, and Sean ate his fill. Charlie was cleaning up the plates when she spoke to Sean without turning toward him.

"We need to head to the general store first thing this morning so you can buy some clothes."

Sean hated to admit it, but wasted no time in doing so. "I have no money."

"I understand that," the redhead continued to talk with her back to him. "When Duncan was here yesterday he pointed out to me that I need to buy you a few things."

Sean said nothing; he couldn't get the words past the lump that suddenly rose in his throat. Duncan was the only person who felt real to him, and knowing that he was still thinking of him and cared enough to see to his needs was almost more than Sean could take.

Twenty minutes later they walked up the street together. The signs of a town coming to life were all around them. Doors were being opened and awnings raised. Sean had no idea where the store was; he simply followed his wife's lead. She suddenly stopped in front of the barbershop.

"Would you like a haircut?"

Sean's hand moved self-consciously to the shaggy hair at the back of his head. Before he could answer, Charlie held out a few coins to him.

"I'll go ahead to the store and find you some clothes. It's just three doors down. If you finish first, come down and find me."

For some reason Sean was hesitant to let her go, but she turned and moved confidently down the street, so he entered the near-empty shop.

There was a man in the chair who had been talking calmly until Sean stepped across the threshold. His face registered shock and then fear as soon as Sean took a chair against the wall.

Sean tried to ignore the man's stare, but his shame was so great that he didn't know where to look or if he should say something. It was a relief a few minutes later when the man left.

Sean stood when the barber swiveled the chair in his direction. For the first time he noticed the man showed none of the apprehension that his customer had displayed.

"Shave and a haircut?" He inquired solicitously.

Sean glanced at the coins in his hands. "Just a haircut, thanks."

As the sheet was draped around him Sean raised his chin. The chair was swiveled to face the mirror, and the barber began to snip.

"I think you got a lousy deal." The softly spoken words were such a surprise to Sean that he didn't immediately answer. The barber met his eyes in the mirror with such understanding that Sean relaxed.

"I had no business being in the bank in the middle of the night. It's a miracle I'm alive."

The barber smiled. "You're just like Duncan said you were. Did you want a shave and can't afford it, or do you prefer the beard?"

"I'm usually clean-shaven."

"Well then, since my sister, who happens to be married to Duncan, thinks you've got wonderful potential, the shave will be on the house."

"Your sister?"

"I believe she brought you a couple of meals while you were still in jail."

Sean remembered her then. She reminded him of his Aunt Maureen in San Francisco. She'd brought breakfast the morning after he had been arrested. Sean now saw the family resemblance in his barber. They were both round with graying hair and had full faces that brimmed with good health.

Sean's face was covered with lather before he could even say thank you, and within the space of about five minutes he was staring at a face he hadn't seen in months. He looked 17 again. What would Charlotte say?

He'd know soon enough since the barber was brushing him off and seeing him to the door. Sean stepped out onto the boardwalk. Replacing his cap, which fit differently without all the hair, Sean headed in the direction of the general store.

Charlie held a shirt up in front of her and wondered again if it was the right size. She had taken special note of how big his clothes were when she'd washed them, but now she felt uncertain. Preoccupied, it took a moment for her to realize someone had come up to stand behind her.

Sean watched her glance his way and then turn back to the shirt in her hands. An instant later her head whipped back around, eyes locked on his face. He watched as she took a hasty step backward, and quickly reached to steady her as she would have fallen into a low barrel of peanuts. He noted absently that his fingers met around her upper arm.

"Are you all right?"

"Yes." Charlie hated how breathless she sounded. "You just surprised me."

"I'm sorry."

"It's all right; in fact, I'm glad you're here. You need to tell me which of these will fit."

"There's no need to guess. Try it on," a man's voice called from behind the counter. "I wouldn't be able to resell it if people knew you'd taken it and brought it back."

The implication was not lost on either of them. Charlie's temper immediately flared, but Sean simply scooped up several shirts and headed into a small curtained room.

"How dare you talk to him like that, Pete!"

"It's the truth, Charlie, and you know it. He's a criminal and people are going to be wary."

"Well, he's never stolen a thing from your store, so there's no call to act like that. And another thing, he's my husband. I give a lot of business to this store, and if you're not going to treat Sean fairly, I'll start going across the street!"

Pete held his hands up in genuine contrition. "I'm sorry, Charlie. I'm just thinking of my need to make a living, and you know how it is in this town. Guilty or not, in the eyes of the people he's no good."

Because he was right, Charlie softened. "I'm sorry I snapped at you. Today we're in here to shop with honest coins and just want to be treated fairly."

"Fair enough," Pete nodded in agreement and, although still somewhat agitated, showed Charlie one of his new catalogs.

Sean had not missed one word of the conversation that had transpired in the next room. How did his wife expect people to react to his walking around town a free man, when most of them believed he should be six feet under ground? He felt sorry for her, since she obviously had more on her hands than she had bargained for. The thought troubled him.

But then without her, Sean would be dead. The sobering thought was enough to bring the young man back to the task at hand. He stepped back out into the store and waited for Charlie and Pete to notice him.

"Does it fit?" Pete asked, since Charlie seemed capable of little more than staring at Sean with his new haircut.

"I think the next size up, if you have it."

"Sure enough."

Sean disappeared back behind the curtain. Charlie wandered around the store then, and with Pete's help, picked up various items that she thought Sean might need. A special pleasure rose within her at his surprised look of gratitude when he watched Pete wrap their purchases.

Fifteen minutes later husband and wife were once again back on the street. Tucked safely under Sean's arm, in a wrapped parcel, were two pair of pants and three shirts, underclothes, socks, a comb and brush set, a razor, shaving mug and brush, and five handkerchiefs.

They received their fair share of curious stares, but no one appeared to be malicious. Even so, Sean was relieved to see the livery come into view. Charlie threw open the doors, and Sean headed toward the forge. The small ovenlike room was already comfortably familiar to him. Here there were no hostile or speculative looks.

The morning slipped away in quiet work. Sean found Charlie more than able as an assistant farrier. She seemed to know what a horse was thinking and second guessed movements on more than one occasion. Some horses tended to rest their weight on the man shoeing them. To call this a heavy burden was a gross understatement. Charlie had a little trick of pushing her small fist into the horse's flank. Most of the animals got the message, and Sean was able to go on with his work without gasping for air. They were just finishing with a high-spirited two-year-old when a young girl appeared with a tray.

"That's our lunch," Charlie said by way of explanation, and after securing the horse, led the girl to a crate.

"You can put it here, Lucy. Tell your mom I'll be in to pay my bill tomorrow."

The young girl, with a few covert glances at Visalia's resident outlaw, exited as silently as she had arrived. Charlie washed and set out their food while Sean had a quick wash himself. The crates were in the stall closest to the rear doors. The high separation wall of the stall shielded them from the people passing on the street, but still allowed the breeze from the back doors to reach them.

Sean looked eagerly at the food before him. Charlie must have been watching since she spoke up immediately.

"I've told the hotel to double your order for both lunch and supper. It might be more than you want, but then it'll be here in midafternoon if you're hungry."

"Thank you, Charlotte." Sean reached for his napkin. "It looks great."

And indeed it did. Large slices of ham nearly obscured one plate and the mix of carrots and potatoes was making Sean's mouth water. A jug of water, although not cold, was more than refreshing.

Sean, after laying his napkin on his knee, simply bowed his head and silently thanked God for the food. He had already reached for his fork and knife before he looked over to see Charlie watching him, her own fork halfway to her mouth.

"What were you doing just then?"

"Praying. Thanking God for the meal."

Sean couldn't hold back a smile as Charlie's head tipped back and she examined the rafters of the livery.

"Do you think Someone really heard you?" Her voice was sincere.

"Yes I do," Sean answered with surety, and Charlie went on to eat her food. Her face, still framed by her hat, gave nothing away.

Seventeen

FRANKLIN WITT DID not have a personal grudge against Sean Donovan. In the hours following the hanging, however, he could think of little else except that he felt cheated. At first he was angry that Donovan hadn't swung from a rope; and then he got to wondering if maybe Sean could be of more use alive. The thought nagged him until he decided to see Duncan with an idea.

"What can I do for you, Witt?" Duncan asked as the suave banker entered his office first thing one morning.

"I've been thinking some more about Donovan." Witt forestalled Duncan with a raised hand when it looked like he was going to interrupt.

"I know you think I'm wasting my time, but the truth is, it's my time and he's still the best lead we've got. I'd just like to talk to him once more."

Duncan looked doubtful, and Witt hurried on.

"No strong-arm stuff, Duncan. I just want to appeal to him as one citizen of Visalia helping another."

Duncan could see how distasteful that last sentence was for Witt and in all honesty he couldn't say as he blamed him. The men talked about the bank robberies a moment more, and then Duncan assured Witt that he'd at least think on the idea.

"You have heard what a good worker he is, haven't you?"

"Yes, Duncan, I'll give him that. He does seem to be faring far better than I ever imagined, but I've got one more thing I need to say before I go. If that bank is hit again in the very near future, it won't matter if *you're* his alibi, you know there will be a lynch mob. Think on that, would you, Duncan?"

Duncan sat very still as Witt rose and left the office. He was right; there was no doubt in that. But right didn't make it fair. Of course, no one ever promised this life would be fair. It looked like Duncan would have to talk with Sean about the robberies whether he wanted to or not.

Sean and Charlie settled into a pattern of sorts that saw them through the rest of the week. Lunch was always eaten in the livery, on the crates that served as a makeshift table and chairs. In the evenings they ate at the small kitchen table and then moved into the tiny living room where Charlie would usually repair a bridle as Sean read silently.

As soon as Charlie found out that Sean liked to read, she had the newspaper sent over. He was quickly seeing how trusted she was in town. Food, laundry, and even the newspaper were delivered without question.

By Saturday Sean was feeling a very definite change taking place in his body. The hours spent with a hammer in his hand pounding iron and pulling the bellows once again became easy.

Both Sean and Charlie went to Sadie's for baths Saturday evening after supper. On the way home Charlie told Sean the livery was closed on Sundays.

"Every Sunday?" Sean was visibly pleased.

"Yes. It used to be open every day all year, but business is always slow on Sunday, and the hotel has a small stable at the rear of the building for folks coming in on weekends. So all I do now is feed and water morning and evening. The doors are shut all day. Sometimes I take a buggy out if one of the horses hasn't had much exercise, but that's not really work."

Sean loved it when she talked to him. It didn't happen often, but when she did open up she usually had a lot to say. And then, he'd watch as an unsure look would pass over her face as though she had said too much, revealed too much of who she was.

"Oh!" Charlie's voice told him she had just thought of something. "I always eat Sunday dinner at Sadie's, so we'll be going there around noon."

"Are you sure that invitation is extended to me?" Regret rose deep from within Sean and shone in his dark brown eyes.

They had arrived back at the house now and Charlie stood in the kitchen looking with great compassion at him. "Sadie likes you.

I can't say that all the people in the boardinghouse are going to welcome your presence, but what Sadie says, goes. She told me tonight when we left that she would see us *both* tomorrow."

Sean was pleased by the invitation, but more than a little wary. He had no desire to cause trouble for Charlie's aunt. His presence at the boardinghouse dinner table would be like inviting it in through the front door.

Sean and Charlie had no more time to discuss Sunday dinner because someone was knocking on the door. It was Duncan.

"I'm sorry to disturb you on a Saturday night, but I need to talk with Sean."

Charlie held the door wide and Duncan removed his hat and stepped into the room. Charlie gestured both men into the living room and followed, taking one end of the sofa. Sean sat next to his wife, and then looked to Duncan who had taken the chair.

"Franklin Witt was in to see me this week," Duncan began without preamble. "He'd like to talk with you, Sean. He's holding out a faint hope that there's something you overlooked that might lead us to Hartley."

"I told you all I know, Duncan."

"I'm sure you did. Witt would like to talk with you anyway. I think it might be a good idea, if for no other reason than to give him some peace of mind."

Sean looked at Charlie, who had tensed when Duncan mentioned Witt and then Hartley. Husband and wife stared at one another for a moment, and Sean would have given much to know what she was thinking.

Duncan didn't stay long, but before leaving he arranged for Sean to come to his office on Monday at 8:00. "By the way, Sean, bring Charlie with you on Monday. There's no reason for her to stay away."

"All right, Duncan. Goodnight."

Sean shut the door and turned to find Charlie on the threshold between the kitchen and living room. Again Sean watched her, wishing he knew her thoughts, or at least what to say.

"I'm pretty tired. I think I'll go to bed."

"Are you all right?" Sean could not hold the question back.

"I don't know," Charlie answered, wondering herself. "Witt just isn't one of my favorite people, and I don't want to see you used by him."

Not knowing how to answer, Sean changed the subject. "If you want I can get up and do the chores in the morning. You could sleep in."

"Thanks, but I'm an early riser. Goodnight, Sean."
"Goodnight."

Three hours later Charlie was convinced that this was anything
but a good night. She'd tossed and turned for what seemed like
days. Never had she known such a myriad of emotions over anything in her life, and certainly never a man.

She had stood and watched Sean pound iron into horseshoes
and then those same hands, as gentle as those of a nurse, slid tenderly along her bruised jaw.

And again, when she had nearly fallen in the general store, he
had grasped her arm ever so lightly, but with enough strength to let
her know she wouldn't fall.

It had taken until the next day for Charlie to find out that Sean
had only thrown one punch before Murphy hit the floor. And then
those same hands, lightly clutching his napkin, had paused to pray
before eating.

Prayer. Sean was the only adult Charlie knew who actually
prayed. She thought such petitions were for children before they
figured out that no one was there listening. Charlie had prayed
until she was 12. She had asked God every night to give her a pony
of her own and to make her grandfather stop hitting her. But there
was no one up there, so naturally her prayers went unanswered.

Sean however, believed in Someone. Charlie could see that. He
didn't seem to be the type of man who prayed without belief. But
what type of man *was* he? The question plagued Charlie until she
fell into a fitful sleep. In the morning she wished she'd taken Sean
up on his offer to do the chores.

Eighteen

SEAN WORE THE still-new pants and shirt on Sunday morning.
The shirt was a blue-and-white check, and the pants were a heavy
denim. Freshly shaved and with his hair brushed into place, Sean
cut a handsome figure.

The moment he opened his bedroom door, he could hear Charlie moving around the kitchen preparing breakfast. He wondered if
his wife was thankful that even though she could cook, she had the
means to have lunch and supper delivered after she'd worked all
day.

Sean's thoughts moved to May Taylor, his sister Kaitlin's
mother-in-law. She was a woman who for years worked all day
in Santa Rosa's shipping office and then went home to prepare
supper for her family. Of course her sons were helpful, but it had
to take some of the edge off one's appetite to be so tired when
eating.

"Good morning," Sean greeted Charlie as he stepped into the
room.

"Morning," she answered, and Sean thought she sounded like
she was getting a cold.

"How are you this morning?"

"Fine."

Sean doubted that, but was hesitant to press her. He thought of another tack.

"Why don't you let me finish breakfast?" Charlie stopped, a cracked egg poised over her bowl, and stared at him. Sean continued, "You've already done the chores, and I haven't done a thing today, so—"

"You can cook?"

"Sure. My brother-in-law taught me."

Charlie turned fully away from the bowl now. "You have family?"

"Yes, I do," Sean spoke as he stepped forward and rescued the dripping egg from her hand. "A father, two sisters, a brother-in-law and two nieces, last I knew."

"Do they know about—" Charlie hesitated.

"About the hanging?"

Charlie nodded.

"No. I haven't seen any of them for two years," Sean said as he stared intently at the eggs in the bowl.

"Where do they live?"

Glad for any question to distract his painful thoughts, Sean answered promptly. "Everyone is in Santa Rosa except my father—he lives in Hawaii. If you haven't heard of it, it's a group of islands out in the Pacific Ocean."

Charlie watched as he held the bowl in his arm and beat the eggs furiously with a fork. Once again she was overcome with curiosity about this man.

"Why is your father in Hawaii?"

"He's a missionary."

Charlie blinked in surprise, and then her face lit with understanding. "That's why you pray before meals," she almost whispered, "because your father is a missionary."

Sean knew he had to weigh his next words carefully. "With missionary parents, I probably did learn about prayer at a younger age than some, but that's not why I pray now."

It was on the tip of Charlie's tongue to say "why do you?" but she suddenly thought she might be intruding. Instead she picked up on something else he had said.

"You didn't mention your mother."

"She died when I was 14." Even now it pained Sean to say those words. "We were at my aunt's house in San Francisco. None of us knew she had tuberculosis until the end. We had a few good weeks together, and then she died quietly one afternoon during her nap."

This time it was Sean's turn to wonder if he had shared too much. Talking about his mother made him feel vulnerable, and once again he concentrated on breakfast.

Some five minutes later they sat down together to a meal of scrambled eggs with bits of salt pork. Sean had also fried large slices of bread. Charlie's contribution was her great-tasting coffee.

There was no conversation about who would wash or dry, but both husband and wife pitched in after the meal to clean the kitchen.

Sean moved into the living room to read the newspaper and was pleased to see Charlie join him. By the time they had finished with the dishes, she'd grown quite pensive, and Sean was glad to see that she wasn't trying to avoid him. There had been something on his mind from the first night he'd come here, and he knew now was finally a good time to mention it.

"Charlotte," Sean called her name and waited for her to look up from her account books. "I've never thanked you for what you did for me at the hanging. It took a lot of courage to come forward and marry a bank robber. I'm not really sure why you did, but I do know I'm grateful and in one sense, I owe you my life. Thank you."

Charlie didn't know what to say. She certainly realized that he'd have hung if someone hadn't stepped forward, but she never expected to be thanked for it

"You're welcome," she finally spoke softly, knowing by the way Sean watched her that he was waiting for a reason.

"I also want to thank you for all you've given me. You didn't owe me a thing, but you've dressed me and fed me like a king, and well, thanks for that too."

He completely flustered her this time. She sounded almost irritated when she spoke.

"Well, it's not as if you haven't worked for it. I mean, blacksmith work is hard, and well, that's why I married you."

It suddenly occurred to Sean as he watched and listened to his wife that she hid her true feelings behind a mask of irritation when she was upset. Sean was usually much better at hiding his feelings than she, even if he did blush every once in a while, and he felt real compassion for the upset he'd caused in her life.

"Would you like to go for a ride in the buggy?" The question seemed to come out of nowhere, and Sean saw that she was trying to make amends for what she had said.

"I think that's a great idea."

"Good," Charlie replied, looking so relieved that Sean smiled. "Sadie doesn't expect us for a good two hours, so we have plenty of time."

Not for a moment did Charlie consider asking Sean to pull the buggy out or hitch the horse. She had gone out ahead of him and was almost finished by the time he arrived. He stood by rather help-lessly as she climbed aboard, and couldn't help but remember how often he'd seen Rigg lift Kaitlin into the wagon. Kaitlin had seemed to expect it, and he knew Rigg enjoyed doing this small service for his wife.

As usual, none of these feelings showed on his face, and Charlie simply looked at him expectantly as she sat on the seat, holding the reins loosely in her grip.

Sean climbed aboard and they headed out the back doors. The day was growing hot, but the top was in good shape. The canopy afforded them plenty of protection from the sun. Cooper's Livery also had a surrey, but there was no need for the extra seat, and it had no top.

Sean got to thinking about what fine equipment and horses the livery had, and said as much to Charlie.

"That's the way my grandfather liked things," she explained. "He believed that if you invested in your own business, people would trust you to do right by them, thus expanding and paying you back for your investment."

"He sounds like he had a good head for business. I take it your grandfather is no longer living."

"He died six years ago. I've been running things on my own ever since."

"And doing a good job, from what I've seen."

Charlie smiled at the compliment, and Sean leaned back in the seat to watch what he could see of her profile. He began to wonder why she was so seldom without her hat. And why, when she obvi-ously had such a prosperous business, she didn't buy clothes that fit.

Her blouse was so full it seemed she might be able to fit another person inside, and her skirt, although the proper length, seemed to have an unusual number of gathers at the waist. The more he thought about it, the more sense it made. After all, she had a very physical job, and to be confined by tight clothing could hinder her work.

Charlie talked as the buggy moved through town. She told Sean about the different people in the area, and once in a while asked Sean questions, but the conversation never ventured to the personal. It was a very relaxed time, and Sean was a little surprised when he suddenly realized Charlie was pulling up in front of Sadie's.

His feeling of contentment evaporated. At that moment, Sean was certain he could relate to those long-ago Christians as they entered the arena filled with hungry lions.

Nineteen

TANSY LANG WAS a flirt, and she made no apology about it. Since she worked in the hotel dining room, it was unusual that she would even be at Sadie's table for dinner on Sunday, but she was there, making Sean wish he wasn't. He had prayed so specifically, asking God to help him bear up under the hostile looks and words he was sure to find. But nothing could have prepared him for Tansy.

She seemed to find it exciting that he'd robbed a bank, and in her high-pitched voice told him so at least ten times. Her dress did a fine job of exposing her cleavage. But it didn't seem to be enough for Tansy, who was intent on drawing Sean's attention to her chest by leaning toward him every few moments. He finally trained his eyes across the table on his wife, who wouldn't look at him, and tried valiantly to get through the meal.

There were six other people at the table besides Sadie, Tansy, Charlie, and himself, but Tansy, who was seated next to him, had so monopolized the entire conversation that Sean had no idea how people felt about his presence.

After the meal, which Sean barely tasted, Sadie directed him and Charlie to a small sitting room back by the kitchen. He was thankful that no one else joined them as they sat down on the long sofa. An uncomfortable silence enveloped them.

"Charlotte," Sean spoke up because he couldn't let the question wait. "Does Tansy eat lunch here every Sunday?"

Charlie was so shocked by the question that she didn't immediately answer. Sean suddenly stood up, his agitation very clear.

"Because if she does," he went on, "I won't be back."

Charlie could do nothing more than stare at him. She had been so intent on her own misery that she never once considered how Sean might be feeling.

Tansy's clothing always showed off her full breasts and tiny waist, and for the first time Charlie had felt like an old crow in her presence. Tansy's nails were attractively long, and her hands were never rough like those of a livery owner's. The woman had stood back while Sean seated her, and then thanked him by leaning close and whispering something in his ear.

Charlie had not waited for anyone to seat her, and she felt her face burn as one of the older women at the table raised a wrinkled brow in her direction. From that point on, Charlie couldn't watch anything that went on across the table.

"Does she, Charlotte?"

The question brought Charlie back to earth. "No. She works at the hotel, and actually she's never here on Sundays. I think she's been under the weather and taking a few days off work."

Sean relaxed, and Charlie searched for something to say. She spotted her aunt's paper.

"You didn't get to finish the newspaper. Why don't you sit down and read Sadie's?"

Sean took up the offer and settled back down on the sofa. There was probably more they should have said to each other regarding Tansy's behavior, but Sean watched Charlie reach for a catalog on a nearby table, so he began to read the paper.

There was no conversation. The only noise was the gentle rattle of paper as Sean turned from page to page. He glanced over a few times to see that Charlie seemed to be stuck on one page in the catalog. It was a listing of blacksmith supplies.

"Can't decide which one you like?"

"No, I guess I can't. I hate it when they don't show pictures of all of them."

"Doesn't it describe the difference next to the prices?"

Charlie hesitated for only a second. "I think it probably does, but I can't read."

Thankful her gaze was on the catalog for a few seconds longer, Sean was given time to school his features.

"Want me to read it to you?"

"You don't mind?"

"Not at all." His voice was gentle.

Charlie scooted closer and handed the catalog to her husband. The front brim of her hat was flipped back and she looked up expectantly as Sean began to read. After starting to read he glanced down to see if she was listening, and for the first time noticed the beautiful color of her eyes—a deep hazel.

He read the whole page with an occasional question from Charlie, and then asked if she wanted him to go on.

"No, you read everything I need to know. I'll just look at the pictures for a while."

Sean returned the catalog and picked up the newspaper, but he couldn't concentrate. On every page of print he saw her eyes and the intent way she held her head as she listened to him read from the catalog. Sean glanced repeatedly out the corner of his eyes to look at her. He noticed at one point that she was falling asleep.

He shifted and pulled the small pillow from his far side and put it against his opposite hip.

"Charlotte," his voice was soft. "Lay your head here and rest a bit."

Charlie turned and blinked owlishly at him, but then did as he bade. Once her head was settled on the pillow, she picked her feet up off the floor and curled her legs on the seat.

Sean gently tugged her hat off and smoothed her hair as she fell into slumber. He sat looking down at her for a long time.

"Sleep well, Charlotte, because tomorrow I'm going to start teaching you to read."

The words were whispered, but Sadie, who had finally finished her dinnertime cleanup, heard every syllable. She didn't enter the room as planned, but turned and went to her sewing room where she pulled a hankie from her sleeve and wiped her suddenly wet eyes.

Twenty

COOPER'S LIVERY HAD opened before 7:00 every morning for as long as anyone could remember, but this was the second day since Charlie Cooper had become Charlie Donovan that the doors remained shut.

Sean and Charlie made a point of being on time to the sheriff's office, and they found both Duncan and Witt waiting.

Witt seemed to be good at his word and did not do anything to put Sean under pressure. Witt was silent as the four adults were seated, but then Sean remembered Charlie's comment about Witt using people, and decided to keep his guard up.

Duncan opened. "Thanks for coming in, Sean and Charlie. Though this discussion was not my idea, I'm not against it. I think I'll just stay quiet while Witt here asks his questions."

Witt's manner was very sedate as he began to question Sean. His voice seemed almost gentle to Sean, and then he realized the older man was in deep thought.

"Are you certain you don't know where Hartley's cabin is?"

"Very certain. I spent some time last night thinking on the terrain, and I know we were in the hills to the east, but beyond that, I haven't a clue."

"Has Hartley contacted you?"

Sean look so surprised that Witt nearly told him to forget the question.

"No, not once. If he did though, I would come to Duncan immediately."

They talked for a while longer, and then Witt surprised Sean by standing and offering his hand. Sean stood also, and they shook hands. Witt thanked everyone in the room and left quietly.

"Well," Charlie breathed after the door shut, thinking maybe she had misjudged the man. He hadn't been at all the tyrant she'd expected, and she said as much to Duncan.

"I've been telling him that Sean is not the man he believes him to be. Maybe he's starting to see that for himself."

"I really wish I could have been more help," Sean admitted.

"You did fine. I know you need to get to the livery, but I need to talk with both of you." Duncan hesitated, praying as he had been for days, about what needed to be said.

"It's time, Sean, that you establish yourself as a law-abiding citizen in this town. Now I don't want to completely upset your life, Charlie, although you did that to some extent when you married Sean. What I'm trying to say is—get involved. Start attending a church, our social events, anything this town has to offer. The townspeople will be watching the way you treat each other. I've already heard about the tongue-lashing you gave Pete the other day. He was stunned that you defended Sean, but also fascinated since your relationship is a curiosity.

"Sean, you need to be in touch with your family and ask them to write you. It would go a long way toward the good for you to get mail. I'm sure most people think you have no previous home or family. They seem to think criminals crawl out from under rocks."

Duncan stopped talking and stared at the thunder-struck couple who both craved privacy in the new and uncomfortable marriage in which they found themselves.

"Why?" Charlie finally asked in a small voice.

"Because," Duncan said gently, "if Hartley hits the bank again, and Sean has stayed aloof and separated from the community, no one will believe he wasn't involved in some way. Your testimony would be of no value, Charlie, because the talk in town is that you're falling for your new husband."

Duncan watched her face heat up like a flame. He knew his words were blunt, but he didn't see any help for it at this point. "Talk it over and don't forget, if you need *anything*, I'm available day or night."

It was a quiet young couple who exited the sheriff's office and then stood outside on the boardwalk. Sean knew that any move they made would have to be initiated by Charlie. He wasn't going to ask or suggest anything. He had turned Charlie's life upside down, and even though the end result could be his being blamed for a crime he did not commit, he was not going to pressure her into an action she couldn't abide.

"He's right, you know."

Sean stared down at the woman next to him, not really believing she'd spoken. But then she continued.

"We do need to get involved, and I think you should pick up some writing supplies today so you can get in touch with your family."

Sean stepped off the walk to lessen the difference in their heights, but still had to dip his head to see his wife's face. She had spoken with her head down, and the rim on her hat completely hid her features from his view.

Not until Sean had dipped his head did Charlie look at him. Her look was such a mixture of fear and determination that he wanted to hold her.

"Are you sure?" he asked softly.

"I'm sure," she said, meeting his gaze for the space of a few heartbeats. When Charlie moved in the direction of the general store, Sean followed her.

Sean had been standing next to Charlie for five minutes while she inspected the writing supplies. He wasn't sure why she was taking so long, but she seemed in no hurry. He put his hands behind his back, rocked back on his heels, and told himself to bide his time.

"I didn't realize how many different things you could buy." Sean heard her soft comment and finally understood. She was fascinated with the paper and ink. She had never even looked at it before. Sean watched her turn, tip her head back, and look up at him.

"Maybe you'd better pick something out. I never buy anything more than the cheapest paper and a pencil to do my accounts."

Sean leaned forward and spoke softly. "Anything you pick out will be fine."

Charlie looked up into his sable brown eyes. *Is this the way you feel about life when you've had such a close brush with death? You don't ask for much and expect even less?*

"Are you always so agreeable?"

Sean's brows rose on what he believed to be a cryptic question, and Charlie looked embarrassed

"I don't think Murphy thinks I'm agreeable." A sparkle entered Sean's eyes. Charlie almost smiled. Sean realized in that instant how little he had seen her smile, and silently begged her to grin at him. But it was not to be. She turned back to the paper, quills, and ink and made a quick selection.

Just as they were walking away from the supplies Sean spotted an elementary school primer. "Get this too." Sean's voice brought Charlie back around, and after one glance at the book in his hand, her startled gaze shot to his face.

Sean remained expressionless as she frowned at him, and when she didn't immediately reach for the book his eyes once again lit with laughter and he spoke.

"Still think I'm agreeable?"

Charlie's eyes narrowed. He was teasing her! The thought so startled her she almost laughed. *But that wouldn't do at all,* she told herself, and snatched the book from his hand, throwing a comment over her shoulder about the horses shoeing themselves.

Sean stood for an instant watching her stalk away to the counter where Pete was waiting. After a brief moment of thought, he followed very slowly.

Twenty-One

DEAR KAITLIN,

I know you're going to be surprised to hear from me, and all I can do is humbly ask your forgiveness for the way I left and the length of time I've been out of touch.

So much has happened, it's hard to know where to begin. Aunt Maureen probably told you I'd been to see her, but I didn't stay long. The way I spent my time from that point to the present is not near so important as where I am today.

Almost two weeks ago I was sentenced to hang for a bank robbery I'd been a part of in Visalia. I was on the gallows, the rope around my neck, when a woman came forward and offered to marry me. (It's a law in this county that you can be pardoned under certain circumstances and by such an action.)

I was married immediately to Charlotte Cooper. She owns and runs the livery and needed me to smith for her. I am thankful to be alive and to finally see that God has been with me all along, but it's a tremendous burden on my heart to be married to an unbeliever. Please pray with me that Charlotte will come to know Christ.

There was no easy way to tell you this; I just hope it's not too direct. Please write me soon. If I could come to you, I would. But in many ways, my life is no longer my own.

There is so much more to share, but knowing that your
worry has been long, I feel an urgency to get this mailed.
How is Marcail? Please tell her I love her. Have you heard
from Father? Apologize to Rigg for me and thank him for the
brotherly love he's always shown. Please kiss the girls and
give them my love.

Sean

Sitting at the kitchen table, Sean broke down at this point. He
asked himself repeatedly how he could have left his loving family,
and why he'd been so blind to how much they cared. What if something had happened to Katie or Marcail and he would never see
them again?

The questions tormented him, causing his tears to come harder.
He prayed and tried to give his hurt to God, but it was some minutes before he was able to contain himself. Even then his heart felt
bruised over all he'd left behind.

Around the corner in the living room, Charlie was crying with
him. She was beginning to care deeply for him and this made her
pain nearly as great as his.

Charlie listened as Sean tried to gain control of himself. She
wanted to join him in the kitchen but was sure she would be intruding. As it was, she didn't have long to wait before he joined her
in the living room.

Sean entered the room and glanced at Charlie as she worked
over her books. He sat on the sofa and picked up the paper. He'd
read just a few sentences of one article when he felt her eyes on
him. He looked over and forced his eyes to lock with hers.

"Are you all right?"

"I think so," he answered honestly. "Thank you for getting the
supplies so I could write."

"You're welcome," Charlie answered and then hesitated. "Do
you think they'll write back?"

"I'm sure they will."

"Then you didn't tell them about the bank robbery?"

Sean understood instantly. She was talking about conditional
love, probably the only kind she had ever known. He chose his
words carefully.

"I did tell them about the robbery and the hanging. They will be
upset that I was almost hanged, but it's been so long since I've been
in touch I think they'll be glad I'm alive and that I wrote to them."

"So you're not afraid they'll never want to see you again?"

"No, that thought never entered my mind."

Charlie was quiet for a long time, and Sean just stared at her. "Your family must be a very understanding one." Sean watched as she went back to her accounts, a sign that the conversation was over.

What type of family life had she known? The question moved through Sean's mind for some minutes before he went back to his paper. As he did, he spotted the school primer sitting on the living room table. His eyes swung once again to Charlie, and he wondered how she even handled her account books. Sean sighed mentally. He knew he couldn't possibly bring it up tonight, but at some point he had to offer to teach his wife to read.

Twenty-Two

AT BREAKFAST THE following morning, Sean's attempt to bring up the school primer failed. Charlie became very brisk and said she wanted to open early since they had been late the day before. Sean headed to the post office to post his letter and then to the livery, praying for a chance to talk with her.

There were several opportunities during the day, but each time Charlie avoided Sean neatly. As the day wore on, Sean became more determined to discover if Charlie was upset with him or just did not want to learn to read. He decided to wait until evening, when she had no place to go, and ask her outright.

"Who does the cooking for the hotel?" Sean asked as they sat down to their evening meal

"Ruth's mom," Charlie replied.

"She's a great cook."

"Most of the town thinks so, and of course her husband does too."

"I haven't met him, have I?"

"You must not have, because you would remember. His size alone will tell you that he's his wife's biggest fan."

"I could fatten up on your cooking too," Sean commented. "Fortunately I work it all off during the day."

"Do you think the work is too hard?" Charlie was instantly concerned, and then embarrassed.

"No," Sean said, ignoring her heated cheeks. "The work is fine. You have some of the best equipment I've ever seen."

They ate in silence for a time and then Sean nonchalantly brought up the primer.

"Charlotte, I wanted to talk to you about the book I had you buy yesterday."

"I think I want to go see Sadie tonight."

Sean knew he shouldn't have been surprised by this, but he was. How long was she going to avoid him? It was a question that went unanswered because Sean decided once again to let the matter drop. Charlie was good at her word, and as soon as the dishes were done, they headed to Sadie's.

"What's this for?" Sadie held out the coins that Charlie had just placed in her lap. Sean was having a piece of pie in the kitchen, and Charlie had gone in search of her aunt. She had found her in the small room Sadie called her private parlor.

"I'm not good with picking out fabrics."

"Fabric for what?"

Charlie frowned, not really wanting to tell, but not seeing that she had any choice.

"A dress."

"For you?"

Charlie nodded without looking at her aunt. Sadie's fingers went under her niece's chin so she would have to look at her.

"What's going on?"

Charlie shrugged and then softly explained what Duncan had said to them. "I think he's right, and I don't have a thing to wear to church."

"So you think you would actually care if Sean had to go back to the gallows?"

Charlie frowned at her aunt. "Of course I would; he's the only blacksmith I've got."

Sadie chuckled. "I guess he is at that. How silly of me to think you might be feeling something for him."

Tears filled Charlie's eyes, and Sadie was instantly contrite. "I'm sorry honey. I shouldn't tease you. I'll go first thing tomorrow and get the fabric. In fact, let me measure you right now, and I'll have a dress ready for you to try on tomorrow night."

"Really?"

"Really," Sadie said with a smile, thinking that Charlie looked young again for the first time in years.

"Sadie?"

"Yes?"

"Can we please not tell Sean?"

Sadie looked surprised, and then her eyes grew round with feigned ignorance. "Tell Sean what?"

Charlie gave her aunt a hug. Sadie went out to check on her niece's husband and give him another piece of pie. Then the two women slipped quietly into Sadie's sewing room so Charlie could be measured.

"There isn't much to you under all these baggy clothes, is there?"

Charlie looked down at her small figure under a nearly worn-out camisole. "You think I'll look all right in the dress?"

"I think you'll look like an angel. Just remember, a man treats a lady like a lady when she acts like one. How you look is not near so important as how you act."

Charlie was quiet as she took this in. Her mind conjured up the scene when Tansy allowed Sean to hold her chair; not just allowed it, but expected it. Charlie's eyes closed in pain as she remembered Sean staring at her those times she had climbed aboard the wagon or buggy like a man.

The more Charlie thought about it, the more she realized she had no idea how a lady acted. Did a man always help a woman with her chair, and how about the wagon? Her grandfather never once helped her or Sadie into or out of a wagon. Of course, her grandfather had been no gentleman, and Sean Donovan was.

Any man who would remove his hat when he entered a room and stand when a woman walked into his presence was a gentleman from the toes up.

"I wonder what his mother was like?"

"Whose mother?"

"Sean's."

"Charlotte," Sean called from the other room before Sadie could reply.

"I'll be out in a minute," Charlie responded, hoping he wouldn't come to find her. She slipped her blouse back on and hurried with the buttons.

Sean was standing near the table, his plate empty once again. That he had wondered where she was and why he had been deserted in the kitchen was obvious.

"Are you ready to go?" Charlie asked.

"Not if you're busy," Sean replied.

Always so considerate, Charlie thought, and then called a farewell to her aunt.

The couple walked side by side toward home in the gathering dusk. They were almost to the livery when a voice, slurred with inebriation, came out of the gloom.

"Well, if it isn't the newlyweds."

"Get out of here, Murphy," Charlie told him in disgust.

Murphy ignored her and began to rain insults down on the livery, its owner, and Sean. At one point he waved his arm expansively and nearly fell over into the street. The action seemed to break his concentration. He stared at Charlie as though just noticing her, and then stumbled on into the night.

Charlie waited only the space of two heartbeats before she started after him. Sean's reactions were quicker, though. In one deceptively fast move his arm shot around her waist, and he pulled her back against his chest.

"Let go of me, Sean," she panted in fury as she struggled against his hold. "I'm going to give Murphy a kick he's never going to forget."

"I think it would be best for everyone if I just held onto you for a while." Sean's voice was so rational that Charlie wanted to scream. She continued to pull at his arms, both around her now, but it was like a dragonfly trying to move a horse's hoof off its wing.

"Weren't you listening to the things he said?" Charlie fumed, trying another tactic. "The things he said about you?"

"I was listening." Again he was infuriatingly calm, his voice almost gentle.

Charlie stopped struggling then and let herself relax against her husband's chest. She felt his chin come to rest on the top of her hat and wished for the first time ever that she wasn't wearing it.

"What am I going to do with you, Sean Donovan?" Charlie asked with a sigh. "You're polite to everyone, even your enemies."

"Had he physically attacked you, Charlotte, I would have knocked him across the street, but that was nothing more than the pitiful rambling of a drunk." Sean's voice was compassionate, and Charlie was more confused than ever.

Charlie turned in her husband's arms, which had loosened to allow her room. She tipped her head back and tried to see him in the now complete darkness.

"What am I going to do with you, Sean?" This time the words were whispered, and the answer was just as soft.

"I'm sure you'll think of something."

Without further words Charlie pushed away from her husband's embrace. Sean let her go, but was more than a little tempted to pull her back. He followed her home in silence, but until he fell asleep much later, his mind dwelt on how lovely she had been to hold.

Twenty-Three

"I CAN'T BE FALLING for her. It's too soon." Sean had been repeating these words to himself for days, and still he was no closer to being convinced than the first time he had said them.

A week had gone by since Charlie had tried to kick Murphy. Charlie's dress had not been quite ready, so she hadn't mentioned going to church again. And even though Sean wanted very much to be in the house of the Lord, his mind was so full of his wife that attending services seemed less important right then.

All Sean had been able to do for the first few days of his marriage was thank God he was alive. But soon he had begun to notice the woman to whom he found himself married. Never in his wildest dreams did he expect her to be a woman who possessed so many of the qualities he admired.

That her life had been no bed of roses was obvious in many ways. She rarely asked for help or allowed Sean to wait on her. She never complained about the hard work or mentioned the past, but there were times when Sean would help her in some small way and immediately find himself under her scrutiny. She would stare at him as though figuring out what type of man he was, was the most important thing on earth.

Sean found himself speculating on Charlie's grandfather a good deal of the time, since he had clearly played such a large part in who Charlie had become. He'd had a good head for business, that much Sean knew, but what had he been like as a person? Sean was unaware both of the new insight he would gain and how swiftly it would come.

The day had flown by as usual, and Sean spent some extra time at the well cleaning up for supper. He knew that Charlie would have the table prepared and the meal set out by the time he arrived. He planned to mention the primer when they did the dishes.

They talked about the customers they'd had that day and even laughed about Sean getting stepped on by a workhorse.

"You can laugh," he teased her. "You weren't the one whose foot was being crushed by a thousand pounds of horse."

"He looked so comfortable too," Charlie said, her eyes lighting. "As if he could have stood there all day."

"He probably didn't even know my foot was down there."

"That's true. There's not a malicious bone in Tiny's body."

"Who in the world named him Tiny?" Sean asked as he pictured the gigantic animal in his mind. Tiny's hoofs were the size of large dinner plates.

"His owner is quite a character. He has a goat he milks every day whose name is George Washington, and a male dog named Dolly Madison."

They shared the light moment together, and then rose to clean up. It was Sean's turn to dry the dishes. He waited only until Charlie handed him the first plate before he brought up the book.

"Charlotte, I want to talk to you about the school primer." She looked startled, and Sean went on in a very gentle voice. "If you want me to return it, I will, but first I want to tell you something."

"No, I don't think that's a good idea." Charlie's voice was one of near panic.

"Charlotte," Sean called after her as she darted out of the kitchen and down the hall. With the drying cloth still in his hand, he followed.

Charlie would have shut her bedroom door, but Sean came through behind her and made the action impossible. She never dreamed he would follow her, and quickly looked about for something to do. She couldn't pick up a catalog and pretend to read, because he knew she couldn't. She didn't sew very well, so mending was out. Charlie settled on rearranging her dresser drawers.

"Charlotte, I just want to talk with you," Sean said from his place near the dresser where he'd followed her, the drying cloth now thrown over his shoulder. "I'm not trying to make you feel bad because you can't read, and if you'll just look at me for a moment I can tell you what I have in mind."

Frustration rose up in Sean as he was *completely* ignored for the first time in his adult life. He knew that if Charlie would just let him explain, the whole matter could be settled.

"Charlotte!" Sean's voice thundered in frustration, and Charlie jumped before turning to face him.

She looked up into his face with a startled kind of fear, and Sean felt more upset than ever, this time with himself. He had scared her, and that was the last thing he wanted. He suddenly raised an agitated hand to his hair, raking his fingers along his scalp. It took no more than a moment to see that his wife had flinched and was steeling herself for a blow.

Sean became utterly still. With his hand still resting on the top of his head, he saw Charlie realize her mistake and try to cover it. She straightened the front of her blouse and touched the rim of her hat as though nothing out of the ordinary had happened.

"You thought I was going to hit you." Sean's voice was strained and filled with pain.

"No, I didn't," Charlie lied.

"Yes, you did."

"No, I didn't," Charlie said, turning away sharply as she spoke. "Don't be foolish." But there was no conviction in her tone, and Sean watched as she went back to work on her dresser.

His next actions were those of a man who felt like he was going down for the third time. He would not leave this room until things were settled between them.

He found his hand gently encircling Charlie's upper arm as he reached for her. He brought her away from the dresser to stand before him, holding her there with both hands on her arms. Charlie looked up at him for a moment and then lowered her head, her hat hiding her face from Sean's view.

"Please take your hat off."

Charlie looked up, startled once again, but did as he asked.

"Look at me, Charlotte," Sean implored her softly and waited for her to comply.

Charlie had never seen a man look the way Sean looked at that moment. His face was a mask of tender determination, and she hoped he couldn't see the tears she felt gathering behind her eyes.

"I want you to listen to me, Charlotte, and listen well. I would *never* hit you. Do you hear me, Charlotte? *Never!*"

Sean watched her eyes carefully and waited until she nodded ever so slightly. Then without permission he pulled her against his chest. Cuddling her full against him, he settled his hands on her back, one thumb stroking idly along her shoulder blade. When he felt her arms come around his waist, albeit tentatively, he began to talk.

"My mother was a teacher. My oldest sister also taught before she started having children, and my younger sister has planned on becoming a teacher for as long as I can remember. I've always taken my reading skills for granted, but there were times when I think they saved my life.

"When we lived in Hawaii there was never enough to read. After coming to San Francisco and living with my Aunt Maureen, I learned what it was like to have a daily newspaper. I've always loved to read, and when I wasn't eating or out seeing the city, I could be found in my aunt's library, reading anything I could get my hands on.

"Then my mother died and my father left for the islands. I remember my sisters and I devoured every word of every newspaper available. I think the pain of my mother's death would have overwhelmed me if I hadn't had something to do with my mind. I wasn't trying to forget her, but dwelling on her loss wasn't doing me any good either. So I read.

"Rarely was a page turned that I didn't thank my mother, because she was the one who taught me to read. And Charlotte, I want to teach you."

Sean's hands slid back to her upper arms and he held her before him so he could look into her eyes.

"I want to open the world of words to you, Charlotte, because I think everyone should know how to read, and because there isn't a more precious gift *I* could give you in all the earth."

"What if I'm too stupid to learn?"

"There's nothing stupid about you."

Sean spoke with such sincerity that Charlie blinked. She did pick up on things rather quickly, but she had never stayed in school long enough to know if she could learn to read. Her grandfather had felt it unnecessary. *You know your numbers, Charlie, and enough words to get by. That's all I've ever learned. It's enough,* he used to say.

"Will you let me teach you to read?"

The question jerked Charlie back to the present, and before she could change her mind, she nodded her head. Sean grinned and pulled her into his arms again. After giving her a tender squeeze, he took her hand and led her back through the kitchen and into the living room, ignoring the unfinished dishes.

A mere moment went by before he had lit the lamp, retrieved the primer, and settled with her on the sofa. Sean read to her from the front of the book and then showed her the letters printed within.

Charlie didn't catch everything he said because she was so busy looking at him. She didn't know that men like Sean Donovan existed.

The talk around town is that you're falling for your husband. Those had been Duncan's words and Charlie felt something almost painful squeeze around her heart at the sight of this man beside her. She also found herself thinking, *the talk around town is true.*

Twenty-Four

SEAN DISCOVERED DURING their second lesson that Charlie had learned the alphabet. She looked so pleased with herself that he wanted to kiss her. When he began teaching her sounds, Sean made a point of starting with words that were pertinent in her world.

While most people learned that *A* is for apple and *B* is for boy, Charlie learned that *A* is for anvil, *B* is for bellows, and *C* is for carriage.

Charlie was as fast a learner as he had expected her to be. The first few days were great, so great, in fact, that Sean was a little confused when Charlie did not want to study on their third night.

"I need to go to Sadie's," she explained, hoping that Sean would not question her.

Sean didn't question her, but he did feel let down. She seemed almost as skittish and hesitant as she had been before they'd talked. It never occurred to him that she was harboring a secret. He was quiet as they made their way to Sadie's, and just as silent as he took his place at the kitchen table. Charlie glanced at him before going to find her aunt. Sean would have been surprised to know she was laden with guilt.

"Why do you look so down?" Sadie asked as soon as Charlie stepped into the small parlor.

"I just feel bad about leaving Sean in the kitchen."

"Well, tell him to come in here and get settled then. We'll measure your dress in the sewing room."

"Is it really ready for me to try on?" Charlie asked, excitement lighting her face.

"It sure is, honey, and I'm sorry I didn't have it ready for you last week."

"It's all right, Sadie; I'm sure the dress will be worth the wait."

"So you think you'll go to church this Sunday?"

"Sean and I haven't talked about it, but I think we'll try the church that Duncan and Lora attend."

"Good," Sadie said emphatically. "Now get Sean in here so we can get to work in the sewing room. I'll have the dress ready for you to take home when you come for your bath Saturday night."

Charlie could do nothing more than stare. Sadie had hurried her into the dress, made a few measurements, and whipped it back over her head before she could even think. Now the dress was hanging again, and Charlie stood before it and looked her fill.

The fabric was an off-white, almost a cream, with the palest of flowers and leaves swirled throughout in a delicate pattern. The only word that would come to Charlie's mind was "soft." The pink and blue flowers, and the green leaves and vines were all soft pastels. The small redhead reached out reverently to touch the fabric.

The sleeves were short and sewn to puff at the shoulders. The waist was gently gathered, and Charlie's hands went to her hips as she remembered the way the fabric fell in a flattering line from her waist.

"Well, what have we here?"

Charlie stiffened at the sound of Tansy's voice.

"My," Tansy said brightly, "what pretty material. I think the neckline is a little too high for my tastes, but then it's probably just right for your figure."

Wishing that Sadie hadn't left the room, Charlie watched as Tansy's shoulders went back to best display her full chest.

"Is Sean here?" Tansy did nothing to disguise the hope in her voice, and Charlie nodded reluctantly.

The voluptuous girl shot out of the room, and Charlie, after another look at her dress, followed slowly. She knew the exact moment Tansy found Sean because her voice went up three octaves in a way she thought men found attractive.

Charlie entered the small parlor to find Sean standing behind the chair and Sadie sitting on the sofa. Tansy was in front of the chair talking to Sean. His look was guarded.

"Why Sean, if I didn't know better I'd think you didn't like me." Her full lips went into a pout, and Charlie watched Sadie's eyes narrow.

"Would it help if I had Sadie make me a dress like the one she's making Charlie?"

Sean's eyes swung to his wife as Charlie, looking utterly crestfallen, turned and walked stiffly from the room.

So that's why we're over here, Sean thought. *Sadie is making a dress for my wife, and Tansy just let the cat out of the bag.* He knew it was time to put the situation in order. He came back around to the front of the chair and stood in front of Tansy. When she put one hand on his chest he removed it none too gently.

The stunning blonde looked with genuine confusion at the man before her and then took a step back.

"I'm a happily married man, Tansy," Sean's voice was implacable, "and you'll do well to remember that. Do not touch me or flirt with me again. I won't put up with it."

Tansy misunderstood, and a sly smile lit her face. "Afraid you won't be able to control yourself?"

"Exactly," Sean said sternly, only to finish by dashing Tansy's hopes. "I've never hit a woman before, and I really don't ever care to, but no one is going to hurt my wife, physically or emotionally, and get away with it."

Tansy looked around in surprise to see that Charlie had left the room. She stared uncomprehendingly at Sean and then Sadie.

"I never meant any harm, Sadie; Charlie knows that."

"No she doesn't, Tansy." Sadie's voice was the angriest Tansy had ever heard. "You've spent a lot of years playing games with men, and Charlie's never done anything but work. Now she has a man and a chance for some happiness of her own, and you're trying to take that away from her. You oughta be ashamed."

The younger woman was dispirited. She carefully turned her face away from Sean as she asked Sadie if she could still room with her.

"If you stay away from my niece's husband," Sadie answered, her voice softening some when she saw the look of regret on her boarder's face.

Sadie was still looking out the door that Tansy exited when Sean kissed her cheek. Her head whipped around in surprise to find Sean grinning at her.

"Thanks, Sadie," he said before going in search of his wife.

"You're welcome," Sadie breathed, even though he was already out of earshot. She sat thinking that if Sean Donovan wasn't married to her niece, Tansy still wouldn't stand a chance. She'd go after him herself.

Charlie stood up from the back steps the moment Sean came out the door. She led the way home and didn't speak or even look at her husband. In fact, she would have gone straight to her room if Sean's voice hadn't stopped her in the hallway.

"I'm a married man, Charlotte, and where I come from that means commitment."

Charlie stopped outside her door and stared at Sean, who stood flooded in the moonlight that came through her bedroom window.

"It's nice if two people are in love, but marriage has to be built on more, or it won't last through the hard times. Even if I found Tansy attractive, which I don't, I'm committed to you and to this marriage."

Sean didn't wait for his wife to reply or even acknowledge his statement before he went into his own bedroom and shut the door.

Charlie looked at that door for a long time before closing her own to prepare for bed. She tried to relax, but she couldn't dispel the idea that Sean would never *really* be hers because he wasn't there by choice.

Twenty-Five

CHARLIE WENT TO the post office first thing Saturday morning. No one ever wrote to her, since she had no family or friends outside of Visalia, but since Sean had been in touch with his family, she checked the mail every few days. Today there was not just a letter, but a *box* for P. Sean Donovan III. Charlie had to stop herself from running back to the livery.

Sean was intent on his work when Charlie arrived, and not wanting to startle him or cause an accident, Charlie waited for him to notice her. When he finally glanced her way, she raised the box excitedly, telling him he'd received a package.

Charlie turned and walked over to put the box on their lunch table. Sean followed her, and Charlie stood back while he worked over the string. She watched as he unwrapped a book. It took her a moment to realize that it was a Bible.

Any words that Charlie might have uttered deserted her as she watched Sean lift the book to his chest. He held it in his arms like the cherished possession that it was. His eyes were shut, and Charlie watched as a single small tear slid out one corner.

Only a minute or two passed before Sean composed himself and sat down to read the letter he found inside, but Charlie could have sworn it had been an eternity. The sight of her husband hugging his Bible and crying would be imprinted on her mind for the rest of her years.

What was in this Bible that Sean found so dear, or it just that he had heard from his family? It was a question that hung in Charlie's mind even as she sat on crate next to her husband and waited until he was finished reading.

My dearest Sean,

There are no words to describe how we felt about your letter. You can imagine how we've prayed and longed to see you. I can't think straight when I imagine you with a rope around your neck. I would love to meet Charlotte and thank her for your life. (We thank God too.) If I understand you correctly, you didn't know Charlotte before you were married. Is that right? Please tell me more when you write back.

Marcail is working on a letter to you, and in fact might arrive before this package. I took the liberty of sending your Bible; I knew you would want it.

You were so young when you left here that it's hard to envision you married. Is there anyone else who could watch the livery so you could both come to Santa Rosa for a visit? We would love to have you for as long as you could stay.

Gretchen and Molly are doing well—in fact everyone is on their feet except me. I'm still resting from having miscarried a baby. It was hard to lose this baby. We were so excited about him, and even though I was only three months along, this tiny infant was already a part of my heart. I know, however, that God's will is perfect. There have been tears, but Rigg and I are comforted in the fact that all through Scripture we read that our God is a righteous and fair God. Knowing this, we believe with all our hearts that this unborn baby is with Him.

What is Visalia like? Is your work steady? Have you found a Bible-preaching church? As you can see, I'm full of questions. I wish we could meet face to face and catch up. Bill, May, Jeff, and Bobbie all send their love. They're also joining us in prayer for Charlotte's salvation. I won't mention this again, so you won't fear Charlotte reading your letters, but know that we are praying.

I love you, Sean, and pray for you always.

Until next time,
Katie

Drained after reading the letter, Sean wondered for a moment why Katie had made no mention of his father. He suddenly became conscious of his wife sitting beside him, and even more conscious of a headache coming on, possibly, due to holding his tears in check.

"Were they glad to hear from you?"

"Yes," Sean answered and turned his head to look at her. "They wish they could meet you. In fact, they invited us for a visit if someone could watch the livery."

Charlie's mouth dropped open. "But they don't even know me."

"That doesn't matter. You're my wife, and they love you."

Charlie turned away from her husband's penetrating look. She stared across the livery at nothing and then spoke in a whisper.

"I'm sorry you can't see your family, but there's no one who could—"

She broke off when Sean's hand moved under her chin. He tenderly grasped her jaw and urged her to look at him. Her gaze was one of apology and regret.

"I didn't mean to insinuate that we should pack up and go to Santa Rosa," Sean said. "I just thought you'd like to know that my family is eager to meet you. I'll have to explain to them that due to the conditions that the judge explained, I can't leave town for five years."

Charlie nodded, and Sean gently caressed her chin with his thumb before he rose and went back to work.

San Francisco

"Rigg!" Maureen Kent gasped when she saw the man her servant had just announced. "What are you doing here?"

"Have I missed Patrick?" Rigg asked about his father-in-law.

"No, he doesn't sail until morning. What's happened?"

"Rigg!"

Before Rigg could answer, Patrick Sean Donovan II had come down from upstairs and joined his sister and son-in-law in the library.

"I'm glad I didn't miss you, Patrick," Rigg breathed with relief, seeing that his presence had upset them. "We received news about Sean after you left."

Patrick sat down hard on the nearest chair, his face draining of color.

"I knew you were going to be here a few weeks before you sailed, and if I'd missed you I'd never have forgiven myself for not sending a telegram—but I wanted to come in person. Then Katie suffered a miscarriage, so I couldn't leave right away."

"Oh, Rigg," Maureen began, but he cut her off gently.

"She's all right. The doctor just wants her to rest."

Rigg stood for a moment, feeling like he needed to catch his breath.

"I have a letter, but I think I should warn you—"

"Is he alive?" the older man cut him off, his voice hoarse.

"Yes."

"Then nothing else matters."

Rigg passed the letter to Patrick and waited while he read. As soon as he had read it silently, he read it aloud to his sister, who cried in her handkerchief for some minutes. The room was silent until Maureen contained herself. Then Rigg spoke.

"Is there anything I can do?"

"Yes," Patrick replied. "You can come with me to tell the captain of the *Silver Angel* that I won't need passage, and then to the stage office so I can buy a ticket for Visalia."

Twenty-Six

"IN THE BEGINNING was the Word, and the Word was with God, and the Word was God. The same was in the beginning with God."

Sean could only read the first two verses from the book of John before his eyes filled with tears. He knew Charlie had supper on the table, but he felt an urgency to spend a few moments in God's Word. He bowed his head and prayed before he left the room. Sean thanked God for his life, his wife, and his family before his mind swung back to Charlotte and dwelt there.

"I don't know if this is love, God," he whispered, "but I care for her so much. Please help Charlotte to understand that she needs to know Your Son personally. Please save her and use us to Your glory."

The moment these words were out of his mouth, Sean envisioned them leaving for Hawaii. He stood from his kneeling place next to the bed and gazed out the window like a man in a trance.

"Back to Hawaii! Oh, God," Sean cried softly, "could that thought be from You, because nothing would make me happier than for me to return to Hawaii with Charlotte, so we could work with Father."

Sean took a moment more to give his future to God and in doing so felt an indescribable peace fall over him. He knew he couldn't tell Charlie how he felt, but he also knew that if the thought *had* come from the Lord, then He would work it out.

"Sean," Charlie called from outside the door. He'd taken more time than he thought. He opened the door to see her waiting in the hall.

"Are you all right?"

"I'm fine, Charlotte. I was reading my Bible. Did I keep you long?"

"No, but I did wonder what had happened to you. Sadie expects us for baths tonight, and I'm tired. I'd like to get over there and home before it gets too late."

Charlie talked as she led the way to the supper table where the young couple sat down and ate. Their conversation was light. Then over dishes, Charlie brought up a subject that nearly made Sean drop the plate he was drying.

"I think we should go to church in the morning."

Sean didn't answer for a moment, and Charlie turned from the dishpan to look at him. "What do you think?"

"I'd like that, Charlotte, if you're sure."

"I'm sure. I think we should go to Duncan and Lora's church."

"That sounds fine." *Fine* was not the way Sean was feeling. Ecstatic, overjoyed, or elated better described his mood, but he wasn't sure he would be able to explain himself to Charlie if he suddenly began to do hand stands in the kitchen.

Ten minutes later they were on their way to Sadie's, and Charlie asked if Sean's family was well.

"They're doing pretty well. I should have read the letter to you over supper."

"You don't mind if I know what's in the letter?" Charlie seemed surprised.

"Not at all. In fact, I'll read it to you when we get home."

Charlie didn't reply, but she was so pleased she wanted to laugh just for the pleasure of it. Sean's family sounded wonderful, and he didn't seem at all hesitant to share them with her. She wouldn't trade Sadie for royalty, but for some reason, Sean's family was fascinating to her.

And the fascination only grew when they returned home and Sean read the letter. Charlie thought the names Gretchen and Molly were beautiful, and she felt terrible over Kaitlin's losing her baby.

Sean made no mention of Charlie's salvation, and so the letter just read that the family was praying for her. Charlie had never had anyone say that to her, and even though she told herself she really didn't believe in such things, the thought warmed her spirit.

Charlie was still thinking on everything Sean had said when he told her he would feed the animals in the morning. She thanked him rather absently and took herself off to bed. Imaginary visions of how Kaitlin, Marcail, Gretchen, and Molly might look filled her head as sleep overtook her.

Twenty-Seven

THE NEXT MORNING Charlie spent over 40 minutes with her dress and hair, and for a woman who usually dressed in five minutes, this was quite a task.

Sean's back was to the hallway when she entered the kitchen. Already regretting her last-minute decision to leave her hat behind, Charlie had just decided to return for it when Sean turned.

Sean had not heard her come into the room. He had been flipping pancakes, and it had taken a moment for him to realize he wasn't alone. He turned unsuspectingly with a ready smile and a morning greeting for his wife, but the words died in his throat.

Charlie's hair was swept up on top of her head in a loose bun that allowed wispy little curls to fall around her neck and forehead. Sean's eyes traveled from her slender white neck to the hem of her flowered dress and then swung back to her face. In those seconds he took in her slim waist, small breasts, and gently rounded hips. She was so utterly feminine that Sean was speechless.

"The pancakes are burning," Charlie whispered softly, having stood silent for his inspection.

Sean spun back to the stove, relieved to have a diversion. *She's darling,* he said to himself, *and she's my darling.*

Charlie took a place at the table and waited for Sean to join her. Sean ate his meal without once looking at his plate. Charlie's face was flushed with embarrassment and something else she couldn't quite define.

"You look very beautiful," Sean said at the end of the meal, easily holding her gaze with his own.

"Thank you." Charlie was so pleased by his words that she felt tears sting her eyes and looked swiftly down at her coffee cup.

When it was time to leave for church, it seemed to Charlie the most natural thing in the world to have Sean hitch up the buggy and help her up to her seat, an act she had never before let him perform. She felt like a lady for the first time in her life as Sean held the reins loosely in his grip and drove the buggy from the livery.

"I haven't been in church since I was a child. I'm not sure I'm going to like this."

"What has you worried?" Sean asked her softly, always alert when she spoke of her life before they met.

"Churches are full of hypocrites."

"Give me an example."

"Well, you know, when you see a man in church on Sunday and then watch him stagger out of one of the town bars on Tuesday night."

"You've seen that happen?"

"No, I guess I haven't, but I hear things."

"Charlotte," Sean asked as he realized his wife's fears were causing her judgmental remarks. "Have you ever been to this church?"

"No," she said softly. She didn't have anything more to say, but fear was closing her throat and she couldn't have spoken had she tried.

"Charlotte, try to relax," Sean bent close and whispered in his wife's ear.

"I am relaxed."

Sean smiled at her reply. Her hands were clenched so tightly in her lap that her knuckles were white. The last song had been sung, and the minister was now at the front of the church behind a small pulpit for the sermon.

The Donovans were seated alone in a rear pew, and Sean was thankful for the privacy. He reached for one of her hands and brought it to the bench between them, where it was nearly hidden by the fullness of Charlie's dress.

Her hand was swallowed up by his own and ice cold. Something in Sean's heart turned over. Not that this was an unfamiliar sensation; his heart had been doing funny things for a week. Sean never dreamed a man could feel this way about a woman, and his hand tightened thinking how *right* hers felt within his own.

His thoughts were cut off when the sermon began. He took a quick peek at his wife and saw that she was attentive, and not as tied up in knots as she had been.

"I'm going to read this morning from John, chapter 3. Feel free to follow along in your own copy of God's Word. 'There was a man of the Pharisees, named Nicodemus, a ruler of the Jews; the same came to Jesus by night, and said unto him, "Rabbi, we know that thou art a teacher come from God; for no man can do these miracles that thou doest, except God be with him." Jesus answered, and said unto him, "Verily, verily, I say unto thee, except a man be born again, he cannot see the kingdom of God."'

"I need to stop here and tell you what I know about this man Nicodemus. As it says here in verse one, he was a man of the Pharisees. This was a sect of men who lived by a very strict code of laws. And the biggest problem wasn't the fact that it was impossible to obey all these laws, but that even if they could have obeyed them to the letter, it would not have saved them.

"Nicodemus must have been one of the few to see the fallacy of the Pharisee's laws. He'd certainly heard of Jesus Christ and the miracles He was able to perform, and his heart must have been hungry to know Him better.

"I find it interesting to note that Nicodemus went to Jesus by night. It's speculation on my part, but I wonder whether Nicodemus was afraid to be seen going to Jesus, or whether he felt an urgency to know the truth and couldn't wait until morning. You see, I don't believe that he doubted that this was God's Son. I know that in the Scripture Nicodemus just says God is *with* Jesus, but Nicodemus is no fool. I believe he understood that he was talking to Jesus the Christ, God's holy Son.

"I want to talk with you more about this passage of Scripture. I want you to know what the Bible has to say about Jesus Christ in the weeks to come. But before I run out of time, I must stop and ask you this: When was the last time you talked to Jesus Christ as Nicodemus did?

"We can't stand face to face with Jesus as he was able to do, but let me tell you, friends, we *can* talk to Christ as though He were in the room. I'm referring to prayer. Maybe you think praying is just for preachers, but I assure you it's not. God wants to hear from each and every one of you. First, He wants to hear you pray and give yourself to Him, or as Jesus said to be 'born again,' as we must do if we want to have eternal life. Then He wants to hear you praise Him and share your every need.

"I'm going to close with my favorite verses in all of Scripture, and they are in the same passage we are in today. John 3:16 and 17 say, 'For God so loved the world that he gave his only begotten Son, that whosoever believeth in him should not perish, but have everlasting life. For God sent not his Son into the world to condemn the world, but that the world through him might be saved.'

"If there is any doubt in your mind as to what those verses mean, please come and see me. Don't let another day pass without settling your eternity. You can know this Jesus Christ as your own personal Lord and Savior."

The congregation was dismissed with a song and then a brief prayer. Sean and Charlie stood and moved toward the door of the church. Sean was unsure what type of welcome he would receive, and afraid that if Charlie saw him rebuffed it would only confirm her belief that some of these people were hypocrites. Sean knew from firsthand experience that born-again Christians were not perfect, and he understood that they might be quite hesitant to associate with a convicted bank robber.

Sean convinced himself that leaving quickly was the best answer to protecting his wife's feelings. They were halfway to the buggy when Duncan called out. Sean and Charlie both turned to see Visalia's sheriff and his wife approaching, each wearing huge smiles of welcome.

Twenty-Eight

"IT'S GREAT TO see you here, Sean." Duncan spoke softy while Lora took Charlie over to meet her daughter and grandson.

"It's great to be here," Sean cheerfully replied, grabbing Duncan's hand.

"How are things going at home and in the livery?"

"Unbelievably. Charlotte treats me like a king."

Duncan nodded. "I knew you would do well together. I'm sure you've caught on that her growing-up years were not easy."

"She doesn't share much, but it's obvious."

"Have you had a chance to talk about spiritual things?"

"Not really. I mean, she's somewhat open when we talk, but I think she's afraid to ask too many questions; fearful of intruding into my past. And I'm wary of pushing her and saying too much."

"I can understand that. We'll keep praying, Sean."

"Thanks, Duncan. I want you to know that my main prayer is that Charlotte will come to Christ. God has already answered so many prayers in my life, so quickly, and I really do understand that oftentimes He asks us to wait. I was saved from hanging, and just minutes later I was married. Now in a very short time I've come to care deeply for my wife.

"My deepest desire is that Charlotte will be saved and we'll go to Hawaii someday to continue the mission work there. It's not going to happen overnight, like it has so far, but God is sufficient, and I know that in His time, we'll be wherever He leads."

Duncan reached out and touched the younger man's shoulder. He seemed unable to speak, and Sean, who turned to watch his wife some ten yards away, was glad for the silence.

Sean lay in bed Sunday night and reflected on the day. There had been nothing but handshakes and smiles of welcome from the pastor and the rest of the congregation. Duncan and Lora had even asked them to dinner, but Charlie had explained with visible regret that her Aunt Sadie was expecting them.

Lora, in her gracious, unpretentious manner, simply asked the Donovans to come the following week, and Charlie had quickly accepted. Sean wondered if anyone had ever tried to reach out to Charlie in the past, or if someone had tried and been rejected. He also wondered how much of this she was doing for him. He felt grateful over this thought, but also prayed that Charlie would soon have an interest in eternal issues.

For the first time he understood the way his sister must have felt as she watched him grow harder and harder toward God. Kaitlin had known that Sean's eternity was secure, while Sean didn't have the same assurance about Charlie's, but that wouldn't stop the ache, the longing, to have your loved one walk in the way of the Lord.

Sean fell asleep thinking about his father. Had he ever made it back to Santa Rosa? Evidently not, since Katie hadn't even mentioned him in her letter. Sean tried not to read anything into that, but he knew in an instant that he was not completely over his anger. Within seconds his mind was immersed in his painful past. How long would Father stay away? How long before he would see that his family needed him? How long before things could be patched up between father and son?

If only we could be in touch, even in a letter. Those were Sean's last thoughts before he remembered he'd written back to his sister just that evening and asked about Father. Now all he could do was wait, or hope that Marcail's letter would arrive with some news.

"Do you believe what that preacher said on Sunday about prayer?"

Sean sighed with relief over the question. Charlie had been very quiet since Sunday morning, and Sean simply didn't know how to ask her what she was thinking. It was Wednesday, and they were relaxing in the living room of their small home as the sun sank low in the sky.

"Yes, I believe it. Is there something in particular you're questioning?"

Charlie looked embarrassed and then quietly admitted, "I'm not really sure there's even Someone up there, let alone talking as though God was in the same room with me."

"Why don't you think God exists?"

Charlie shrugged. "He never answered my prayers when I was young, so I knew He wasn't there and just stopped praying."

Sean wasn't sure what to say. He believed that God's will was perfect, even when it hurt, but how did you explain that to someone whose faith was nonexistent?

"What types of things did you pray about?" Sean felt he had picked a safe question and was certain when a smile came over his wife's face.

"I wanted a pony of my very own," Charlie sighed. "All the horses were always so big for me, and I wanted one I could mount and ride on my own. But a pony wouldn't have been an asset to the business, so Grandpa said no."

Sean was quiet, hoping that she would continue. He never suspected that his feelings, already very protective, would forever deepen in their intensity.

"I also asked God to make my grandfather stop hitting me." Charlie didn't look at Sean as she continued, "It seemed that I couldn't do anything right when I was growing up, and Grandpa's answer was always an openhanded blow. Sadie said it wasn't me, that he was just like that. He used to slap her all the time too.

"Sadie also believes that he hit my mother so hard that she died having me. My mother would never tell him who my father was, and even though she'd always been his favorite child, Grandpa wouldn't forgive her.

"Sadie married Harry just to get away from Grandpa, and they had a good life together. They even tried to take me in, but Grandpa fell in love with my red hair. Even though he acted like he hated me half of the time, he wouldn't let me go."

Charlie had stared out the window for this emotionless recital, and Sean couldn't take his eyes from her. How could anyone have mistreated this girl? How could anyone have laid a violent hand on this woman? They were sharing the sofa, and an instant later, Sean, overcome with his newfound emotions, covered the distance that separated them and took his wife in his arms.

Charlie whispered in his ear as she let him hold her close, "I'm all right, Sean."

"Well, I'm not," he whispered back and settled her head more comfortably on his shoulder. "I'm not going to let anyone else hurt you."

His hold was almost crushing her, but Charlie didn't resist. After a few moments she sighed, "It was all a long time ago." She sounded very reasonable. "You are really too sensitive, you know, and I don't know what I'm going to do with you."

Sean didn't answer. He pressed his lips to her fore-head and his arms tightened slightly. Charlie turned her head to look up into his face, glad that she was once again without her hat. Sean's eyes traveled caressingly over her features and emotions flooded through him, ranging from fierce protectiveness to tender desire.

He realized in that instant that he was truly in love with this woman. He ached to declare his love for her, but a tiny fear of rejection lingered in his mind. The desire to kiss her was overpowering, and almost of its own volition his head began to lower. His lips were just a breath away from Charlie's when a knock sounded at the front door.

Sean drew back reluctantly. He rose from the sofa, but the look of longing on his wife's face made him sit back down and reach for her. The knock sounded again.

"Later," Sean said in a strained voice as he once again pulled away. "We'll finish this later."

The sun was still casting an orange glow in the sky as Sean answered the summons at the door. There wasn't much light, and the man at the door was now a stranger, but Sean knew him. His face was older, and he looked thinner than the boy of 14 remembered, but Sean would have known his father anywhere.

Twenty-Nine

PATRICK FELT AS if the air had been knocked from his body at the sight of his son. He had left a frightened 14-year-old boy and come back to find a man, strong of limb and features. In fact, he felt like he was looking at a younger version of himself.

"Hello, Sean." The older man spoke softly.

Sean was silent as he moved back and held the door for his father to enter. Patrick stepped across the threshold and stood with his hat in his hand. Sean made no move to touch him, and the two men stood in the lantern light eyeing one another. Sean wished he could say just one of the things he had rehearsed while he waited for this man. Patrick was also quiet, not wanting to say anything that might drive an even bigger wedge between them.

Charlie, curious about the silence in the kitchen, came from the living room and stood beside her husband. Patrick's gaze swung to the small redhead and he smiled in relief.

"You must be Charlotte?" he guessed. Setting his small bag down, Patrick held out his hand. Charlie was quick to offer her hand to this stranger, having weighed the situation up in an instant. "I'm Patrick Donovan, Sean's father."

"It's nice to meet you," Charlie offered sincerely.

"How did you know this was Charlotte?" Sean asked, speaking his first words.

"I was just in Santa Rosa for a visit, and then I was at your aunt's with plans to sail when Rigg showed up with your letter."

125

"This is your first visit back then?"

"No, actually it isn't," Patrick said somewhat reluctantly. "I was back two years ago, but when I arrived in Santa Rosa, Katie told me I'd missed you by about six weeks."

"*Six weeks,*" Sean said the words in a stunned whisper as pain crowded in around his chest. After a moment he seemed to mentally shake himself. "Well, come in and have a seat. Are you hungry?"

"Thank you, no."

Once in the living room, Charlie and Sean took the sofa and Patrick took the chair. Again silence prevailed.

"Was it a rough trip over from San Francisco?" asked Charlie.

"Not bad," Patrick smiled at his daughter-in-law for the lifeline she had tossed him. "This is hot country over here, but I met some interesting people."

"You came by train?"

"For the most part. It's a good way to see the area." The remark sounded ridiculous even to his own ears, but nothing else came to mind.

"I've never been on a train," Charlie continued, thinking that the elder Mr. Donovan looked rather lost.

She wished that Sean would get involved in the conversation. He was sitting ramrod straight, his eyes taking in Charlie and his father with measured glances. Sean's face, Charlie noted, gave away none of his feelings. Charlie talked with her father-in-law for the better part of an hour before he rose.

"Well, it's been good visiting with you, but it's getting late. If you could point me in the direction of the hotel, I'll go get a room for the night." He tried to keep the disappointment from his voice.

"You don't need to stay at the hotel," Charlie said as she and Sean both stood. "We don't really have room for you, but my aunt runs a boardinghouse and I know she'd be glad to have you. It's very clean, and you would have your own room."

"Well, if you're sure it wouldn't be an imposition."

"I'm sure. Sean and I can walk you over."

It was a silent threesome that made their way to Sadie's. Sean stood with his father in the kitchen while Charlie went in search of Sadie.

"Sadie is very hospitable," Sean told his father. "Don't hesitate to ask for whatever you need."

"I won't."

Again the heavy silence fell.

"I smith for Charlotte at the livery," Sean began again. "I have to work tomorrow, but you're welcome to come by anytime."

"Thank you, Sean," Patrick responded, working again to keep the emotion from his voice. "I'll plan on that."

Sadie bustled into the room a moment later, and before following her to his room, Patrick bid his family goodnight.

Seeing how badly he needed time to adjust to his father's presence, Charlie wasted no time in getting Sean out the door and home. As soon as they were within the walls of their own home, Charlie told Sean she was going to bed.

"I'm tired, and I suspect you need some time to think." Charlie turned toward the hallway and then hesitated. "If you need to talk, Sean, just knock on my door."

"Thanks, Charlotte."

Sean waited until she had gone into her room before moving toward his own. He did need some time, she had been right about that, but what was he to do with that time? Did he pray and ask God to erase all the years of hurt and confusion, or did he walk straight back to Sadie's and confront the father he believed had deserted him and his sisters when they needed him most?

Sean opted for prayer. Not so that he could forget all the hurt, but so that he could put aside the anger and bitterness that still rode him. If he didn't, he was sure to have even more regrets after what was certain to be a brief time with his father.

Why didn't you come back? Didn't you realize how much we needed you? I was so angry with you, I think I must have hated you. I can't believe you could put the work at the mission ahead of your family . . .

Sean's thoughts gave him little rest through the night. But the anger in his heart was abating, and Sean was pleased because he didn't want to face his father with angry words. The questions that came to his mind again and again, however, *had* to be answered.

One look at Sean's face the following morning, and Charlie knew just how bad his night had been; hers hadn't been much better. As soon as she had shut her door, she wished she had asked Sean to move into her bedroom. They needed each other, for love and companionship. It was impossible to say when the time would be right again. The thought saddened her.

The conversation over breakfast was subdued, and both husband and wife were glad to get into the livery to start their daily tasks. Sean was in the midst of shoeing one of their own horses when his father appeared.

Sean's back was to the stall opening, and Charlie, not wanting to break his concentration, did not alert him of his father's presence.

Patrick watched in fascination as his son worked. Katie had written about the fine blacksmith Sean had been when he was 16 and 17, but as Patrick watched Sean's capable hands, he realized that her letters didn't do him justice. Patrick also took note of Charlie, who assisted her husband with quiet efficiency. They made an ideal partnership.

He prayed silently as the couple finished, asking God as he had last night and all this morning to ease the way between Sean and himself. He knew he deserved his son's anger, but he also knew that he would go nowhere until things between them were settled. Sean had been so silent the night before that Patrick had no gauge as to how long that could take. He prayed that his emotions as well as his finances would hold.

The task complete, Sean emerged from the stall, effectively breaking into his father's thoughts. Again Patrick spoke the first words that came to mind.

"Your grandfather was a blacksmith back in Ireland, Sean. I don't know if you remember me telling you that."

"Actually, I'd forgotten," Sean's said, surprise filling his voice. Then the memories flooded back. "You helped him from the time you could walk."

"That's right, I did—right up to the day before I left for America."

An uncomfortable silence fell for the space of a few heartbeats, and then Sean began to show his father around the livery. Patrick was as impressed as Sean had been on his first day. Charlie joined them, and Sean moved from stall to stall with his arm around his wife. It was a comfort to touch her; his life with her seemed more concrete to him than being able to call this man Father.

The day was not as uncomfortable as Sean would have thought. In fact, although impersonal, the next three days were very relaxed. Patrick spelled Charlie in the livery whenever he could, and Charlie, although she missed Sean's company, left father and son alone often, knowing they needed to talk.

Charlie could have stayed without worrying. In the end, the showdown between father and son was to come at a time no one could have predicted.

Thirty

I<small>T</small> <small>FELT VERY</small> odd for Sean to be taking his father to church. He wondered at the tenseness he felt, and then realized how much he craved his father's approval of the church he attended.

As the pastor had said, they were once again studying the life of Jesus Christ. Each time Sean looked down at his own Bible, his eyes drifted to his father's lap and the Bible resting there, remembering the Christmas his mother had given it to him.

Sean had been about nine that Christmas, and very interested in boats and sailing. He simply couldn't understand why his mother was so excited to be giving her husband a new Bible. A *Bible?* Surely his father would be disappointed. To Sean's surprise, he wasn't.

On Christmas morning it was the last gift to be opened, and Sean had watched his mother sit on the edge of her chair. He had no idea how long she had waited for that Bible to arrive, praying it would be on time and undamaged.

Sean could see in an instant that his father was thrilled with his gift. He caressed the leather binding and touched the pages before turning unsuspectingly to the front where his mother had written some well-chosen words.

Sean recalled the way his father's eyes swam with tears as he looked across the room at his spouse. It was some time before Sean was able to see what his mother had written, but he knew they were words he would never forget.

129

My darling Patrick,

No day passes that I don't rejoice in our marriage. No month goes by that I don't see you growing in the Word. With each new year our love increases. And when at last we stand in heaven, I'll thank our eternal Father for blessing our life together here on this soil.

All my love,
Theresa

The Bible was no longer new, and the woman who had written the message had gone on before them, but her message was as powerful to Sean now as it was the first time he had read it. Sean suddenly felt overwhelmed with the loss of his mother. It wasn't really his mother's death that grieved him as much as his father's having to be alone, and how little he now knew his father because of the mistakes he had made.

With an effort Sean pulled his mind back to the present. He had missed half the sermon while his mind wandered to events of the past and things he couldn't change. There was the present and the future to think about, and in those he could play a part. It was time to talk with his father; not the small talk they'd been uttering for days, but *real* talk.

Having come to this decision, Sean remembered they were going to Duncan's for dinner. He prayed for patience over the delay, and then asked God to bless them when the timing was right.

The conversation over dinner was lighthearted and fun. Duncan and Lora were thrilled to meet Patrick and welcomed him into their home with all the love and graciousness that Charlie and Sean had come to expect.

The party of five was just finishing their coffee and dessert when Duncan's deputy came to the door. He said he had a problem at the office that would not wait. Duncan regretfully bid his wife and guests goodbye.

Sean and Patrick both offered to help the women with cleanup, but Lora said the kitchen was too small for so much help. She showed them into a spacious, comfortable living room and left them alone.

Patrick was silent as his gaze took in the room, and it was a few moments before he realized Sean was staring at him. Their eyes met, so alike in shape and color, and Sean finally asked the question that had been on his mind for more than five years.

"Why didn't you come back?"

Patrick's eyes slid shut for just an instant, relieved that his son finally wanted to talk.

"At first, it was because they needed me, Sean."

"We needed you too."

"I know you did, but at the time, I believed they needed me more."

Sean was quiet as the remembered pain flooded back in upon him, and then he realized exactly what his father had said.

"What did you mean—at first?"

Patrick seemed reluctant then, but Sean never took his eyes from his father, forcing Patrick to take a deep breath and tell his story.

"As selfish as this is to admit, it was almost a relief to have a catastrophe on my hands the moment I returned to the islands. I was so busy for the first seven months that I had little time to miss you kids and your mother.

"But then things began to regulate. Not enough so that I felt I could leave, but enough so that I had more time on my hands—time to think about all I'd lost. The evenings were the worst. When daylight disappeared and there was nothing more I could do for the day, I'd go back to our empty little house that had miraculously survived the hurricane and sit alone until I thought I would die of loneliness, or worse yet, have to keep on living. Then the lies began."

"The lies?" Sean broke in softly, not fully believing what he was hearing.

"Yes, lies," Patrick admitted. "It was easy, you know, to lie in the letters and tell you I was doing well and praying for you. But I wasn't. I was so eaten up with bitterness that God would take my wife when I believed I needed her most that I stopped praying."

"But you continued to minister to the people there?"

"Yes, I did, and only a select few knew I was struggling. When I finally made it to Santa Rosa, Katie told me how your backsliding had been slow in coming. I couldn't help but think how alike we are.

"Not that I was happy about such a comparison, but three years had passed before I made it back to California and spiritually, I was still on shaky ground. In fact, it was in Santa Rosa that I got things straight, and in a way I have you to thank."

"Me?"

"Yes, Sean, you. When I watched your mother's health decline, I thought I'd felt as helpless as a man could, but at least I knew where she was. It was worse with you. I'm thankful that Katie spared me nothing. She told me, sometimes at the top of her voice, how disappointed she was, and how I'd missed you by only a few weeks. I can't tell you the pain I felt to think that my 17-year-old son was out wandering the state and possibly the country, on his own. The decision to leave was yours, Sean, but I should have returned sooner. I just kept telling myself that I couldn't face all of you. You thought I was a pillar of spiritual strength. In actuality, I was a mass of pain and anger."

"I still don't understand where I came into the picture."

Patrick took a breath; remembering was painful. "The helplessness Sean—that was my final downfall. You were gone and I didn't know where. I had no other choice but to call on God and give myself back to Him completely. My despair was so great that I don't believe I would be here today had I not done just that."

Patrick fell silent at this point, giving Sean time to think. Of all the scenarios he had conjured up in his mind, the idea of his father living in bitterness against God was not one of them. But so much made sense now. Sean could never reckon the man who left California with a man who could leave his family for years, but now Sean saw that it could happen.

Sean wanted to thank his father for baring his heart so completely, but there was a little more he had to know.

"You said you had been in Santa Rosa for a visit, so I assume you went back to Hawaii two years ago."

"Yes, I did. I stayed with Rigg and Katie for about two months and then with Maureen for a few weeks."

"Did you take Marc with you?"

"No," Patrick smiled. "Your sister had become quite grown up, and she told me very seriously that she wished to remain in Santa Rosa. I felt it was for the best, so I went back alone."

"What brought you back now?"

"Time. When I left two years ago I decided I would not stay away for more than a two-year period, no matter what was happening on the islands."

"Were you in Santa Rosa when Kate had her miscarriage?" Sean's voice was as impersonal as it had been during the entire conversation.

"No." Patrick suddenly looked older than Sean had ever seen him. "Rigg told me when he got to Maureen's. He also told me that she deliberately kept from mentioning me in her letter to you because she didn't know if Rigg would catch me before I sailed."

"I'm glad he did." Sean spoke thickly, no longer able to hide his breaking heart.

"Are you really, Sean? Are you really glad?" Patrick's voice was desperate, and Sean saw the tears in his eyes.

Lora and Charlie planned to join the men at that moment, but the sight of Patrick and Sean embracing in the middle of the room stayed their action.

As they turned away, Lora saw the tears in Charlie's eyes and assumed they were tears of joy, as her own were. She would have been surprised to know that Charlie's tears came from believing she had just lost the most precious thing she'd ever found.

Thirty-One

THE NEXT THREE days were a time of joy and laughter for Sean and his father. They talked almost nonstop. Sean learned of his sisters' activities and those of his beloved nieces. Aunt Maureen had sent her love also, and Sean had even taken time to write to her.

Patrick also spent time getting to know his daughter-in-law, and joined the family with renewed purpose in prayers for her salvation. But it was obvious that something had changed between husband and wife.

That Charlie was trying to give Patrick and Sean time together was clear, but she seemed to be doing so at the expense of her own marriage. Patrick said as much to Sean one evening when they were alone in the living room.

"It's time for me to go, Sean."

"So soon?"

Patrick nodded. "It is soon, but my presence is not helping your marriage, and I think that needs to be a priority right now."

Sean's face was a mask of confusion. Finally he spoke. "She seems to have drawn farther away from me every day you've been here, and yet I know she likes you."

"Have you had a chance to ask her about it, like when you retire for the night?"

Sean hesitated for only a moment. "We don't share a bedroom."

Patrick was not surprised at the lack of intimacy in the marriage. He had been happily, *intimately*, married for over 20 years himself,

134

and he knew the signs. He had seen Sean touch Charlie, but they never looked at each other the way Rigg and Katie did—in a way that told how one found the other to be wonderful and desirable.

Patrick decided to keep most of his thoughts to himself, and when he spoke his look was kindness itself. "You're nearly strangers, Sean, but I can see she cares for you, and unless I miss my guess, you're in love with her."

"You're right. I do think I'm in love, but how can I be?" Sean voiced the question that would not leave his mind. "As you said, we're practically strangers."

"I've always believed that love can happen very fast. Believe me, love is what gives a marriage joy, but the factor that's going to stand the test of time is your—"

"Commitment," Sean finished for his father, and Patrick's eyes grew suspiciously wet.

"Yes, commitment. Some people feel this is some sort of duty, but in fact it gives a marriage very real stability." They talked for the next hour and then spent another hour in prayer.

Sean went to bed in a quandary of emotions, at peace with God and his father, but saddened to see the parent he had come to love all over again leave. He knew Patrick planned to tell Charlie the next day that he would be leaving the day after.

Suddenly Sean didn't feel quite so sad. He was more than ready to work on his relationship with his wife, and his father was right— his presence was something of a hindrance. If only he and Charlie had already come to the point of conversing as husband and wife should, Sean would have felt on more stable ground. As it was, he felt only confusion.

Charlie had constantly put Sean and his father together as though she approved of the relationship, and yet she suddenly seemed to disapprove of Sean. The smiles he had begun to see more and more frequently had disappeared altogether, and in the evenings when they had some time to work on the reading, Charlie would take herself off to her room and not come out before morning.

Sean prayed about the time he could approach Charlie, wanting desperately to lean on God for this. He fell asleep as he always did, asking God to bring his wife to a saving knowledge of Jesus Christ.

"I really would like to pay you for the room and board."

"I won't even discuss it with you," Sadie told Patrick in a no-nonsense voice. "You're Charlie's father-in-law, and that makes you family. I don't charge family."

Sadie's hands were on her hips, her eyes daring Patrick to argue with her. Patrick eyed her for just a moment before he spoke graciously.

"Then I thank you, Sadie, for your hospitality."

"You're welcome," Sadie told him simply and turned away, looking for something to do with her hands. He was the most handsome man she had seen in years, and for some reason, Sadie felt a bit flustered in his presence. But flustered or not, she felt it was a pity he had to leave.

Sadie's wayward thoughts were interrupted by the arrival of Sean and Charlie. They were there to walk Patrick to the train station. Patrick, his manner once again quiet and gracious, thanked Sadie for the last time. He was unaware of the way she stood in front of the boardinghouse and watched him leave.

"Charlotte, I can't thank you enough," Patrick said as he pulled his daughter-in-law into his sturdy embrace. The walk to the train station had been very quiet. Charlie realized in that instant how much she'd come to care for her husband's father.

"Do you really need to leave?" she asked in all sincerity.

"I'm afraid so. Taking the afternoon train like this will make for a long evening and a sleepless night, but I really must be on my way. I'll write, and you know I'll be praying for you."

The words made Charlie feel like crying, and she nearly broke down as she watched Patrick and Sean embrace unashamedly for long moments. She moved a few yards down the platform to give them some time alone.

"I know that God is going to do mighty things in your life, Sean, and I believe one of the first will be the salvation of your wife." Patrick's voice was low, but Sean caught every word.

"I'm praying you're right."

"Pray *believing*, Sean." Patrick spoke with conviction. "God loves her more than you do, and nothing would give Him greater joy than to bring Charlotte to Himself."

Sean wondered how he'd gotten along for so many years without this man. The thought caused him to put his arms around his father once again.

The next few minutes passed in a flurry of activity as last-minute passengers boarded and the final whistle blew. Patrick hugged his beloved children one last time, and they stood waving after he boarded and until the train was out of sight.

Both husband and wife were very quiet as they headed home for the evening. They were done working for the day, but the hour wasn't at all late. Sean's thoughts turned to his marriage, and he hoped they might be able to talk as soon as they were home. Charlie, however, surprised him and put an immediate stop to any such plans.

Just as they approached the back of the livery, Sean watched Charlie veer off.

"I've got some things I need to do in the livery, Sean."

The young husband was so surprised that he didn't speak for a few seconds. "Is there something I can help with?" he finally asked.

"No," Charlie answered a little too emphatically as she moved toward the barn. "I'll be in later."

Sean didn't have a clue as to what he should say to that, so he stood still until she disappeared into the rear door of the livery. He spent a few moments in prayer before turning and going on to the house.

Thirty-Two

HE'LL STAY, Charlie told herself as she stood in the warm, dim barn, *but only because he has to. He'd have left today if he could have, and after seeing his father he'll probably be watching for a chance to run.* The thought caused an ache in Charlie that she would not have believed possible. It also started her tears.

As a child it had become familiar to hurt inside, knowing that her grandfather would often have liked to rid himself of her. With Sean it was much more than just hurt, it was . . .

The thought hung on like a bad headache, and Charlie's arms went around her middle, as though the pain was centered there. It wasn't. The pain was higher and squeezed around the region of her heart like a cruel fist.

She wondered during one brief moment of near insanity what Sean would do if she went back into the house and told him she was in love with him. He might go down on his knee and declare his own love and then take her in his arms. After all, he did care some; she was sure of that. And then she knew it would never happen.

"He'd laugh in your face, Charlie, and you know it."

Sean was so surprised to hear his wife's voice that it halted his progress through the back door. He had stayed in the house until he could no longer stand it. It had never occurred to him that she wasn't alone in the livery. Maybe someone was trying to hurt her.

It was this thought that propelled him forward, his face a mask of worry.

"Charlotte?" Sean blurted as soon as he spotted her in one of the stalls, instantly feeling contrite over the way he had startled her.

Charlie had come away from the wall of the stall where she was leaning and was now kneeling on the ground. She frowned when she realized she hadn't brought her gun. After all, it could have been anyone.

Sean didn't like that frown, but he came forward anyway. Charlie watched as he lowered himself to the ground and leaned against the wall of the stall, as she had been doing. He just stared at her as she sat back on her heels, her knees just inches from his outstretched legs. The window above them lit the stall, casting a soft light around Charlie's red hair.

"I hope that frown isn't for me."

"It's not," Charlie answered and then looked away, knowing no matter how kind he was, she mustn't let herself get more attached to this man than she already was.

"Are you all right?"

"Why wouldn't I be all right?" Charlie's tone was suspicious.

"Since you're the one who's been crying, you'll need to tell me." Sean's voice was soft, and Charlie turned her head slowly back to look at him. Her look was filled with surprise, and Sean had to speculate for only a moment on what she might be thinking.

"How did you know I'd been crying?"

Sean smiled; he couldn't help it. "Charlotte." Again his voice was very low. "Haven't you ever looked in the mirror after you've cried?" Sean raised one finger and tenderly touched one corner of Charlie's red-rimmed eyes.

The act was too much for the confused redhead. Her eyes filled with tears once again and before she could even draw a breath, Sean gathered her to himself.

Charlie told herself to pull away, but his arms felt so good, and he smelled wonderful. She suddenly remembered the regret on her husband's face when he realized that he had missed his father by six weeks. Knowing that he was never even supposed to be here, and that he would never really be hers, was enough to make her cry all the harder.

"Charlotte, Charlotte, please try to stop. You're going to make yourself sick." Sean stroked her hair with his free hand and thought his heart would break. If only she would confide in him. Theirs had become a strange relationship all over again. Husband and wife, but not lovers. Housemates, but just barely friends.

Charlie, in an attempt to stop her tears, drew in a shuddering breath and tipped her head back to look at her husband. She told herself to thank him and move out of his arms, but no words would come. She watched Sean's gaze drop from her eyes to her mouth, and still she couldn't move. Not even when she watched his head lower and felt his hand holding the back of her head, was she able to put any space between them.

The kiss was like nothing Sean had ever dreamed of. He honestly believed he was going slowly, but when Charlie whimpered he knew he was crushing her in his arms. He loosened his hold without breaking the kiss, shifting his wife onto his lap as he did. She was kissing him back now, and Sean felt as lightheaded as a man who had gone for days with an empty stomach.

Empty. That word perfectly described Sean's arms a moment later when Charlie suddenly pushed away from him and stood a few yards away. Sean took several deep breaths and had to clear his throat before he spoke.

"I'm not going to apologize for that, Charlotte, because saying I'm sorry would be a lie. I like kissing you, and I hope someday you'll enjoy it too."

"I enjoyed it." Charlie could have pulled her own tongue out.

"Then why are you way over there looking terrified?"

"I don't know. There's so much between us, and I think if we had continued it would have complicated things further." The words were stilted, and Sean wished with all his might that he knew what she was talking about. Complicate what things?

"Charlotte, I'm not sure I understand."

"And I'm not sure I can explain."

Sean realized he would have to be satisfied with that. He stood, determined not to press her, but equally determined not to leave her in the barn alone.

"Why don't we head inside now. Maybe we can talk some more tomorrow."

Charlie seemed relieved by his understanding and went willingly with him to the house.

"While you're here I want to get a lot of this done. Everything is pretty small, and I guess that's why it has been sitting for so long. They are just the jobs I never seem to get started."

Sean listened silently as Charlie spoke over lunch. She was communicating with him now, but all was strictly business. She had also insinuated often in the last three days that Sean was going somewhere. It was always subtle, but Sean never missed it. To his surprise Charlie had been eager to resume her reading lessons. At first it made no sense, but as Sean listened to his wife, he realized she wanted him to teach her before he *left*.

Well she's going to be in for a surprise, Sean thought to himself, *because I'm not going anywhere*.

In fact, he was going to be beside her even more, as much as it was in his power to do so, and his plan of attack was going to begin that very evening.

As had become their routine since the day after Patrick left, Charlie quickly cleared the kitchen table and retrieved the primer. She turned the lantern high and waited for Sean to join her.

"Why don't we study in the living room tonight?" Sean suggested as he picked up the lantern and pulled out his wife's chair. She looked surprised, but preceded Sean into the other room, primer in hand.

Sean sat very close to Charlie on the sofa and took the book from her grasp. He opened to the page where he wanted her to start and stayed close as she read. She was doing exceptionally well, and Sean uttered only a few corrections as she read the simple story. She stumbled over the word "ear" and Sean helped her, but before she could read on, he interrupted.

"You have very nice ears," he said softly. "I wonder why I've never noticed them before."

Charlie's hand came up. She touched her ear self-consciously, turning slightly to look at her husband. He was nearly touching her with the way he was leaning to read over her shoulder, and as soon as her eyes caught his, he winked at her.

Charlie nearly dropped the book, and Sean smiled as she cleared her throat and tried once again to read. But Sean could tell she wasn't concentrating. She stumbled over words she had never had any difficulty with, and after a few moments Sean took pity on her.

"Could we skip the reading lesson tonight, Charlotte?"

"Skip it?" Charlie's voice was several octaves higher than normal, and she looked ready to panic at the way Sean shifted even closer.

"Yes, skip it. I want to ask you something. Do you like children?"

Charlie did drop the book then. Her head turned at a nearly impossible angle to look at the man beside her. What in the world had gotten into him? Charlie wasn't really sure she wanted to know.

"I think maybe I'd like a bath tonight." Charlie's voice was breathless as she moved to get up, but Sean leaned so close that his nose was brushing her temple. She froze in her place.

"You don't need a bath. You smell wonderful."

Charlie could only gawk at her spouse.

"What happened, Charlotte?" Sean entreated softly, his face close to hers. "What happened after the last time we sat on this couch together and acted like husband and wife?"

Charlie knew exactly the evening to which he referred. It was the night Sean had been about to kiss her, and they had been interrupted by his father. She answered without looking at him.

"I'm not sure what happened, Sean, but I know your father's interrupting us was for the best."

"Why do you say that?"

"Because it's true. You don't belong with a girl like me. You belong with someone beautiful and feminine like your sisters. I can only guess at how much you miss them. I was a fool to think you'd ever really be mine."

Sean's hand gently grasped her face and turned her gaze back to his.

"Charlotte, you're my wife!" Sean's voice was urgent. "It's true that I miss my family, and it was hard to see my father leave, but this is where I belong, here with you."

"But you wish you could be elsewhere."

"Not without you," he told her simply. "Whenever I think about visiting my family, or even going to see my father in Hawaii, you're with me. The idea of leaving you behind or leaving you at all is inconceivable to me."

Charlie searched his face and learned in an instant that she had been blind to Sean's true feelings about her.

"Charlotte, will you please ask me the question that you wanted to ask me days ago?"

Charlie didn't know how he knew about that, but neither did she care. "Sean, how do you feel about sharing my room?"

Sean's smile was so tender that Charlie's breath left her in a rush. They leaned toward each other at the same time, and Sean suddenly understood the silly look Kate always had on her face after Rigg kissed her—he would have sworn he was floating.

He also knew that he could now tell Charlie he loved her, but he knew he had time—all the time in the world.

Thirty-Three

It TOOK SADIE exactly five seconds to notice the new intimacy between Sean and Charlie. If there *had* been any doubt in her mind, and there wasn't, it would have been resolved when Charlie stayed in the kitchen to talk with Sean during his bath. Naturally Sadie approved wholeheartedly, and would have approved all the more had she known the whole story.

Rarely had two people been so lovingly compatible. Evening lessons with the primer were now spent in the bed they shared as husband and wife, and Sean was always ready with a kiss for a job well done.

Sean learned in no time at all that Charlie loved to have her back scratched. In fact, she was downright greedy about it! Her request for him to scratch a certain spot on her back for a minute always turned into a half-hour. She was disappointed when he stopped, even when he told her his arm was ready to fall off.

Their favorite times were Sunday mornings, because they were able to sleep in. Since the livery was closed, the only chores were feeding the stock and checking the forge. They were usually able to cuddle and talk in bed for more than an hour before they needed to get ready for church. It was during this time that they had their most important discussions.

"Sean, can I ask you something?"

"Sure."

"The night you moved into my room, you asked me if I liked children. Why?" Sean's shoulder vibrated under Charlie's cheek and jaw. "What's so funny?"

"Me," Sean answered her, his voice still full of laughter." I couldn't for the life of me figure out how to bring the conversation around to intimate things, so I thought if we talked about babies, you'd understand that I wanted a marriage in every way and that I was *going* nowhere."

"Oh," Charlie replied thoughtfully. Sean shifted so he could see her face.

"By the way, you never answered me. *Do* you like children?"

"I think so. I haven't been around them much."

"What was your own childhood like?" It was a question Sean had wanted to ask for a long time, and he prayed even now as he waited to see if his timing had been right.

"Not much fun," Charlie admitted softly. "I could never do anything right."

"You mean in your grandfather's eyes?"

Charlie sighed. "He was not an easy man."

"Tell me about him," Sean entreated, attempting with his voice and eyes to tell her just how much he wanted to know.

"Sadie told me he'd always been the same," Charlie began. "Even when she was a little girl she remembers him being over-bearing and cruel. Sadie thinks his own father must have treated him that way; it was the only way he ever knew. She also thinks it would have been better if either she or my mother had been a boy."

"You didn't know your mother did you?"

"Not personally, no, but Sadie has been telling me about her forever. She was a lot like Sadie I think—warm, caring, and nurturing."

"Were you ever able to talk to your grandfather?"

"He wasn't the talking type. Once, when I had a crush on a boy, I tried to tell him about it, but Grandpa got so mad I lit out for Sadie's and stayed away for the better part of the day. He had cooled down by the time I got home, but I never tried again. When I got a little older, and I knew he was about to hit me, I would threaten to run off like my mother had. That would calm him down for a while, but there was no reasoning with him."

"How is it that your mother ended up back here to have you?"

"Sadie said my father was a married man who lived in another town. When my mother ran off and took up with him, I don't think she was worried about getting pregnant, just about staying away from my grandfather for the rest of her life. It's funny, isn't it?"

"What is?"

"That the man she was most afraid of was the man she came back to when she found herself alone, hungry, and scared because she was eight months pregnant and not married. If only Grandpa could have been a little more understanding."

"What did he do?"

"He hit her. Knocked her to the floor. Her water gave way just about then, and I was born 15 hours later. Sadie thinks my mother gave up after that. I didn't cry right away, and she was certain I was dead. Sadie tried to tell her otherwise, but she wouldn't listen. She just lay there, fell asleep, and never woke up."

"Who took care of you?"

"Sadie found a wet nurse. I was pretty scrawny, but I must have something of Grandpa in me, because I survived."

"Where was your grandmother during all of this?"

"She died when Sadie and my mother were just girls."

They were both quiet for a few moments, and then Sean asked one final question. "Do you have *any* good memories of your grandfather?"

"Not many. When I was 12, I remember being thankful that he only hit me. A friend told me that her dad would touch her the way a husband touches a wife."

Sean pulled her very close then and held her securely against his chest. *She's known such awful things, Lord. It's a miracle she's as wonderful as she is.* Sean desperately wanted to tell her that as hard as this life was, it was only temporary and if she chose, she could someday live forever with God, but now did not seem the time to talk of eternal things.

As Charlie cuddled into his side, Sean prayed silently. *Please, Lord, open the door in Your time and use me if it's Your will.*

Sadie had made Charlie a second dress for church, and she wore it that very morning. It was a pale yellow print that brought out the gold color in her hazel eyes. Sean whistled when he saw her in it, and even with their newly discovered love Charlie was so flustered her face turned three shades of red.

They were again having dinner with Duncan and Lora, and this time Charlie was taking a basket of muffins she had baked the day before. Just as they left the house, Charlie stopped Sean with a question. She had copied a word onto a small scrap of paper and, holding it out to him, asked how to pronounce it and what it meant.

"Remission," Sean told her. "Where did you read this?"

Charlie looked uncomfortable. "In your Bible."

"Oh," Sean said simply, as though it didn't matter in the least. "Well, if it's from the verse I'm thinking of, about the shedding of blood, it means forgiveness."

He led the way to the buggy then, his heart pounding in his chest. He kissed Charlie softly as he helped her into the seat, and prayed once again that God would use him to show Charlie that God was the true Forgiver.

"John, the son of Zacharias and Elizabeth, is often referred to as the forerunner of Christ." Pastor Miller had begun his sermon. "We're still studying the life of Jesus Christ, but right now I'd like you to get to know John a little better. We read about John in the books of Matthew and Mark as a man whose 'raiment is made of camel's hair and whose diet is honey and locusts.'

"I think it's important that the Scriptures tell us what John eats and how he dresses so we get a picture of the overall man. They help us to see that John is a man of consistency. But consistent about what? Let's check Mark 1:7. Let me read it to you. 'There cometh one mightier than I after me, the latchet of whose shoes I am not worthy to stoop down and unloose.'

"There isn't a one of us that hasn't heard the phrase, 'He's not good enough to tie my shoes.' This is what John is saying about himself in regard to Jesus Christ. Mark records here that John said he was not worthy even to untie Jesus' shoes.

"What I'm trying to point out to you is that John was a man of great humility and singleness of purpose. He could have sought a life filled with riches, but we see in his food and clothing that he didn't. His purpose was to prepare the way for the Savior, to tell others that the Christ was coming. John knew that nothing was more important than this task.

"John's mission on this earth as the forerunner of Christ was a great one, but he knew he was not *the* Great One. John couldn't save; he pointed the way toward the One who could. John baptized with water, but the One he pointed to would baptize with the Holy Spirit. For salvation we can look only to Christ, as John states in chapter 20, verse 31, 'But these are written, that ye might believe that Jesus is the Christ, the Son of God; and that believing, ye might have life through his name.'"

Charlie could not get Pastor Miller's words out of her mind. He made it sound simple, but it was all so foreign to her. Salvation, the need to be saved, even words and phrases like "forerunner" and "life through His name," were not in her vocabulary.

Charlie had tried to read Sean's Bible in an attempt to please the husband who meant so much to her, but very little of it had made sense. She hoped that as her reading skills improved, more would become clear. Charlie wouldn't have hesitated to ask Sean what something meant in the newspaper, but his Bible was different.

She was afraid to let him know just how limited her knowledge of the Bible was. He said he wasn't going to leave her, but in many ways Sean was just too good to be true, and Charlie was still just a little afraid she would wake up someday and find him gone.

Thirty-Four

TWO WEEKS LATER Charlie awoke to discover she was alone in bed. She lay still and tried to calm her frantic heart. She and Sean always got up together. Even when one was awake first, the other lay quietly and waited for the other to waken.

Charlie's mind was racing. It wasn't Sunday, so she knew Sean was not feeding the stock, and the stillness of the house told her he was not fixing breakfast.

Charlie rose from the bed and stood clutching the front of her nightgown, not wanting to face what she had feared from the moment Patrick left town. She walked out to the kitchen on limbs that were stiff with dread, limbs that came alive with action when she spotted the note on the table.

Charlotte,

I've gone to Duncan's. Hartley has been in touch, but he's gone now. I'll be home soon, so stay where you are. Stay out of the livery, and for my peace of mind, don't even answer the door.

Sean

Charlie read the note through twice before running to the bedroom with plans to disobey her husband's every word.

"About what time did you hear the noise?" Duncan asked Sean.

"It was just beginning to get light, so I guess around 4:30."

Duncan consulted his pocket watch. "It's been two hours; there's no point in trying to track him now."

"Do you think he's hit the bank?"

"No. I'd have heard by now. You don't seem overly surprised, Sean, that he was able to track you down."

Sean's eyes narrowed in thought for a moment. "I guess it's because I know Hartley so well. I can't say as I've ever felt that Charlotte and I were being watched, but the man has eyes everywhere, if you catch my meaning."

"Connections?"

"Right."

Lora put a plateful of food in front of each man, and Sean was opening his mouth to say he couldn't stay, when all three heard a horse approaching at high speed.

Charlie burst into the kitchen without even knocking, her hand going to her mouth and her eyes closing in relief when she saw that Sean was all right. The young husband rose from the table and took her into his arms. They stood for a few moments in silence, unaware of the older couple watching them, and then Sean led Charlie to the table.

He put her in the chair next to his own and brushed a stray curl from her cheek. He spoke tenderly and without rebuke.

"I know you read the note or you'd have never found me. You also knew I wanted you to stay home and out of the livery."

"Would you have stayed if I'd left you the same note?"

"No," Sean admitted without hesitation, and leaned to press a kiss to her forehead.

Charlie still had hold of Sean's hand when she began to calm down enough to look at the other people in the room. She looked across the table to find Duncan grinning at her.

"Good morning, Charlie."

Charlie couldn't help but smile back. "Hi, Duncan."

A moment later she had her own plate of food, as did Lora, and Duncan was saying grace as though having people interrupt their breakfast was an everyday occurrence.

"Father in heaven, I thank you for this food and for Lora's work; please bless our bodies this day. I would also ask Your guiding hand on our plans concerning Hartley. Protect us, Lord, in Your will, that we might glorify Your name. In Christ's name I pray. Amen."

Charlie ate and listened in silence as the conversation between Sean and Duncan continued. She learned that Sean had heard a noise outside at daybreak. He had gone out dressed in nothing more than his jeans to find Hartley standing by their well.

In the space of a few seconds Hartley told Sean that Rico had been killed in a bank robbery in Los Angeles, and Hartley needed to pull another job because he was out of money. He wanted Sean's help to hit the Visalia bank.

Before Sean could make any reply, the two men heard noises on the street. Hartley left quickly, but told Sean where to meet him on Sunday night, only three days away, so they could make plans.

"He fascinates me, Duncan, because he seemed genuinely shook when he told me about Rico, and then he went on to tell me where I was to meet him, assuming I'd be a part of his gang again."

Duncan shook his head. "He doesn't fascinate Witt. Did you see which way Hartley headed?"

"No, he went around the house."

"But this place where he wants to meet you is only about a 30-minute ride?"

"Right. He didn't give me a time, so I'm going to head out when there's still plenty of light."

"You can't be serious?" Charlie said softly, but no one acknowledged her.

"If he doesn't show, I'll leave him a note and maybe we can still trap him. I still can't believe I went outside without the gun. When Witt finds out he'll be furious."

"You can't be serious?" Charlie's voice, although still an incredulous whisper, was louder this time and heard by everyone. Sean looked at her with great compassion and then explained softly.

"Duncan is not pushing me into this, Charlotte; I volunteered. Hartley would have hit the bank here whether I'd been with him or not, but the truth is, I *was* with him, and now I want to do something to bring him to the law."

Charlie was silent. She stared at Sean as though seeing him for the first time. Without thanking Lora for breakfast or bidding anyone goodbye, she rose from the table and walked out the door. The Duncans and Sean stayed in their places even as they listened to her ride away.

"We'll be praying for you, Sean," Duncan finally said. "And if you change your mind, there will be no hard feelings. I won't talk to Witt until I hear from you."

Sean thanked both husband and wife after those words and went back to the livery to try to reason with his wife.

On their own once again, Lora rose from the table to pour more coffee for Duncan. She would have returned the pot to the stove, but he moved his chair out and patted his knee invitingly. Lora, never needing to be asked twice, sat in her husband's lap. It had been their special way of cuddling since the day they had been married.

"What were you thinking just now as you poured the coffee?"

Lora sighed on the question.

"Don't want to tell me?" he questioned as his arms settled around her waist.

"I guess I don't because it means admitting how faithless I am."

"Charlie," Duncan said in instant understanding. Lora nodded.

"I know all about fears, Lucas, and if she would just turn to God, He would comfort her," Lora said with tender conviction.

"You don't sound very faithless to me."

"My faithlessness comes when I see the complete lack of hope on her young face. She's not the hard person I always believed her to be, but at times she seems so closed to spiritual matters."

"We've got to look at how far she's come already," Duncan told her assuredly. "When you think how quickly they've made their situation livable, it does make you want to see it as the miracle of which Sean talks."

Suddenly Lora hugged him back. "Thank you, Lucas. I needed to hear that."

Still wrapped in one another's embrace, they took a moment to pray, each thanking God for bringing the Donovans into their world and for whatever purpose He had in doing so.

Thirty-Five

CHARLIE HAD NOT touched or spoken ten words to her husband since leaving the Duncans. Sean tried to bring her out, but she refused to talk to him.

By Friday night Sean was at the end of his tether. He knew Duncan was waiting for his answer, and even though he wanted to please his wife, this was something he had to do. If only she would talk to him.

Sean pulled the double doors in the front of the livery shut and went to his wife, who was making an expectant mare comfortable for the night.

"Charlotte, can we please talk?" Sean had started the conversation just that way on many occasions, and as before, Charlie ignored him. But Sean had had enough. When Charlie moved away from him he reached for her, but Charlie had second-guessed him and begun to run. A second later she found herself tackled in a stall full of sweet-smelling hay.

She struggled under her husband's weight, but he held her easily. In fact, he simply captured her hands within his own, buried his face in the side of her neck, and waited for her to stop struggling.

It took a little time, but Sean began to feel the tenseness leave her body. The hands he held began to hold him back and Charlie angled her head so that she could kiss her husband's forehead.

"Please don't go," she finally whispered.

"I have to."

"Then let me go with you."

"That's out of the question."

Sean heard her sigh. "Sean, I'm afraid you won't come back alive."

"I know you are," Sean said simply.

Charlie fell silent again. "You're not afraid of death, are you?"

"No. I've settled my eternity with God."

Charlie began to struggle this time so suddenly that Sean let go of her. He watched in surprise as she sprang up and faced him, her hands doubled into fists at her sides.

"I wish someone would tell me what that means!" She was a picture of frustration, and Sean could only gawk as she turned and stormed from the livery.

All this time he had been expecting her to show interest in the things of the Lord, waiting for her to ask questions, when she hadn't even understood what she had been hearing.

Sean would have liked to have taken a few days to pray over this new revelation, but he didn't have time. Charlie was right; he might not come back alive. He had to be certain that Charlie understood before he left. Maybe she wouldn't make a decision, but he had to map it out for her. He would start by apologizing for not explaining in the first place.

"Instead of working on your spelling words tonight, Charlotte, I'd rather we talked."

"About Hartley." Charlie's voice was flat.

"No, about something more important than Hartley."

Charlie looked over at Sean from her end of the sofa, only to find him watching her. She couldn't take her eyes off him as he began to share.

"First of all I want to tell you how sorry I am that I haven't explained my faith to you, and how sorry I am that I took for granted you would understand. I'd like to explain now, if you'll let me."

Sean waited for Charlie's nod and then began.

"When I was four I memorized my first two verses from Scripture—John 3:16 and 17: 'For God so loved the world that he gave his only begotten Son, that whosoever believeth in him should not perish, but have everlasting life. For God sent not his Son into the world to condemn the world, but that the world through him might be saved.' I could say the words both frontward and backward but I didn't understand that they applied to me personally until I was six.

"When I was six I began to notice for the first time that my sisters and I looked different from the Hawaiian children with whom we were growing up. I remember asking my mother about it, and she told me it was because we were from a different background. I, of course, wanted to know where all the other people like me were. When she explained, I then wanted to know why we even lived in Hawaii in the first place. When she told me that we were there to tell people about the love of Jesus Christ so they could believe in Him, I told her I'd never prayed and told God I believed in his Son.

"To my surprise she told me she had known that all along, but she never worried because she was certain that as soon as I understood, I would believe, and then I would make that step. She was right. We knelt right there on the sand, and I told God I was a sinner who believed He sent His Son to save me, and Charlotte, that's what I was trying to do with you.

"I was certain that as soon as you heard the words from me or Pastor Miller, you would make a choice for Christ. I lost sight of the fact that I grew up hearing words like 'saved' and 'eternal life,' forgetting that not everyone understands." Charlie was taking in every word, so Sean continued.

"I need to tell you why I believe. First of all, belief is a choice. One of the first acts of faith is believing that the Bible is God's Holy Word, and that the words inside can be trusted and need to be obeyed.

"The Bible tells us that our life on earth is not forever; everyone's physical body dies, but there is life after death. It also says that all men sin and sin separates us from God, but Charlotte, honey, I honestly didn't know how to tell you any of this.

"I've been so afraid that you would think I was saying I'm better than you are, so I held back. I didn't want you to think my love was conditional. Am I making any sense?"

Charlie could only nod, and Sean moved on.

"The Bible teaches that this life on earth is temporary, and following this life is eternity. I know you're not certain that God is there, but I believe with all my heart that He is. And when the time comes for you to die you can either meet God as your Savior, as I will, or you can meet Him as your judge. If you meet Him as your Savior, then you will spend eternity in heaven. If not, then you will spend eternity in hell, separated from God. I have accepted Jesus Christ as my Savior. That's what I meant when I said that my eternity is settled.

"Should I die on Sunday, I know without a doubt that I'll go to be with God. That's why I'm not afraid. I'm not wishing that I'll die, but I'm not afraid either. You can make that choice also, so you don't have to be afraid, Charlie, for yourself or for me."

It was the first time he had called her by her nickname, and it was said so tenderly that it made Charlie tremble.

"Please hold me, Sean," she whispered.

Sean was more than happy to comply. He knew he had given her a lot to think about, and she obviously needed time to take it in. All he could do for the moment was pray that he would be there when she needed him most.

Thirty-Six

CHARLIE SPENT THE night wrapped in her husband's arms. Even in sleep she clung to him. In the morning, Saturday, Sean told her he had to meet with Duncan and Witt. Charlie was proud of herself when she didn't argue or cry.

She walked over to Duncan's with him. While the men talked in the kitchen, she stayed in the living room with Lora and tried not to think about the conversation in the other room. She wasn't denying what was to come, but she didn't think she could handle hearing plans that were certain to lead to her husband's death.

"I want us to head out around 4:00. Since I'm sure he won't be there until after dark, I've written a note to leave him. I want to play things my way, so the note tells him where we can meet again in a few days."

"I still think we should go after dark," Witt interjected.

"Then tomorrow night would be our only chance, and I don't like those odds," returned Sean. "My way is better. When he finally arrives, he will see tracks made by three horses and know that I'm not coming alone."

Witt was frustrated. "Where is *your* meeting place for Tuesday night?"

"It's only 15 minutes outside of town, but it's far enough away from the bank that he will be lulled into a false sense of security."

156

Duncan agreed wholeheartedly with Sean's plan, and between the two of them they won Witt over to their way of thinking. The men continued to plan their actions of the next few days with careful precision.

Sean was the first to leave, and Duncan and Witt were able to discuss something that had been on both of their minds. When Witt finally left, Duncan sat down and wrote a letter to the judge who had sentenced Sean to hang.

Charlie tried to act normal at Sadie's house on Sunday, and in fact fooled everyone at the dinner table except the man who loved her. Sean could see the strain in her face, and prayed that she would turn to God for comfort.

Sean knew his life on earth held no guarantees, so he didn't dare tell Charlie he would be back. He was confident, however, that they would not see Hartley this day. Still, he said nothing.

In fact, they had barely said a word to each other on any subject when Sean realized it was 20 minutes to 4:00. With a heavy heart he moved toward the livery to saddle Buddy, their best mount. He dreaded leaving Charlie when she was so upset, but he could not for the moment see any help for it.

Charlie stood at the window as Sean tied Buddy's reins to a tree limb and came inside. He wasted no words, but came directly to Charlie and took her in his arms.

"Charlie," he again used her nickname, and she loved the sound on her ears. "If you find you have time on your hands in the next few hours, I want you to do me a favor."

"Lora invited me over."

"I know she did, and I could tell when you thanked her that you didn't plan to go."

"That's true. What did you want me to do?"

Sean reached down to the kitchen table for his Bible. "If you stay here and feel restless, start reading in the book of John." Sean turned to the first chapter and left the Bible open on the table.

"Take down a few notes if something confuses you, and we'll talk about it when I get back."

"Will you be back, Sean?"

"If it's within my power to be here, nothing will keep me away." Charlie thought she would drown in the emotional depths of her husband's eyes.

"I love you," he whispered before his lips covered hers. Charlie clung to him.

When they both heard the approach of other horses, they exited the house together. Sean climbed on his mount and stared down at his wife. He dragged his gaze from hers and stared out in the direction of the meeting place. A second later he leaned from the saddle and pulled Charlie up to his lap. He kissed her long and hard, and then set her back on the ground. This time he didn't look in her direction as he heeled his horse and went with the other men.

Charlie paced for 15 minutes before she picked up the Bible and carried the precious Book to her bedroom. She lay down on the bed, snuggled into Sean's pillow, and began to read the first verses.

Charlie made an effort not to get slowed down by unfamiliar words. Reading steadily, she came to John 3:16 and 17 and remembered Sean reciting them to her. Several times her eyes focused over each word before continuing.

Time ceased to exist as she read about Jesus and Nicodemus. Her eyes devoured the story of Jesus and the Samaritan woman, and then on to the sick boy in Capernaum whom Jesus healed, sight unseen.

Chapter after chapter fell away. The feeding of the 5000, Jesus walking on the water, the healing of the blind man, the raising of Lazarus—all became real to her. Page after page revealed Jesus as Shepherd and Lord. With tears pouring down her face, Charlie arrived at the final chapters where God's perfect Son was mocked and crucified for the sins of all men.

By the time Charlie read the last verse in the last chapter, she had cried until her head hurt, and she was wrung dry. She told herself she had to get up and watch for Sean, but before her mind could make her body obey, she fell into an exhausted sleep, with Sean's Bible held in her embrace.

Thirty-Seven

THE MEN RODE out of town with the sun at their backs. There was little talk, and Sean by necessity took the lead. Their pace was steady for about 20 minutes, and then Sean eased off as the terrain became rocky.

Hartley chose his meeting place well; it was secluded from three directions. The hair at the back of Sean's neck stood on end. He knew that Hartley could have them in the sight of his rifle at that very moment. Since he had been the one to betray Hartley, Sean knew he would be the first to die.

But all was quiet. They rode into rocks that resembled a small canyon with no sign of anyone or anything. With plenty of sunlight still available, they completely scouted the area. Had it not been for the fear of Hartley showing up and surprising them, the entire trip would have been anticlimactic.

Sean left his note in a conspicuous place, and the three rode home by way of what was to be the meeting place two nights hence. They didn't tarry and were back in town just at dusk. Witt asked both men to his home in order to go over their plans one more time.

It was well after dark before Sean rode toward home. Seeing from a distance that all was dark, he stopped and checked first with Lora and then with Sadie. He went back home with his heart pounding in his chest. The fear that Charlie might be harmed made his anxiety over Hartley seem a small thing. Without bothering to

159

attend his horse, he tied Buddy outside the house and entered, his heart pleading with God for the safety of his cherished wife.

The lantern light flickered over the bedroom walls as Sean's hand trembled. He had come in and called Charlie's name as he lit a lamp, and then after a quick peek into the living room, walked with dread toward the silent bedroom.

Even in the dim light he could make out her puffy eyes and the signs of tears. He set the lantern on the nightstand, turned it high, and eased down beside her. Sean didn't try to remove the Bible from her grasp. He just put his arms around her and kissed her softly on the cheek.

It took a few moments for her to come fully awake and then she only blinked at him, as though she believed herself to be dreaming. One moment she was staring at him, and the next the Bible had fallen to the side and her arms had his neck in a stranglehold. She was sobbing uncontrollably.

"My darling Charlie," Sean crooned softly.

"Are you all right . . . are you really all right?" Charlie gasped through her tears, touching his arms and chest as though checking for injuries.

"I'm fine. We didn't even see Hartley. I just need a bath, since I smell like sweat and horses."

"Sadie won't mind," Charlie hiccuped, thinking they would do anything he wanted, just as long as he was home, safe and sound. "We can go right now."

Sean laughed to himself at her enthusiasm. She had never been easily offended by unpleasant odors before, and he wondered at her nearly frantic state. She grew very quiet on the walk to Sadie's, and Sean told himself he was going to hurry so they could get back home and talk.

Charlie, still agitated, was trying to scrub the skin off Sean's back when she broke her silence.

"I wanted to wait until we were back home, Sean, but I've got to talk to you."

"All right," he agreed with some relief.

Scooting around the side of the tub, Charlie stayed on her knees and leaned so close to Sean that she soaked the front of her dress. He watched in confusion as fresh tears puddled in her eyes and she began.

"They killed him, Sean—they killed Jesus Christ. He had healed them and fed them and proven to them over and over that He was the Son of God, and they still crucified Him. Why, Sean? If He's really God's Son, He could have saved Himself. Why didn't He?"

Sean's wet hands came up and tenderly cradled her face. His heart was beating so fast he was breathless.

"Because we needed a Savior. Our sin debt to God had to be paid. He loved us enough to be that Savior. Man's sin placed a ravine between God and man, but God in His infinite love bridged that ravine with His own dear Son."

"Oh, Sean." Charlie's tears began in earnest.

Sean's water was quite cold by the time Charlie was done crying and talking about all she had read. She apologized to him several times, but the night was hot and he only smiled. Did she really think a little cold water was important in light of her meeting Jesus Christ? But that wasn't the only question on Sean's mind, and he waited only until they were home in bed before he broached it.

"Charlie, in all your reading, did you understand that you, Charlotte Donovan, must make a decision?"

"You mean the faith and believing you were talking about before?"

"Yes. I don't want to push you; I just want to make sure you understand."

"I do understand, Sean, but I don't think you do. I haven't been a good person and Jesus, well, He's *God's Son*. I don't think He really wanted me—"

"Charlie," Sean called her name softly. "I want you to listen to John 3:16 and 17 again."

"I've read those verses through several times."

"I'm sure you have, but I want you to hear them one more time: 'For God so loved Charlie, that he gave his only begotten Son and if Charlie believes in him, Charlie will not perish, but have everlasting life. For God sent not his Son to condemn Charlie, but that through him, Charlie might be saved.'"

Sean watched her face closely. He saw her struggle, her desire to be loved and accepted, but he stayed quiet and prayed.

"I didn't even believe He existed for a long time."

"That sin and all others were covered on the cross where He was crucified." Again Sean waited and prayed.

"Do you really think He loves me?"

"Absolutely."

Charlie gave a small nod, as though confirming in her mind what she must do. Sean helped her with the words, and in a soft, confident voice she prayed, telling God of her sins and confessing her belief in His Son.

Charlie finally knew peace as she fell yet again into exhausted slumber, this time in her husband's arms. Sean, very mindful of starting Charlie's tears again, held his own until she was asleep.

"I would have waited years, Lord," Sean cried in the dark. "But You've given me another of Your miracles. For this, I thank You."

Sean followed his wife into slumber a few minutes later, but not before he pictured himself and Charlie in the Hawaiian Islands, living and working with the island people he loved so well.

Thirty-Eight

CHARLIE'S FACE WAS puffy in the morning, but the smile she gave her husband when he kissed her awake was beautiful. They were up a little earlier than usual, and Sean answered many questions about the Bible as they readied for work.

Over breakfast the questions continued, and then Sean knew he had to mention Hartley. He prayed that with her newfound faith, Charlie would turn to God with her fears.

"Charlie, I need to tell you some things."

The seriousness in his tone immediately arrested her attention, and even though alarmed, Charlie listened.

"It's true that we didn't see Hartley yesterday, but we did set up another meeting time at a different place."

"How could you have done that?"

"I left him a note."

"When do you meet?"

"Tomorrow night."

"Is Duncan going with you?"

"Not this time; for the plan to be successful both he and Witt are needed here in town."

"You're going out alone?" Charlie's voice was strained.

"Yes. It has to be that way." Sean reached across the table and claimed Charlie's hand. "Would you like me to explain what's going on?"

163

Sean could see that it took an effort on her part, but she nodded. He explained the situation calmly, and Charlie's mouth dropped open in surprise.

"Whose idea was this?"

"Mine. After working with Hartley, I have a pretty fair idea of the way he thinks." Sean shrugged and then became serious. "Now, long before dark tomorrow night, I'm going to deliver you to Lora's or Sadie's: The choice is yours. But after I take you there you *must not* leave."

"Oh, Sean." Charlie looked as helpless as she felt, but Sean was relentless.

"There will be no discussion on this, Charlie. You can't go with me, and you can't follow me." His look was very stern, and Charlie knew he was right. She would probably get in the way and get them both killed.

"Now, where do you want to go?"

"Lora's," Charlie said with resignation. "She knows more of what's going on, and I know she'll pray with me if I ask her."

Sean's smile was a picture of tenderness. "Speaking of prayer, why don't we ask God right now to protect both of us in the next few days?"

Charlie nodded, and Sean thought his heart would burst as he heard her sweet voice in prayer. She talked to God as she talked to anyone else, only now there was an element of confidence in knowing that she was very loved.

Even though they were now running a little late, husband and wife followed their prayer time with a long embrace before heading out the door for work.

If Lora hugged Charlie once she hugged her ten times when she shared the news of how she came to know Jesus Christ. The older woman cried, and just as Charlie expected, Lora was more than happy to pray with her.

Their conversation was animated during the hours they had together. The fact that their husbands might be in danger hung in their minds, but Charlie was full of questions that Lora was happy to answer. They both felt God's presence and His blessing in the time they shared.

Sean Donovan was nowhere near as calm as he appeared to be. He had ridden out to the meeting place just as the sun was setting and leaned against a tree as though he had all the time in the world. He was in fact praying until he thought his heart might burst.

"I can hardly believe I'm in this position, Lord. It could have been me. It could have been me they're trapping right now. So many of the choices I've made have been for myself and not You. Thank You, God, for sparing me and giving me another chance.

"Please protect Duncan, Witt, and the others as they put their lives on the line tonight. Please protect them. And Hartley. Oh, God," Sean groaned, "if only I could talk to him about You. I don't know if he would listen, but I'd just like the chance. Help the men to bring him in without harm."

Sean would have prayed on and on if his thoughts had not been interrupted by the sound of approaching hoofbeats. Thinking the entire plan had backfired, he came away from the tree with the rifle cocked and ready. He sagged with relief when he heard Duncan call his name. The older man reined in his horse and sat looking down at Sean in the moonlight.

"It's all over."

"Hartley?"

"In custody."

"So he's alive?"

"He was wounded, shot in the arm, but he's very much alive. It was over so fast I didn't see any point in letting you sit out here much longer."

"Was anyone hurt?"

"Only Hartley. He was alone, and it all happened just like you said it would. He came in the back door, and with his attention riveted on Witt's silhouette in the moonlight at the front of the bank, he never even heard me approach."

"How did he get shot?"

"After he felt my gun at his back he turned and started to draw. His eyes looked a little wild with shock, and I can't say as I blame him. He must have been certain we would all be out here waiting with you."

Sean nodded with resignation. "I want to talk to him."

"I don't see any problem with that, but I think I should warn you—he'll hang, Sean, as sure as I'm sitting here, Hartley will hang."

Sean said nothing to this. He swung himself up into his own saddle and followed Duncan back to town.

"I heard you had found God, but I just couldn't believe it." Hartley's mocking voice was like a whip over Sean's back.

The men had been talking for about 20 minutes, and Sean could see that Hartley still believed himself invincible. Any attempt Sean made to discuss God or eternity was met with open contempt. He couldn't really blame him, but it hurt. Unfortunately, that wasn't the worst of it.

"You're completely unrepentant," Sean commented to the older man, his voice soft with pain.

"Now you sound like a preacher," Hartley sneered through the bars, and turned away.

Sean could see the conversation was over. He was turning away himself, but before Sean could leave Hartley made it clear that he didn't want to see him again. Sean really couldn't blame him, but it hurt more than he could have imagined.

"He was a bank robber before the two of you ever met, Sean. Try to keep that in mind." Lora's words and gentle manner were like a balm applied to an open wound. *"You* did not make him choose the life he did, and even today when he had a chance to discuss eternal things, he again made his choice."

Sean thanked her softly and held his wife's hand a little tighter. Sean had turned down refreshments in the Duncans' living room, needing for the moment only to sit and be ministered to emotionally.

"When is the trial, Duncan?" Charlie wanted to know.

"Tom should be here by Thursday, so the proceedings should be no later than Friday afternoon."

There was little conversation after that, and finally, a little before midnight, Sean and Charlie both received hugs from Lora and went home. They stopped outside the front doors of the livery long enough to post a note, stating that they wouldn't be open before noon. It was wise planning since they both slept until 11:00 A.M.

Thirty-Nine

SEAN SEEMED PREOCCUPIED for the next two days. He and Charlie prayed together at every meal and then before bed, but his heart was so burdened for Hartley (and how clearly he remembered being in the jail cell himself) that he was a bit quiet and withdrawn.

Charlie didn't know what to say or do for her husband, so she too was quiet. Quite unexpectedly, Kaitlin came to the rescue by sending a box just for Charlie.

"Lunch is here, Sean," Charlie called to her spouse, who went immediately to wash up for the meal. They had thanked God for the food and begun to eat when Pete's son, from the general store, arrived with the box.

"My dad asked me to bring this over. It's for you, Charlie, from Santa Rosa."

Charlie didn't do anything more than look at the box, even when the boy placed it at her feet and went on his way. She glanced at it several times, and then felt her husband's eyes on her.

"Aren't you going to see what it is?"

"I think I'll wait until after lunch."

Sean was a bit surprised that she wasn't more curious, and for the first time since Hartley had been caught he realized how little conversation they'd had in the last two days.

He was on the verge of telling her his feelings when they were interrupted by a customer who wanted his horse shod. The afternoon gave no time for anything save hard work. Again, conversation between man and wife was delayed.

At closing time, Charlie went to the house to set the table for supper, and Sean closed up the livery. He took one final look around before heading toward the door, and that's when he spotted Charlie's box. He tucked it under one arm and went to have his meal.

The box wasn't mentioned until after the supper dishes had been washed and dried. It had been Sean's night to wash, and Charlie, thinking he had finished up and gone into the living room, turned away from hanging her drying towel to find he was sitting back at the kitchen table, the box next to him, watching her.

She looked decidedly uncomfortable, and Sean's mind raced to figure out why. And as Charlie had done so many times past, she put Sean's questions to rest with the first sentence out of her mouth.

"Why do you suppose your sister sent me a box and not you, her own brother?"

"Well," Sean thought a moment. "She already sent me one, and there's nothing else I really need." He smiled encouragingly and pushed the box in her direction.

Charlie looked unconvinced. She touched it tentatively and then with a quick look at Sean, opened the top.

"Oh, my," Charlie breathed as she held up very feminine linen undergarments and bed attire. There were two shifts, a camisole, a nightgown, and a pair of bloomers. Charlie stood fingering all of them for some minutes before she remembered Sean.

"Oh," she said in dismay as she held the nightgown in her arms. "There's nothing for you. I really thought there would be."

Sean's eyes twinkled as one dark eyebrow lifted. "On the contrary, I think everything in there is for me." He laughed softly and pulled Charlie into his lap when she blushed to the roots of her hair.

"Why didn't you want to open the box?" he asked as Charlie leaned against his chest.

Charlie sighed. "The past few days have been so hard for you, and I wanted to do something to make them easier. Instead, all I've done is sit back and watch you. Then this box arrived not addressed to you, and I thought that might make you feel even worse."

"I love your honesty," he told her simply. "And it's my own fault that the last few days have been hard. I've been picturing myself in Hartley's shoes, and believe me, it's easy to do when you've been there. But that's not the worst of it. I've been so worried about Hartley's future that I've forgotten the here and now."

"The here and now?"

"You, Charlie. You are the here and now. I can't do anything for Hartley. The judge will determine his fate, and unless Hartley asks to see me, I won't talk to him again before he hangs or goes to jail for the rest of his life. There is nothing I can do about that. But my darling wife, who happens to be a new believer in Christ and needs much nurturing and guiding, well, let's just say I can see now that I've been neglecting her. I'm sorry."

Charlie kissed him and told him she didn't feel at all neglected. Sean wasn't convinced, but the door was opened for a full evening of sharing. Sean told Charlie everything he was feeling, and Charlie, who had been holding off with more questions about God, was able to question Sean to her heart's content.

It was past the time they both should have been asleep when Charlie ended the night with one more question.

"Sean," she said in a sleepy voice, "why do you call me Charlie now and not Charlotte?"

He answered after a moment. "Charlie was too familiar when we were first married, and then after getting to know you, I wanted you to understand that I look at you as a man does a woman. The name Charlie wasn't very fitting in that case. But suddenly you just became my darling Charlie, and I rarely even think of calling you Charlotte anymore. Which name do you prefer?"

"Charlie," the sleepy redhead answered with a tired sigh. "Or my darling Charlie. Either one will do."

Forty

DUNCAN'S PREDICTION FOR the trial proceedings proved to be very accurate. At 1:30 on Friday afternoon the courthouse was jammed with people, and Judge Harrison was up front trying to silence the crowd.

Sean, on hand because both Duncan and Witt told him he might be needed, found that if given a choice, he would not have been present. His own trial came back to haunt him. The chairs in the room, the fear he felt, the very smell of the place were all too evocative, and Sean felt himself break out into a cold sweat. He repeatedly thanked God for sparing him until he was once again able to breathe normally.

Charlie had decided not to come, even though both Lora and Sadie were in the courtroom. It did Sean's heart good to know that she was waiting for him at the livery.

As it was, Sean's testimony was not needed. Witt had done his homework well, and the evidence stacked against Hartley was more than enough to convict him. Surprisingly, Sean felt nothing but a calm acceptance when he heard the judge announce that Hartley would hang on the following day.

Sean was one of the first out of the courtroom, but he had only been back at the livery for some 20 minutes when Duncan showed up. He was more than willing to accompany the sheriff back to the jail when Duncan said Hartley wished to see him.

Another 20 minutes passed before Sean exited the jail once again, heavy of heart. He had been so certain that Hartley had wanted to discuss his eternity. Instead, all he had wanted from Sean was help breaking out of jail. Sean had stared at him incredulously, but Hartley had been very serious. All talk of anything else was rejected, and Sean went on his way.

Charlie had only to look at her husband to know it had not gone well. She put her arms around his waist. They stood inside the door of the forge without speaking. Charlie knew Sean would share when he was ready.

"I prayed for you," she whispered.

"Thank you, darling."

It wasn't the first time Charlie had said such a thing to him, but it never failed to give him a tight sensation in his chest. She was so precious, and knowing they were going to spend eternity together only heightened the love in his heart.

Before Sean went back to work he took a moment to remind himself of his own words to Charlie concerning Hartley.

"You've taken it out of my hands, Lord. Please help me to leave it with You."

Thankfully, Sean knew peace in his surrender, even though he felt pain over the loss. Hartley was executed the next afternoon. The date was July 1, 1876.

Forty-One

SEAN FELT IT was very odd to have a hanging in town on the first of July and a celebration on the fourth, but that was just what Visalia had.

Nearly all businesses were closed on this special centennial day, and the livery was no exception. It felt just like Sunday to the Donovans, and they took advantage of the time to lounge in bed and talk. For the first time in days the conversation was not about Hartley.

"I love the letter your sister included with the clothes she sent. I'm going to write back to her this week."

"I should have known why Kate wanted to know your size."

"She asked you about my size?" Charlie was surprised.

"That she did. Both she and Marcail have a weakness for frilly underclothes, and I think they figure all women do."

"You must have told her the terrible shape all my clothes are in."

"Charlie!" Sean was shocked. "I would never tell my sister such a personal thing."

"I guess you wouldn't." She sounded apologetic.

"But while we're on the subject," Sean went on, "why don't you buy some more new underthings? You're always picking up new things for me, but neglecting your own wardrobe."

"I just don't care to shop for myself, and I don't have an eye for just the right thing like Sadie does. Do you hate my things an awful lot?"

"I don't hate them at all, but everything has holes in it. It's not as if business is slow and we can't afford it."

"That's true. Does your sister order her things through the mail?"

"No. Rigg carries everything imaginable for the mercantile, and Katie and Marcail usually have their pick." Sean's voice had softened, and Charlie became very attentive.

"You miss them, don't you?"

"More than I can say," he admitted. "Kate usually organized a picnic on the Fourth of July, and then of course there were always fireworks."

"I know it won't be the same, but we'll have fireworks tonight. Everyone says they're to be spectacular, since it's the centennial celebration!" Charlie spoke enthusiastically, trying to erase the lonely look from her husband's face.

Sean was quiet, and Charlie rolled on her pillow so she could better see his face. He appeared resigned to the situation, but she could see the sorrow in his eyes. It took a moment for Sean to realize he was under her scrutiny, but Charlie spoke before he could question her.

"Five years is a long time, isn't it?"

"Yes, it is, but in light of never seeing them again, it's no time at all."

"If you could leave town, Sean, I would try to get someone to take the livery."

"Thank you, darling," Sean said simply, reaching to hold her and thinking the subject was settled. But Charlie had more on her mind.

"Sean, if you didn't have to be here for five years, would you want us to move away?" Charlie didn't know why she asked; she just needed to know.

The white-sand beaches of Hawaii immediately swam before Sean's eyes as he answered. "I want us to live wherever God wants us to live. Since I'm bound here for five years, I don't even need to ask God about moving right now. After that time, if we feel led to move on, I'm confident that God will show us where and when."

"I think I knew you would say that, but what I want to know is, where? Where would you like to move if you could?"

"Well, I've thought about Santa Rosa and even San Francisco, but Hawaii was home for so long, I guess my mind always goes there first."

"Would I like Hawaii?"

The question so surprised Sean that he raised up on one elbow to look down at her.

"Why did you ask me that?"

"I don't know. It's just that since I've been married to you, I'm a little restless, and even though you're a great smithy, you always look just a little out of place working in the forge."

Sean couldn't believe what he was hearing. "You mean you would be willing to give up the livery and move away from Sadie?"

Charlie thought for a moment and said yes, but she knew it was safe to do so because they wouldn't have to make a decision for nearly five years.

The subject was dropped then, but Sean was very pleased. *It's a long time in the future, he thought, but it sure feels good to know that Charlie is receptive to the idea of moving.* It never once occurred to him that she was agreeable partly because the possibility was years away.

Sean and Charlie went for a midmorning breakfast over at Sadie's. They prayed together before they left the house since Sean knew that Charlie was waiting excitedly for a time when she could share with Sadie what had happened in her life. But Charlie told him she knew how busy Sadie was going to be on this day and was certain there would be no opportunity.

The town's festivities began at noon with a huge potluck lunch. Sean and Charlie sat with Lucas and Lora Duncan, and as always, Sean felt the mix of emotions from townspeople. He was greeted with both smiles and glares, something he had learned to take in stride.

It would have surprised most of the people to know that he understood completely. Not many knew of the part he played in Hartley's arrest, and wanting to be accepted for himself, Sean preferred it that way. But Duncan had been at work, and all of this changed when Judge Harrison, who had been asked to speak at the centennial ceremonies, was closing his speech.

"It's a scorcher out here today, so I won't keep you much longer, but recently something has been brought to my attention, and I've acted upon it. I feel now is the best time to share it with you.

"When I was called here in April, I judged a young stranger who had helped rob your bank. Well, most of you know that through fortuitous circumstances, one of your own townswomen came forward and married that young man, thereby rescuing him from the hangman's noose. This was done within the bounds of the law and it still stands, but I've amended the document I read to you back in April.

"Patrick Sean Donovan III, 'Sean' to most of you, is now a free man. The clause in the aforementioned document, stating that he must live in and serve the community of Visalia for no less than five years, is now amended.

"In case any of you feel outrage at this change, I will tell you this." Judge Harrison's voice rose with intensity. "It was Sean Donovan's plan and his willingness to risk personal injury that brought Hartley to the law this week past. Hartley, a man who has long plagued your town, is dead and will torment you no more because of the efforts of Sheriff Lucas Duncan, Franklin Witt, and Sean Donovan."

The judge said no more, but the applause was thunderous as he exited the platform. Most of the people had stood, but Sean and Charlie sat still in their seats, feeling nothing but shock.

They finally stood and Sean reached for Charlie's hand. A moment later they were surrounded by people. There were still many who hung back, but most of the townsfolk came up to thank or congratulate their local outlaw-turned-hero. Even when the throng pressed close, Sean never once let go of Charlie's hand, so he knew the exact instant she collapsed.

Forty-Two

"IT'S INCREDIBLY HOT out there, Sean. I'm surprised more people haven't fainted."

"But you're not certain it's just the heat?"

"No, I can't really tell you anything else until I talk with Charlie."

"Sean?" Charlie called to him in a confused voice.

The frightened young husband turned swiftly at the sound of his wife's voice. They were at the doctor's house, and Charlie was stretched out on the sofa in the dining room that had been converted into an office. Sean quickly knelt by her and cradled her pale cheek with his hand.

"Hi." He spoke the small word, unsure if he should say more. Charlie's complexion was ashen, and she looked completely disoriented.

"Sean," her voice was desperate now, "I'm going to be sick."

The doctor stepped in, and Sean felt every bit of his wife's pain as she vomited into a basin. When she was done, Sean was equally pale.

Charlie wanted to sit up after the doctor mopped her face with a cool cloth. When she did, Sean sat next to her. She leaned her head against his shoulder, and the doctor pulled a chair close to question her.

"Was it the heat, Charlie, or something more?"

"I don't know, Doc. I did feel pretty warm, but there was no warning. Suddenly everything started to get fuzzy and then black. My head hurts now."

"I can probably give you something for that, but first I need to ask a few questions."

Charlie was questioned about whether or not the heat had ever bothered her before, her diet, sleeping habits, alcohol intake, everything. Charlie answered all questions with calm patience, until the last one.

"Is there a chance you're in a family way?"

Charlie blinked at the man across from her, and then turned to look at Sean. They had talked of children, but neither one had given much thought to the fact that Charlie could be expecting.

The doctor took in the comical looks on the young couple's faces, and had to stop himself from shaking his head. To what did they think the intimate side of marriage led?

"I take it there is a possibility?" the doctor questioned dryly. When Charlie nodded he became much more specific. His questions made her eyes go wide, not because she was offended, but because he was able to tell her exactly what had been happening in her body of late. Nothing very noticeable, but distinct nevertheless.

"I thought women got sick when they were pregnant," Charlie commented. "I'm eating like I always have."

"No, you're not," Sean cut in. "You haven't wanted any coffee in the morning for a couple of weeks, and you're taking in more food than I've ever seen you eat."

Sean left them alone while the doctor examined Charlie, who told her as he finished that she was going to have a child in about seven months. He advised her to go home for the rest of the day, and even though she didn't want to miss any of the festivities, she complied after Sean promised to let her attend the fireworks that night.

Duncan, Lora, Sadie, and most surprisingly, Witt, were all waiting for the Donovans outside. Upon hearing the young couple's news, hands were shook and hugs were given before Sean ushered his wife home and into bed.

Charlie slept for two hours, and Sean sat in the living room and prayed. He marveled at how swiftly things had changed from this morning's conversation to Judge Harrison's announcement.

He wondered how Charlie felt about it. He knew she desperately wanted to please him, but if they were supposed to go to Hawaii or even Santa Rosa, it had to be because *both* of them knew they were to move from their present home.

The idea of leaving Duncan and Lora was painful, but the thought of seeing Kate, Marcail, and the family, or possibly living near them or Father was so exciting it took his breath away.

Sean prayed for calm. The change in the document did not make every dream come true. Charlie was his wife, his most precious possession, and if she wanted to stay in Visalia, they would stay. Sean decided right then and there not to mention it to her. He would give her time, and when she was ready, she would talk to him.

For an instant Sean's mind had completely forgotten the baby. As he remembered, he suddenly found himself smiling at absolutely nothing. His darling Charlie was going to have a baby. He once again bowed his head in prayer, this time in praise to God for the miracle in his wife's womb.

Lying on her back, Charlie woke slowly and without moving. She frowned at the ceiling for a moment, trying to figure out why she was in bed. When she remembered, her hand slid to her still-flat abdomen. She was going to have Sean's baby.

A smile of pure contentment crossed her face. She had fallen asleep dreaming of a little boy with his father's black hair and eyes. Charlie was still praying, thanking God for the baby and praying for a safe arrival, when Sean came quietly into the room.

"Hi," he whispered. She grinned at him.

He lowered himself to the edge of the bed and bent to kiss her. When Sean sat back there were tears in her eyes.

"Anything I can do?" he asked gently, and Charlie bit her bottom lip as a single tear spilled down her temple.

"There's just been so much, Sean, so much. I never dreamed there could be so many changes, but in the months since we've been married, my life has been completely altered. I mean, they're good changes, but sometimes I'm a little overwhelmed. Like right now."

Charlie couldn't go on, and Sean leaned over to put his arms around her. She had summed it all up rather nicely. They were good changes, but they were a little overwhelming.

They talked about the baby for a long time, and then had a light supper before joining Duncan and Lora, this time to watch the fireworks display. All agreed it was a perfect end to a wonderful day.

Forty-Three

CHARLIE'S TWENTY-FOURTH birthday was five days away when Sean went to the general store hoping to find her a present. The attitudes of the townspeople had changed toward Sean, and even though he had never felt threatened, he was surprised over how many smiles now came his away. Sean was not at all offended by the changes. He only hoped that with the new acceptance he would have opportunities to share about the One who had changed him.

Pete, the owner of the general store, sported an attitude which was remarkable different than in his first encounter with Sean. He greeted the younger man warmly when he walked through the door.

"Hello, Sean. You must be here about Charlie's birthday."

Sean's mouth dropped open in surprise, and the older man chuckled. "Sadie was just in," he said by way of explanation. Sean smiled in return.

"What did she buy?"

"Fabric. I would guess for a skirt or something."

Sean nodded and began to look around. He lingered over the fabric himself, but he wouldn't have known what to ask Sadie to make. The tools distracted him for a time, but then he got down to business. He studied the writing supplies for a long time, and after picking out what he thought to be perfect, a lone book on the shelf caught his eye.

He picked it up and checked the spine. He nearly did a double take when he read the words *Holy Bible*. Sean emptied his hands of all else and inspected the fat volume. He could hardly believe what he was seeing. The top was dusty, but the book itself appeared to be brand new. He carried it over to Pete.

"Pete, is this Bible for sale?"

"Yeah, although I've had it for years. Some woman ordered it, but she never came back to collect, so it's just been sitting here all this time."

"How much do you want for it?"

The price Pete named was more than reasonable, and, intending to purchase it, Sean set the Bible down on the counter. His hands had gone to the pocket of his jeans when he spotted a small case of jewelry with a glass top. His eyes caressed the 14K gold wedding bands, ranging in price from $1.19 to $4.79. His look was tormented when he glanced back at the Bible.

"Why don't you give her both?" Pete spoke softly.

Sean's hand went again to his pants pocket, and he dug out the money he had brought along.

"If you don't have it now, you can bring it to me later. I won't even put it on the bill."

Sean hesitated for only a moment. "Thanks, Pete," he said gratefully, and in a few minutes was back on the street, the Bible wrapped in plain brown paper and the simple gold band tucked safely in his pocket.

Charlie's birthday was on a Sunday, and her first surprise of the day was breakfast in bed. As Sean set the tray down, he looked so satisfied with himself that Charlie couldn't help but laugh.

"You're looking very pleased with yourself." She spoke as she shook out her napkin, and then started as something fell from it and hit the tray. Charlie stared at the small gold band that had landed near her coffee cup and then at her husband.

His smile was shy, and Charlie's heart melted. She didn't talk but picked up the ring, gave it to her husband, and presented her left hand. Sean gladly did the honors, and Charlie's eyes shone as the smooth gold band slid onto the third finger of her left hand.

"Happy Birthday, my darling," Sean whispered when the band was firmly in place, and Charlie leaned close to kiss him.

The breakfast was more than Charlie alone could handle, so she and Sean sat together on the bed and shared from the tray. As was the norm these last days, they talked of the baby, which Charlie had figured was due in early February. But as was also the norm these days, Sean sensed that something was bothering his dear wife.

Knowing she was genuinely excited about the baby, he couldn't help but wonder what was troubling her. Though she never mentioned it, he speculated often as to whether or not she was thinking about what Judge Harrison had said on the Fourth of July. Sean prayed every day about God's purpose in such a pardon. He believed with all his heart that God would lead them in His time, so he felt it best not to press her.

Sadie had asked them to a special dinner that afternoon, so they headed in the direction of the boarding-house as soon as church was dismissed. To Charlie's delight, Sadie had also asked Duncan and Lora.

The meal was a great success, and Charlie was surprised again when both Lora and Sean handed her packages. She had already opened a package from Sadie containing a skirt and blouse, and of course her ring from Sean.

The five of them were crowded into Sadie's private parlor. Lora and Duncan exchanged a glance as Charlie peeled back the wrapping paper on the hard, flat gift.

"Oh, my," Charlie said in disbelief as she held up a beautiful daguerreotype of the livery. "Where did you get this?"

Duncan smiled at how pleased she looked. "One of the photographers who wandered around town the week of the Fourth was in and tried to sell me a picture of my office. When I spotted the one he'd done of the livery, he told me he was headed to see you. I couldn't resist buying it myself."

Charlie passed the picture to Sean, and his face split with a grin. He knew in an instant that it had been taken the day before the Fourth because he remembered seeing the photographer setting up and wondering what he wanted. Sean was smack in the middle of the picture, framed by the double doors and reaching toward his back pocket for his handkerchief.

Framed in beautifully etched wood, the photo was examined by each and every one. Charlie thanked both Duncan and Lora, and Sean asked her to open the last gift. Charlie threw him a suspicious look before giving her attention to the gift he had placed in her lap. The whole room erupted with laughter at the way she babbled after the gift was unwrapped.

"Oh, Sean; oh, my! My very own Bible! I can't believe it! Do you know how badly I've wanted one? Where did you find this? Oh, look at the pages! Isn't it beautiful? I can't believe it—my very own Bible!"

Charlie moved to her husband's chair and threw her arms around his neck. He laughed as she tried to squeeze the life from him. She thanked him repeatedly and had to stop herself from sitting down to read it right on the spot.

Sadie went to ready the cake and coffee after the presents were put aside. Charlie joined her in the kitchen, giving the younger woman a chance to mention her Bible.

"You must wonder how I could be so excited about receiving a Bible," Charlie began tentatively.

"It has crossed my mind that there's been a change in you," Sadie said matter-of-factly.

"I'd like to tell you about it sometime, Sadie."

The older woman turned her full attention to her niece. She studied the fervent young face for a moment and tried to put her finger on the change. At first she had attributed it to having a happy marriage with a handsome husband and a baby on the way, but Sadie could see there was more.

"This means a lot to you, doesn't it?" Sadie asked quietly.

"Yes, it does."

Sadie suddenly smiled. "Well, honey, if it means that much to you, I'll listen to all you have to say."

They were not given any further time for talk, but Charlie praised God for opening a door. Even as the cake was served by Sadie's capable hands, Charlie prayed about the future opportunity she would have to speak with her aunt.

When Sean and Charlie did head home, Charlie immediately sat down to read her Bible. She had read Sean's on many occasions, but this was somehow special. As always, Charlie prayed that God would show her just what He would have her to see as she read the words, but she never dreamed of the things she would discover in the weeks to come.

Forty-Four

"IN OTHER WORDS we should never have been married?" Charlie was looking very distressed, and Sean searched for some way to explain something he didn't fully understand himself. They were studying in 2 Corinthians, the sixth chapter.

Sean began carefully. "People who have made a decision for Jesus Christ are commanded not to marry someone who does not share that belief, and I was no exception. But everything happened so fast. I want to say that I had no choice in the matter, that I probably could have spoken up and stopped everything, but the truth is, such a thing never occurred to me.

"I had come to a complete peace about dying, even though I was scared of the way that rope would feel. When Duncan removed the noose, I was in a state of shock. Less than ten minutes later, we were husband and wife."

Sean paused before continuing. He wanted Charlie to understand that God never condones sin, but that God's sovereign will is always in play. "Darling," Sean went on gently, "believing that God has complete command of life and death, I have to assume He sent you to keep me on this earth for a while longer. Had we met under normal circumstances, it would have been wrong of me to even court you."

Charlie looked at Sean for a moment and then down at her Bible to read verses 14 through 16 again: "Be ye not unequally yoked together with unbelievers; for what fellowship hath righteousness with unrighteousness? And what communion hath light with darkness? And what concord hath Christ with Belial? Or what part hath he that believeth with an infidel? And what agreement hath the temple of God with idols? For ye are the temple of the living God; as God hath said, 'I will dwell in them, and walk in them; and I will be their God, and they shall be my people.'"

"Who is Belial?" Charlie asked softly.

"That's one of the many names for Satan."

Charlie nodded. "I rather figured you would say that, considering everything else written here."

"Charlie, tell me what you're thinking."

The confused redhead gave a small shrug. "It's just hard to think of our marriage as a sin." Charlie held her hand up when Sean began to protest.

"What if I hadn't come to Christ?"

"I've thought about that. First of all, I know my love for you would never change. Second, I've confessed the sins of the past and known God's forgiveness and fellowship. Nevertheless, there have been numerous consequences from those sinful years. I've hurt people I love dearly, and all I can come up with is, God *did* spare my life, so I would have tried to serve Him as best I could, even with an unsaved wife."

Charlie gave a small sigh and looked again at the Bible in her lap. "There's so much to learn, isn't there?"

"Yes there is, but God is infinitely patient." Sean reached for her hand. "He knows our hearts and understands each and every struggle."

Charlie didn't answer because she didn't want Sean to know what she was *really* struggling with. Finding out what the Bible taught about marriage between believers and unbelievers was a little upsetting. But after some thought Charlie could see how much sense it made.

On the other hand, her real struggle was much harder to define. It was a mix of knowing how right Sean looked with a Bible in his hand, and less so with a hammer, and also knowing that if they so chose, they could leave Visalia whenever they wanted. Charlie was well aware of the fact that Sean, after all these weeks, had never mentioned the surprising announcement made on Independence Day. This told her one thing—he was waiting for her to bring it up. But as much as Charlie wanted to talk about it, she was scared. It would be some weeks before she understood that God was waiting to take care of that fear.

Charlie, now six months along in her pregnancy, stood rubbing her back. The dishes were put away, and Sean had already retired to the living room to read the paper. With her free hand, Charlie felt the very distinct swelling in the front of her skirt. She was not very big, but the baby moved constantly, telling her there was indeed a little person growing inside.

Charlie looked at the doorway of the living room and still she hesitated. It was time to talk with Sean. She was still a little afraid of the future, but it was time to bring her fears to her husband. God had shown her many places in Scripture that assured her of His love and control, and Charlie found comfort in these verses. But God had also given her a husband, a man who loved God and wanted His will. It was time she talked to him about those fears.

Sean smiled as Charlie took a place on the couch beside him. Reaching for her hand, Sean studied her face in the lantern light. The pregnancy was making her tired, but she was far and away the most beautiful woman in the world to him.

Quite often when they sat together in the evening, Sean would lean over her swollen tummy and talk to their baby. But tonight he perceived that Charlie needed all of his attention.

"Anything I can do?" It was Sean's standard line when he sensed that Charlie needed to talk, and as he had hoped, it did the trick.

"*I'm* being a baby," Charlie admitted softly.

"About what?"

"About our moving away."

Sean didn't reply to this, and after a silent moment Charlie continued.

"You're a good blacksmith, Sean, one of the best I've seen, and I've seen a few. But something hasn't been right from the very beginning, and it took my coming to Christ to understand what that *something* is. You look better with a Bible in your hand.

"I don't know if that makes any sense, but I just can't see you pounding on horseshoes for the rest of your life. It's taken me awhile, but just after you said that you always think of Hawaii when you dream of us living elsewhere, Judge Harrison publicly pardoned you. I just knew that someday God would direct us away from here, and the truth is I'm scared to death."

Sean reached for Charlie and pulled her into his arms. "And you thought," he finished gently, "that the second I knew you were willing to move, I would make you pack and drag you out of town."

"Something like that," Charlie admitted softly.

"Well, it's not going to happen that way, darling, because I don't know if we're supposed to go anywhere. I picture us working as missionaries, just as my folks did, but I don't know where, and God might have Visalia in mind for another 20 years."

"And you could be happy, Sean?"

"Definitely. Now I have a question for you. Could you be happy if God shows us in an unmistakable way that we're to move from here?"

Charlie was silent for only a moment. "You know, for the first time in my life I think I could. Some of the fear is still there, because everything beyond this town is unknown territory to me, but if you're beside me and we know we're headed where God wants us to go, I'll be fine."

Sean watched the front of Charlie's skirt lift with the baby's movement. His hand when to her abdomen as it often did to feel the baby move within her. No words were necessary for a time.

"Do you still wish we could serve the Lord in Hawaii?" Charlie asked.

"Yes, but not before spending some time with my family in Santa Rosa. It's been far too long since I've seen them."

"We could go for a visit, you know."

"That's true. Maybe after the baby is born."

"Let's plan on it."

"All right. Who will run the livery?" Sean wanted to know.

"I don't know, but if we're supposed to go for a visit, then God will send just the person we need."

Sean hugged her again. She'd grown so much in the last weeks, and he couldn't begin to tell her what an encouragement she was. He ended their evening by calling her his darling Charlie and telling her she was the love of his life.

Forty-Five

Two weeks had passed since Sean and Charlie had talked about moving. The conversation had opened new doors between them, and they were now able to pray and discuss all possibilities with ease. But the real test of faith was upon them, and it was delivered in the form of their new friend, Franklin Witt.

All Charlie had ever heard about Visalia's banker had been put to rest as she got to know the man better. He had become something of a champion to the young Donovans, even before the judge's surprising announcement. He never failed to inquire over Charlie's health with real concern, and it was not at all unusual to see him lounging in the livery, sharing friendly conversation.

Never before had he come on business, but this particular morning things were about to change. The morning had flown by, and the livery owners were just finishing lunch. Sean, always very concerned about Charlie overdoing, had almost convinced her to go to the house and lie down.

"I can take care of everything here," Sean urged.

"Mrs. Franks' mare doesn't like you, and she still needs shoes."

"I'll leave her for last so you'll still have plenty of time to take a nap before coming to help me."

"I'm not tired," Charlie replied stubbornly.

Sean shook his head. She was exhausted. Charlie had not slept well, but she wouldn't hear of it when Sean tried to convince her to stay in bed that morning. He could see that he was going to have to become very stern.

"I want you to go to bed, Charlotte, and I mean now."

Charlie frowned at his tone and the order, but Sean leveled her with a look that told her he meant business. She turned ungraciously for the back door just as Witt came in the front.

"I'm glad I caught you together. Have you got a minute? There's something I need to tell you."

"Actually Charlie was just headed to the—"

"Now is fine, Witt," Charlie interrupted, ignoring the look Sean gave her.

"Well, I just had a man come into the bank who wants to set up a livery in this town. He told me he'd rather buy this one, but didn't really think it would be for sale. Either way, he plans to borrow money to open a livery."

"What's his name?" Sean asked suspiciously, and Witt answered, "Zach Carlton."

Husband and wife exchanged a glance. A man named Zach Carlton had been in just two days ago to rent a horse. He had been far from casual about his interest in every square inch of Cooper's Livery. Sean had tried to question him about whether he had business in town or was just passing through, but he'd been very evasive.

"I can see that I've surprised you, and I don't expect you've ever given it any thought, so why don't I come by tomorrow and you can tell me if you're at all interested?" The Donovans agreed and thanked Witt for his trouble before he went on his way.

"We definitely need to talk about this," Sean quietly told his now-pale wife, "but not until after you've slept."

This time Charlie did not argue, and after Sean put out the sign saying he would be back in 15 minutes, he escorted his wife to the house. He stayed with her until she was asleep, which took less than five minutes, but it was far more than five minutes before Sean was done praying and able to concentrate on his work.

Sean had been desperate for a bath that night, so husband and wife decided that when they returned from Sadie's they would go to bed early to talk about Witt's news. Neither one had taken the time to open the mail, so when they were finally snuggled in bed, Charlie started with the letter from Aunt Maureen, and Sean read a letter from Katie. Kate's letter ended with news about Father.

"Don't be concerned if you don't hear from Father for some time. He wrote that he was so busy with the work there, he didn't know which way was up. He said that God is moving in mighty ways throughout the villages. He also asked us to pray with him that God would burden other families to come and join the work there, and of course for the furtherance of the gospel of Christ.''

When it was time to trade, Sean hesitated. Charlie looked at him with some surprise.

"Bad news?"

"No, but Katie reports something Father said, and I really want us to talk before you read it.''

Charlie looked at Sean for the space of a few heartbeats, her brows raised in surprise. Sean suddenly realized he was selling her short and handed her the letter. His desire not to pressure her about moving wasn't even valid. She could just as easily have been the first to read Kate's letter and know what Father had said.

Sean also realized it was unfair of him to believe that God would pressure them at all. He was, most likely, giving them some direction. A few minutes later the letters were put aside and Charlie used that very word.

"This is what I've prayed for, Sean," Charlie began. "This is exactly what I've prayed for."

"What is that exactly?"

"Direction. I've prayed that God would show us what direction He wanted us to go and in a way that we could never doubt. I think we know that now."

Sean was speechless and for some reason, fearful. "Charlie, when we were first married, I could tell that you wanted desperately to please me. And now I'm just a little afraid that you're doing it again and—"

"I'm not," Charlie said with a smile. "I mean, pleasing you is important to me, and you don't fear moving because you've been where we're probably headed, but none of what I've said stems from any desire other than to follow God's will."

Sean's heart overflowed with praise to God. He realized then that his wildest dreams were coming true. Charlie saw the emotion in his face and moved close to hold him.

"Oh, Charlie," Sean's voice was breathless, "I thought my life was over, and then you came forward and rescued me. Then I thought I would have to live forever with an unsaved wife, but God brought you to Himself, and now this. My darling Charlie, I can't tell you how I've dreamed of our going to see my family, and then going to Hawaii to work with Father."

"I know," Charlie whispered softly. "Did you think we could live together as husband and wife without me learning to read your thoughts?"

This caused Sean to laugh deeply, and he wrapped his arms fiercely around her. They prayed together, surrounded by each other's embrace. It was a prayer of surrender for the future, near and far. They both fell quickly asleep, their hearts filled with prayers that God would be glorified in their lives.

The next morning they made their way to the bank. In the space of a few minutes, their hearts at peace, they told Witt they were willing to talk about the sale of the livery.

Forty-Six

"YOU'RE REALLY LEAVING, aren't you?"

Charlie nodded and bravely fought the tears that threatened. She knew Sadie had wanted to tell her she couldn't go anywhere, but the fact was, they were leaving in two days and the time for facing reality was at hand.

"What about the baby, Charlie? Should you be traveling when you're so far along?"

"The doctor says I'm in great shape, and we're taking the train for most of the journey."

"You've changed, Charlie." Sadie sounded almost despondent. "I'm not saying it's a bad change; it's just that I don't understand it."

Charlie couldn't bear the dejected look on Sadie's face. Gently grasping her aunt's arm, she led her to the sofa in Sadie's small parlor.

In the minutes that followed, Charlie learned a great deal about her aunt's knowledge of the Bible. She hadn't realized that her late Uncle Harry had read the Bible regularly.

"Your Uncle Harry was a good man, Charlie. He deserved God's love."

"And you don't think you do?" Charlie asked softly.

Sadie let out a small sigh. "I'm nearing 60, honey."

"You're only 56," Charlie replied, wondering why Sadie believed her age mattered.

"Yes, but I've lived those 56 years for myself, and I don't really think God would be interested in me now."

"I don't believe that, Sadie." Charlie spoke with quiet conviction.

"I know you don't. You believe that everyone is redeemable— but I just don't know."

The conversation continued on in this vein for nearly two hours, and even though Sadie listened intently to all Charlie shared, Charlie could see that she was not convinced.

When it came time for Charlie to leave, however, she did not go under a cloud of depression. She believed that God really would save her aunt in His time.

When Sadie saw how much Charlie loved Sean, and how badly she wanted to go and do this "missionary thing," as she called it, Sadie was able to send her with her blessing.

Charlie told her aunt, without offending, that she would be praying for a change in her heart. Knowing that this would be their only private goodbye, their embrace was long and tearful.

The church family gave Sean and Charlie a loving send-off. There was a potluck supper, served at the church, the night before they were scheduled to leave. Pastor Miller asked Sean to share his testimony with all present, and Sean praised God for the opportunity to give Him the glory for all that had transpired in the last months.

Most of what he shared regarding his years in Hawaii, his mother and father's departure, and the way his heart turned from God was a surprise to those who attended. The sincerity they saw as he told how God had changed him gained him numerous hugs when he finished and came down into the crowd.

Pastor Miller quieted everyone so he could pray for their journey, and then presented them with a generous gift of money to help them on their way.

The potluck followed and went quite late into the evening. Though it made it hard to rise in the morning, excitement rode them and they rose with hearts of anticipation for the day's travel. Once at the train station, they found Duncan, Lora, and Sadie on hand to see them off. Lora gave them a basket of food for the trip.

Few words were said, but all promised to write, and after a round of hugs was shared and tears were shed, the Donovans were on their way. Charlie didn't cry as Sean had expected. She was very quiet for the first five miles, and Sean didn't press her into conver-

sation. Sometime after the fifth mile, she fell into a sound sleep on
Sean's shoulder.

At the end of their first day, they were both sticky with perspira-
tion and felt cramped from sitting so long. But on they rode, taking
trains and two stages, whatever was needed to speed them on their
journey. Charlie was beginning to think they would never stop
moving when the stage they were on pulled into Santa Rosa late
one evening. It was after 8:00, so the shipping office and all other
businesses were closed for the night. The streets were quiet.

Sean thought Charlie looked about ready to collapse, but she
told him it felt so good to stretch her legs that she could ignore the
fatigue. They didn't rush their walk, and since they had left their big
trunk at the stage office, they had only one small traveling bag
each. Once they stood in front of the Riggs' home, Sean paused.

"This is the place."

"It's big, isn't it?"

"I guess it is pretty spacious," Sean agreed, but he didn't speak
again or move toward the house.

The last days, as well as the walk from the stage office, were
beginning to wear on Charlie, but she sensed Sean needed time, so
she stayed quiet. When he finally stepped toward the house, she
moved after him, praying that her legs would hold.

Charlie stood behind Sean and watched as a man opened the
door, shouted Sean's name, pulled him inside, and grabbed him in a
bear hug. Smiling at the sight of the reunion, Charlie was making a
move forward when the door was shut, almost in her face.

Strangely enough, Charlie did not feel hurt or rejected. In fact
she chuckled just a little. Originally they had planned on Sean coming alone for a visit, returning to Visalia before the baby was born
and then heading to Hawaii from there. Charlie knew that none of
Sean's family was expecting her.

Charlie mentally counted the seconds before the door was
wrenched open. Eight seconds passed before she was once again
seeing Sean's face, which registered shock over what had happened.

"I'm sorry," he spoke softly, his expression telling Charlie he
was slightly aghast over her being so totally ignored.

"It's all right, Sean," she smiled to reassure him. "But could I
please sit down somewhere?"

Sean ushered Charlie into the living room in time to hear Kaitlin
scolding Rigg.

"I can't believe you left her standing on the front porch!"

Rigg was fighting laughter. "Honestly, Kate," he tried to placate her, "I didn't see her."

Kate frowned at the sparkle she saw in his eyes before enveloping her new sister-in-law with her embrace.

"Oh, Charlotte, you must be exhausted! Come right over here to the sofa."

Kate then proceeded to issue orders to Rigg and Marcail like a drill sergeant, and within the space of a few seconds Charlie was alone with Sean. Sean smiled at the wide-eyed look on her face.

"She's not always so bossy."

"I think she's wonderful," Charlie whispered as tears filled her eyes. As always, the sight of Charlie's tears melted his heart. He sat beside her and pulled her against him. She didn't cry, but her breathing was uneven and her whole frame shuddered with suppressed sobs.

A few minutes passed, and Sean could tell without looking at her that she was no longer sobbing. That she was asleep was not apparent to him until Marcail came in with a mug of hot coffee. He watched his sister stop halfway across the rug, and then tip-toe to set the cup on the sofa table.

"She's asleep, Sean," Marcail whispered and Sean nodded. "If you want to carry her upstairs, your room is all ready."

"Maybe I'd better."

Kaitlin and Rigg came back in time to see Marc leading Sean up the stairs with his precious bundle. As their feet disappeared from view, Kate spoke.

"I'm so glad they came together, but we didn't even get to meet her."

"We'll have plenty of time for that."

"I almost ran upstairs to wake the girls."

"Since tomorrow is Sunday, we'll all have the entire day to get acquainted."

"So tell us your plans!" Rigg encouraged Sean as both men, Katie, and Marcail sat around the kitchen table.

"Well," he said slowly, "I probably should have explained everything to you before moving back, bag and baggage, but—"

"You misunderstand me, Sean," the older man assured him gently. "I'm not trying to pin you down to any schedule. I'm just excited to have you here and want to know what you have in mind."

"I guess I just wanted the baby to be born here," Sean began again. "Everything happened so quickly with the sale of the livery. I know we'd have been welcome at Sadie's if we had to stay, but we honestly believed the trip would be easier for Charlie and the baby *before* the baby was born." Sean's gaze traveled upward to where his wife was sleeping. "She's so tired right now," Sean continued, "I wonder if we made the right decision."

"I think she'll be fine, Sean," Katie told him. "You know that we'll do all we can to make her comfortable. And we're just thrilled that your baby will be born here." Kate's voice caught just a little.

Sean could only nod, his heart full. It had been so long since they'd been together, and so much had passed. Marcail, quiet as she was, seemed to be having the hardest time. She kept touching Sean as though making certain he was really there.

They talked late into the night before Rigg said they'd better get some sleep. No one argued, and after a few yawns and another round of hugs, Sean made his way upstairs.

"Sean?" Charlie's voice was heavy with sleep as she felt the bed shift beside her.

"I'm sorry I woke you."

"What time is it?"

"I'm not sure, I think about 2:00 A.M."

"Oh, Sean," Charlie pleaded as she remembered where she was. "Please tell me I didn't fall asleep before a proper introduction to your family."

Charlie buried her face in the pillow when he laughed softly. Forgetting the hour, she told herself to get up and apologize, but before she could work out the time or force herself out of bed, she was back to sleep.

Forty-Seven

CHARLIE LOOKED AROUND the breakfast table at the people surrounding her and smiled. Marshall Riggs, a man whose frame was even larger than Sean's, was a big sweetheart. He had taken Charlie's hand as soon as she had come downstairs and humbly asked her forgiveness for closing her outside in the cold. That he was still amused over what he'd done was immediately evident to her, and they ended up grinning at each other like old friends.

Kaitlin, so obviously Sean's sister, was a model of tenderness. Charlie had apologized about falling asleep, but all Kaitlin did was laugh and hug her again. She then went on to tell Charlie some great stories about the way she had behaved when she was expecting, putting Charlie so at ease that she laughed until she had tears in her eyes.

"Beautiful" was the only word Charlie could mentally formulate to describe Marcail Donovan. Kaitlin was extremely attractive, but Marcail's exquisite features and huge dark eyes were so fetching that Charlie caught herself staring on more than one occasion. Marcail had a genuine desire to help, and her lovely mouth would draw into a smile at the slightest provocation. Her frame and height were petite. Charlie, who never considered herself tall, found that Marcail looked up to her.

The last to come under Charlie's scrutiny were Gretchen and Molly. The sight of them caused Charlie to smile. Both girls were darling, with big dark eyes and the coal-black hair that seemed to be

196

the hallmark of this family. They were perfect little ladies at the breakfast table. Since Gretchen was only four and Molly was just two, Charlie mentally congratulated Rigg and Kate for the work that must have gone into the last years.

There was a bit of a squabble in the wagon on the way to church, showing Charlie that the girls were not always so well behaved. But their quick response when reprimanded, and the way they snuggled close to their Uncle Sean and Aunt Charlotte as if they had known them for years, was enough to win over even the hardest of hearts, let alone one like Charlie's that was waiting to love them.

Charlie desperately tried to keep the names of everyone she had met clear in her mind. So many from Rigg's family had come to meet her that she was beginning to think that he was somehow related to the entire church.

"We're all going to Taylors for lunch," Sean told her as the wagon pulled out of the church yard.

"Rigg's family?"

"Right."

"Which ones were they?" Charlie looked very worried.

Sean took her hand and squeezed it. "Don't try to remember. They'll understand if you need to ask their names."

Charlie wasn't at all convinced, and with Molly trying to get Sean's attention, he missed the look of distress on his wife's face.

"It's all a little overwhelming, isn't it?"

Charlie turned and found one of Rigg's brothers smiling down at her. He joined her on the sofa, and Charlie gave him a tried smile.

"I've never had any trouble with names before," Charlie stated apologetically.

"I'm Gilbert Taylor, Rigg's brother, and please don't apologize," Gil forestalled her.

Charlie smiled. "I won't, although it seems as though all I've done in the past 24 hours is apologize. Actually," Charlie paused, looking a little surprised, "I haven't been here that many hours." She looked even more exhausted after realizing that less than a day ago she was on a stage just coming into town.

Gilbert, always sensitive to the feelings of others, talked quietly to Charlie until her lids began to droop. The house was noisy, but she fell asleep beside him, and he stayed close to keep the little ones from disturbing her.

It wasn't long before Sean came in from the kitchen. He had been talking with Bill and May Taylor, and Rigg and Kaitlin. When he saw Gilbert guarding Charlie, he grabbed the newspaper and with a softly spoken word of thanks took his place.

Charlie was able to catch almost an hour's sleep before someone slammed a door and woke her. Sean had done very little reading as he sat beside her. He had been praying, and as soon as Charlie's eyes focused on him he spoke to her in a soft tone.

"I think I owe you an apology."

"Over what?" Charlie blinked slowly at him, but she had heard every word.

"About taking you out of the house today, even for church."

"I don't understand what you mean."

"I mean, we're going to be here until after the baby is born, so you'll have lots of time to meet folks. I had no business taking you out today, introducing you to dozens of people, and then bringing you here for lunch, when all you needed was rest."

"I hope you know you're being very silly," Charlie said, her voice still very sleepy. "I wanted to go to church, and you've told me how long all these people have been praying for you. Sean, you *needed* to see them."

Sean only shook his head and moved close enough to put his arm around her. With one arm holding her close, he reached with his free hand to the roundness of her stomach. It seemed she was increasing daily.

While Sean held her close he whispered in her ear that she was the most important person on earth to him. He told her that from now on, he would be taking much better care of her. Charlie tried once again to tell him she was fine, but he silenced her with a kiss.

Neither one of them realized that Kaitlin had come into the room just in time to witness that kiss. She turned back to the kitchen with a smile on her face. The only thing better than having Sean come home was having him home with the woman he loved and who loved him in return.

Forty-Eight

CHARLIE HAD BEEN in Santa Rosa for about eight days When the dam that carefully held her emotions in check shattered. It was a Sunday morning, and while still in the bedroom getting dressed for the day Sean innocently teased her about once again falling asleep when conversation was going on around her.

To Sean's utter amazement, Charlie burst into tears. He apologized several times, but she seemed inconsolable. Staying with her until the harsh sobs had passed, Sean left her still crying softly on the edge of the bed to tell Kate they would not be joining the family for church.

When he returned to the room, he found that she was once again readying for church. In a soft voice Sean told her that he didn't think they should go; they needed some time alone to talk. Sean stood helpless as she once again erupted into tears.

He stood back for only an instant before going to her and taking her in his arms. With gentle movements he removed her dress and slipped her back into the nightgown she had just changed from. Charlie was still crying into the handkerchief that Sean had pressed into her hands when Sean lifted her and put her back beneath the covers of the bed.

He expected her to fall back to sleep immediately, but after some minutes, with her eyes still closed and voice shuddering, she began to speak.

"I can't do it, Sean, I just can't do it. I can't remember anyone's name, and I think they're offended when I forget. My back hurts constantly. And it's almost Christmas! We don't have gifts for anyone. I'm tired all the time. I'm so tired."

Sean listened to all of this in silence and then climbed onto the bed beside her. He smoothed the hair away from her wet cheek and used the handkerchief to dry her face. She had developed a body-shaking case of the hiccups by the time Sean's arms were back around her.

"You're frightened about a lot of things, Charlotte, and I hate to think how long you've been keeping all of this to yourself." His voice was compassionate and coaxing.

"I want you to be proud of me." Her voice faltered with suppressed sobs. "I don't want to do anything to stand in the way of our going to Hawaii."

"No man could be more proud of his wife than I am," he told her with tender assurance. "And as far as Hawaii goes, I'm glad you brought it up because I've been praying about that very subject."

Charlie shifted so she could look at Sean's face. "You've changed your mind? You don't think I'll be a good missionary?"

"You will be a wonderful missionary," he told her with a kiss. "But I don't think there's any hurry. Our money is in the bank, and after Christmas I think we should find a place of our own. That will take the pressure off as to when we should leave. It might be two months after the baby is born, and it might be two years. Rigg has already asked me to work part-time for him at the mercantile, and I don't think I'll have trouble finding other employment."

"But if it weren't for me, you'd leave now?" Charlie looked utterly despondent.

"No, my darling Charlie, I wouldn't. There is still one person whom I haven't even been able to talk with about all of this, and that's my father. His opinion means a lot to me, and I need to write and ask for his counsel. Now, I have a question for you. Are you sorry we left Visalia?"

Charlie answered immediately. "No, in fact I can see why you talk so fondly of Santa Rosa; it's a wonderful town. But I *do* miss Sadie, and my world feels turned on end right now, and—"

She couldn't go on, but she didn't need to; Sean understood completely. They talked until Charlie yawned expansively.

"I'm sorry I'm so tired all the time."

Sean laughed and shook his head. "You're way too hard on yourself. When Katie was pregnant with Gretchen, all she did was sleep. It was even worse with Molly, since she had Gretchen to care for at the same time." Sean kissed her softly. "Go to sleep. When you wake up I'll make you some breakfast."

Charlie was too tired to reply, and almost before Sean could remove his arms from around her she was asleep.

Sean took advantage of the quiet house and sat in the living room to read his Bible. He then spent a long time on his knees praying for Charlie. He asked God to help her to know Him better, and to understand that God's love for her was all-encompassing. He prayed for her physical needs and for those of the baby.

He then went on to pray for himself, especially that he would accept whatever future God had for him. He asked for sensitivity to Charlie's needs, and about when they should move on from Santa Rosa. Still very peaceful about being there, he asked God to show him in an unmistakable way when Hawaii, or anywhere else, was right for them.

Charlie awoke more than an hour later, and after they ate breakfast she and Sean spent some time in prayer before reading the newspaper.

The next morning Kaitlin took Charlie to meet Dr. Grade, the doctor who had delivered both Gretchen and Molly. He gave Charlie a good report on the baby's position, as well as a clean bill of health for herself. Kate, who was very cognizant of Charlie's fatigue, watched her face closely when she asked if Charlie wanted to do some Christmas shopping.

"Do you have time?"

"Sure," Kate told her easily. "Sean is playing with the girls, Rigg is working, and Marcail is at school. I have, for the moment, time on my hands." Katie gave a little shrug and Charlie laughed.

The women went to Rigg's Mercantile, and Charlie was able to cover over half of her Christmas list. The only gift she hesitated on was a pair of black stockings for Marcail.

"Won't she be embarrassed to open these in front of everyone?"

Kaitlin chuckled. "Not Marc; she is quite drawn to feminine attire. I promise you, she'll love them."

Kate knew that she still had plenty of time before her girls would even ask about her, but after making her purchases Charlie was flagging. Kate asked if they could finish on another day, and Charlie was more than willing to comply. Their conversation on the walk home was light and carefree.

"I would have said that running a livery was the hardest job on earth," Charlie commented. "But now that I'm pregnant, I've changed my opinion."

"And to think," Kaitlin said with wonder in her voice, "for a while you did both."

"Not really, Katie. Sean has been rather hennish since I fainted on the Fourth of July."

"Well, since you're obviously not a person who will ease up, I can see why."

Charlie knew she was right, so all she did was smile. Kate did not miss that smile. She decided that as soon as she was home, she would have a talk with her brother and sister-in-law.

"How did you know we were thinking of moving?" Charlie asked Kaitlin.

"I didn't, not for certain. But Rigg and I talked about it last night. We both think that getting your own place is fine, but we think you should wait until after the baby is born."

Sean and Charlie exchanged a look. He knew Charlie thought she was a great burden because no one let her wash clothes or do work of any kind, but he also remembered how sick his mother had been when they first came to San Francisco. Aunt Maureen had not let her lift a finger. While it couldn't change the fact that she was very ill, it did remove the weight of housework. With the baby coming, it was doubtful that Charlie would have another chance to receive such a rest.

"I think it's a great idea, but I know Charlie is concerned about being a burden."

Charlie gave Sean a look that told him she wished he hadn't said that, but he was not sorry. As he hoped, Kaitlin knew just the right thing to say.

"I can't quite describe to you, Charlie, how long we've waited to see Sean like this. I'm not talking about physically; I'm talking about spiritually. I don't know if you'll understand this, but it's our *privilege* to help you. I think you both need nurturing right now, and the fact that we get to reach out to you means more than I can say."

There was nothing Charlie could say to this, except thanks, and she did. It didn't change her desire to help, and she hoped Katie would agree, but Charlie knew she needed to take herself off and spend some time in prayer.

She put aside her pride and was able to admit to herself how badly she needed the rest they were offering. She also found a verse that became very special to her in the days to come, Philippians 4:19: "But my God shall supply all your need according to his riches in glory by Christ Jesus."

Forty-Nine

TWO DAYS BEFORE Christmas Charlie sat in the living room with Gretchen, listening to her chatter on about people whom Charlie thought she remembered *might* be her cousins. Why it was so hard to learn everyone's name and relationship, Charlie was still not sure. To add to the confusion, when Gretchen got excited her speech was not as clear, and names like Cleo, Willy, Joey, Paige, and Sutton flew at her so fast that she couldn't keep them straight.

Marcail entered the room in time to see Charlie looking utterly bewildered. A few minutes later Gretchen jumped down from the couch and went happily on her way. A look of determination crossed Charlie's face. Had Sean seen it, he would have laughed, since it usually meant she had work for him. Marcail smiled in her sweet way, unaware of the fact that Charlie was going to keep her in the living room for the next hour.

"Marcail," Charlie said with quiet determination. "I wonder if you could do me a favor?"

"Sure."

"I'd like you to start at the top and tell me the names of the people in this family. I want to know who Sutton and Paige are, and all the others. Not just their names, but how they're related to Sean."

Marcail smiled. Charlie looked ready to take the world in her hands. Marcail thought she was wonderful.

"That's a pretty tall order, but I'll give it a try."

Charlie nodded, her brow furrowed in concentration. She made herself a little more comfortable on the sofa, and Marcail began.

"I guess the main family is the Taylors, so I'll start with Bill and May and their kids, the oldest of whom is Rigg. Rigg is a Riggs and not a Taylor because his father died when he was little and May married Bill. You, of course, know who his wife and children are." Marcail waited for Charlie to nod and then moved on.

"Next is Jeff Taylor. His wife is Bobbie, and their children are Cleo and Sutton. Bobbie's parents are Jake and Maryanne Bradford. Bobbie also has an older sister named Alice. Alice and her husband have twins named Paige and Wesley. Bobbie's brother is Troy. Troy is married to Carla, and they have a little boy named Jacob, after his grandpa."

Charlie nodded again, this time with a little more understanding, and Marcail continued.

"After Jeff is Gilbert. You met him two Sundays ago. He's not married and still lives with Bill and May. After Gil comes Nathan. Nathan's wife is Brenda and their little guy is Willy."

"Who is Joey?"

"Oh, Joey Parker," Marcail looked almost apologetic. "He's my age. We go to school together. He's not related to us, but is a good friend of the family. Gretchen talks about him because she thinks he's wonderful."

"Is there anyone who's going to be at Taylors on Christmas Day you haven't mentioned?"

Marcail thought for a moment. "Joey's dad, Mr. Parker, will be there. Not everyone will be there for the meal, Charlotte. Some have other family in town, and they'll just come for dessert."

Charlie smiled at her understanding tone. "Marcail, has anyone told you lately that you're wonderful?"

Marcail only smiled and then looked at the front door as a knock sounded. She made a move to answer it, but Charlie stopped her.

"I'll get it, Marc. I've been sitting too long as it is."

Charlie was a little stiff in her movements as she waddled toward the door, and the person on the other side knocked a second time before she could get there. Charlie swung the door open and even though there was plenty of light, it took her a few moments to respond.

Patrick Donovan's face broke into a huge grin as he took in his daughter-in-law's startled face and swollen form.

"Well now," he spoke softly. "I thought I would be the one doing the surprising, but I can see that the surprise is on me."

Charlie beamed and moved to hug Sean's father. The door
opened directly into the living room, so it only took a moment for
Marcail to see that her father had arrived. Her happy shout brought
the household running.

Patrick was not able to get a word in for some minutes. He was
hugged, pulled this way and that, and questioned until he could do
nothing but laugh at the pandemonium. When the family settled
down, Patrick's gaze settled on his son. Sean smiled at him, but his
look turned curious when Patrick continued to stare.

"So tell us how you came to be here," Kaitlin asked when the
silence lengthened.

"I think Sean is the only one who can tell me that."

"What do you mean?" Marcail spoke this time.

"Just that I knew I had to come. I knew he planned to be here
from Katie's letter and that I had to see him."

This time it was Sean and Charlie who looked at each other.
Charlie's face lit with such a peaceful smile that Sean felt his throat
close. She knew Sean had written to his father asking how he felt
about their coming to Hawaii, but the letter had obviously missed
him.

Father and son did not get a chance to talk just then, because
both Molly and Gretchen wanted their grandpa's attention, but the
adults knew their time would come that evening when the children
were in bed.

Rigg kissed his wife and thanked her for supper before asking
her if she wanted him to play with the girls or do the dishes. Kate
was more than ready to give her daughters over to their father, so
Rigg ushered them into the living room for games.

They started with "horsey" rides around the room, and when
everyone was flushed with laughter, they settled onto the sofa with
a book. Patrick and Sean were still in the kitchen with Kate and
Marcail. Charlie was in the living room, enjoying the story along
with the children.

It seemed like no time at all before the girls were kissing everyone goodnight and being carted off to bed by their loving, but somewhat tuckered, father. Kate served coffee in the living room and
when all was quiet, Patrick spoke.

"Knowing how seasick I always become, getting on that boat
was the last thing I wanted to do," he admitted softly. "Although I
must admit it seemed a little better this time. But no matter; I *had* to
come. I didn't even stop to see Maureen. Now, Sean, tell me why
I'm here."

"I wrote to you that we were leaving Visalia and coming here, and even though it seems you missed my letter, you would have known that from Kate's." Sean went on to explain how Charlie had come to grips with leaving, Witt's unexpected visit to announce a buyer for the livery, and all the other details leading up to that moment.

"I laid it out in the letter, but the main point was not to give you information, but to ask your advice. Charlie and I value your opinion, and we want to know what you think of our coming to Hawaii to work with you."

Patrick couldn't answer. Sean had shared with him during the summer about this very desire, and Patrick suspected this was the reason it had been so heavy on his heart to be here, but hearing it with his own ears brought him more joy than he thought possible.

"We've prayed for so long that God would send willing workers, Sean." Patrick's voice was thick with emotion. "Come, Sean. Bring your family and come as soon as God leads. I understand that you may want to wait to travel with the baby, but come. We need you in the islands."

Everyone tried to talk at the same time after that. Above the conversation Rigg could be heard telling Sean and Charlie that he wanted them to continue living at the house until they left. When some of the excitement died down, Charlie found herself to be the center of attention.

"Charlotte," Kate implored, "would you mind telling us a little of how you and Sean met?"

Charlie chuckled. "It wasn't exactly what you'd call conventional. In fact, until I came to know the Lord, I couldn't have told you why I was at that hanging, but I see now that it was all a part of His plan."

"When did you fall in love?" Marcail asked with a teenager's curiosity about romance.

"I think it happened for me when Sean punched a man in the face to protect me."

Every mouth in the room dropped open. Charlie and Sean couldn't help grinning at each other, even though it hadn't been at all funny at the time. Everyone in the room was gawking at them. Sean finally took pity on his family and explained. Katie looked ready to punch Murphy herself when she found out he had assaulted Charlie.

The conversation moved to how Sean had spent the years prior to meeting Charlie. His family was at once captivated and grieved for all he had been through because of the choices he made. The last question of the evening came from Patrick, and it was addressed to Charlie.

"How did you come to know that you could move away from your home?"

Charlie smiled at the eldest Donovan. "It was the Lord again. For years I'd been so content, and then I suddenly had this black-smith to whom I happened to be married, and one of the first things I noticed was how he looked more natural with a Bible in his hand than a hammer. I knew then it was just a matter of time." She paused and turned her smile to Sean. "And now our going to Hawaii—that too I think is just a matter of time."

Fifty

THE CHRISTMAS SEASON passed with a full slate of activities and fun. Sadie's box of gifts was a little late, but it arrived filled with clothes for the baby. Charlie was delighted with each tiny hand-made article.

With a prayer in his heart that Sean and family would join him soon, Patrick said goodbye to his family two days after the new year.

When February arrived and her due date was still two weeks away, Charlie became discouraged. She was so big and uncomfortable that it felt as if she would be pregnant forever. She was poised to tell Sean just that when the first contraction hit. Charlie's startled gaze flew to Sean, who was already dressed for church and reading his Bible. He did not immediately notice her distress. She gasped softly as the pain eased, causing Sean to look her way.

"The baby?" Sean's voice was instantly urgent when he saw his wife's horrified face.

"I think so," Charlie said breathlessly.

Sean was out the door and down the stairs to alert his sister before Charlie could make a move. Upon entering the bedroom moments later, Kate hardly had to question Charlie before telling her to put her nightgown on and get back into bed.

Rigg took the girls and went for his mother. On the way home he stopped to let Dr. Grade know that Charlie's labor had begun. She was in the midst of another contraction when May Taylor

208

walked in. May's countenance was calm, and Charlie found her voice very soothing in the midst of her agony.

Hours passed. Thinking he would burst if he had to watch his wife's suffering for one more moment, Sean was in and out of the room often. He almost wished she would cry out or rail at him, but she bore her pain silently.

The sun was setting when Dr. Grade came for the last time. He told Charlie her delivery would happen any minute, and in less than five, a tiny baby boy slid into his waiting hands.

The room buzzed with activity, and Charlie heard someone calling down the stairs that it was a boy, but beyond that she heard and saw nothing. Her eyes were locked on the tiny, howling infant that was being wrapped in a dry sheet and placed in the crook of her arm.

She ached from head to foot, but at the moment nothing mattered save her baby. She began to croon softly to him and watched in fascination as he stopped crying and turned his face toward hers. The room emptied of everyone but Sean before Charlie looked away from the little boy who had captured her heart with just one glance.

"Isn't he beautiful?" Charlie breathed softly as she held Sean's eyes with her own.

Sean's smile was infinitely tender, but he was actually thinking that their little son was as funny-looking at birth as Gretchen and Molly had been. He sensed immediately that he should keep this particular comment to himself.

"What are we going to call him?" Sean chose a safe subject.

"Ricky," Charlie answered softly.

"Ricky?"

"That's right. It's short for Patrick Sean Donovan IV."

"I like it," Sean said with a smile, thinking he would never have thought of it. In fact, they hadn't even discussed names, and that struck him as being a little unusual.

Sean leaned and kissed his wife to thank her for their son before pressing a kiss to the tiny dark head of his namesake.

"I have a son." Sean said the words aloud as though he was finally believing it. Charlie passed Ricky into his father's arms and watched as tears flooded his eyes. Neither of them spoke for some time after that. It was enough just to sit and watch the tiny movements of the little miracle God had placed within their arms.

In the next several weeks Ricky Donovan grew quickly and seemed to take an unusual interest in his surroundings. He had occasional bouts of colic, but nothing severe. Charlie seemed to have unfailing patience even when he cried for no apparent reason.

Most nights he slept well, and having a good night's sleep was always enough to send Charlie forward for a full day of activity. Sean's family had thought she was wonderful from the day they met, but nothing could have prepared them for a post-pregnant Charlie.

She never sat still. If she wasn't taking care of Ricky, she was mending clothes or baking bread. One day she even went to the livery where Sean had found extra work to lend a helping hand.

After watching Sean and Charlie move nonstop from day to day at what appeared to be their normal activity level, it came as no surprise to the family when Sean announced their plans to leave. Ricky was only four weeks old.

It was the first of March, and Sean said that he would write a letter to Aunt Maureen relaying their plans to be in San Francisco for one week at the end of the month. Everyone understood then that the Sean Donovan family had only three more weeks in Santa Rosa.

As well-prepared as Kaitlin thought she was, she felt bereft at their announcement. It had been so much fun to have them, and she knew it would be at least two years before they would be together again. It therefore came as a surprise to her that she wasn't more upset when the time to say goodbye finally arrived. She strongly suspected that it had plenty to do with the peace and joy she saw glowing from the faces of her brother-and sister-in-law as they boarded the stage. Confidence that they were going exactly where God wanted them to go showed in their every move.

Not only were Sean and Charlie confident, they were thrilled with the idea of going to Hawaii. Sean had been coaching Charlie in the Hawaiian language, and she knew enough to give her a great start once they arrived. A letter had been sent to Father to inform him of their approximate sailing date. The young couple knew there was nothing else they could do except head to San Francisco where they would board a ship that would take them to an exciting new life—a life that Sean knew well, but one that Charlie had only dreamed about. A life of service to their God and prayers that their service would bring honor and glory to His name.

Fifty-One

AUNT MAUREEN, WHO was not a grandmother herself, fell instantly in love with Ricky. Charlie was rarely able to hold him for the nine days they visited.

Two days before their scheduled departure Sean and Charlie had a "Hawaiian" day. Neither one spoke English, and Sean even attempted to teach Charlie how to cook his favorite Hawaiian dish. They were having a great time, but in one quiet moment Charlie spoke quite seriously, and in English.

"It's all a little like playing house, isn't it? But it won't be all fun and games, will it, Sean? Being missionaries is a lot of hard work."

"That's true, but I think the fact that we're both so burdened to be there means that God will bless and provide for us.

"And Charlie," Sean's voice grew urgent. "This doesn't have to be forever. If we get there and you or Ricky are miserable, then we don't have to stay. Who knows? Maybe I'll be the one who can't take it. It might not be anything like I'm remembering, and if that's the case God will show us where He wants us to be.

"We haven't discussed the way my father left us, at least not in detail. Even though I've forgiven him, I would never follow in his footsteps. We're going to stay together; the three of us are a team. I don't want you to ever forget that."

Charlie was thankful for her husband's words. With a kiss and a whispered word, she let him know of her love for him.

Maureen came to the docks to see them off, but the wind was cold and she stayed in her coach as they boarded. Sean had grown very quiet, and Charlie knew that he was remembering how ill he had been on his one previous trip. They talked about a plan of action if Sean was completely out of commission on the ship as he'd been before. Even though Charlie prayed it would be otherwise, she believed she could do what she had to do.

They stayed at the balustrade as the ship pulled away from the dock. Sean held his tiny son, swathed in blankets, close and spoke into his sleeping face.

"We're leaving now, buddy. We're headed to our new home, to Hawaii, where we will serve others and share Christ's love."

Charlie, having heard every word, found her heart swelling with love for this man God had given her. Never did she believe in all her life that she would have the things she had now. Even if God should choose to remove someone or something from her world, she would never again doubt that He was there and that He loved her unconditionally.

Sean looked over to see Charlie's face turned skyward, a look of profound serenity filling her eyes.

"What are you thinking?" he asked softly.

"Only that it's all so wonderful. I never dreamed I would have all that God has given me."

Sean's smile was huge. "And to think that a little over a year ago, we were married strangers."

"Oh, Sean!" Charlie's eyes grew wide as she realized his words were true. Then she grinned and proceeded to tease Sean about one of his favorite sayings. "I guess miracles don't take as long as we once believed."

Epilogue

Hawaii—1879

THE HALF-MOON CAST a faint glow on Charlie as she waded into the waters of the Pacific Ocean. Sean was already splashing in the light surf, but he stopped to watch her. She had on a light shift that she was again able to use for their private nighttime swims.

It had taken longer after her second pregnancy to fit into that shift, but now that little Callie was three months old, Charlie was slim as a girl once again.

They swam, as was their Sunday night ritual, for the better part of an hour before stopping to talk and play in the waves. Grandpa Patrick was home with the baby and a now two-year-old Ricky, both of whom were asleep, or so their parents hoped.

"What did you think of your father's announcement this morning?"

"I think he did a good job, and I'm certainly glad he warned the two of us about his plans a few days ago."

"But you weren't surprised, were you—not even when he shared with us in private?"

"No, I guess I wasn't."

"I can't imagine being here without your father, but I'm certainly excited about where he's going and the possible impact he could have on Sadie."

"I can't imagine him gone either, but it's time—I can see that. He has been praying about it for the better part of a year. Taking the pulpit for Pastor Miller in Visalia is perfect for his needs right now.

213

It's not a large body of believers, and there are several good leaders."

"To hear you, Sean, you'd think he was an old man."

"No, I know he's not an old man, and he assures me that his health is good, but the work here is so widespread now and he just can't stop himself from putting too much on his plate. Did he show you Marcail's letter?"

"Yes, I read it and I really admire her decision, Sean. She's at the end of her schooling, and her home has been with Rigg and Katie for years. As hard as this will be for her, I have to agree that her place is with your father."

"I think so too. I would guess that she's doing this out of love and respect for Father, since she doesn't know him very well after all these years, but I believe that God will bless her for her actions. Plus, it's always been Marcail's dream to teach school. Father will help her to that end."

"Do you really think he will want her to go to work?"

"I think when he sees how badly she wants to teach, he will. He might be protective of her, but he'll do the right thing."

They continued to discuss Sean's family, Sadie's last letter and need for salvation, the mission work, and a myriad of other subjects during their swim. When it was time to head home, they found their towels on the beach and stood wrapped in the cloths and each other's arms, staring up at the crescent moon.

"I love knowing that no matter what happens, God is in His heaven and loves unfailingly."

"You sound a little worried about the days ahead," Sean whispered.

"Not worried really, just aware that there will be changes in the future."

"The changes will be necessary, including some that will cause pain and take adjustment. But as you said, God is in His heaven, and His sovereign will is always at work. By the way, have I told you lately that you're beautiful?"

Charlie turned her head to stare at Sean, who was still looking at the sky. "Where in the world did that come from?"

He looked down at her then. "I was thinking about it when you stepped into the water and realized I don't tell you often enough."

"Oh, Sean," was all Charlie was able to say before his lips covered her own.

As they walked hand in hand toward their house, Charlie wondered if there was anything more beautiful than being married to the man God has chosen for your life.

Charlie let her mind dwell on the hand that held hers. A hand that swung a hammer with strength and surety, a hand that grasped the Bible with confidence during a sermon, a hand that held their children with tenderness, and a hand that would claim her own with loving care every day of their lives.

Charlie didn't have to speculate for very long as to whether or not there was anything more beautiful. With her hand engulfed within Sean Donovan's, she knew she had her answer.

Book II

Donovan's Daughter

*This book is
dedicated with love to my nieces,
Jessica Wick, Julie Kolstad,
Katharine Arenas, Johanna Wick,
Barbara Wick, and Mary Wick.
I praise God for each of you,
and pray that you will grow
in the grace and knowledge of
our Lord and Savior, Jesus Christ.*

*W*illits Families–1881

Alexander Montgomery (Willits' doctor)

Marcail Donovan (Willits' schoolteacher)

Cordelia Duckworth
Sydney Duckworth (Cordelia's grandson)

Allie Warren

The Austin Family
Husband—Dean
Wife—Kay
Children—Marla
Daisy

*S*anta *R*osa Families–1881

The Riggs Family
Husband—Marshall (Riggs)
Wife—Kaitlin (Katie)
Children—Gretchen
Molly
Donovan

March 25, 1881
Santa Rosa, California

Dear Marcail,

Happy Birthday! It's hard to believe that we're not together on your nineteenth birthday; it's the first time I can remember our being apart. You know my love and prayers are with you and Father. Let me know what the two of you did that was special. Tell Father I hope be baked you a cake!

Rigg sent your birthday box in plenty of time, so when you read this, you should be able to write and tell me if the dress fits. I know all-white is impractical, but you look so pretty in white.

The girls talk about you constantly. I tell them that you'll come to see them when you can. Donovan is growing like a weed, and I so wish you could see him. The girls were nowhere near his size at this age. I think he's going to rival Rigg before he's done. And speaking of Rigg, you can't believe the joy in his face when he holds his own little son. God is so good, Marcail.

I just couldn't resist writing to you on your birthday. Write back soon and catch me up on all the news. I don't know about you, but it feels to me as if you've been gone for three months, not three weeks.

Love, Katie

April 6, 1881
Visalia, California

Dear Katie and Family,

I love the dress. It's beautiful and fits like a dream, Thank you so much. I've been saving a white ribbon, and now I have a dress with which to wear it. From whom did Rigg order the dress?

I wanted to take my time to tell you about Father's gift to me, but I'm so excited I can't wait. Father told me I could start taking the special studies class with my teacher, Miss Wilkins, and get my teaching certificate. It means staying after school every afternoon, but I should be done by midsummer and be able to apply for teaching positions this fall!

I can hardly believe it's true, Katie—I'm finally going to be a teacher! It's what I've prayed for and dreamed about for as long as I can remember. I think it was hard for Father when I told him I did not want to be married right away, but after he took some time to get used to the idea, I could see he was going to wholeheartedly support my decision.

I think his change in attitude might have something to do with his watching me tutor. He can tell I love to teach. I'm not sure if he can understand that it's not the same as having my own class, but I am really enjoying it. Mitchell, the little boy I tutor every afternoon, has a crush on me and tells me he's going to marry me. Renee, the little girl I teach, is just the opposite. She resents my presence, and I have to coax nearly every word out of her. Please pray for both of us.

Give Rigg and the girls my love, and kiss Donovan for me. I've found a pair of matching dolls for Gretchen and Molly, but I'm not going to send them. I'd rather bring them when I can visit, to see their faces when they open them. I might hold onto them until Christmas.

I wish I could tell you I'll see you soon, but with my studies intensifying, I just won't be able to get away. I hope this finds you all well.

Love, Marcail

June 17, 1881
Visalia, California

Dear Katie,

I stood at Miss Wilkins' side today and watched her sign my teaching certificate. I can't really explain the way I felt, except to say that I was excited and scared all at once.

I knew that the Lord would want me to trust Him, as you trusted Him so many years ago the first time you taught in Santa Rosa without Mother's help. I loved the schoolhouse there, and I love thinking back to your gentle way of teaching; so often you reminded me of Mother. I think she would be thrilled with the decision I've made.

I don't believe for a moment that I would be receiving my certificate if you hadn't been such an encouragement to me. Thanks, Katie, for all you've taught me, and for being the pillar of love and strength you've been in my life.

Love, Marcail

May 28, 1881
Santa Rosa, California

Dear Marcail,

Well, summer is upon us. The weather is hot in the extreme and all the grass in Santa Rosa is already brown. Every window in the kitchen is open as I write this letter.

Rigg's mood has been nothing short of nonsensical tonight. He keeps coming through the kitchen and giving me messages for you. The last one was that a man was here, a doctor; seven feet tall, and he was asking for your hand in marriage. Honestly, Marc, he certainly can be outrageous when he makes up his mind!

Business picked up at the mercantile, and I was able to order a new rug for the girls' bedroom. You remember how worn the old one was. I know Rigg hated to see it go since it had been his grandmother's, but Molly's foot catches on the loose threads time and again, and I'm afraid she's going to hurt herself. I cut them, but I can't seem to stay ahead of it.

We painted your bedroom a soft peach color. It really brightened things up. Wish you could see it. (That was a hint, in case you didn't catch it.)

I'm glad your studies and tutoring are progressing well. We're praying for you, Mitchell, and Renee. I have every confidence you'll have your certificate in record time. I'm so proud of you. Write me soon.

Love, Katie

July 25, 1881
Santa Rosa, California

Dear Marcail,

I prayed this morning about the perfect teaching position for you, and then found myself asking God to open the doors here in Santa Rosa. Then I realized that I was trying to help God with your life, and I was not trusting.

This letter is to inform you that I've given you over to the Lord and His tender care. Here are some verses that I know you love and have shared with me in the past. As I read them this morning, I found them a real comfort. Thanks, Marcail.

Isaiah 55:8,9, ''For my thoughts are not your thoughts, neither are your ways my ways, saith the Lord. For as the heavens are higher than the earth, so are my ways higher than your ways, and my thoughts than your thoughts.''

All my love, Katie

August 12, 1881
Visalia, California

Dear Katie,

I've received letters from three school boards who have seen my credentials and want to hire me. Father and I talked and prayed before finally deciding on the school in Willits, which is only about five hours from Santa Rosa by train.

I'll be coming through Santa Rosa on August 25, on my way to Willits. I can't stay any longer than the train does, but if you're at the station around 10:00 a.m., we'll have a few moments.

The conduct and dress code laid down by this school board is very strict, but I think that's part of the reason Father liked it; that and knowing how close I'll be to you and Rigg. I know he wants peace of mind over how I'm being cared for.

Father can't get away to come up with me, but he asked me to tell you he's planning on coming to Santa Rosa for Christmas, and we'll all be together then. If this won't work for you, be in touch. I won't write again before I leave, but don't forget to write me once I get to my new home. Thanks for all your prayers.

Love, Marcail

Prologue

Santa Rosa, California— August 25, 1881

MARCAIL DONOVAN WAVED from the window as the train pulled away from the Santa Rosa station. Her sister, Kaitlin, brother-in-law, Marshall Riggs, and nieces, Gretchen and Molly, all waved furiously in reply. Her nephew, eight-month-old Donovan, sitting comfortably on his father's arm, was too busy working on the thumb in his mouth to notice his aunt's departure.

When the train station was out of sight, Marcail settled back against her seat with a smile and a sigh. How good it had been to see them, however briefly. It was an unexpected blessing amid numerous blessings of late from the Lord.

If Marcail had had the luxury of time, she would have loved to stay and visit, but knowing her teaching position awaited her further up the tracks was enough to keep Marcail's mind from how deeply she missed her family.

Marcail suddenly thought of her father, Patrick Donovan, and again she smiled. It wasn't every girl who had a full-time father for the first nine years of her life, saw him only occasionally for the next ten years, and then had him come back into her life to stay when she was nearly 19.

It had taken some weeks, but father and daughter had become close. At first Patrick had struggled with the fact that his little girl was now a grown woman, and there were times he had treated her like a child. But he was always swift to apologize when he saw the disappointment in her eyes. He soon saw that her manner of life, and the loving way she responded to his affection and counsel, showed that Marcail was level-headed enough to know what she wanted.

And what Marcail wanted was to teach school. Patrick's first reaction when she expressed this desire had been enthusiastic, until she informed him that she was willing to travel anywhere in the state to acquire a position.

"Wouldn't you like a teaching position here in Visalia?" he'd asked her in some surprise.

"Yes, I would. It would be wonderful to teach close enough to live here, but if nothing is available, then I'm going to look for a position somewhere else."

Marcail could see that her words surprised her father, and she did not push the point. She also did not tell him that she felt it was time to be on her own. Marcail knew that if he was totally against the idea of her teaching elsewhere, she would drop the subject, but as she hoped and prayed, he came to her a few days later and told her to follow her heart.

And follow her heart was just what Marcail did. She began submitting her resume whenever she found a school board advertising for a teacher, and in a surprisingly short amount of time, several responded.

Marcail had been careful to consult her father on all the correspondence she received, and in just a matter of days, Patrick advised her to take the job in Willits. It was a long way from where they were now living in Visalia, but not too far from Katie and Rigg. And with the strict code of dress, Father was certain the townspeople would be upright and moral.

Marcail had plenty of time to grow nervous as the train drew ever closer to her destination. She had prayed for most of the journey and worked at overcoming her anxieties. There was so much she could panic over if she allowed her mind to wander; little things, like living alone for the first time, taking care of all her own finances, and being the sole authority in the classroom.

Marcail had known responsibility for numerous tasks over many years. She had always risen to the occasion and seen to every need, but she suddenly found herself asking, what if something entered her world that was beyond her control? What if she became sick or the schoolhouse burned down?

Marcail realized she was working herself into a fine frenzy and immediately prayed for calm. It was true that any of those things could happen, but worrying about them would change nothing. *If* and when the time came to handle any and all disasters, she knew the Lord would lead and guide her to His good work.

She was completely calm by the time the conductor called Willits as the next stop. As the town came into view, however, Marcail's heart began to pound once again. This time there was no fear, only excitement.

One

MARCAIL PEERED THROUGH the window as the train pulled into the Willits station. There was nothing unusual or remarkable about what she could see of the small town, but the fact that it was her new home made it, along with the moment, a thing to be treasured.

The train came to a complete stop. Marcail stood in the aisle, her carpetbag in one hand. As she stepped forward, her heart beat against her ribs so hard she was certain the fabric on her dress was moving. She glanced down at her simple black gown with the long sleeves and high collar, and suddenly found herself hoping it would hold up under the censuring eyes of Willits' school board members.

There were a few other people disembarking with her at the train station. Marcail, wanting to soak up every person, every nook and cranny of this small town, smiled and greeted anyone who met her eyes.

Her letter of introduction, held firmly in one hand, said she was to locate a Mr. Stanley Flynn. He was, the letter explained, the local banker. Because Marcail's only piece of luggage was her one over-stuffed bag, she carried it in one hand and the letter in the other.

More than one shop owner stepped to the boardwalk in front of his store as she passed, and Marcail took time to smile and greet each one. She didn't tarry long, however. Her desire to meet Mr. Flynn gave her a singleness of purpose that took her swiftly to the door of the bank and over the threshold. Once inside the small building, Marcail approached the single clerk who stood behind the counter.

"May I help you, miss?" Marcail noticed he was very business-like, his speech and manner proper in the extreme.

"Yes, thank you. I'm looking for a Mr. Stanley Flynn."

"May I tell him who is calling?"

Feeling much younger than her 19 years, Marcail gave her name and watched the bank clerk walk to a private office at the rear of the building. She looked around admiringly at the elegant surroundings of the compact room, taking in the gleaming wood-work. She thought she detected the faint odor of linseed oil.

Moving to the windows that looked out over the street, Marcail spotted a cobbler shop, hotel, dry goods store, and what appeared to be a doctor's office. When she heard footsteps behind her, she turned with a ready smile. A man was approaching, his smile cor-dial but his eyes watchful. He extended his hand to Marcail, who was well aware of his scrutiny. She was quite conscious of the fact that she looked like a girl on the threshold of womanhood, and not a woman fully grown. But Marcail was confident of her ability to teach, and in her posture and the very tilt of her head she uncon-sciously relayed just that.

"Miss Donovan, it's a pleasure to meet you." Stanley Flynn must have liked what he saw because his manner became very solicitous, his smile genuine.

Marcail smiled in return. "It's a pleasure to be here, Mr. Flynn."

She might not have been so confident or ready to smile if she could have read the banker's thoughts, the first of which was that she was beautiful. The second was that she looked innocent enough to be malleable. It would be some time before Marcail would find out that she was Willits' ninth school teacher in three years.

Ten minutes later Mr. Flynn put Marcail's bag in his buggy and drove Marcail to her house. As they appeared to be headed out of town, he explained that the builder of the schoolhouse and teacher's home, some 30 years before, had not liked how noisy children could be. It had been his opinion that the school should be located on the outskirts of town. Since he had supplied most of the funds, the town had acquiesced.

Willits was larger now, and the last houses on that end of town were within sight of the school. Still, a small group of trees on the town's side of the school gave it a very distinct feeling of isolation. Marcail spotted one small farmhouse in the distance, but she asked no questions concerning the owner. She was much too captivated with her first glance at the small house into which Mr. Flynn was now leading her.

Mr. Flynn did not tarry. Only five minutes passed before Marcail saw him to the front door, waved to him after he was back in his buggy, and shut the door. She turned back to the room, her hands going to her mouth, her eyes sparkling with pleasure. This was her house, her own little home! And some 50 feet away was the schoolhouse where she would start work on Monday.

Marcail's gaze roamed the room with pleasure. It couldn't have been more perfect if she'd designed it herself. The main room of the house was spacious, with a kitchen in one corner. The one doorway led to a small bedroom. It was a house intended for one person, holding only two kitchen chairs at the table and a rocking chair near the stove.

Marcail moved into the bedroom. The bed she found was very small, but then so was she, making her feel that everything was all the more perfect. The curtains on the window and the quilt on the bed were both a soft, sky-blue plaid.

After throwing the curtains back to let in the sunlight, she went to work unpacking her single bag. She hung her other two dresses and put her undergarments in the drawers of the small dressing table. Her entire outer wardrobe consisted of three dresses—one brown, one dark blue, and the black one she was wearing.

She set a few of her personal books on the nightstand, and put the others on the bed to be taken to the school. A picture of her mother as a young girl went on the dressing table, as did a picture of herself and her siblings taken in Santa Rosa. Marcail smiled at the homey touches.

She stopped before the mirror that hung opposite the bed to check her hair. She was not accustomed to wearing it up because of its length and thickness, but her hairstyle and the dark-colored clothing were all a part of the stipulations set down in her contract.

The last item Marcail removed from her bag was her Bible. She sat on the bed and held it in her arms, and then prayed aloud in the stillness of her home.

"Thank You, Father, for bringing me to this place. It's more wonderful than I could have dreamed." Marcail didn't speak again, but sat quietly and dwelt on verses from Psalm 46: "Be still, and know that I am God. I will be exalted among the heathen; I will be exalted in the earth. The Lord of hosts is with us; the God of Jacob is our refuge."

Two

MARCAIL SPENT THE next hour inspecting every inch of the schoolhouse. It was spotless and well equipped. She had brought along a few of her books and stood for a long time just looking at the way they sat on her desk. The platform in front of the blackboard, on which her desk sat, was raised about eight inches from the rest of the schoolroom floor. Marcail, whose height and frame were so diminutive, was very pleased.

After she finished at the schoolhouse, she went home to make out a complete list of all the supplies she thought she might need. She was eager to take a walk into town. The schoolhouse and her home sat on the west edge of the community. A quick scan out the schoolhouse window had earlier confirmed that the only visible structures beyond were the small house and barn that she had spotted on her arrival.

It didn't take long for Marcail to reach the houses of town, but the shops were a bit further. She was flushed from the weight of her dress, as well as the warmth of the day, by the time she reached a storefront that said Vesperman's General Store above the entrance. The building appeared to be half the size of Riggs' Mercantile in Santa Rosa, but once inside there did not seem to be any lack.

Marcail's eyes took in pins and measuring cups, fly traps and thread, composition books and soap flakes, eggbeaters and blotters, cookie cutters and bibs, fabric and shoes, checkerboards and muffin tins. She chose a basket near the door and began to shop. Not until she was near the candy counter did Marcail meet the proprietor. He was a smiling man with a sandy mustache, who introduced himself as Randy Vesperman.

Marcail liked him instantly. He answered all of her questions and informed her that his children, Erin and Patrick, would be in her classroom Monday morning. The friendly sparkle in his eyes confirmed that she had made her first friend. He encouraged her to take the basket in order to carry her purchases home.

Marcail's next stop was the bank. The tutoring she had done in Visalia for the two children who, for different reasons, were unable to attend the schoolhouse, allowed her to come to Willits with something of a financial cushion. She spent a fair amount in gaining supplies for the next month, but with the exception of a few coins to get her by, she deposited the rest into a savings account.

It soon became obvious that the townspeople knew who she was. Several people approached her in the bank. One couple, the Whites, introduced themselves and their children, allowing Willits' new schoolmarm to meet two of her students.

Marcail was moving toward the door when it opened and a woman of immense proportions, both in height and width, swept in. She was dressed in black crepe, and Marcail felt instant sympathy for her mourning. It took her a moment to realize that the woman was not going to let her pass, causing her to finally look up into her eyes.

"You must be Miss Donovan." The voice was cold.

"Yes, ma'am," Marcail replied and swallowed hard. The woman had the hardest eyes she had ever encountered.

"I am Cordelia Duckworth," the woman said, as if this explained everything. "I trust that Mr. Flynn made you aware that I'm expecting you for lunch tomorrow?"

"Yes, Mrs. Duckworth. I was planning on it."

"Well, see that you are. I'll finish your interview then."

Mrs. Duckworth moved toward the teller without giving Marcail a chance to reply. Marcail left feeling a bit dazed. Interview. The woman had said interview. Marcail wondered suddenly if the teaching position was really hers.

The basket was now starting to weigh on her arm. Turning toward home, she intended to reread every bit of correspondence she had received from the Willits school board.

Dr. Alexander Montgomery closed and locked his office door before heading toward Rodd's livery. Rodd always kept his horse, Kelsey, in exchange for free medical services. But considering that

Rodd's wife had had four babies in the last four years, Alex sometimes wondered who had gotten the better end of the deal.

Kelsey, a rather high-spirited bay gelding, was more than ready
to escape the confines of his stall. Alex could tell that he was ready
for a run, but was careful to keep the animal on a tight rein until
they were past the houses in town. Ready to heel his mount into a
gallop, Alex spotted a lone, darkly garbed figure walking ahead of
him on the road.

She moved to the far edge of the road when she heard the horse
approach, but Alex had the impression that she would not have
even looked at him if he hadn't stopped beside her. It took him an
instant, even after she stopped, to figure out who she was and
where she was headed.

"Hello," Alex called cheerfully. "You must be Miss—"

"Donovan." Marcail supplied the name and tried to see the man
addressing her. The lowering sun was directly in her eyes, and even
squinting didn't give her a clear view of the rider. Having switched
arms so many times while carrying the basket that she now held in
both hands, she was afraid to lift her hand to shield her eyes for fear
of dropping her load.

"I can't really offer to give you a ride, but why don't I drop that
basket on your doorstep?"

"Oh, that's all right. I'm almost—" Marcail stopped midsentence
because he was already bending low from the saddle and taking the
thick handle from her grasp.

"I'll just take this ahead for you. It was nice meeting you, Miss
Donovan. By the way, I'm Dr. Montgomery."

Marcail did little more than raise her hand in a gesture of thanks
before the rider was once again on his way. She continued her
walk, knowing that if she passed that man on the sidewalk and he
didn't speak, she would have no idea who he was. Well, no matter
really. He was a doctor, and Marcail knew she would have to be
dying and then some before she'd have anything to do with him.

Three

By THE TIME Marcail climbed into bed that night she was very tired, but not discouraged. She had searched through her documents, and beyond her being listed as one of the school board members Marcail could not find any mention of a Cordelia Duckworth. There was nothing to indicate that she would be interviewed once she arrived. As much as Marcail wanted to stay in Willits, she trusted that if the door closed in this small town she was already coming to love, God had another teaching position for her elsewhere.

Marcail was able to blow out her lantern with a peaceful heart. Having eaten only a light supper, she fell asleep dreaming about the bread she planned on baking the next morning.

At 11:30 Saturday morning, having finished her baking earlier, Marcail started out for her luncheon appointment. Feeling as though Mr. Vesperman would welcome her inquiry, she stopped and asked for directions to Mrs. Duckworth's home. He was more than happy to oblige, but Marcail caught what she thought might be pity in his eyes. She prayed that her imagination was working over-time.

Following the directions she was given, Marcail headed through town, passing businesses she had seen only from a distance. When she met people on the street, they were friendly, and Marcail found herself hoping she would be able to stay. Mr. Vesperman had told her that she wouldn't be able to miss the Duckworth house, since it was as far to the east of town as the schoolhouse was to the west. It was set apart and seemed all the more grand as the ground rose to meet it. Marcail had to move up a slight incline to the front steps.

The Duckworth house was an imposing structure, and Marcail felt rather intimidated as she approached. The sensation intensified after knocking on the massive front door. Marcail began to feel like a child waiting to see her teacher. She scolded herself over ground-less fears.

As she might have expected, a servant answered the door. Marcail was led toward the rear of the house to an elegant dining room. She paused on the threshold, her head tipped back to take in the massive chandelier that seemed to fill the ceiling. The sound of a sharply cleared throat brought Marcail's head around.

Mrs. Duckworth was already seated, and with a regal nod of her head, bid Marcail to enter. She did so and took the chair being held for her by a nervous-looking manservant.

"You are very prompt. I like that," Mrs. Duckworth declared stoutly. Several more servants joined the first two, and the food began arriving. Before Marcail could think twice, her plate was filled with a sumptuous piece of roast beef and all the trimmings.

Marcail watched as her hostess picked up her fork. She was about to follow suit when the interrogation began.

"So tell me, Miss Donovan, are your parents living?"

"My father is."

"And your mother, did you ever know her?"

"Yes, she died when I was nine."

"Siblings?"

"Yes. One sister and one brother."

"Older or younger? Do they have families? Tell me about them."

Marcail took a breath. "They are both older. My sister, Kaitlin, is the oldest. She's married to a man named Marshall Riggs, and they live in Santa Rosa. They have three children. My brother is also married. He and his wife, Charlotte, live in Hawaii with their two children."

Mrs. Duckworth ate while her guest answered questions, but Marcail, not knowing when the next question would come, did nothing more than hold her fork in her hand.

"And this is your first teaching assignment; is that correct?"

"Yes, ma'am. I've been a private tutor, but I've never had my own school."

"And you understand the terms of the contract, that your clothing and conduct *must* be above reproach at all times?"

"Yes, ma'am." Marcail watched her hostess take another bite of food and thought this might be the only chance to ask a question. "I'm a little confused, Mrs. Duckworth. I didn't expect to be interviewed. I thought the job was already mine."

"The job of teaching the town's children is yours," the older woman answered without hesitation. "I am interviewing you, however, to see if you are suitable to teach *my* grandson. Right now Sydney is with his parents, but he lives with me much of the time. He's a delicate child, and they simply do not understand him. I usually hire private tutors to see to his education, but I thought it might be time for him to try the classroom again. And since you are the person at the head of that classroom, I must make certain you are sensitive to Sydney's needs."

A small warning bell was ringing in Marcail's mind. "I'm not a teacher who plays favorites, Mrs. Duckworth. If Sydney does his work and is respectful to my authority, we'll get along fine."

Unfortunately Mrs. Duckworth did not appear to have heard her.

"You haven't told me about your father, Miss Donovan."

Marcail blinked at the change in topics, but was willing to accommodate nevertheless.

"For years he was a missionary to Hawaii, but now he's a pastor for a small church in Visalia."

"Is he remarried?"

"No."

"And you, Miss Donovan, are you looking for a husband?"

"No, ma'am. I want to teach school." It sounded like a platitude even to her own ears, but it was the truth. "I'm not saying that I'll never be married, but I don't wish to be now, and probably not for quite some time."

"You understood that your conduct is to be *above* reproach?"

"Yes, ma'am. The contract was all very clear to me." Marcail's voice was losing some of its congeniality after being questioned time and again over a matter she felt was settled.

Marcail glanced in front of her to see that her plate had been removed. She hadn't had a bite. Setting her fork down, she leveled her eyes on her hostess. She watched as Mrs. Duckworth looked at her own soiled napkin and then to Marcail's empty place setting. To her credit she had the good grace to look momentarily ashamed.

Marcail would have loved to ask what her little game was, but she knew the question would have been disrespectful. When dessert was offered, the young guest declined, and not long after, thanked her hostess and went on her way. As far as Marcail was concerned, the interview was over.

Marcail would have been surprised to know that Mrs. Duckworth watched from the living room window until she was out of sight. The older woman was torn between consternation and admiration. Consternation because Miss Donovan wasn't going to be as easy to manage as she hoped; admiration because in a very respectful way she'd stood up to her, and that was something few people had ever done.

Four

MARCAIL SPENT THE rest of the day in the schoolhouse preparing for Monday morning. Her mind was never far from her luncheon with Mrs. Duckworth. However, each time she felt her worries assail her, she prayed and asked the Lord for wisdom.

Marcail was writing her name on the blackboard, her last job before heading back to her house to prepare some supper, when someone knocked and entered.

"I really thought they were exaggerating. Well, it wouldn't be exaggerating because that means something gets bigger. What's the opposite of exaggeration, when you really mean something is small?"

Marcail stared at the round, pink-faced young woman in the doorway and smiled. "I'm afraid I don't know. Maybe if you tell me what they were exaggerating about." Marcail was beginning to think she'd walked into the middle of a bad theater performance.

"Your size. I mean, they said you were tiny, but I never dreamed . . ."

Marcail couldn't help but laugh. The other woman was talking again, so she tried to control herself.

"And here I thought we were going to be good friends, but being with you is only going to accentuate my size." The talkative visitor moved closer.

"Your hair is really black, isn't it? I mean, *really* black, and mine is so blonde it's almost white."

242

Marcail laughed again, and the rotund blonde smiled also, thinking the new schoolteacher was just wonderful.

"My name is Alice Warren. But you can call me Allie because we're going to be friends."

"I'd like that." Marcail smiled a genuine smile. "My name is Marcail Donovan, and you can call me Marcail, since we're going to be good friends."

"Marcail." Allie tested the word on her tongue. "Do you spell it with a *k?*"

"No, it's *M-a-r-c-a-i-l,* but the *c* is hard."

Allie beamed. "I like it. It suits you." Allie's face turned to a sudden frown. "But I don't think Alice suits me. I've always pictured myself as a Mirabelle." She finished this last sentence with a dramatic sigh.

"Mirabelle?" Marcail bit her lower lip to camouflage her smile. "You don't think so?"

The smaller woman shook her head apologetically, and they both laughed.

In the space of the next few minutes, Marcail discovered that Allie's family ran the sawmill at the other end of town. She had two older brothers, both of whom were the bane of her existence, or so she proclaimed.

They talked for the better part of an hour before Allie jumped up with a hand to her mouth.

"I completely forgot why I was here. Mother wants you to come to dinner after church tomorrow."

"Oh, I'd love to. Thank you."

"Good. I'd better go now. By the way, how old are you?"

"Nineteen."

Allie sighed. "I'm 20. Do you think we'll ever find husbands?" She sighed again and flew out the door. She'd have returned to hug Marcail if she could have read her thoughts.

I don't need a husband, Allie—not when I've found a friend like you.

Church was not at all what Marcail expected. The building was fairly large and packed with people. They sang good hymns of faith for most of the service, but not a word of Scripture was read, even during the short sermon. Marcail wondered if this was something out of the ordinary and not the norm. She certainly hoped so.

Marcail met just about all other students that day, and by the time she emerged from the building, she was certain the Warren family must have left without her. They had not.

Marcail exited the building to find Allie standing with two well-built, good-looking men. She approached with a smile, and as soon as she reached them Allie said something outrageous.

"Marcail, these are my brothers, Logan and Mallory. I believe they are about to make absolute fools of themselves where you are concerned."

Marcail's gaze flew to the faces of the men flanking their sister, but they didn't seem to be the least put out by her remark. Both of them smiled as through Marcail were a dream come true, and reached at the same time to escort her to the wagon. Allie pushed their hands out of the way with an unladylike snort and took Marcail's arm herself.

"Just ignore them, Marcail, or we'll be here all afternoon deciding who is to help you into the wagon."

The boys were on hand to see the ladies into the rear seat, and Marcail soon learned that Allie was right—her brothers couldn't seem to take their eyes off her.

With both men turning to look at her every few minutes, the ride seemed to take forever. Their actions caused Marcail to stop and think of how few young women she had seen in church that morning.

Allie's parents had gone ahead of their children, so dinner was nearly on the table when the young people arrived. Mr. and Mrs. Warren were gracious, hardworking people, and they welcomed Marcail into their home as if she were a long-lost daughter. But when the dishes were passed and everyone began eating without a prayer of thanks to God, Marcail began to wonder if there wasn't something very important missing from the lives of these dear people.

Allie and Marcail took a walk after the meal. Marcail was greatly relieved to escape the interest of the Warren boys. It wasn't that she found them repulsive; they were nice-looking and seemed very kind. But their quiet watchfulness was beginning to unnerve her.

"How do you fill your days, Allie?" Marcail asked her new friend.

"I keep the accounts for the mill and help Mama around the house. I know she likes my company, but she is so anxious to see one of us marry and make her a grandma that it seems that's all I hear."

"So you don't really care that much if you get married?"

Allie was quiet a moment, and Marcail apologized for intruding.

"You didn't intrude, Marcail, but I'm not sure a girl like you can understand what it's like for me."

"I don't know what you mean by 'a girl like me.'"

"I don't know either. It's just that the girls who have no desire to be married are the ones all the boys chase, and girls like me, who really want a husband and family, can't seem to draw anyone's attention."

"I guess it does seem that way at times, Allie, but I believe that if God wants a person to be married, then He shows that person exactly whom they're to marry, and when."

Allie stared at her new friend uncomprehendingly, and Marcail knew that all she'd just said was completely foreign to Allie.

The subject of marriage and God was dropped for the time, but Marcail asked God to open the door someday. She wanted to introduce Allie to the Man, Jesus Christ, who would change her life forever if only she would let Him do so.

Five

ON THE FIRST day of school Marcail had the worst attack of nerves she'd ever experienced in her life. The coffee she drank made her feel sick to the stomach, and when she burned the piece of bread she was going to eat, she decided to go without.

Too excited to stay home, she was over at the schoolhouse an hour before the children were expected. There was no need to ring the bell when the time came because the children were already on their way. Marcail rushed to the door when she spotted the first group heading toward the schoolhouse.

Mr. Flynn had given Marcail a list of whom to expect. She noticed that Sydney Duckworth's name was not on the list. Without him she had 19 students, the youngest of whom was seven and the oldest 15.

Marcail introduced herself to the children as they entered the classroom, and then requested their first and last names, even if she'd met them the day before. She told them to take any seat for the time being. They did as they were told, but each and every one turned in his seat to stare at the new teacher. Marcail felt compassion for them. Up to the time she was ten, her mother and then her sister had been her only teachers. When that changed she clearly remembered how worried she'd been about the new instructor liking her.

"Good morning, class," she greeted her students once she was in front of the blackboard. Marcail smiled at them with sincere warmth and felt her heart melt over some of the shy smiles she received in return.

She proceeded to tell the class a little bit about herself before asking each student to stand and introduce himself again. From that point forward, the day flew. Marcail could hardly believe her eyes when the big clock on the wall read 3:00.

A few parents came in wagons to claim their children, and two students had horses they had stabled for the day in the small barn out back. Most walked, however, and Marcail stood at the door until they were far from view. She stepped back into the room and stood smiling at the little signs that clearly showed children had been there: a crooked chair, marks on the board, the globe on the floor.

"Thank You, Lord." She whispered the words. "Thank You for a wonderful day."

Marcail had been teaching school for ten days with no sign of Sydney Duckworth. It wasn't hard to figure out that Mrs. Duckworth had decided against sending him. Even though Marcail would like to have met him, she had other things on her mind, specifically, the lunchbox social scheduled for the next day.

When Marcail got up on Saturday morning she had already planned what she would put into her basket to be auctioned. The proceeds went to the school, and Marcail was determined that everything be perfect.

She found a small-handled basket in the cupboard, and after lining it with a yellow linen hand towel, she began to fill it with the lunch she had prepared. All the women of the town, married or single, were encouraged to attend and bring their baskets. The auction would start promptly at 10:30, so all baskets could be auctioned off in time for a noontime picnic for the entire town.

Marcail used a little piece of string and paper to label her basket. She held the paper for just a moment and stared at the name. Miss Donovan. She felt a little thrill each and every time she wrote it.

Not certain where the auction was to be held, Marcail left the house a little early. She should have known not to worry since the noise from people gathering in the town square could be heard from 300 yards away. From a distance it sounded as if all 296 of Willits' residents were in attendance.

Marcail greeted the families she knew as she made her way to the blanket Mrs. Warren had laid out for her family. Allie was the only one seated, and Marcail joined her.

"Hi, Marcail. Is your basket all set?"

"I think so. What's in yours?"

The girls traded baskets, and then exchanged compliments and conversation until a good-looking, dark-haired man walked by. Marcail's gaze followed him as he passed.

"Handsome, isn't he?" Allie sounded almost smug.

Marcail laughed over being caught looking. "Yes, he is," she said with an unrepentant grin. "Why haven't I seen him before?"

"Oh, he keeps to himself. Some say he's still mourning his wife. But she's been gone for over four years."

"What's his name?"

"Dr. Alexander Montgomery," Allie answered and chattered on, but Marcail caught little of it. Her mind was conjuring up a man bending from the saddle to relieve her of her basket, his manner solicitous, his voice kind. But a cold feeling had swept down her spine on hearing the word "doctor." His good looks and the previous kindness he'd shown her were overshadowed by his title. Marcail knew that if they met and talked she would be cordial, but past experience told her she would never be completely at ease in his presence.

More thoughts on Willits' doctor were cut short when the auction began. The women carried their baskets and hampers forward and joined the crowd around the stand.

Mr. Flynn from the bank was the auctioneer, and the first basket belonged to Mrs. Warren. It was customary for the woman whose basket was on the table to step forward to the platform during the bidding. Mr. Warren knew his job and bought his wife's basket. It went for a good price and that seemed to get the ball rolling. Baskets and coins were exchanged amid a backdrop of laughter and great fun.

Marcail's basket was one of the last to be auctioned. She moved toward the platform and took the hand offered her as she stepped up. Her eyes briefly met those of Dr. Montgomery's before he released her hand and she turned to face the audience.

There was a moment of silence that caused Marcail to become a shade nervous. What she couldn't know was how she appeared to the townspeople at that moment. She wore her dark blue dress with the white collar. Her black hair, braided and then wrapped into a fat bun, shone in the sunlight, and the young, vulnerable look she sported on her beautiful face was enough to stop the men of the town dead in their tracks.

"Well now," Mr. Flynn said softly, as though shouting would spoil the moment. "Most of you have met our new schoolmarm,

Miss Donovan. Let's give her a grand welcome to our small town by bidding high on her basket."

The bidding started at two bits, and Marcail smiled when it swiftly went to 40¢. There seemed to be four young men bidding—the Warren boys and two men Marcail did not recognize. She felt her face flame when her basket went over a dollar, and the crowd began to cheer with each accelerated bid.

Mr. Flynn didn't yell *sold* until the bidding stopped at $2.75. Marcail had never heard of such a high bid for a lunch basket. She moved in a state of shock and once again felt the doctor's hand before suddenly being grabbed by someone and nearly pulled from the platform.

"Take it easy, Rowie." Marcail heard the smooth tones of Dr. Montgomery's voice. "You've won the basket fair and square; there's no need to pull her arm off."

"Sorry." The young man apologized but did not relinquish his hold on Marcail's arm.

"Do you two know each other?" Again the doctor spoke.

Marcail could only shake her head as she stared first at the doctor and then at the burly stranger who held her arm in a possessive grip.

"Miss Donovan, this is Jethro Kilmer. Rowie, this is Miss Donovan."

"How do you know her?" Rowie's jaw suddenly jutted forward, and if Marcail had recognized the signs of jealousy, she would have backed completely away from this squarely built man who had bought her lunch basket.

"She's my closest neighbor, Rowie. You know I live past the schoolhouse." The doctor's voice was once again honey smooth, and the younger man calmed visibly.

Marcail was given no chance to thank Alex for his help before she was pulled across the grass to the area where everyone had placed their blankets. When Rowie stopped to look around, Marcail gently disengaged her arm.

"Which blanket is yours?"

"I was sitting with the Warrens."

Rowie's head spun around so quickly to face Marcail that she thought he might have hurt himself.

"You like one of the Warren boys?"

Marcail blinked at the aggressiveness in his voice. "Allie and I are friends," she explained calmly.

Again she watched him relax. She could tell he was going to take her arm again and drag her off to who-knows-where, so Mar-

cail turned and walked with steely determination to the Warrens'
blanket.

Mr. and Mrs. Warren were already seated on the blanket. Seth
Porter, a man Marcail had not met, bought Allie's lunch. He and
Allie were headed their way. Allie introduced Marcail to Seth, and
they talked for just a few moments. Marcail immediately noted the
excited gleam in Allie's eyes and the lovely blush on her cheeks
each time Seth looked in her direction.

Everyone was in high spirits as they began to eat, but Marcail
soon discovered that this lunch was going to be work. Rowie sat as
close to her as she would allow. She did her best to keep her small
basket between them. He didn't have much to say, but she felt his
eyes on her much of the time. When he wasn't watching Marcail,
he was looking at the other people on the quilt as though he wished
they would disappear into another state.

Logan, who had not bid on anyone else's lunch, stared at Marcail also, putting something of a damper on her afternoon. Mr. Warren seemed to sense what was happening and sent his gawking son
on an errand as soon as he was finished eating.

People began to mill around, and Marcail was tempted to rise
also. Weighing how safe it would be to wander around town with
this man, she hesitated. When Seth, Allie, and Mr. and Mrs. Warren
left, leaving only Rowie and Marcail on the blanket, he spoke.

"You don't have a boyfriend back home or anything like that, do
you?"

"I'm sorry, Jethro, but I don't feel that's something you need to
know."

"I like it that you call me Jethro."

Marcail sighed with frustration. He hadn't heard a word she
said. Rowie went on to ask Marcail a score of questions about how
she liked children and housework. That he was in the market for a
wife was more than obvious. Marcail decided to nip his thoughts in
the bud, at least where she was concerned.

With a gentle tone, she told him in no uncertain terms that she
was not in the market for a husband. Rowie looked crestfallen until
Marcail told him it wasn't personal, and that she didn't want to be
married to anyone. Rowie didn't push the point, but Marcail had
the distinct impression that he believed he could change her mind.
When they parted company later that day, Marcail did so with a
prayer that Jethro Kilmer would not push her, because if he chose
to, his feelings were certain to get hurt.

Six

Alexander Montgomery helped himself to a serving of potatoes and then passed the bowl to the young girl on his right. He was having dinner, as he did most Sundays, with his best friends, Dean and Kay Austin.

The Austins had two children, nine-year-old Daisy and 11-year-old Marla, both of whom were in Miss Donovan's class. Before the girls left the table the conversation turned to the high price Miss Donovan's lunch basket brought at the auction. As soon as the girls were out of earshot, Kay teased Alex.

"Honestly, Alex," Kay spoke in feigned rebuke. "You didn't even try to bid on Miss Donovan's basket. You can't tell me that you don't find her attractive."

Alex's eyes sparkled with laughter. "You're right, Kay, I can't tell you I don't find her attractive, but it's a good thing I didn't bid, since I had only 25¢ in my pocket."

Kay became instantly alert, an action Alex did not miss.

"Calm down, Kay, I have a sufficiency. My last three patients all paid with food, and you know when I go hungry, I land myself on your doorstep."

"Well, just see that you do!" Kay spoke the words with a gruffness she didn't feel and left the table. Dean took a sip of his coffee and leaned back in his chair.

"She worries about you."

"I know she does, but I'm fine, really."

"Tell me something, Alex. If Miss Donovan's basket hadn't topped out so high, would you have been interested?"

"I don't know," the younger man answered honestly.

"Linette has been gone for over four years, Alex. Does it still feel unfaithful to you when you think about marrying again?"

"No, but sometimes I think I've lived as a bachelor for too long. I feel set in my ways."

"I can see why you would, since you're all of 30." Dean's voice was dry, and Alex smiled. Both men were quiet for a few minutes, and then the youngest Austin girl joined them.

"Do you want to see what I made, Uncle Alex?"

"Sure."

Alex took the offered picture. It was a pencil drawing of an open field of grass and wildflowers. Daisy showed real talent, and Alex's compliment was sincere.

"Thank you," she told him. "It's for Miss Donovan because I think she must like pretty things."

"Why is that?" her father wanted to know.

"Because she's so pretty," the young girl spoke in a matter-of-fact tone, as if this must be obvious to everyone.

Daisy went on her way, and Dean started to ask Alex a question but found him studying the picture Daisy had left on the table. For some reason the look on the younger man's face caused him to keep still.

Marcail dropped the last of her hairpins onto the table and shook her head carefully. She massaged her temples as her hair fell out of its braids in a mass of waves down her back and to her hips. She sank into the rocking chair and prayed that her headache would go away.

Until the last few weeks she had never worn her hair up for more than a few hours, and by the time church was over and she'd eaten with the family of one of her students, her head was throbbing. She fingered a few strands and thought with regret over the way Allie had responded when she asked her to cut it. Allie had been more than willing until they had arrived in Allie's bedroom and Marcail had taken her hair down.

"I can't do it, Marcail."

"What do you mean, you can't do it?" Marcail had been truly dismayed.

"I just can't," her friend spoke apologetically. "I mean, I had no idea it was so long and beautiful. I just can't cut your hair."

Marcail had sighed. "Who can I ask?"

Allie shrugged. "I could ask Mama, but I'm sure she'll say no."
"Will you check with her anyway?"

Allie had gone to her mother then, but just as she predicted, Mrs. Warren would not touch Marcail's blue-black locks.

Marcail didn't know what to do. She had to wear her hair up in public, and there was nothing wrong with the school board's request. But Marcail was young, and Kaitlin had always encouraged her to pull her hair away from her face, letting the back hang free. Her hair curled naturally at the ends, so she never did anything but wash it and brush the tangles out.

Marcail let her head fall back against the back of the rocker. It was a depressing thought, but it looked as though she would have to wait until she was in Santa Rosa for Christmas. Then she would ask Kaitlin to cut her hair.

Seven

On MONDAY MORNING, the children had just taken their seats when a large black carriage pulled up in front of the schoolhouse. Marcail, having heard the horses, moved to the door. She watched as a frail boy of approximately 11 years stepped down and moved toward the school. Marcail spotted Mrs. Duckworth in the dark interior and knew that at long last Sydney had arrived.

Marcail greeted her new student warmly and felt instant pity as she looked at his pale, pinched features. He was polite, but there was a hesitant, almost defiant look in his eye that, strangely enough, made Marcail want to hold him.

Most of the children in class were familiar with Sydney, so Marcail wasted no time in long introductions. The day moved along very smoothly, and Marcail learned in no time at all that Sydney was in line with the others his age, if not ahead of them, scholastically.

Not until the afternoon of Sydney's second day in class did he show any sign of behavior beyond the ideal. Marcail asked him to come forward and take his turn reading aloud, but he told her he didn't feel up to it.

"Are you ill?" Marcail questioned him.

"No, I just don't want to."

"I'm sorry, Sydney, that you would rather not, but this is not a time when you have a choice. Please come forward and do your reading assignment."

Sydney stared at Marcail without moving from his seat.

Considering this was Marcail's first confrontation, she was very calm. "You will come up and read, Sydney, as I have instructed, or stay in your seat for the afternoon recess."

With ill-disguised boredom, he shuffled to the front. Marcail listened attentively as he read. He did an excellent job, and she told him as much, but he pouted for some time in his seat.

Marcail sat on the schoolhouse steps during recess, and for the first time had to break up an argument between two boys, one of whom was Sydney. She was almost relieved when it was time to dismiss the children and wondered if the rest of the year was going to be like today.

Marcail went straight home and stayed on her knees for over an hour in prayer for Sydney and the rest of her class. By the next morning she thought she was ready to tackle anything, but when Sydney disappeared during the morning recess, Marcail nearly panicked. One of the other children found him hiding behind the outhouse, and Marcail, not doing anything to hide her anger, made Sydney write sentences on the board until lunch.

Thursday was perfect. Marcail was not lulled into a false sense of security, but it did give her hope that Sydney could behave when he put his mind to the task. It also made the events of Friday all the more painful.

By Friday at lunchtime Marcail had corrected the older boys on more than one occasion about talking out of turn. Sydney had been the worst offender. Marcail hoped that some time outside during lunch would help and that he would come back in ready to work.

For an hour after lunch everything seemed to be more settled, but there was an anxiousness about Sydney that concerned Marcail. She turned to write something on the board, thinking as she did that she would ask him if he was feeling well. But as she turned back to the class, a rock flew seemingly out of nowhere and struck her on the cheek.

Marcail's head snapped back, more out of surprise than anything else, and she grabbed the edge of her desk to keep her balance. When Marcail looked up, her students were as still as death. She searched their faces and felt frightened over the searing pain on her own.

Marcail finally reached with a shaking hand to touch her face. She stared for a long time at the blood on her fingertips. Her voice shook as she addressed the class.

"Throwing objects in this classroom will not be tolerated. Do you understand?" Marcail didn't wait for an answer before going on, but she did notice that more than one head turned toward Sydney.

"I find, children," Marcail's entire body had begun to shake, "that I'm not feeling well. School will be dismissed a little early today."

It took a moment for the children to understand that they could leave, but within the space of ten seconds they exited the room with unusual haste.

Marcail stayed on her feet until she reached her house where she collapsed on the bed. Unable to stop shaking, she lay as still as she could for some minutes before rising and wiping her face with a damp, cool cloth. She stood before the mirror and cleaned the cut, which was much smaller than it felt. In fact, with the blood gone, it was barely noticeable. The effort of cleaning, along with the deep feeling of disappointment within her, tired her. Again she sought her bed.

Once there, Marcail curled onto her side, her uninjured cheek pressed into the pillow, and tried to pray, but she must have dozed because she lost all track of time. A sound woke her, and she sat up wondering why she was in bed during the day.

The pain in her cheek brought her thoughts quickly back to earth as someone knocked on the door. Realizing that it had been the knocking which had awakened her, she halfway hoped that whoever it was would go away before she answered. On legs that were just a little bit shaky, she moved toward the door. The person standing on the other side was Dr. Montgomery.

Marcail stared at him for five full, silent seconds before realizing she was being rude. He was the last person she wanted to see, but the least she could do was invite him in.

"Please come in, Dr. Montgomery."

Alex stepped over the threshold, and once in the room, turned to face Marcail. He didn't recognize the fact that he'd just wakened her. She was as white as a sheet, and if he'd had any closer relationship with her, he'd have ordered her immediately to bed.

"I don't wish to disturb you, Miss Donovan, but Marla Austin came by my office. When I asked why she wasn't in school, she said you weren't feeling well. Is there anything I can do?"

"No, no," Marcail spoke and took a step back toward the door. "I'll be fine, but thank you for checking on me." Marcail opened the door, relieved that this was all he had come about, and stood expectantly.

Her message was more than clear to Alex, and he moved toward the opening but paused in the doorway. Because he was not com-

fortable with her color or the way she wanted to be rid of him, he
was on the verge of breaking his own rule about pushing medical
attention on someone who was sane enough to refuse him.

"Are you sure I can't do something for you?"

"Yes, I'm sure." This time her voice was emphatic. "But thank
you for stopping."

She seemed to be a little more at ease with him heading outside,
and Alex, assuring himself that she looked a little better than before, went on his way. He sat astride Kelsey for a few seconds before starting down the road, wondering as he did so how she'd
obtained the little cut on her cheek, and knowing in light of her
almost frightened response to him that he would probably never
find out.

Eight

MARCAIL SPENT A long time studying her Bible and praying on Saturday morning. She read in the book of Philippians, the second chapter, that she was to put others first, but one of her students had acted in violence toward her and that was not to be tolerated. Marcail knew she had to go for help and advice.

By 10:30 she was on her way to see Mr. Flynn at the bank. The scratch on her face was very small, unnoticeable really, but Marcail was quite conscious of it.

The bank teller gave her a searching look when she asked for Mr. Flynn, and she forced herself not to reach toward her face. She watched him disappear into the back office and reappear with the bank manager.

"To what do I owe this pleasure, Miss Donovan?" Mr. Flynn smiled cordially until he got a close look at Marcail's tense features.

"I have a problem I need to discuss with you, Mr. Flynn. Is this an opportune time?"

"Yes, certainly." He'd become somewhat tense himself in the last few seconds, and his movements were agitated as he led Marcail to his office. Marcail took the chair Mr. Flynn gestured toward and watched as he sat behind his desk. She was on the verge of explaining her visit when Mr. Flynn spoke.

"Is there a problem with someone in your class?"

"Yes, sir, there is."

"I hope it's not Sydney Duckworth. I can go to the parents of anyone else in town, but if Sydney's been difficult, well, you'll just have to do your best."

Marcail couldn't believe her ears, and her look must have registered her surprise.

Mr. Flynn continued: "I know I've shocked you and probably caused you to think I don't deserve my position as head of the school board. However, Mrs. Duckworth will make the town miserable if I go to her and complain."

"He threw a rock at me, Mr. Flynn." Marcail's voice reflected her mounting anger. "It hit me in the face!"

"You *saw* him do this?"

"You can't possibly be questioning my word?"

"No, *I'm* not." Mr. Flynn's voice was kind. "But please understand, Miss Donovan—Mrs. Duckworth will."

Marcail was silent for an entire minute. This was inconceivable to her.

"I guess I'll have to go to Mrs. Duckworth myself," Marcail said, thinking she had come up with a logical solution.

"I really hope you won't do that."

"Why not?"

"Because the last five times a teacher went to Cordelia and complained about Sydney, she pressured the rest of us into keeping our children out of school until the teacher quit. We've had to hire other teachers in the middle of the year. In fact, you're the ninth schoolteacher we've had in three years."

"And you let her get away with this?" Marcail was incredulous. "Just because you're afraid she won't speak to you the next time you pass on the street?"

"I wish it were that simple," the banker's face was drawn." You see, Mrs. Duckworth owns over half the town, including this bank. When things don't go her way, our rents go up or we find ourselves completely out of work.

"Having to wear dark clothing and put your hair up at all times is part of her belief that the schoolteacher must be a shining example to the children of town. *But,* she's completely blind to her own selfishness or the deeds of her grandson."

Marcail felt something grow cold inside of her. It chilled her to think that one person had this much power.

"You could just up and quit; others have. You certainly have grounds, but we're very pleased with your work and hope you'll stay."

For just an instant Marcail's heart grabbed at the word "quit." How easy it would be to run home to Father, but then Marcail remembered how badly she wanted to prove to herself that she could do this.

She also realized the word "quit" was not a part of her vocabulary. She shook her head ever so slightly.

"I take it that means you're not quitting. Well, I'm glad to hear it. I'll start making surprise visits to the school-house every few days. I think if more than one person is watching, Sydney will be less likely to act up."

Marcail nodded almost numbly. She could see that nothing more was going to be offered to her. As Mr. Flynn saw her to the door and she began the walk home, her mind worked over the options before her. Quitting was out, but she could go to Mrs. Duckworth. However, Mr. Flynn's initial response to her predicament had shown her that such a move would cause trouble for the entire town.

Marcail was tempted to write her brother-in-law, Rigg, or her father and pour out her entire story, knowing instinctively they would show up in Willits within hours or days of hearing from her. But all her life she'd been protected, and she so wanted to stand on her own this time.

Marcail's mind played over every second of the previous afternoon, and she realized that in throwing that rock, Sydney had succeeded in shocking even himself. With that in mind, Marcail decided that she would confront Sydney on Monday so he would know where he stood, and then pray there would be no more outbursts.

"Hello, Miss Donovan."

Marcail was startled out of her musings by the sound of Dr. Montgomery's voice. She'd been so intent on her walking and planning that she had not heard his approach.

"Hello, Dr. Montgomery." Marcail's hand had gone to her throat in surprise. She tried to smile pleasantly, but as usual he made her nervous, and she was a bit embarrassed over how preoccupied she'd been. She watched as he swung from his mount to stand before her.

"How are you feeling?"

"I'm fine, thank you," Marcail replied, actually mustering up a smile.

Alex nodded and continued to watch her. He had wanted a closer look at her than his mounted position would allow, and now he was able to see that her color was much better than the day before. In fact, she was rather flushed. On the other hand, her discomfort in his presence hadn't changed in the least; she was obviously afraid of him. He wondered absently if it was just him, all doctors, or men in general.

Marcail was standing as far from him as propriety would allow, and for some reason Alex was torn between turning on his best bedside manner or laughing. The latter won out, and Marcail watched as his eyes lit with some inner amusement.

Alex witnessed the raising of her chin and knew that the voice she used to address him was one she used with her students.

"Was there something you needed to see me about, doctor? If not, my schedule is quite full, and I'd like to be on my way."

Alex caught a light of vulnerability in her eyes, slight, but nevertheless evident to him. All humor fled.

"I'm glad to see you're doing well, Miss Donovan. Please don't let me keep you."

Marcail nodded to him by way of answer and turned even before he mounted his horse. She felt his eyes on her back for some steps, but before long her mind was back on Sydney and she didn't give Willits' handsome young doctor another thought.

Nine

"I'M SO SORRY, Miss Donovan. I'll never do it again," Sydney told Marcail with heartbreaking sincerity, his bottom lip quivering pitifully, his face nearly ashen. Marcail had been correct—he had shocked even himself.

"I'm glad to hear that, Sydney," she told him gently, "because if you do, I'm going to have to punish you severely." The young boy nodded, and Marcail reached to give him a hug. It was not the first time she'd hugged him, but for the first time he reciprocated. His thin arms clung to her, and Marcail's heart thundered with emotion.

They were the only ones in the schoolhouse, and Marcail, realizing that the children would be returning from recess very soon, knew she had to quickly say what was on her mind. Holding Sydney gently at arm's length, she began.

"I understand, Sydney, that people have days when they feel upset, but no matter what you're feeling, you must *never* deliberately hurt someone."

"I understand, Miss Donovan." Again Sydney's lip quivered, and Marcail believed he meant it. They talked for a few moments more, Sydney apologizing for the third time and Marcail telling Sydney she forgave him.

As he returned to his desk, Marcail realized that something special had happened between them. Sydney was looking at her with new eyes, and as much as Marcail regretted his action, she prayed that this incident would make a difference in their future relationship. Some of the shock over being struck was still there, but Sydney was as precious to her as he'd always been.

In the weeks to follow God sustained Marcail in a way she would not have dreamed possible. She was growing very close to her entire class and knew that some of the students thought the world of her. The Austin girls had even come after school one day to tell her they prayed for her every night. Marcail had been so moved she had nearly cried. She asked the girls to also pray for Sydney, and for Marcail's relationship with him.

The girls had readily agreed, and Marcail felt their prayers. There were days when Sydney was a school-teacher's dream and days when he was a nightmare, but amid the ups and downs they grew closer. Marcail was swiftly learning to take each day as it came.

Sydney had not turned into a model student, but neither had he shown any signs of aggression since the day he'd thrown the rock. Marcail suspected this was because he was becoming slightly infatuated with her.

They were able to talk with ease, but Marcail's prayers were many on Sydney's behalf. She hadn't mentioned her fears to anyone else, but she recognized the fact that he was a child who was prone to acts of violence when angered. It frightened her a little that she had no idea what had set him off the last time, but she kept an eye on him, and Mr. Flynn was making his visits as promised.

Teaching school was harder work than Marcail had anticipated. Her sister had made it look so easy. This made the weekends a time of relaxation and recuperation. She liked to work on her lessons and bake Saturday morning. Often she would walk into town in the afternoon.

One Saturday, when the weather was beginning to turn cold, Marcail ran into Kay Austin in the general store.

"Miss Donovan," Kay greeted her warmly, "did the girls give you my message about tomorrow?"

"Yes, Mrs. Austin, they did, but tomorrow is—"

"The pie auction," she finished for her. "That's no problem because I want you to bring the young man who buys your pie."

"Oh," Marcail said with genuine pleasure, "that sounds wonderful. I'll plan on it."

Kay squeezed her arm and smiled before telling her she would see her on the morrow. Marcail thought that Mrs. Austin would never know what a relief the invitation was. Rowie Kilmer had seen Marcail just the weekend before and made it quite clear that he was going to bid on her pie. Marcail had been gracious, but in her heart she sighed and wished that he would turn his attention elsewhere.

She had crossed his path from time to time, and although he made no move to press her, he questioned her very carefully as to whether or not she'd been seeing anyone else. Her comments on the privacy of her own business seemed to roll off him like boulders on a hill-side.

The next morning Marcail went to church. Since the auction was to follow the service, she brought her apple pie in a basket, as did most of the other women in town.

Allie's pie was mince. She whispered to Marcail during church that it was Seth's favorite. Marcail smiled at the joy in her friend's eyes. She had missed Allie since she'd started seeing Seth, but Marcail recognized the signs of love and told Allie, in all honesty, how thrilled she was for her newfound happiness.

No social time had been planned, since the weather was cooling, but spirits were high as the bidding began, raising funds that were once again to go to the school.

Marcail's pie came up in the middle of the bidding, and just as Rowie had said, he was on hand and bidding like a rich man. It looked as if Marcail's basket was going to go high, and the young schoolmarm kept her eyes on Mr. Flynn as two men took the price over $1.00. She recognized one voice as Rowie's, and the other as Allie's brother, Logan's.

Marcail, preparing herself for an afternoon of being gawked at or pulled around, was praying for patience. A deep voice from the back of the crowd startled her with a bid.

"Three dollars!"

Marcail's eyes slid shut on a sudden rush of tears. She was barely aware of the way Mr. Flynn stuttered to a halt or how still the crowd had grown. Moments passed before Mr. Flynn declared the pie sold and Marcail turned and made her way back off the platform.

A massive hand was there to take her basket and then her hand, but Marcail didn't dare look up until the man had led her away to the semiprivacy of a nearby tree. As soon as he stopped she let her tear-filled eyes meet his, and a second later she was crushed in Rigg's arms.

Marcail didn't know when anything had felt so good. She let herself be cuddled against his chest and tried not to cry.

"I've missed you," Rigg whispered in her ear, feeling as though he could cry himself.

He couldn't love this girl more if she had been his own child, and in a way she was. He was only 17 years her senior, but she had come into his life as a nine-year-old girl whose mother had just died and whose father was overseas. Their's had been a love-at-first-sight relationship, a brother-sister type of love.

A year later he was married to Marcail's sister, and she was living with them. Not even the birth of his own three children had diminished his love for her. He'd gone into a state of near mourning when her father had returned to California and she had moved downstate to live with him.

Rigg released Marcail and tenderly wiped a tear from her cheek. There was so much they wanted to say to each other. They had just began to share when Jethro Kilmer came on the scene.

"Who is this, Marcail?" Jethro demanded unexpectedly.

Rigg only glanced at the younger man before turning his surprised gaze to his sister-in-law.

"Rigg, this is Jethro Kilmer. Jethro, this is my brother-in-law, Marshall Riggs." Marcail's voice was polite, but Rigg heard the note of longsuffering.

"Oh, he's married! Why didn't you say so?" Rowie's voice was so filled with relief that Marcail felt angry. She would probably have spouted off at Rowie if Rigg hadn't put his hand on her arm.

"It's nice to meet you, Jethro," Rigg's voice was steady. "But I'm sure you'll understand my wanting to spend some time with my sister."

Rigg led Marcail away without further explanation. Marcail was so pleased over the way he'd handled Rowie that her smile nearly stretched off her face.

"Do you need me to talk with this young man?" The question came softly to her ears as they walked. When they stopped, trying once again to steal some privacy, Marcail shook her head.

"No, but thank you. As you've probably guessed, I'm not encouraging him, even though I'm sure he would welcome any interest on my part. I'm certain he'll grow discouraged and eventually leave me alone."

Marcail grew silent then and simply drank in the sight of her sister's husband. He had seemed bigger than life to her when they first met, and even now he was one of the largest men she'd ever known. But there wasn't a mean or malicious bone in his body, and from the first he'd always made her feel loved and secure.

"How's Katie?" Marcail asked softly.

"She has a bit of a cold."

Marcail nodded. "And the kids?"

"Colds too. They miss you almost as much as I do."

They grinned at each other again, and Marcail reached to give him another hug. She explained the invitation for lunch, and as they talked they made their way toward the Austin home.

Marcail had a myriad of questions, as did Rigg. They had exchanged most of the pertinent information regarding family and friends by the time Rigg knocked on the Austins' front door.

Unfortunately, some of the joy went out of Marcail's afternoon when the door was answered by Dr. Alexander Montgomery.

Ten

TWO HOURS LATER Alex knew with a certainty that Miss Donovan's fear was not of men in general. She was at complete ease with her brother-in-law, as well as with Dean Austin. This left only him, or doctors in general. Alex wondered why the thought was so discouraging to him.

He figured it might have to do with the fact that after 15 minutes of conversation around the dinner table, he knew that both Rigg and Marcail were believers. This made the young teacher safe enough for him to drop his guard, but no more approachable.

Alex knew that everyone in town believed he was still too much in love with his first wife to even look at another woman, but that was not true anymore. What the towns-people didn't understand was how earnestly Alex took his relationship with Jesus Christ, and in so doing, he was serious about finding a wife who shared his belief.

Without a doubt, the first criteria was that the woman be a Christian. Alex found himself thinking, however, that it certainly didn't hurt that her hair was so black and shiny it appeared blue in the right light, or that she had eyes like big brown pansies. Her eyes, along with the tiny dark mole near her lower lip, drew his attention to her smiling mouth and her beautiful teeth when he least expected it. No, none of those things hurt at all; and, added to the fact that she loved the Savior, they made her more distracting by the minute.

Alex had worked hard at not staring at her all afternoon, but surprisingly, he found himself alone with her in the living room after the dessert dishes had been cleared. Alex could almost hear her telling herself to relax. After a few minutes of tense silence, she smiled at him. It gave him hope, and he spoke, his excellent bedside manner coming to the fore.

"It was certainly nice of Rigg to surprise you today."

Marcail smiled a little wider because he didn't seem at all threatening to her at that moment. Her voice revealed her relief when she answered.

"It was, wasn't it? I don't think I knew how much I missed him until I heard his voice at the back of the crowd."

"How long has it been?"

"I saw them for a few minutes when the train stopped in Santa Rosa, but I moved away in late February. I wish Katie and the children could have come, but Rigg said everyone has colds."

"You're an aunt then?"

Marcail beamed with pleasure, and Alex sucked in a sharp breath at her enchanting beauty.

"Several times over, actually," Marcail answered easily, not having noticed the doctor's reaction. "Katie and Rigg have Gretchen, Molly, and Donovan. My brother, Sean, and his wife, Charlotte, have Ricky and Callie."

Alex smiled at her, a smile of genuine warmth. Marcail returned the grin until Alex shifted in his chair. Marcail thought he was rising to join her on the sofa. She tensed and moved a little further down the cushions, an action that Alex did not miss.

"Is it me, Miss Donovan, or all doctors?"

Marcail's face flamed with humiliation, and she stuttered an apology.

"Please don't apologize." Alex's voice was tender. "It's just that if I've done something to upset you, I'd like to ask your forgiveness."

"No, no," Marcail assured him swiftly. "You've been very kind; I just—that is—I'm rather—" The young woman came to an awkward halt and was surprised to find the doctor smiling at her, his eyes filled with understanding.

Marcail met his gaze for just a moment and then unintentionally spoke out loud. "I guess you might not be so bad after all."

Laughter erupted from Alex's chest, and Marcail's hand flew to her mouth. Her face had heated all over again, and she began to rise from her seat. Alex waved her back with his hand, still chuckling over her remark.

"Please don't go, Miss Donovan. I assure you, I'm not easily offended. I find your honesty refreshing."

Marcail eyed him carefully to gauge his sincerity. She finally relaxed back on the sofa, and they continued to talk. If Marcail wasn't exactly at ease in the situation, she found it tolerable. What she didn't know was that Kay Austin was beyond the door, hesitating before entering. She was also listening to every word and hoping that before long Marcail would find the situation much *more* than tolerable.

"I can't believe how swiftly the day went."

"I can't either. I sure enjoyed the Austins' hospitality."

"I really hadn't known them before, but they's wonderful," Marcail agreed and added, "Are you sure you have to go first thing in the morning, Rigg?"

The full moon shone on Rigg and Marcail as they stood at Marcail's front door recalling the afternoon. Rigg was headed to the hotel for the night, and this would be the last they would see of each other.

"I really do, Marc. Jeff is going to open the mercantile for me, but I've got to get back. Christmas is only about two months away, and we'll all be together then."

Marcail nodded, and they hugged one last time. She stood in the doorway and watched him walk toward town. When she finally shut the door, it was with a prayer of thanksgiving for her family, and for the way God had sent Rigg on the day she needed him most.

"But don't you think she's perfect for Alex?"

"Kay," her husband spoke patiently as he slipped into bed, "that still does not give you an excuse for eavesdropping."

Kay looked somewhat rebuked, but she was so excited about the little she'd overheard that she was not very sorry.

"I can see you're not at all sorry."

"I am sorry that I listened. I should have walked right into the room instead of waiting, but I'm not sorry about what I heard."

Dean frowned at his wife's line of reasoning, but she was too wound up to notice.

"You should have heard his voice. When he found out she was afraid of him, he was so tender with her. I just know she's the one."

Dean shook his head, kissed his wife good night, and turned down the lantern. Kay listened as his breathing evened out into sleep. She was planning ahead and much too excited to sleep. Alex came to lunch every Sunday afternoon; maybe she should ask Miss Donovan to join them more often. It was a delightful plan.

Eleven

An entire month passed before Alex saw Marcail again. It was not for lack of trying on his part, but he wanted to be careful about how often he went to the front door of her home, and there was really no other time when he ran into her. Since she would probably have to be dying before she would call on him, he knew better than to hope she would need medical attention.

On this particular Saturday morning he was a little late heading into his office in town. For the first time he saw Marcail at the side of her house. He did a double take when he saw that the tiny, black-haired woman was chopping wood, or at least making an attempt. Knowing that he was getting a glimpse of Marcail Donovan's determined personality, Alex dismounted and stood watching her.

Marcail balanced a fat log on end, and then lifted the ax in front of her, bringing it down on the log. A small piece of wood flew off as the remainder of the wood landed on the ground. Alex watched in fascination as she added the piece to a small pile of chips and started again.

Just as Marcail raised the ax again, she spotted her neighbor. She repeated the process and then stood breathing heavily as Alex approached.

"I can't believe you're doing this yourself."

"Well, I said I would," Marcail was still panting, "So I'm going to."

271

"And just who did you say that to?" Alex reached for the ax and tried to ignore the surreptitious way Marcail backed away from him.

"Jethro offered to chop wood for me, but I didn't think that was a good idea, so I told him I would take care of it myself. In fact, I think you should give the ax back to me."

Alex stared at her for a full ten seconds, shook his head, and began to chop. In 20 minutes he had a large stack of burning logs and a smaller stack of kindling. They worked together carrying the logs to the house and dumping them into the box by Marcail's stove. On the last load Marcail turned to thank the doctor, but found him standing and watching her from the door. With his gaze leveled so intently on her, it took a moment for her to speak.

"Thank you for your help."

"You're welcome. Will you do me a favor?"

"What is it?"

"Will you do it?" he persisted.

Marcail hesitated. She knew it was unfair of him to ask for a commitment before explaining, but he *had* chopped her wood, and she could see his desire to help was out of kindness and not selfish motives.

"All right."

"Come by my office and let me know the next time you need wood."

Marcail nearly panicked. That would mean he would be around more often. She had to make him see this wasn't necessary.

"There really is no need. I, uh, well, I mean, that is, I didn't think that you would, I mean, I really appreciate, but I don't want to bother, and I—" Marcail came to a breathless halt when she saw laughter in the depths of his blue eyes.

Marcail took a breath and tried again. "Thank you for your help, but I'll be okay now."

You're not about to let me near you, are you, little one? These were Alex's very tender thoughts. What he said aloud was much less personal.

"I don't want to push in where I'm not wanted, but if you'll let me, I'll just keep an eye on your woodpile. I won't come into the house; I'll just stack it by your porch when it looks like you're getting low."

Marcail's mouth had suddenly gone dry. She did not want to be beholden to this man, but she couldn't go on as she was. Every day was colder than the day before, and as hard as it was to accept his help, she didn't really have much choice.

"Thank you" was all Marcail could muster, and then she scolded herself for her rudeness. But the doctor must not have minded. He smiled at her, raised a hand in a small wave, and went on his way.

It would be a long time before Marcail knew that Alex found her delightful, especially when she stood looking very proper and composed, unaware of the strands of hair that hung in her face and the dirt that was smeared on her cheeks and forehead. Delighted, captivated, fascinated—Alex's emotions ran the gamut, and much to his chagrin, he found he could think about little else.

Marcail was invited to the Austins for dinner again the first Sunday in December. As much as she wanted to, Kay had not had the courage to ask the girls' teacher to join them the week after the pie auction, and every week to follow. So on this day, she decided to pull out all the stops.

Alex was the first to arrive, and spotting the extra place setting and fancy dinnerware, he turned a curious eye on his hostess.

"Who's joining us, Kay?"

"Who?" Kay sounded much like an owl.

"Tell him, Kathleen," her husband commanded as he entered the room.

Kay turned aggressively on both men. "I happen to know that she eats by herself every evening, and I think the least we can do is ask her to join us on the weekends!" Kay stormed back out to the kitchen and left the men to stare at each other.

"I take it the lovely Miss Donovan is joining us today?"

Dean only nodded and watched the younger man. "I'm sorry, Alex, if that's a problem for you."

"It's no problem for me, Dean. I find myself daydreaming about the next time I'll see her. However, I don't know how Miss Donovan is going to feel about *my* being here."

A moment later they both heard the knock on the front door.

"Well," Dean spoke again, this time softly, "we'll know soon enough."

Marla answered the door and stood grinning at her teacher. Marcail was just as glad to see her because the Austin girls were some of her best students. The fact that they prayed for her gave them a bond she did not share with any of the other children. They were also bright and well behaved, and looked at her with something close to adoration, which was good for any teacher's confidence.

Daisy joined them as they made their way to the dining room. Even though both girls were talking at once, Marcail didn't miss the sound of Alex's well-modulated voice. Surprisingly enough, she did not feel like running away. There was a constant supply of chopped wood next to her door, and Marcail wanted to thank him. Unfortunately her mouth went dry the moment she felt his eyes on her.

"Hello, Miss Donovan," Kay greeted her warmly. "Come in and make yourself at home."

Marcail had to clear her throat before any words would come out, and only then was she able to thank her hostess. Dean greeted her, and then Marcail had no choice but to meet the doctor's eyes.

"Hello, Dr. Montgomery," she began. "I want to thank you for the firewood."

"You're welcome. Has there been ample?"

"Yes, more than enough, thank you."

Alex had to hide a smile. Such a speech had obviously cost her, and he found the look of profound relief on her face adorable. He realized in an instant that he wanted to court this woman. With Linette, his attention had been welcome; with Marcail, he didn't know whether he even stood a chance.

Alex had sudden visions of the young men in Santa Rosa, just waiting for her to disembark from the train when she returned for Christmas. He couldn't believe the wave of jealousy that overwhelmed him at the thought.

"Dinner is ready," Kay called as she added a soup tureen to the table and everyone gathered around.

Marcail found herself next to Marla and across the table from Daisy. Alex sat on Daisy's left, and even though Marcail told herself not to, she looked at the young doctor almost constantly.

Her mind ran in two directions. One moment she found herself enjoying his handsome face, dark hair, and blue eyes, but regretting the fact that he was a doctor. The next moment she wished his features were pale and washed out, and that she found him repulsive.

Alex did not miss the way Marcail's gaze strayed to him repeatedly. He tried to squelch the hope rising within him that she might be interested, but it didn't work. When Marcail said her goodbyes, Alex did the same so they could leave together.

Marcail was looking uncomfortable all over again as they walked out the front door. But Alex so wanted to be with her that he ignored her look, took a big breath, and asked if he could see her home.

Twelve

MARCAIL'S MOUTH WAS dry and her palms were wet. She felt like some type of small prey that was being stalked by a larger animal. She told herself she had no one to blame but herself, as she realized her looking at Dr. Montgomery had given him the wrong impression.

"Why don't I just rescind that question, Miss Donovan, since I've obviously upset you?"

Marcail's heart broke just a little at the dejected tone in his voice and the look of resignation on his face, but she felt she had to be honest.

"I'm sorry." Marcail's voice was soft, and Alex saw very real regret behind her fear.

"Don't be," he assured her. "It's nice to know right up front that my suit would not be acceptable." He mustered up a gentle smile intended to ease her guilt and went on his way. Marcail stood still until he rounded the house to retrieve his horse and watched as he started toward home.

Alex stretched his stocking feet out in front of him and relaxed back in one of the kitchen chairs. The supper he'd just eaten had been filling enough, but he was feeling a bit empty inside. His Bible lay on the table. He reached for it, but didn't open it.

"I thought she might be the one, Lord," he said out loud in the quiet house. "I can't push in where I'm not wanted, and not until

275

she apologized did I realize how badly I wanted her to want me. I don't know why I feel this way, Father, but I somehow think that she needs me . . . that we need each other."

Alex believed that his was the God of all comfort, but the truth was he hurt right then in a way that he'd never hurt before. Losing Linette had given new meaning to the word loneliness, and his hurt over her loss had been very real. But this was different. This was rejection.

Alex opened his Bible to the book of Genesis. It always comforted him to read the account of creation and to marvel again at the perfect, orderly way God had constructed the world. When Alex read in chapter 2, verse 18, that man should not be alone, he stopped to pray.

With a heart honestly seeking to be the man God would have him be, Alex committed his thoughts of Marcail to the Lord. He lay his own desires at the feet of a holy God and prayed that God in His timing and will would provide someone special to share his life. At the moment the only face Alex could see was Marcail's, but he trusted that God could change his heart and turn this fresh pain into glory for Himself.

Marcail brushed through her hair with long even strokes as she sat on the edge of the bed and thought about Dr. Montgomery. She knew she was being silly, since he couldn't be nicer, but fears were never logical, and the truth was that she was afraid of him.

Marcail lay in bed thinking of the humble way Alex had accepted her rejection. She wondered for a moment if her fear wasn't causing her to pass up what could be a wonderful relationship. How would she know either way? She fell asleep before she could come to any solid conclusions.

Thirteen

Santa Rosa—
December 18, 1881

MARCAIL BEAMED ACROSS the living room at her sister, who mirrored her look as though they alone shared a secret. They were silent for a moment, a relaxed, easy kind of silence that sisters who are also friends can share. Kaitlin was the first to break the spell.

"I can't believe how good it is to have you here. It's been so long."

"That quick hug back in August when the train came through didn't count."

"You're right, it didn't."

Again they smiled at each other. Marcail had arrived the day before. Now it was Sunday afternoon, and they'd already been to church and eaten lunch. Little Donovan was napping, and the girls were with their dad at their grandparents' farm. The house was quiet.

"You look good, Marc. You must be happy."

"I am. I mean, the job isn't without its drawbacks, but I really do love it."

"It's what you've always wanted to do, that's for certain."

"The biggest difficulty," Marcail spoke with a twinkle in her eye, "is that both you and Mother made it look so easy."

"And you're finding out different?"

"In a hurry." Marcail spoke fervently this time.

"Have there been some problems?"

"Yes, but I believe I'm handling them."

277

"Why didn't you write about them?"

"Because I wanted to stand on my own, and if Rigg had known about the one problem, he'd have rushed to Willits. I didn't want that."

Kaitlin looked concerned. "Were you in some sort of danger?"

"In a way I was, but the situation is under control now, at least I pray it is."

"Want to tell me about it?"

Surprisingly, Marcail did. She told her older sister all about Mrs. Duckworth, Sydney, and the town's refusal to stand up to this family. She half expected Kaitlin to be angry, both at her for not sharing and at Mrs. Duckworth's manipulation. But instead Kaitlin looked very thoughtful.

"Mother had a problem like that once."

"She did?" Marcail was astounded.

"Um hm. In Hawaii. You were probably too young to recall. One of the leaders in the village wanted his son schooled, but without the slightest bit of correction. And believe me, this boy needed to be disciplined."

"How did she handle it?"

"She wouldn't allow him into the schoolhouse. He ran home to his father, who stormed over to Mother in a fury, but she stood up to him. When he left he took not only his own son, but every child who was related to him by blood or marriage. Half the school was missing."

"What did Mother do?"

"She taught the children who remained," Kaitlin stated serenely, obviously agreeing with her mother's choice of action. "Within a week's time, all but the one boy were back in school. It took another month before we saw him again, but there was never any trouble after that."

Marcail was silent as she digested this new picture of her mother. Their situations were not identical, partly because of the position of respect and administration her parents always held in the villages, but Marcail did see similarities. She wasn't completely sure she'd have handled it the same way.

True, most of the children had come back within a week, but what if they hadn't? How long would Mother have let the children go without their schooling before trying to find another solution? It was a question only Theresa Donovan could have answered, and she was no longer there to ask.

"I'm not saying that you should do the same thing, Marc." Katie's voice cut into her thoughts. "Please don't think that. You have to follow your heart. At least you're able to talk with Sydney and reason with him. Unless I miss my guess, you see him as a mission field."

She smiled at how easily Katie could read her. Marcail did see Sydney as a freshly plowed field, just waiting for planting, and she prayed every day that God would help her sow the seeds of truth. He was a little boy much in need of a personal relationship with Christ Jesus, and Marcail's constant prayer was to be used of God to that end.

Donovan cried then, and Katie went to check on him. Once alone, Marcail's mind wandered to her last day of school and the lovely lace handkerchief Sydney had given her. Most of the children had brought her something, and she was grateful for every gift. But none of the children had sported Sydney's look, a look that begged her to find him as special as his gift.

Well, he was special, and Marcail took time right then to pray for him as the new year approached. She also prayed that she would return, renewed in spirit and body for the remainder of the year. She didn't know what tomorrow would bring, but she believed it was in God's hands.

Fourteen

THE WEEKS MARCAIL spent at home for Christmas were some of the best that year. She loved Willits and Visalia, but Santa Rosa had been home for such a long time that it was hard to think of it in any other way.

Free from the cares of the classroom and lessons, Marcail felt like a schoolgirl once again. Her father, thinking she would be in Santa Rosa more often, had brought most of her dresses from Visalia when he came for his Christmas visit. Marcail dressed in her best to go out with friends on drives and to dinner, enjoying the time of her life.

Christmas was like old times, even though everyone was sorry that Sean and Charlotte weren't able to leave the mission in the Hawaiian Islands to be with them.

The girls loved the dolls their Aunt Marcail had brought, and she was thrilled with their reaction. Marcail herself said she made out like a bandit, with more lovely gifts than she'd ever received before.

It was great fun to sit around and catch up on all the latest news, the most wonderful of which was Rigg's brother Gilbert's decision to go into the pastorate. With his gentle manner and love for God's Word, it was no surprise to Marcail. His mother, May, also told her he'd already met someone special, and it looked like her last son would soon be leaving the nest.

Mr. Parker and his son, Joey, special friends of the family, also filled a part of her time at home. Joey had been in Katie's class when she first taught in Santa Rosa. He and Marcail were the same age, but the difference between them had been marked. Joey's father had been drunk whenever the coins in his pocket had allowed, and Joey had been one of the most neglected children Kaitlin had ever encountered.

Kaitlin's heart had been instantly softened toward this boy and his father. With the help of Rigg's family, they were brought into the circle of their fellowship.

Joey had come to Christ in a very short time, and the family had watched with awe and praise as he grew stronger in the Lord with each passing month.

Mr. Parker had only recently made a decision for Christ, but their ten years of friendship, years when the family helped him overcome painful obstacles such as illiteracy and alcoholism, had given them a bond that transcended most other relationships.

Joey was a foreman at the feed mill, and Mr. Parker worked part-time for Bill Taylor at the shipping office. They had a comfortable house in town, and Mr. Parker was seeing a lovely widow he'd met at the church. Marcail met her one Sunday and thought she was very special.

It was wonderful just to be back under the solid Bible teaching of Pastor Keller. Marcail couldn't help but feel saddened when she thought of her Pastor Zimler in Willits and his complacent attitude toward the Word of God.

As difficult as it was to go back to what seemed a spiritual wasteland, Marcail found as the days passed that she could hardly sit still for the thought of returning. She missed her students and her little house so much that she dreamed of them the night before she left. She knew she would miss her family once again, but strangely she found herself thinking of Dr. Montgomery as she boarded the train for Willits.

Fifteen

MARCAIL COULDN'T BELIEVE how good it felt to step off the train in Willits. The scenery on the ride north was a little more familiar this time. As the train lumbered its way through the mountains and valleys en route to her home, Marcail reveled in the beauty from the window.

There was a slight pang of loneliness when no one was at the train station to meet her, but then she hadn't been able to tell Allie exactly when she was scheduled to arrive.

Mentally thanking Rigg and Katie for the new coat she wore, Marcail started her walk home. She felt snug and warm as she pulled the high collar around the back of her head. Her new boots, a gift from her father, were a little stiff at first, but they were already feeling better by the time her house came into view.

Marcail breathed in the crisp, cold air as she walked, and not until she drew near her front porch did she recognize the sound of someone chopping wood. She peeked around the corner of the house to find Alex in shirtsleeves and swinging an ax.

He had come into her thoughts at odd times while in Santa Rosa, and each time Marcail had prayed very specifically about her feelings. If she was very honest with herself—and she usually tried to be—he still made her uncomfortable. But she was also fascinated.

Lost in her thoughts, Marcail stood long enough that Alex eventually noticed her. Marcail watched as he set the ax down, drew a handkerchief from his rear pocket, and came toward her.

"Welcome home," he said as he wiped the back of his neck. He stopped before her and couldn't hold the smile that stretched over his face at the very sight of her.

"Thank you. It's nice to be back."

Alex's smile deepened over the sincerity he saw in her eyes. When she had boarded the train to Santa Rosa he had wondered if he would ever see her again. The thought had given him no peace of mind. When she still hadn't returned on Saturday and school was scheduled to resume on Monday, he became concerned. He purposely left her wood until Sunday in hopes that he would be there when she returned.

"Did you have a nice Christmas?" Marcail's voice was tentative, telling Alex how hard it was for her to make simple conversation with him.

"Yes, I did, thank you. How about yourself?"

"It was very nice."

"Did you get a new coat?"

"Oh, yes, I did." Marcail's voice told of her surprise that he had noticed. She didn't realize he noticed most everything about her. She touched the lapel on the long, single-breasted navy coat.

"Thank you for chopping the wood," Marcail blurted suddenly, just remembering she hadn't done so.

"You're welcome."

The silence between them deepened, and after a few moments Alex rescued Marcail by going back to work. Once in the house, Marcail listened to the sounds from outside. Her mind ran in numerous veins, and unfortunately she stood daydreaming even after the chopping stopped and all grew quiet.

It was then that Marcail noticed that Alex had lit a fire in her stove. Her heavy coat must have kept her from noticing the heat when she first walked in. Marcail moved swiftly to her front door, opened it, and looked out. But she was too late. Alex, astride his horse, was almost back to his own house and much too far to hear her voice.

Nearly a week had passed since Marcail had returned to work, and it was now Saturday, her day to bake and shop in town. She was just about to walk into the dry goods store when Mrs. Duckworth's stringent tone sounded in the cold January air. The sound of her voice could be heard from down the block.

"Don't tell me I don't have the right! I own this building, and if I request to see your books, then I expect to see them!"

Marcail did not hear the hotel owner's reply, but she did spot Sydney sitting in his grandmother's carriage out front. She approached with a smile.

"Hi, Sydney."

"Hello, Miss Donovan." Sydney smiled with genuine pleasure at the sight of her. It was obviously one of his good days.

Marcail nearly shook her head in wonder. She'd never met a more cordial child when he determined to be so. His manners were perfection itself. Get on his wrong side on a bad day, however, and look out! Anything could happen.

"It's getting colder all the time, isn't it?"

"Yes, it is," the boy replied. "My grandmother says that because last year was so mild we'll have a heavy snowfall this year."

"Well, she is the person to listen to, since she's lived here so many years."

As if sensing she was the topic of discussion, Mrs. Duckworth suddenly appeared at Marcail's side.

"How do you do, Mrs. Duckworth?"

"I am well, Miss Donovan. I understand you went to Santa Rosa for Christmas." This last statement sounded like a rebuke.

"Yes, I did. It was nice to see my family." Marcail's voice was friendly, but she struggled with the feeling that she'd done something wrong by not checking with Mrs. Duckworth before leaving. The feeling increased when she noticed Mrs. Duckworth's scrutiny of her new coat and boots.

Marcail's chin rose slightly as Mrs. Duckworth's gaze met her own. The younger woman's eyes were calm, and there was no sign of the groveling this tyrannical woman was usually afforded from the Willits townspeople.

Mrs. Duckworth found herself wondering how she could have admired the girl's spunk on their first meeting. At the moment she found Marcail's confidence quite rude. Were it not for Sydney's admiration of her, she'd be tempted to give her the sack for such impertinence.

"I won't keep you," Marcail said after a moment. "I'll see you on Monday, Sydney. Good day, Mrs. Duckworth."

Marcail waved and went on her way. She wasn't long in town that day, and once she got home and began her laundry she found her mind straying back to Mrs. Duckworth. No one should have the godlike power that Mrs. Duckworth wielded. Of course, that was the problem—no one was bold enough to tell her so.

Marcail realized with a start that *she* was bold enough, but knowing the people of Willits would suffer for her words stopped her in her tracks.

Marcail spent the day thinking about why, beyond her teaching position, God might have brought her to Willits. Often she was tempted to quit, but God always detained her with a gentle reminder that her example to the townspeople, her students, and especially Sydney might bring them to a saving knowledge of Jesus Christ.

Sixteen

MARCAIL'S HAND WENT to the back of her neck to rub at a sore spot. It was a cloudy Friday afternoon, and the children had been gone for about 15 minutes. From her place at the desk, Marcail glanced outside and stared for a moment.

It took some seconds to realize it was snowing. A few inches had already accumulated on the ground from the two different nights it had snowed, and for an instant Marcail thought her eyes were playing tricks on her.

Finally convinced that snow was falling, Marcail rose quickly from her desk and hurried toward the door. She pulled the school door shut behind her and stood for a moment, her face lifted toward the sky.

Marcail Donovan had never seen it snow. Having grown up in the tropics and then living in Santa Rosa, where it had snowed only twice and at night when they were all asleep, left her more than a little curious and excited about actually watching it snow.

In a near trance she walked down the steps with her hands spread wide to catch the white particles falling to the ground. Her tongue came out as she tried to taste a snowflake.

She had not taken time to grab her coat and was surprised at how warm it felt outside with only her sweater. Marcail began walking toward the trees that lined the road in the distance, loving the way the snow looked against the backdrop they formed. She entered a small copse of oaks and spent the next 20 minutes alternating between standing under their shelter and dashing out into the snow to make new tracks and feel the cold flakes on her face.

Marcail became aware of the cold about ten minutes too late. She wrapped her sweater a little more tightly about her and scolded herself for not taking her coat. The clouds had thickened and the wind had picked up suddenly, and as Marcail came back onto the road she realized that having the snow blowing in her face was no longer fun.

She squinted against the sting in her eyes and wondered how she could have been so foolish as to come this far from the school. She decided to make a run for it, and ran a good 30 yards before realizing she was going in the wrong direction. She turned back, but the wind caught her breath so suddenly that she decided to take refuge once again under the trees.

At what she assumed to be the edge of the road, Marcail tripped. She fell hard onto her face, her dress suddenly feeling very wet. Marcail began to shiver so severely she could hardly stand up. When she finally pushed off the ground, she was certain she was heading toward safety, but only a few steps told her she was guessing.

She pressed on, praying for help. Suddenly a dark object loomed before her. For an instant Marcail thought she had found the schoolhouse, but by then she didn't really care. Her only concern was to escape the freezing wind and somehow warm her icy limbs.

The exterior of the building was rough under her hands as Marcail felt her way around a corner. She nearly missed the odd latch on the wall before her. She fumbled for just a moment before the door slid open and the wind nearly blew her inside. Marcail gasped for every breath as she slid the door shut. She turned and leaned against the wall and then blinked in confusion. Dr. Montgomery was headed toward her with a lantern held high.

"I got caught in the snow," Marcail's voice shook as the doctor approached in disbelief.

"Where is your coat?" Alex asked, as he moved to the single window by the door and peered through the glass.

Marcail couldn't answer. Every part of her body was beginning to go numb, and all she could do was shake her head.

"Let's get you to the house," Alex said, more to himself than anyone else. As he moved to hang the lantern, he heard Marcail's softly spoken "No."

Alex turned back and stared at her.

"I'll just stay here until I get warmer," the young schoolteacher stuttered as she rubbed furiously at her arms.

Knowing that now was not the time for discussion, Alex did not hesitate for a moment. He hung the lantern, blew it out, and moved toward Marcail. She couldn't see him approach, so she jumped as a hand touched her in the darkness.

"Put this on," Alex was saying, and Marcail felt a coat surround her.

Before Marcail even had time to enjoy the warmth of the coat, the barn door was thrown open. She let out a small scream when she was suddenly tossed over the doctor's shoulder. Marcail had no time to comment on her position, since Alex was already moving swiftly through the blizzard toward the house.

"No" was the emphatic reply. "I'll be dry in a little while."

Staring at the tiny woman before him who was shivering from head to toe, Alex pulled to the fore what was certain to be the last of his patience.

"You can't stay in that dress," Alex said for the fifth time. "It's wet and you're *freezing*. Now please go and change into the nightgown I've laid out for you, because if you don't take yourself out of those wet things, Miss Donovan, I'll do it for you."

"You can't treat me this way. I'm a grown woman."

"Then act like one," Alex snapped.

Marcail stood mute with embarrassment. Alex's jaw tensed, and a moment later he had his guest by the arm and was leading her to the bedroom. Once inside, he pulled her sweater off before she had time to think. He then spun her around and unbuttoned the back of her dress. Marcail gasped in surprise, but was given no time to respond before she was spun once again, this time to face the doctor, her eyes so big they nearly swallowed her face.

"You will remove *everything* you are wearing," Alex held Marcail's shoulders, his head bent close to her face, his voice unrelenting, "and put on the nightgown. You will then come back out to the kitchen and sit by the fire. It's the only way you're going to get warm."

Alex's face and manner softened slightly as he felt her tremble under his hands, but he exited the bedroom and shut the door before she had time to notice.

Marcail stood alone in the bedroom, so angry and humiliated that she wanted to weep. She told herself that he was overbearing and rude. She also told herself that he was right; she was freezing.

Shame nearly overwhelmed her as she pulled the bodice of her dress down and remembered his unbuttoning the back. It took some minutes, but eventually Marcail had a pile of damp clothes on the floor and a white flannel nightgown in her hands. She was trembling so violently that she could barely lift it over her head. Once she did, she found herself enveloped in cloth. The nightgown was huge on her slight frame.

"Miss Donovan," Alex's voice called through the door.

"Yes?"

"Are you dressed?"

Marcail's answer was to open the door. Alex barely glanced at her attire before he placed a hand on her back and led her to the large upholstered chair that he'd drawn up in front of the stove. Before he gave Marcail a small push into the chair he wrapped her in a thick quilt.

In her frozen misery, Marcail was unaware of the way Alex retrieved her clothing, hung it to dry, and then fetched a mug and the pot from the stove.

"We have to get you warm, Miss Donovan" was all she heard before Alex bent over her with a steaming cup. He placed it against her mouth with one order.

"Drink."

Marcail did so, only to bury her face in the quilt a moment later in an attempt to evade the cup, as well as breathe past the acrid taste in her throat. He had given her the strongest coffee she'd ever tasted.

Alex tried to get her to drink more of the thick liquid, knowing how quickly it would warm her, but the sound of her small, choked voice begging him to stop was too much for him. He put the cup aside.

After Alex reached to put the mug on the table, he then shifted Marcail in the chair, moving her as though she were a doll so he would be certain every part of her was warm. He made sure her arms and shoulders were tucked into the quilt and then tugged one corner of the quilt up over her head until only her face showed. He pulled another chair close, sat down to face her, placed her feet in his lap, and wrapped yet another quilt around them.

Marcail looked at him through eyes that were beginning to blur, wishing he would go away. Her last thought before her body began to warm and sleep came to claim her was that this couldn't really be happening to her.

Seventeen

ALEX WOULDN'T HAVE believed that anyone could be sleeping as soundly as Marcail. She had fallen asleep over an hour ago and not moved a muscle, not even when he carried her to his bed and tucked her in. He assumed she would awaken before he was ready to go to bed himself, but she never stirred, not even when he banged around in the kitchen fixing some supper. He found himself checking her often to assure himself she was okay, but her breathing was regular and her pulse normal, so he had to assume that she was exhausted.

The snow was still falling steadily as Alex tried to make himself comfortable on the sofa in the living room. This was no easy task since the sofa was nearly a foot shorter than his 5' 10' frame.

He was covered with a warm quilt as he turned the lantern low and settled back to think on the events of the evening. Alex wondered if he would ever forget the way Marcail looked when she defied him about changing her clothes, or how small she had felt under his hands as he'd tucked the quilt about her.

A sudden feeling of dread overcame him. Alex wondered if Marcail would have any idea how a situation like this would be viewed by the town of Willits. He began to pray that God would uphold them both in the days to come, and that the townspeople, specifically Mrs. Duckworth, would be reasonable.

Marcail woke up and stretched luxuriously in the large bed. The smell of coffee assailed her senses, and for just an instant she smiled. A second later she sat up with a start and stared through the dim light at the strange dresser across the room from her and then at the bed in which she slept. Marcail's heart began to beat so hard she felt breathless. The bedroom door was open, and, moving very slowly, she walked to that door and looked at the man sitting at the kitchen table.

Alex, fully dressed for the day, looked up from his Bible to find his houseguest standing in the bedroom doorway, clutching the front of her nightgown.

"What time is it?"

"About 6:30."

"In the morning?" Marcail whispered.

Alex looked at her with tender compassion and rose to retrieve her clothing. "These were by the stove all night, so they're dry now."

Marcail took her clothes and thanked him, her voice stilted.

"I'll fix some breakfast whenever you're ready."

Again Marcail thanked him and stood staring at nothing, trying to come to grips with the fact that she'd spent the night at the doctor's house.

"Why didn't you wake me?"

"First of all you were so exhausted and sleeping so hard, I'm not sure I could have awakened you. And second, it was still snowing, so I didn't see any point."

Marcail didn't look to the window until he mentioned the snow. Alex watched as she moved slowly toward the window by the door and looked out. A white blanket stretched for as far as her eyes could see, and snow was still coming down. Strangely enough, the sight gave her comfort. The doctor had been given no choice, and Marcail's fear of her situation, if not the doctor, lessened to some degree.

She turned from the window, thanked Alex for drying her clothes, went into the bedroom, and shut the door. Her voice told him she was coming to accept the situation. Alex stood for a few moments outside the door, thinking as he did that Marcail didn't have an inkling of how the folks in town would react if they ever found out what had happened.

"What will you do if someone needs you in town?" Marcail asked from her place in front of the dishpan, relieved over having something to do.

Alex picked up a plate and started to dry. "If the bell rings, I'll try to get through."

"The bell?"

"Yes. Since I don't live in town, I have a bell outside of my office so people can call me here at home."

Light suddenly dawned for Marcail. "I've heard that bell at times and wondered what it was."

Alex didn't answer. He was too busy smiling over how long she was taking to wash a few dishes. She'd been extremely nervous at breakfast and had hardly eaten a bite. This surprised him because he knew she'd missed supper. He remembered then how wary she was of him, and found himself wishing he'd get called into town so he could leave her in peace.

"Will you take me home if you get called into town?"

The question seemed to come out of nowhere, but Alex had an answer. "I really doubt I'll be called."

"But if you are?" Marcail pressed him.

Alex didn't even hesitate. "No, it's too risky."

Marcail began to gnaw on her lower lip. Alex had seen her do this several times at the breakfast table when the silence between them had lengthened.

When Marcail was finished with the dishes, she turned to Alex with her hands clasped nervously in front of her. "All done," she said, stating the obvious.

"Thank you for your help."

"You're welcome. Is there anything else I can do?"

"Sure," Alex began, and Marcail missed the sparkle in his eyes. "I have several shirts that need to be mended and washed, and the bedroom needs dusting."

Once again, Marcail caught her lower lip between her teeth and nodded her head, taking in the orders with wide-eyed agreement. Alex's heart melted just a little at the sight of her.

"I'm teasing you," Alex said softly, and watched as she visibly relaxed and even laughed quietly. He also noticed that her cheeks were just a bit flushed.

"How about a game of checkers?"

Marcail agreed and looked as though Alex had thrown her a lifeline. He set up the checkerboard on the kitchen table, poured fresh cups of coffee, and settled down to play.

$\mathcal{E}$ighteen

THE TALK ACROSS the checkerboard was light for the most part, and Alex noticed that Marcail was relaxed around him until the conversation led to her calling him Dr. Montgomery, a name she nearly stumbled over.

Marcail noticed that Alex was an easygoing host who seemed to be a genuinely kind individual, but like all doctors she had encountered, he seemed just a bit too sure of himself. She wouldn't have called his demeanor outright arrogant, but it wasn't far off.

As they played, Alex coaxed Marcail into talking about her class, and when she was relaying something that Daisy Austin had said, he interrupted her.

"Since we're going to be spending the day together, why don't you call me Alex?"

Marcail hesitated, and Alex allowed her a few moments to think it over. "All right," she finally said and fell silent.

"You missed your turn."

Marcail stared at him in confusion. He'd just watched her move one of her checkers.

"It's your turn to tell me your name is Margaret, and that I can call you by your first name," Alex explained.

Again Marcail hesitated. "What if my name isn't Margaret?"

Alex blinked in surprise. "Didn't I hear your brother-in-law calling you Marg?"

"No. You heard Rigg call me Marc." She emphasized the hard c. "My family's nickname for Marcail."

"Marcail." Alex tested the name on his tongue and spoke sincerely. "That's a beautiful name. It fits you."

Marcail smiled at the compliment. The smile gave Alex courage.

"And may I call you Marcail?"

As he watched her with eyes that were a beautiful sapphire blue, he didn't seem quite so arrogant to Marcail. She found herself liking him just a little.

"That would be fine," Marcail told him, and then watched as he concentrated on his next move on the board. Alex took a little extra time, and Marcail's attention began to roam. A glance out the window told her it was still snowing steadily. Her gaze wandered around the room, and she noticed what a meticulous housekeeper Willits' doctor seemed to be.

There were wooden pegs by the back door, and his coat, her sweater, and some scarves were all hung neatly in line. Not a dish was out of place in the kitchen. There were high shelves along the wall, which led Marcail to believe his wife must have been a tall woman. All the cups, bowls, and plates were stacked in tidy rows, and beyond them sat Alex's black medical bag.

Until now, Marcail had taken little more than a glance at the living room, which sat in the long part of his L-shaped house. It was as neat as the kitchen, with a small sofa and chair, two tables, and a bookshelf.

Marcail's gaze moved to the bedroom door, where she remembered an orderly setting with two wardrobes, a dresser, and the bed. Her eyes slid back to the table where Alex's Bible was placed before one of the chairs.

Looking at his Bible made Marcail wish she had her own copy on hand. Realizing she couldn't remember where Alex's checkers had been, she glanced at the board suddenly and then at the man himself. She found him sitting back in his chair, one hand resting on the table, the other laying casually in his lap. He was studying her intently.

Marcail sat mute under his inspection, not able, for some reason, to take her eyes from his.

"Is there someone special back home, someone who tells you on a regular basis how beautiful you are?"

Marcail could only give a negative shake of her head.

"Since you don't hear it that often, I'll tell you. You're very beautiful."

Alex watched as she caught her lower lip under her teeth. His voice was filled with laughter when he spoke this time. "You're beautiful even when you're trying to chew off your lower lip."

Marcail's hand came up as though she'd never realized it was habit. Her action made Alex's eyes sparkle all the more. Not wanting to make her suffer overly long, Alex stood in one fluid motion.

"I need to go out to the barn to check on Kelsey." He threw these words over his shoulder as he headed for his coat and boots.

Marcail stood also. "Will you be all right?"

"I'll be fine. The wind has died down some, and I've strung a rope from the edge of the house to the barn. I use it as my guide. That's why I carried you over my shoulder last night; I needed one hand free."

Marcail blushed over the remainder, but Alex pretended not to notice. His hand was on the door when she called his name.

"Alex?"

He turned back, his brows raised expectantly.

"Thank you for bringing me out of the cold last night."

"You're welcome," he told her softly, before opening the door and disappearing into a flurry of snow.

"I can't think why this has happened, Lord," Marcail prayed in the empty house. "But I want to keep my eyes on You. Alex has been so nice, and he's not as scary as I first thought, but this feels very strange—this being snowed in with a stranger.

"It was silly of me to come out without my coat," Marcail continued to share with God from her heart, "but somehow I don't think it would have made any difference."

Marcail hovered at the window and continued to pray until Alex came back. She was unaware of the fact that Alex was lingering in the barn and doing a little praying himself.

"Please bless Marcail, Lord, and ease her anxiety over doctors. Help me to be gentle with her, and give her no reason to fear me. I'm so drawn to her, but I fear if I'm not careful, I'm going to scare her away forever."

Alex continued to pray and think of ways to make Marcail feel at home. Having many books in the house, he hoped she would feel free to sit down and become absorbed in one before he returned.

In an attempt to give Marcail some privacy, Alex didn't rush back to the house. He eventually slid the barn door back and made his way through 15 inches of wet snow. The wind was still blowing, but not as hard, and Alex thought he might be able to get Marcail home.

But then, why risk it, he reasoned to himself. *The damage is already done.*

Nineteen

"ARE YOU ALL right?"

"I'm fine, Marcail. Why wouldn't I be?

"You were gone so long, I thought you might have become lost."

Alex shook his head. "The wind has died down, and I could see the house as I moved from the barn."

"If it's that clear maybe I should head home. I mean, you've been very kind, but I really hate to take advantage of your hospitality or wear out my welcome."

Alex was tempted to tell her she could stay for the next 50 years and not wear out her welcome, but he kept this thought to himself.

"Even though the wind has died down and it's stopped snowing, the sky looks like it could dump again at any moment. I'm sure you have things to do at home, but we had both better stay put for the time being," Alex told her reasonably.

Marcail nodded and then glanced around uncomfortably for something else to say. It was still a little unbelievable to her that she was snowed in with this man. Since it was still early, it was also hard for Marcail to face the fact that they were going to be together for the remainder of the day. She was wondering what they would find to talk about when Alex spoke.

"By the way, what were you doing out in the snow, and where is your coat?"

"My coat is at the schoolhouse. I was working after the children left when I noticed the snow coming down. I'd never seen it snow before, and I—"

"You'd never seen it snow before?" Alex interrupted her.

"No, and I never meant to wander so far from the school—"

"But I thought it snowed in Santa Rosa once in a while."

"It does, but I've only lived there since I was nine. The two times it did snow, it was in the middle of the night and had stopped before I got up." Determined not to let Alex interrupt her again, Marcail quickly finished her explanation. She then fell silent.

Too busy thinking about how terrified she must have been, Alex wasn't about to break in again. He pictured her wonder and delight over the snow, and then without warning, her terror in finding herself blinded by the wind and stinging flakes, lost and freezing. A thought suddenly occurred to him.

"Were you hurt yesterday in any way?"

"No, I'm fine."

"You didn't fall or anything?"

"I did fall once, but I'm not hurt."

Alex eyed her speculatively, wanting to believe her but afraid her fear was overruling her good sense. "I think you might find that, as a doctor, I'm really not so bad," he told her quietly.

Alex watched as Marcail's face heated. It made the skin on her cheeks look as soft as rose petals, and even though Alex told himself he was embarrassing her, he could not drag his eyes away.

"Could I have another cup of coffee?" Marcail finally said in a small voice, all the while telling herself not to bite her lip.

"Sure." The question was enough to tell Alex that even if she was hurt, he was not going to know about it. He turned toward the stove, and Marcail once again sat at the kitchen table.

"If you like to read, I have a shelf full of books in the living room." Alex said as he filled her mug. "I need to do a little baking, so please, make yourself at home."

"Can I help with anything?"

"I don't think so, but I'll let you know."

Marcail wandered into the living room then, and even though the light was dim, she could see the titles. She selected a fat volume from the lower shelf and went back to the kitchen table.

Alex had to quell the impulse to turn and begin talking to her once again. She fascinated him, and he found that he couldn't hear enough of her voice, or watch too many of the expressions on her face when she talked. Alex worked in silence for about 20 minutes, mixing dough for bread, before Marcail spoke.

"Where is the ulna?

Alex turned to her with a wide-eyed expression, but Marcail didn't notice. She was bent over one of his medical textbooks, studying it intently.

"In your arm," he told her simply.

"Where?" Marcail finally looked at him.

Alex raised his right forearm, pinky side toward his curious houseguest, and then drew the fingers of his left hand down the outside of his forearm from wrist to elbow.

"It's the bone right here on the little finger side of the forearm." Alex watched as Marcail inspected her own forearm and then went back to her reading.

Alex returned to his mixing bowl with a smile on his face. He found himself selfishly hoping it would continue to snow for days—anything to keep this precious girl close to him.

The sun broke through the clouds at about 2:30 that afternoon. The day had been spent in various pursuits, some idle, some intense, but all enjoyable. Marcail was becoming less tense as the day wore on, and Alex, as he offered to take her home, hoped that she would be a little more receptive to his suit in the very near future.

Even as the thought occurred to him, another thought, much more painful and dark, crowded into his mind. It came to fruition as he and Marcail approached her house and found several men from town, including Rowie Kilmer, in her front yard.

"Miss Donovan," Mr. Flynn called to her as Alex held her under the arms and lowered her to the bottom step of her porch. "We were just about to organize a search for you."

"Oh, Mr. Flynn, I'm sorry you were worried."

"Well, we're just glad that Dr. Montgomery found you," he assured her warmly. "You must have gone out early this morning, since the fire is out in your stove."

"Actually," Marcail explained with an embarrassed smile, "I got caught out yesterday."

Marcail failed to notice the change on Mr. Flynn's face or how still the other men had become. Alex, on the other hand, did not miss a single expression.

"Are you saying that Dr. Montgomery is just now bringing you home?" Mr. Flynn questioned her softly.

"Well, yes," Marcail continued, still unsuspectingly. "I got caught in the white-out yesterday, and as you know, the sky didn't clear until just a short time ago."

Since she was moving up the steps toward the door, Marcail again missed the men's faces. She called over her shoulder that the men could come inside out of the cold, but she didn't immediately notice when they failed to follow her or respond.

Once she was out of earshot, Alex spoke to Mr. Flynn, whose eyes were leveled on the younger man.

"You know better than to think what you're thinking, Stan."

"I realize that, Alex," he answered, his voice measured. "But have you given any thought as to how this is going to be received?"

"I've given it plenty of thought, but there wasn't much I could do. Maybe the board would feel better if you had found Miss Donovan's body frozen somewhere here in the woods, instead of healthy and completely innocent about what is going through your minds."

Mr. Flynn nodded, his expression pained, and Alex let his gaze wander to the other men. Most were very worried. One wore a smirk that Alex wanted to wipe off, and Rowie was clearly furious.

Marcail came back to her front door. When she could see that no one was going to come in, she thanked the men, closed the door, and restarted the fire in the stove. It briefly crossed her mind that the men were acting strangely, but within minutes her thoughts were on the late hour of the afternoon and how much she wanted to get done before bedtime.

Twenty

ALEX HAD TO turn his face away from the pain and confusion he saw in Marcail's eyes. He had not approached her at church for fear of making a bad situation worse, but the desire to sit next to her, put his arm around her, and tell her everything was going to be fine was over-whelming.

But telling her such a thing would be a lie. Everything was not going to be fine, at least not for a while. Alex knew with a dreaded certainty that in order to make things "right," Marcail was going to have to make some painful decisions. He missed every word of the sermon while he prayed for Willits' young schoolteacher.

Marcail was cut to the quick when Allie Warren walked past her without a word. She knew her friend had seen her, but Marcail watched as Allie kept her face averted, even when she called a greeting to her.

It had taken half the morning, but the innocent Miss Donovan finally understood that this sudden, cold treatment from the people at church had to do with her spending a night at Dr. Montgomery's home. Her first reaction was shock, and then outrage at what they must have been thinking.

It didn't seem to matter that she'd have frozen to death if Alex hadn't rescued her. In the eyes of the towns-people, she had acted outside the bounds of propriety, and that was not to be tolerated. Feeling lonely and rejected, Marcail walked home from church alone. It was the first week she hadn't been asked to join one of the town's families for Sunday dinner.

She spent the day praying, overcoming her hurt, and working on her lessons for the following week. It was almost a relief to realize that she wouldn't have to see anyone but her students until the following Sunday. Marcail, who still did not grasp the severity of the situation, hoped that everyone would be over their upset by then.

Marcail looked into the uncertain faces of the six children in her class and wanted to cry. She had hovered around the door for an hour after she rang the bell, finally accepting the fact that most of the town's families were not going to send their children to school.

The Austins, Vespermans, and Whites had sent their children, and after Marcail directed them to read silently in their readers, she sat at her desk and decided what course of action to take.

First of all, she knew that the children who *had* come to school deserved her undivided attention as well as all the instruction she could offer them. Second, she would dismiss a little early and pay a visit to Mr. Flynn. Marcail, after coming to these conclusions, settled down to the teaching at hand.

"Mr. Flynn, I would be happy to stand before Mrs. Duckworth and the entire school board and attest to the fact that Dr. Montgomery was the soul of propriety while I was in his home."

"I have no doubt that he was, Miss Donovan, but you've watched Mrs. Duckworth; you've seen the way she runs things in this town. You know that the hands of all the people whose buildings and businesses are owned by her are tied."

"In other words," Marcail spoke with a sinking feeling of dread as his words finally became clear to her, "you want my resignation?"

"I'm afraid I do." He spoke with visible regret. "I was coming to see you about it this afternoon."

"And if I refuse?" Marcail asked, telling herself not to cry.

"Then the majority of your class will not be receiving an education, because they will be kept out of school as they were today."

Marcail had thought the way Mr. Flynn's hands were tied concerning Sydney was awful, but this was atrocious. Her voice said as much when she spoke.

"And if I went to Mrs. Duckworth myself?"

"As before with Sydney, it would only make matters worse."

Marcail sat in silence for a moment. Mr. Flynn could only watch her. At length she stood.

"The word 'quit' has never been a part of my vocabulary, Mr. Flynn, and I don't care to add it now. I'm going to continue to teach at the Willits school whether there is one child in my class or 30. Maybe when the people in this town grow tired of having their lives dictated by one woman, they'll send their children to be taught. It's my hope that if enough of you take a stand, you can make a difference."

Marcail walked out of Mr. Flynn's office without saying goodbye, wondering as she went if she could really hold to all she said.

Twenty-One

Marcail's emotions were in tatters by the end of the week. She'd had only six children to teach and was beginning to regret everything she'd said to Mr. Flynn.

For the first time in her life she was honestly thinking of quitting. In fact, this idea pressed upon her so strongly she walked to the train station to check the schedule for southbound trains.

It was late Saturday afternoon, and even though she was low on flour, sugar, and coffee, she had not come into town for any other reason that day. She felt curious eyes on her as she walked, and nearly turned back home before reaching her destination.

The train station was very quiet at that time of the day. Feeling like a coward, Marcail walked toward the far side of the train office, knowing it would be even more deserted. She slipped around to the front of the office just long enough to read the departure times, and then quickly back to the far side of the building—and into the arms of Rowie Kilmer.

Marcail gasped in surprise and would have taken a step backward, but Rowie had a hold of her arm and drew her up close to the side of the small structure.

"It was all a lie, wasn't it?"

"What was?" Marcail's voice was breathless with fear and a little bit of pain.

"All your talk about teaching. All your denials about wanting to get married. They were all lies."

"No, Jethro, they weren't. I'd have frozen if Dr. Montgomery hadn't taken me in."

As usual, Rowie wasn't listening. "Wasn't I good enough for you? Didn't you think I could take care of you like he could?" His hand tightened on Marcail's arm, and she flinched. "You didn't do nothing but lie, telling me no and then giving favors to the doc in front of the whole town."

If Marcail could have moved she would have slapped him. She began to struggle, but he was so much stronger it did no good. A feeling of panic began to overtake her. She would have cried out, but again he tightened his hold and her cry turned into another gasp.

Marcail watched Rowie looking around as if he planned to drag her somewhere. With his attention momentarily diverted, she threw back her head to yell, but a voice stopped her.

"I might be mistaken, Rowie, but I believe you're hurting Miss Donovan."

Marcail and Rowie's heads turned sharply with surprise, and Marcail could have wept at the sight of Alex Montgomery. This time when Marcail pulled her arm, Rowie freed her. She walked on trembling legs toward the doctor.

"So that's the way it is between you two?" Rowie said with a shake of his head. "Well, you haven't let anyone know, so you can't blame a guy for thinking she's up for grabs."

Alex saw no point in arguing with him, even though he was sickened by Rowie's words about Marcail. It was hard to stay silent, but it helped to have Rowie leave as soon as he'd had his say. Alex looked at Marcail as the other man backed out of sight. She looked devastated. He felt her trembling as he took her arm and led her from the train station.

Marcail didn't speak as Alex led her to the livery. He claimed Kelsey and began the walk toward Marcail's house, leading the horse. When Marcail still hadn't spoken at the edge of town, Alex began to question her.

"Are you all right?"

"Yes." Marcail wasn't, but she didn't know how to begin telling him how much she hurt inside. And besides, he was a doctor of the body, not the heart.

Alex knew she was far from "all right," but he had no idea how to question her. She didn't thank him or even look at him as he opened her door and waited for her to go inside. He stepped in behind her.

"Will you be okay now?"

"Yes, thank-you" was the wooden reply.

Alex felt concerned over her lack of response. He reached out and touched her shoulder.

"Marcail, I'm going to come by in the morning. We need to talk."

"In the morning?"

"Yes, but right now I think you should get some rest."

She was finally looking at him.

"Did you hear me?"

Marcail nodded slightly.

"I'll be by in the morning before church."

Again she nodded, and Alex felt there was nothing more he could do. With a heavy heart he turned toward the door, praying that Marcail would get a good night's sleep.

Twenty-Two

ALEX WAS AT Marcail's front door nearly three hours before church was scheduled to begin. She was up and dressed, her hair in place, but looking so pale Alex feared she might be ill. She greeted him soberly, and Alex thought she might be working hard at fighting the fear over why he was there.

"Would you like some coffee?" Marcail offered while Alex removed his coat.

He accepted the offer, taking a place at the kitchen table. He thought to kill some time before he asked Marcail something that was sure to upset her. But while he still had coffee in his mouth, Marcail spoke.

"I'm not really sure why you've come by this morning, Dr. Montgomery."

So *we're back to Dr. Montgomery,* Alex thought before he answered her question.

"I think we need to talk about what's happened in the last week," he told her quietly. "In fact, I have a question to ask you, maybe two." He paused until he was sure he had Marcail's full attention.

"Marcail, are you going to leave the teaching position here in Willits?"

Marcail did not understand immediately. She sat for long moments in quiet thought. When she did speak, her voice was soft and sure.

"No, I'm not. I've thought about nothing else all week, and I just can't leave these children. I might be sorry, and I might change my mind later, but right now I'm going to stay here and teach."

"Then I'll ask my second question." Alex cleared his throat. "Will you marry me?"

Marcail stared at him, completely nonplussed. Alex could see that he'd shocked her speechless, but he'd given this idea much thought and prayer in the last week, and he honestly believed it was the best course of action. He began to explain his position before Marcail could voice her thoughts.

"I'm not going to tell you that your decision to stay here is wrong, but I can tell you that it's not safe for you to remain single. I think Rowie proved that yesterday. And if you do stay single, you'll not have any children to teach."

Marcail looked crushed. "I thought that if I could only tough it out, that they would all send—"

Marcail stopped speaking as Alex slowly shook his head.

"Marcail," Alex implored her. "Try to understand Cordelia Duckworth. She has an impossibly strict code of morality; it's like a sickness with her. In her eyes you've sinned, and our marriage would make an honest woman of you."

"You can't really be telling me that my class is going to come back if I marry you?" Marcail's head was beginning to clear, and a myriad of questions buzzed through her mind.

"That is exactly what I'm telling you. I've lived in this town for seven years, and I know the way these people think. By little choice of their own, most of their lives revolve around Cordelia Duckworth. If she disapproves of you, you're finished."

Marcail came to her feet. Alex watched as she paced the small area in front of her stove.

"I've prayed so fervently that I would be a light to this town, and now my testimony here is ruined. In fact, by marrying you, I'm really saying that I do have something to be ashamed of."

"I'm sure some will see it that way, but they'll have the same opinion if you leave."

Marcail wished she could wake up from this nightmare. "I just want to teach school," she finally said, her hands spread wide in what might have been supplication.

"I realize that," Alex's voice was compassionate. "And you could do that in another town. But unless you're willing to be married, you're not going to teach in Willits."

Marcail began to pace again and then stepped to the window and looked out. *It would be so easy to run away,* she told herself. *I*

*could pack my bag and go to Santa Rosa or Visalia; everyone in the family
would understand. But I've always done that. I've always run to them for
help, and this time I want to stand on my own. I want to show them that
I've really grown up.*

He makes it sound so simple. Just marry him and I can teach school.
Marry him! *I didn't think I'd be married for years. And he's a* doctor!
I'd be married to a doctor!

Such were Marcail's thoughts for a good ten minutes as she
stood before the window. Knowing how upsetting his offer had
been, Alex remained silent.

Alex, on the other hand, found the idea of being married to
Marcail nothing short of splendid. He knew that it wouldn't be easy
at first, but Alex recognized that she wasn't a quitter, and neither
was he. He truly believed they could make a go of it.

He was beginning to wonder how long he would have to wait
for an answer when she suddenly turned and asked him when he'd
come to know the Lord. He didn't really need to answer, because
Marcail could tell by his very life that he was set apart. Many people
in town attended church, but only a few, Alex included, were obviously sold out for God.

He answered her briefly, and since she shared her own testimony as soon as he was finished, she must have been satisfied.
Marcail fell silent and again Alex waited, knowing that she was
going to say yes, but obviously still struggling to accept it all.

"When were you thinking we would do this?" Marcail asked
softly, as the immensity of the situation began to weigh upon her.

"This afternoon." Alex could see he had shocked her once
again.

"This afternoon?"

"Yes. I thought we should go to church together and talk to
Pastor Zimler right after the sermon. Word will be out by this evening, and your classroom will be full in the morning."

Your classroom will be full in the morning had been Alex's exact
words. Marcail couldn't help but wonder if he didn't feel a little
used. She was standing in Dean and Kay Austin's bedroom collect-
ing herself to become Mrs. Alexander Montgomery.

The morning had fairly flown by. She and Alex had attended
church together, drawing speculative glances from every corner of
the building. After the service they immediately approached Pastor
Zimler about marrying them. He had seemed quite honored by the
request and agreed immediately.

Marcail knew her father, before agreeing to anything, would have questioned them at length, as he did all couples seeking to be wed, but Pastor Zimler didn't seem to have a single reservation. Marcail wondered if he wasn't a little oblivious to all that was happening in his own town.

Dean and Kay Austin must have sensed something was afoot; they stayed at the rear of the church until Alex and Marcail were through with the minister. When Alex saw them and explained their decision, the Austins offered their home for the nuptials.

It's not too late, Marcail, she told herself. *If you want, you can walk out there and tell Alex that it won't work.* But as soon as the thought of never seeing Alex again formulated, Marcail felt something akin to grief.

He's giving you a chance to repair the damage that's been done. And you know he must care for you to some degree or he would never have offered. You could leave, but it's time to grow up and face this problem! Marcail's thoughts continued to run in all directions until someone knocked on the door.

"Come in," she called, and watched as Alex slipped into the room and shut the door. He came and stood directly in front of her.

"Change your mind?" he asked softly.

"I don't know," she answered honestly. "The situation is terribly overwhelming, Alex, but I'm terribly afraid that I could be making the biggest mistake of my life."

Alex reached with a gentle hand and smoothed the hair over Marcail's ear. His eyes were loving, as was his voice, when he spoke.

"I don't believe this will be a mistake, Marcail. It's true that we don't know each other, but I've prayed for a long time about another wife. And now you need to either leave town or take a husband. If you choose the latter, I'm more than willing to be that man."

It was one of the most precious things Marcail had ever had said to her. A peace settled over her as she looked into the kind eyes of this gentle stranger. Her expression was serene when she nodded her head. Alex took her hand within his own and led her out to stand before the preacher.

Twenty-Three

MARCAIL MONTGOMERY STOOD in the kitchen of the little house next to the school and knew that she would not be back, at least not to live. After leaving Austins, Alex had dropped her off so she could collect her things. Now she was ready and feeling just a bit bewildered over the events of the day. One hour ago she had married a near stranger.

Her mind moved abruptly to her brother, Sean, who had been forced into a marriage with his wife, Charlotte. When Marcail had first heard their story and seen the love that had grown between them, she thought it was the most romantic thing on earth. But in truth, this business of being married to a stranger was rather frightening.

A knock at the door interrupted Marcail's tempestuous thoughts. She hadn't heard Alex's horse, and not wanting to see anyone from town, she opened the door tentatively. Allie stood on the porch, her face a mask of pain. Marcail swung the door wide and as soon as it closed, the friends embraced.

"I'm sorry, Marcail. I'm so sorry." Allie was openly sobbing. "I feel just awful about last week, but Mama insisted I stay away." Allie sniffed, calmed somewhat, and then went on quietly.

"I told her you weren't guilty of anything, but she just kept saying I wasn't to have anything to do with you. We had a big fight just now, and I stormed out and came over here. My only regret is that I didn't do it a week ago."

"Oh, Allie—"

"Don't say it, Marcail," Allie cut her off. "Mama is in the wrong. If we've had a fight, it's our own fault not yours."

Marcail felt terrible, but stayed quiet. She watched as Allie suddenly noticed the table where her one bag sat, filled once again with her belongings. The shopping basket that Mr. Vesperman had given her, filled with the few food items she'd had on hand, was also on the table.

"Where are you going?" Allie asked, her eyes begging Marcail not to leave.

"Dr. Montgomery and I were married an hour ago. When he saw how impossible it was for me here, he offered his hand. He'll be here any minute to take me . . ." Marcail hesitated, "home."

Allie burst into tears all over again, and nothing Marcail could say would comfort her.

"This isn't what you want, Marcail," Allie wailed. "That old hag on the hill has forced you into this, and I know you'll just be miserable."

"I'm all right, Allie, really," Marcail tried to assure her. After a few moments the older girl calmed down enough to listen.

"Alex has been very kind, Allie, and I *agreed* to marry him. No one is forcing me. I'm sure it's going to be a little strange at first, but I'm trusting God to take care of me and the marriage."

Allie nodded, the misery on her face receding. Although she didn't agree with Marcail's belief that Jesus Christ was God, she admired her for her faith and stamina. The young women continued to talk for a few minutes, and when Allie saw that Marcail was really all right, she said she had to be going. They planned to talk again soon, and the new Mrs. Montgomery saw her friend to the door.

Marcail, thinking Allie was alone, was surprised to find Seth Porter outside in the cold, waiting in a small buggy. He didn't seem put out; his warm smile and wave were genuine. He jumped easily to the ground to assist Allie with tender care into the small seat. As they drove away, Seth's arm around Allie, Marcail couldn't help but envy the obvious love between them.

Alex walked out of the barn with Kelsey, wishing, not for the first time, that he owned a buggy. He had a feeling that Marcail would never complain, but he certainly wished he didn't have to take his bride home on the front of his horse.

As it turned out, Alex found himself wishing Marcail would complain, or at least say *something*. She was totally silent on the ride to the house. He hadn't expected her to share her life story the first evening, but her silence concerned him.

The reason didn't really occur to him until he saw her into the house. Then he noticed that she looked everywhere but the bedroom. He thought to bring up the subject of their sleeping arrangements after supper, but since his wife was obviously scared to death, he knew he'd have to mention it as soon as he got in from the barn.

Marcail's view of Alex's house was vastly different this time—she knew it was now her home. Standing in the opening between the kitchen area and the living room, she looked her fill. Nothing had changed except herself.

At last Marcail forced herself to look toward the bedroom door. Her lower lip went unconsciously between her teeth. This was her wedding night, and she was terrified. Marcail and Kaitlin had talked on several occasions, and her older sister had assured her with complete confidence that there was nothing whatsoever to be afraid of when a husband and wife loved each other. It was glaringly evident at the moment, however, that Katie had never mentioned the possibility of the couple *not* loving each other.

Alexander returned to the house to find Marcail's face completely drained of color, and his bride biting on her lower lip as though she no longer had need of it.

"Marcail," Alex spoke her name and watched as she turned to him with wide, terrified eyes. That she'd been working herself into a fine state of panic was obvious.

"Marcail," he started again. "I don't feel there is any reason to rush anything. I mean, we both need some time to feel a little more comfortable with each other."

Marcail looked very surprised at this announcement. What she couldn't know was that the fear Alex saw on her face was enough to stop him in his tracks. The last thing he wanted was to scare her, and since she'd already been doing a fine job of that herself, he knew that his next words, although difficult, were necessary.

"I want you to take the bedroom, and I'll sleep out here on the sofa."

"Do you mean that?"

Alex nodded, seeing that he'd instantly freed her from a load of fear. He moved toward the bedroom, intending to clear some dresser drawers for her, but spun back on her softly spoken "No."

"I mean," Marcail explained to Alex's shocked countenance, "that you should stay in the bedroom and I'll take the sofa."

"No, I think—" Alex began to protest, but Marcail forestalled him.

"It's silly for you to be on a sofa that's obviously too small for you. I would fit very nicely, and I won't put you out of your bed."

Alex was shaking his head, and Marcail asked him a question that settled the entire argument.

"How well did you sleep on the sofa the night I was here?"

Alex opened his mouth and then shut it again. She was right, but he wanted to make her feel comfortable and at home, and he knew she would have less privacy in the living room.

Marcail could see she had won, and with a decisive nod of her head took her bag into the living room and set it next to the sofa.

Twenty-Four

MARCAIL WAS UP, dressed, and out of the house Monday morning before Alex stirred. It felt odd for her to wake up in his home, and Marcail, not knowing Alex's schedule, had been careful not to wake him. She skipped breakfast in order to be quiet, but she had packed some bread and two cookies for lunch.

As she moved toward the schoolhouse, Marcail skirted the sloppy areas of the road where the snow had melted into giant puddles. She prayed that her class would arrive as Alex predicted. Questions ran through her mind about what she would do if the children didn't show, but she prayed and gave her worry to God every time it reared its ugly head.

The stove was a bit stubborn, but Marcail was determined to ward off the chill in the air. The logs had finally lit when Alex walked in and joined her by the stove. Marcail felt herself blushing, although she didn't know why.

"Good morning." Alex's voice had that distinct early morning growl.

"Good morning."

"Do you always come to school this early?" he asked his new wife.

"Only on Mondays. The stove hasn't been lit all weekend, and I usually need a little more time."

"It didn't look as though you had any breakfast or even coffee. Were you afraid of waking me?"

Marcail looked uncomfortable. "I'll be all right, and I have some bread for lunch."

"Maybe we should sit down tonight and compare schedules. I like to get up early, and I never intended for you to walk all this way in the mud."

"Please don't feel like you need to give me a ride, Alex. I really didn't mind the walk."

Alex didn't reply right away. "I'll see you this afternoon. Have a good time with the kids today."

With that, Alex cupped Marcail's jaw in his long-fingered hand and placed a kiss on the tiny mole that sat at the corner of her mouth. He had kissed her the same way moments after they'd been pronounced husband and wife.

Alex didn't look back as he left or he'd have found his wife watching him, her lower lip tucked neatly between her teeth, and her finger on the spot he'd just kissed.

It took most of the day for Marcail to really believe that her marriage had brought her students back to school. Her classroom was full, and other than a slight change in Sydney's disposition, things were as usual.

She told the children her new name and wrote it on the blackboard. Except for Sydney, very few children made mistakes with her new name as the day progressed. Marcail knew he wasn't even trying to call her by her married name.

It had never occurred to Marcail that the 11-year-old's infatuation with her would cause him to experience such violent jealousy, but it became suddenly evident with the way he grew angry when she gave special attention to any of the other boys. Now that she had married, he was becoming impossible.

Marcail was filled with compassion for the way he felt, but she knew she had to redevelop the respect they'd shared in weeks past. She decided to give him a few more days before she took him aside to insist that he call her Mrs. Montgomery.

The day flew by as Marcail knew it would, and just as she was dismissing the children, Alex came in the door. Most of her students greeted him cordially and by name. Marcail was amazed at how accepting they all seemed of the situation.

"I came by to give you a ride home," Alex offered. He knew he was staring, but Marcail appeared as fresh to him as she had been that morning, and he knew she'd just taught 19 children for seven hours.

"I appreciate the offer, but I was planning to walk into town. There are a number of things I—that is, *we*—need." It felt a little funny to be discussing this with Alex, but Marcail knew she was going to have to get used to it, and he didn't seem to notice her slip.

"All right," Alex agreed. "I'll walk with you, but then I need to return to the office. When you are finished, come by."

Marcail agreed and after gathering her things, preceded Alex out the door. They didn't talk much on the way into town, and Alex touched her arm by way of farewell when he left her at the door of the bank.

Marcail had to stand in line at the teller's window. She couldn't see around the tall man in front of her, but as soon as he moved, she was surprised to see that no one was there to help her. She waited only a moment before Mr. Flynn himself came from the rear of the bank.

"How are you, Mrs. Montgomery?" He hesitated over the name, but his eyes sought hers, begging her to understand his position.

"I'm doing very well, Mr. Flynn," Marcail told him graciously, even though she disagreed with the way he had handled things. She could see that her words lifted a burden of guilt from his shoulders, and he told her he would handle her transaction himself.

"I need three dollars from my account," Marcail explained. "And then I'd like you to close my account and move my money into Dr. Montgomery's account. I haven't checked with Alex, but is it all right to add my name to his account?"

"It's fine." Mr. Flynn's voice was hoarse, but Marcail didn't notice. For some reason, Marcail's request to join her funds to her husband's touched him deeply. His wife had told him she thought Miss Donovan was a very special young woman who deserved to be treated better than she was. Now he was convinced of it himself.

Marcail's next stop was Vesperman's General Store. She shopped carefully, thinking that she didn't really know Alex's tastes. Figuring she couldn't go wrong with the essentials, Marcail opted for flour, sugar, salt, soda, coffee, rice, and yeast. Her last item was a tin of salted peanuts. She knew it was an extravagance, but Marcail was in the mood to bake and knew these would be good in cookies.

The street was quite slushy, but Marcail took a long route to Alex's office and avoided most of the mud. She wasn't thrilled about being there, but with her hand on the door, she took a deep breath and went inside.

Twenty-Five

MARCAIL STOOD VERY still and looked around the small waiting room without really seeing anything. Her heart thundered in her chest, and even though she told herself to calm down, fear gripped her. She tried to examine the reason for her anxiety, but as in the past, the only thing that came to mind was her mother's face.

It wasn't at all logical, but for so many years it seemed to Marcail that it was the doctor's fault her mother had died. They had been a happy, settled family. Then, when Marcail was nine, the doctor had come to see Mother. He hadn't caused her illness, but he had diagnosed it, and Marcail had struggled for years to believe that none of her mother's rapid decline had been his fault. To this day she was terrified of doctors and everything relating to them.

Maybe her sister hadn't handled the situation very well; maybe Kaitlin should have insisted that Marcail see a doctor when she was sick. But because the mere mention of a visit from this dreaded man was enough to make any condition Marcail had worse, Katie had never insisted she go. Instead Katie herself talked with the doctor to find out how to treat her. Thankfully, there had never been anything more serious than a bee sting or a spring cold.

Now she found herself not only standing in the Willits' doctor's office, but actually married to the doctor himself. "Hi."

Marcail jumped at the sound of Alex's voice and wondered from where he had materialized.

"You looked lost in thought just then."

"I guess I was," Marcail answered as her gaze roamed the room. "I'm still getting used to the idea of being married to a doctor." Marcail didn't realize how that might have sounded until it was out of her mouth. Her gaze flew to Alex, but he was smiling.

"You're not easily offended, are you?" Marcail asked softly, more to herself than anyone else.

"No, I'm not," Alex answered, having heard her clearly. "As I said before, I like your honesty. Come, I'll take you home."

As with the few times she had ridden with Alex, Marcail tried to make herself as comfortable as possible without leaning on her new husband. Alex, however, had clearly tired of her trying to put space between them. His chest and arms surrounded her as he held the reins in an easy hold. Marcail wasn't sure how she felt about this, but the ride was brief, and she wasn't forced to examine her feelings too closely.

Alex tied Kelsey at the door and walked his wife inside. Marcail put her basket on the table and was removing her coat when she noticed that the furniture had been rearranged.

The kitchen table was closer to the bedroom door than it had been, and Marcail could not see the living room sofa from where she stood. She stepped into the living room and her eyes widened with surprise.

The small sofa was on another wall, giving Marcail's "bed" almost complete privacy from the kitchen area. One of the wardrobes had been moved from the bedroom along with a small chest of drawers. Alex had done a nice job of fitting in the added pieces to go with the tables, chair, and bookshelf. In short, he had given Marcail a very private area for sleeping and dressing.

"I put your blanket and pillow in the bottom of the wardrobe. That little dresser was in the barn, so you might want to wipe it out."

Marcail turned to the man who spoke softly behind her. "Thank you, Alex."

"You're welcome. I have to get back to the office, but I'll be home around 5:00."

He left then, and Marcail stood for a long time at the window watching him go. He was nothing whatever like she had imagined. What kind of man stepped in to rescue a woman in need and then rearranged his home to suit her when she was little more than a stranger?

No answers came to mind. Marcail knew that she could stand there all day and speculate, but that would accomplish nothing. With a determined stride she attacked her basket of groceries, putting everything away. She started supper, and then moved to the living room to settle her clothing in the dresser drawers and wardrobe.

The now-familiar headache was beginning, and Marcail had to stop herself from ripping the pins from her hair. Both she and Alex were swiftly losing all privacy, and Marcail couldn't dispel the feeling that she would be further embarrassed in front of Alex if he came home and her hair was down.

No one in Willits, save Allie and her mother, had ever seen her hair down, but Marcail knew that at least part of the reason for her maintaining the severe style lay elsewhere. She looked very young without the piles of thick hair atop her head.

But headache or no, there was work to be done, and Marcail set about her tasks. By the time Alex came in the door, supper was ready and Marcail's personal effects were all put away. They ate in companionable silence. After Alex helped with the dishes, he asked Marcail to come back to the table so they could discuss their schedules.

"Do you feel all right?" were the first words from Alex.

"Yes, I'm fine," Marcail answered him without thought.

What she didn't realize was that her pain showed on her face. Her forehead was slightly furrowed, and her eyes told Alex that she was tired, worried, or in some type of pain. He knew he couldn't push her, but he honestly wished she would tell him what was wrong.

Indeed, it was a good thing that Alex didn't push her, because Marcail wouldn't have known what he was talking about. Since she couldn't always take her hair down when she liked, her headaches had become a way of life with her. Had Alex pressed her, she'd have lost some of the ease she was beginning to feel around him.

"Now, about our schedules," Alex began, and they sat for over an hour comparing times and preferences for the weeks to come.

Alex's schedule was much more flexible, so he told Marcail he would be taking her to school and bringing her home each day, at least until the roads dried out.

They found that they both liked to go to bed at the same time and, with the exception of Saturday morning, got up within a half hour of each other. Marcail brought up the problem of disturbing Alex if she moved about in the kitchen. His response was a broad smile.

"If your banging around means that I get to wake up to a hot cup of coffee, you can bang all you want. At least I don't have to worry about waking you."

Marcail looked uncomfortable. "You know about that, do you?"

"Um hm. In fact, you scared me a little the night of the snowstorm. I kept checking your breathing to see if you were still with me."

"I sleep very soundly," Marcail explained unnecessarily.

"That, my sweet Marcail," Alex told her with a chuckle, "is a gross understatement."

Marcail couldn't help but smile in return. "My brother loves telling people how soundly Katie and I sleep. His favorite story is about the time he held me by my feet one night, my head nearly brushing the floor, and I slept through the whole thing."

"I can believe it. When I carried you to bed that night, I thought you would wake the moment I placed you against those cool sheets, but you only curled into a ball and slept the night away."

A faint blush began to cover Marcail's cheeks, and Alex's eyes sparkled impishly. "I have a sister who blushes as easily as you do, and I think I'd better warn you, my brothers and I tease the life out of her just to see it happen."

Alex shouted with laughter when Marcail's face became even redder. He watched as she bit her lip and sobered instantly.

"What does that worried look mean?"

"I've just never thought about meeting your family. I mean, I didn't realize you had a family." Marcail realized how silly that sounded as soon as she said it, but as she was coming to expect, Alex was amused.

"You must think that doctors crawl out from beneath rocks."

His words brought such a hysterical image to mind that a small laugh escaped Marcail before she could muffle it.

"So you think that's funny?" Alex tried to look indignant.

Marcail shook her head, but her eyes were brimming with laughter, and Alex would have been a fool to believe her.

"Well, you can laugh now, but I can tell you they'll show no mercy the first time they see those rosy cheeks."

Alex watched as Marcail suddenly grew very serious. It was on the tip of his tongue to ask what he'd said wrong when she spoke.

"Will they like me, Alex? I mean, your family. Will they be disappointed that you've married someone they don't know?"

"No." Alex's voice was now as serious as hers. "They'll love you the first time you meet. It's true that they're all a big bunch of jokers, but their hearts are warm and caring. You'll be taken into their hearts and lives as though you'd been there all along."

Marcail nodded, wanting so much to believe him, but still feeling uncertain. "How big is your family?"

"I'm the youngest of five. I have two brothers and two sisters. They're all married with children. My oldest sister and I are the only ones who live away from our hometown."

"And your folks—are they still living?"

"Yes, my father has been a doctor in Fort Bragg for years."

"Fort Bragg? That's out on the coast, isn't it?"

"Right. I think you'll like it when we get there. We have to take the logging train when we go, but once there, it's a great little place."

"Are we going soon?" Marcail asked tentatively, thinking it sounded like they were leaving in the morning.

"About ten days," Alex said with a wide-eyed look, realizing how presumptuous he'd been. "I always go home the weekend before my birthday. I just assumed you would go with me. I'm sorry I didn't check with you."

"Don't apologize. I'd like to meet your family; that is, if they really won't mind our being married and—"

Alex shook his head, and Marcail stopped.

"It's a long ride on the train, Marcail. I was wondering if you would have a problem with my asking Stan Flynn if you could have two days off?"

Marcail looked surprised, but didn't deny his request.

"I thought we would leave first thing Friday morning. That puts us in Fort Bragg in the afternoon, and I thought we'd come home on Monday."

"I don't have a problem with it. It would be a nice break, but I don't know how Mr. Flynn will feel." Marcail sounded as dubious as she felt.

"I'll talk to him. He knows he can be honest with me. Since I know he feels partly responsible for our being married, I somehow doubt he would deny us a little time away."

Marcail agreed, and they continued to talk for a while longer. She found out Alex's exact birthday and that he was going to be 31. With her birthday coming in March, it wasn't hard to figure that he was almost exactly 11 years older than she was. Marcail wasn't sure how she felt about that.

A half hour later it was heavenly for Marcail to finally take her hair down and crawl onto the sofa for the night. As she fell asleep with a dull headache, Marcail wondered if she should try to explain to Alex about her hair. As she pictured herself trying to do just that, the image caused her to blush all over again. Marcail told herself she was going to have to suffer through the headaches.

Twenty-Six

THE NEXT DAY Marcail sent a note home with Erin Vesperman in regard to Alex's birthday present. Marcail prayed that there would be enough time to order the new black leather satchel she'd spotted in one of Rigg's catalogs when she was home for Christmas. Why she'd been looking at the medical supplies, she wasn't sure, but she knew what she wanted and could only hope that Mr. Vesperman dealt with some of the same suppliers as Rigg.

Alex was a little late in claiming Marcail, but she had some work to do at the schoolhouse and didn't miss him. Their evening was much like the previous, with a quiet supper and talk across the table. Again, Marcail went to bed with a dull ache around her forehead, but as always, she slept soundly and woke up refreshed and ready to take on the day.

Alex had made the coffee that morning, and when Marcail was enjoying her second cup, he surprised her with a question.

"I don't want to put you on the spot, Marcail, but I was wondering—how do you feel about Dean and Kay Austin?"

"I think they're very nice." Marcail was a little taken aback by such a question.

Alex nodded. "The three of us have been meeting for Bible study on Wednesday nights for a long time, and I was wondering if you'd be interested."

"Alex," Marcail thought she understood, "you don't have to ask me. I know you have things you want to do that don't include me."

"That's just it—I *want* to include you. I want you to join us, but I don't want you to feel like you should."

"How do the Austins feel about my joining you?"

"Kay was in yesterday, making sure I planned on bringing you."

Marcail warmed with his words. It had seemed the majority of the town was against her. Then both Mary Vesperman and Cindy White had talked to her in the bank, telling her how much they appreciated her stand. And now knowing that the Austins wanted to include her in their Bible study meant more than Marcail could say.

"So you'll come?" Alex had seen the look of pleasure in her eyes.

"Yes, I'd love to."

"Great," Alex too was feeling very pleased himself. His Wednesday night study was important to him, both spiritually and emotionally, and he'd have definitely felt the void if Marcail had stayed home.

When Alex picked her up from school that afternoon, he surprised her with the news that Kay had asked them to supper that evening. He told Marcail when he would be back for her, and she took advantage of the time to do a little baking.

By the time Alex returned, Marcail was flushed from her baking efforts, but the cookie tin was full. Marcail also had a basket to go to the Austins.

"You've been busy," Alex commented with pleasure as his nose tested the air. "What is that I smell?"

"Probably the peanuts. I like cookies with peanuts in them."

Marcail held one out to her spouse and waited for the verdict. Her smile was triumphant at the look of rapture on his face.

"I take it you like them?"

Alex quickly schooled his features into a blasé mask. "They're pretty good, but it's hard to tell after just one. I'd better try another."

He started toward the basket, but Marcail neatly scooped it up with one hand and held it behind her back.

Alex's brows rose, along with the corners of his mouth, at her impertinence, and he came to stand very close to his wife. When Alex leaned very close and put his arms around her, Marcail began to wonder if she should have hidden the basket. He seemed to take an inordinate amount of time stealing a second cookie, and Marcail's face was a dull red by the time he finished.

Alex never took his eyes from his wife's face as he reached around her slight form and retrieved the cookie without ever touching her. As she watched him, Marcail had the sudden impression that Alex was not all that interested in the baked goods. The idea scared her a little and caused another emotion, one she could not define.

Alex kept his place by Marcail as he ate the second cookie, and did nothing this time to hide his pleasure.

"These are really excellent, did you know that?"

"I'm glad you came to that decision after only two; one more and you wouldn't want any supper."

"Now you sound like a teacher," Alex told her as he wiped the crumbs from his hands.

The smile Marcail gave him was brilliant. "I do, don't I?"

Alex only laughed, shook his head, and escorted his wife out the door.

Kay Austin said little to the new Mrs. Montgomery when she first walked in the door. Not until they were in the kitchen, and alone, did Kay give any hint as to what was on her mind.

"Are you all right?" Kay asked the question while looking directly into Marcail's eyes, and Marcail suddenly felt tears stinging her own.

Marcail nodded a little. "Why do you ask?" she whispered.

Kay hugged her before answering. "Because there was not one bit of color in your face when you were here on Sunday to marry Alex. I know Alex well enough to know that he's a very gentle and compassionate person, but this can't have been easy for you. So tell me, are you really okay?"

"It doesn't seem real yet," Marcail admitted softly. "And you're right, Alex couldn't be more kind, but he's still—" Marcail hesitated.

"A stranger," Kay finished for her. Marcail nodded. The older woman reached out and gently squeezed Marcail's arm.

"You can talk to him about anything," Kay told her. "He's very understanding, and he's also a man who really strives to obey God every day of his life. I know he prayed about marrying you and believed it to be the best thing, or he never would have asked.

"Maybe you think I'm being too optimistic, but years ago my older sister Addie was widowed suddenly while she had four children under the age of five. So her children could eat, she married a near stranger three months later. She and Hank have had a wonderful life together. In fact, Hank is a lot like Alex, with his gentle ways and quiet humor. As hard as it must be for you to believe this, I really think that the two of you will make a go of it."

Her words did much for Marcail's spirits, and the evening proved to be both relaxing and refreshing. After supper, Marla and Daisy went off to bed, and the adults gathered around the kitchen table for the Bible study. As they studied in the book of James, Marcail found out in a hurry that Alex, Dean, and Kay were serious about knowing God better and dedicating their lives to His glory.

Twenty-Seven

ALEX HAD BEEN in his office for two hours on Saturday morning before Marcail stirred from her sofa-bed. Sleeping in seemed almost decadent, but as tired as she'd been on Friday night, Marcail needed the extra rest.

There was cleaning to be done, clothes to be washed, and baking to be tackled. Alex had told Marcail he would not return until midafternoon, and Marcail took advantage of the privacy to bathe and wash her hair. She luxuriated in the water a little longer than she should have, but it felt so soothing that after scrubbing every inch of herself, she just wanted to relax.

Fifteen minutes later, Marcail was dressed in her undergarments and looking over her dresses. They all needed to be washed, but she wouldn't have anything to wear if she got all three of her dresses wet. She wished she'd brought a couple of work dresses from Kaitlin's until she suddenly remembered the several dresses hanging on the far end of her wardrobe. Marcail opened the second door, something she hadn't needed to do as yet.

Marcail had given little thought to the previous Mrs. Montgomery, but now as her hand went to the fabric of the dresses, her mind began to wander. What had she been like, and how much did Alex miss her? How long had she been gone? Did Alex know where she was spending eternity? And many more questions.

There were five print dresses and two solids. Marcail looked with some envy at the bright calico and gingham cloth, and then

328

noticed the sleeve of the blue gingham was torn. Marcail pulled this dress out and saw in an instant that it was different from the rest. It was faded and the top button was missing. Marcail knew by looking at the other gowns that this one was a wash-day dress.

Without giving herself much time to think, Marcail pulled the dress over her head. It had barely settled on her shoulders before one of Marcail's questions regarding Alex's first wife was answered—the dress was huge on her. Marcail suddenly remembered the nightgown Alex had given her the night they'd been snowed in, and wondered how she could have forgotten.

"Well, Marcail, what are you going to do?" the small brunette asked herself as she looked down at the way the dress hung on her frame. She knew she was wasting valuable time thinking about how she looked when her only plans were to wash and clean. Marcail swiftly buttoned the front that bagged enough to hold another person, and rolled up the sleeves that hung past her fingertips.

Her hair was still very wet, so after pulling the heavy tresses away from her face with a comb, she let the back hang free and went to work.

Alex was glad to leave the office for the day. He knew the bell could ring at any time, but he was looking forward to seeing Marcail and was anxious to discover how she had spent her day. It was incredible how often she was on his mind. After stabling Kelsey, Alex's step was swift to the front door.

Marcail had just taken two loaves of bread from the oven when the door opened. Thinking she'd heard Kelsey's hooves, she wasn't at all surprised when Alex walked in the door.

"Hello," Alex spoke as he hung his coat. Still wearing the workdress, Marcail was standing near the stove, bending over a pan of cookies. She missed the way he turned with a ready smile that died abruptly on his lips.

"Hi." Marcail spoke without turning. "I'm just about to put these cookies in so you'll have some dessert to eat after your lunch. You must be hungry, since you—"

Marcail didn't finish the sentence. She'd finally turned to find Alex staring at her, his face holding an expression she'd never seen before. They stood in silence for a moment, and then Marcail watched his gaze slide over her dress. A sinking feeling settled around her heart.

"I'm sorry about the dress, Alex," she said softly. "I wanted to wash all my dresses and just acted without thought. I should have checked with you before wearing one of your wife's dresses. Please forgive me. I won't do it again." Marcail could tell she was babbling, but he seemed so pensive.

"I never thought of Linette as being big," Alex finally said, "but that dress swallows you."

"I'll change just as soon as something is dry."

Alex shook his head and smiled. "There's no need. You should wear them if you can. As you said, they are my wife's dresses, and you're my wife."

Marcail nodded, but because he was still watching her, she was not convinced.

"I wouldn't have believed that you were hiding so much hair in that bun you wear." Alex's eyes took in the way her hair, so black it was almost blue, hung to her hips, each strand falling in a glossy wave and curling of its own accord at the end.

"I'll put it up," Marcail spoke, unable to keep the disappointment from her voice. It was the first time in days she didn't have a headache. She turned to find her box of pins.

"Don't pin it up on my account. I like your hair down."

Marcail turned back, afraid to believe what she'd heard. "You don't mind my wearing it down?"

"Not at all." Alex's voice was matter-of-fact.

"And you don't think I look 16?"

Alex smiled. "Sixteen," Alex let out a slow whistle. "That would make you roughly half my age, and that scares me a little. Right at the moment, you look like a girl playing house in her mother's dress, but no, Marcail, you do not look 16 with your hair down."

Marcail's relief was so obvious that Alex smiled again and wondered for an instant why she wore it up if she didn't want to. When she continued to smile, he wondered if she would still be smiling if she knew how much he wanted to hold her, letting her fill his arms the way she already filled his heart, or if she knew how badly he wanted a real marriage, and not just a marriage of convenience to salvage her testimony before the townspeople.

As he constantly did these days, Alex prayed for patience. He believed that if he could just give this woman time, court her, and tenderly care for her, they would someday have a marriage in every sense of the word.

That Marcail was unaware of his thoughts was obvious in the way she went about her business in the kitchen as though they'd been married for years. Alex silently congratulated himself for keeping the emotions he felt from showing on his face.

"How did things go at your office today?" Marcail asked as she poured Alex a second cup of coffee.

Alex was so surprised by the question that he didn't answer for a moment. He realized then that no one in Willits ever asked him that question. Linette had been burdened with a weak stomach and never wanted to talk about his work. His parents checked with him on a regular basis and nearly picked his brain dry when he went home, but that was only a few times a year. Alex suddenly recognized that he'd been lonely before Marcail, and that he'd missed someone taking a personal interest in his work.

"Things were fine. Saturday mornings are usually pretty hectic, but today was quiet. I was able to restock my bag, so if I'm called out, I'll be all set. Oh," Alex said abruptly, "I made some lotion for one of my patients who suffers with dry skin. I added some fragrance after filling her bottle and brought you some."

Alex went to where his coat hung by the door and returned to hand Marcail a glass bottle filled with a thick yellow fluid. Marcail pulled the cork and inhaled the fragrance. It smelled like summer flowers, and she smiled as she held the bottle beneath her nose.

Alex watched as she rubbed a small amount on her arm. That she was more than pleased with the gift gave him tremendous satisfaction. Acting as though he'd given her a diamond instead of a small bottle of perfumed lotion, Marcail thanked him in her soft voice.

In that instant Alex wondered what type of home she'd grown up in, where she had obtained such an appreciation for small things. His thoughts made him realize, not for the first time, how little he knew about his wife.

Twenty-Eight

THE REST OF Saturday flew by in a buzz of activities. Alex was not called away, so he chopped wood and worked in the barn. Marcail finished the baking and worked on her school lessons for the following week. At one point Alex came in to find Marcail standing on a chair, putting dishes away.

Before she could take another breath, he was taking the dishes back down, and telling her he was going to lower the shelf. Marcail tried to explain that she didn't mind using the chair, but he had become a man with a mission and didn't even answer her. When she saw how determined he was, she worked with him for a time, but as he began to pull the shelf from the wall, nails creaking and dust flying, she moved into the living room to get out of his way.

By the time Marcail was ready to start supper preparation, the shelf and dishes were back in place, and she went to work on the evening meal. Alex washed up and helped her. In no time at all, they had put a filling meal on the table.

As the evening progressed, Alex noticed that Marcail was more animated than he'd ever seen her. He wondered how stressful it was for her to teach. On the other evenings they'd spent together, she'd been communicative but not enthusiastic. He then pondered if her bubbly mood had anything to do with the lotion he'd brought. He told himself with an inner smile that if this was the effect he could expect, he'd bring her a different bottle every night.

Alex took a bath in his bedroom after supper. Marcail helped him heat the water, and then to give him as much privacy as she could she took herself off to the living room to a book she was reading. An hour later, when Alex was still behind closed doors, Marcail decided to get ready for bed, telling herself she could use the extra sleep.

Alex took an unusually long time with his bath that night, but not because he was overly dusty or wanted to put space between him and Marcail. Once away from Marcail, he found his mind trying to work through the puzzle of the change in her that night. His mind lingered on the fact that she hadn't taught school that day, but then he put that idea aside. Marcail never seemed beaten down or tired when he picked her up in the afternoon.

Alex dried off and sat on the edge of the bed. He let his mind see her as she'd been when he'd come home from work—bent over the stove, looking adorable in that huge dress, her hair falling in thick waves down her back.

Her hair! Alex realized with a start. He jumped up, pulled on his pants, and opened the door as he slipped into his shirt.

"Marcail," he called before rounding the corner into the living room.

"Yes?"

"May I come into the living room? I need to ask you something."

"Sure," Marcail answered from her place on the sofa. She was already in her nightgown and robe, but was sitting on the sofa with her Bible. She watched as Alex came in and sat beside her, even though the sofa was already made up for the night.

Alex had not carried his lantern from the bedroom, and Marcail's was turned rather low. Alex reached and increased the flame before he spoke.

"I need to ask you about your hair," Alex began, watching her face closely in the lamplight.

"My hair?"

"Yes. Does it give you a headache to put your hair up?" Alex came straight to the point, and Marcail blinked at him.

"Yes it does, but how did you know that?"

"Because every other evening you've seemed to be upset about something or in some type of pain. And tonight you weren't, so I figured either your job is very stressful or you get headaches from putting all of this on top of your head."

Alex's hand came out and brushed back the locks that had fallen over her left shoulder. "Marcail," Alex continued, "why do you wear your hair up if it hurts you?"

Marcail was surprised he didn't know the answer. "It's part of my contract with the school," Marcail explained softly. "I must wear my hair up at all times."

Alex was stunned. *What a bizarre rule,* he thought incredulously. The next instant he realized why she always wore such dark clothing.

"Your dresses, I should say the *dark color* of your dresses—are they a part of the contract too?"

Marcail nodded, and Alex could only look at her. He asked himself just how badly he wanted to take on the Willits school board.

"If you're thinking of going to Mr. Flynn, please don't." Marcail had accurately read his mind. "I've learned to live with the situation, and I knew the terms of the contract before I signed it."

"So before you taught here, you would normally wear your hair up, and just live with the pain?" Alex just barely managed to keep the speculation from his voice.

"No, not exactly. I seldom had occasion to wear my hair up, and when I *would* get a headache, I didn't relate it to my hairstyle. Such a thing never occurred to me until I moved here."

"So you didn't actually know it would be a problem?"

"No, I guess I didn't."

"Before we were married, did you go home each day and take your hair down?"

"Most days, yes. As long as I knew I was home for the day."

"Did that help?"

"Yes. I mean, I would still get a headache, but it would be gone before bed."

It occurred to Alex that they could cut her hair, but the thought made him cringe, and he mentally shook his head no.

"You need to come home each day and take your hair down. Lie down if that will help. If you find that still doesn't alleviate the pain, then we'll have to think of another solution."

Marcail didn't reply. She was again thinking how different he was from her original view of him, and that most of the time she didn't even remember his title of "doctor."

"You're looking rather pensive," Alex commented softly. "Want to share?"

Marcail gave a small shrug. "You're just different than I first thought."

"Good different, or bad different?"

"Good."

Alex nodded, feeling satisfied and thinking absently how lovely she looked in the lantern light. "Have you started to *feel* married yet?"

"Not yet. I mean, I wrote my family and all, but even after seeing it on paper it's still pretty unreal in my heart."

"Would it help if I kissed you good night, or would that scare you?"

Marcail hesitated.

"You can be honest," Alex encouraged her.

"I think right now it would scare me, but I'm afraid if I say no, you'll never offer again." Marcail could hardly believe she'd been so open with her feelings.

Alex was thrilled with her answer and chuckled softly as he left his place on the sofa and stood before his wife. The sound of his laugh, as well as the way he stood looking at her, sent a chill down Marcail's spine.

"Make no mistake, Marcail, I *will* offer again—I will *definitely* offer again."

Marcail sat very still as he turned and moved on bare feet out of the room. She had wanted to get some extra sleep, but as it was, it took some time before she found her rest.

Twenty-Nine

MARCAIL, USUALLY A morning person, exercised great effort to haul herself from the sofa the next morning. Her nose lifted toward the smell of coffee coming from the direction of the kitchen, and almost of their own volition her feet moved to the table. She sat in a kitchen chair, yawning and looking very fuzzy around the edges.

Alex, having been up for nearly an hour, placed a mug of hot coffee in front of her, took a chair opposite, and worked at not laughing. He'd never seen Marcail this way—without her robe, her hair a disaster, and struggling to focus on the cup before her. Alex realized then that he'd never seen her anything but cheerful in the morning. He wondered which Marcail he liked best.

"Good morning," Alex finally spoke when she looked a little more lucid.

"Good morning." Marcail attempted a sleepy smile. "I can't seem to wake up this morning." Alex watched as she took another sip of coffee, propped her elbow on the table, and leaned her chin into her palm.

"Did you sleep well?"

"Once I got to sleep, yes."

Alex was tempted to ask if his question and their discussion the night before had upset her, but he kept his thoughts to himself.

"How did you sleep?" Marcail said without blinking as she stared at some spot over his right shoulder. Alex wondered if she was headed back to sleep.

"Fine." This time he could not keep the laughter from his voice. Marcail, even in her sleepy state, noticed.

"You're laughing at me."

"You're right," Alex chuckled.

"If you keep it up, I'm going to go back to bed."

"If you do that, we'll be late for church."

Marcail sat up straight, sobering instantly. "I'd completely forgotten it was Sunday." Marcail, who never gave up or hid from any task, was tempted for the first time to tell Alex she was not up to going.

"This first Sunday will be the hardest." Alex accurately guessed her thoughts. "And don't forget that families like the Austins, Vespermans, and Whites will be there. You'll also see Allie, who has shown you her loyalty."

Marcail nodded, trying to convince herself of his words. "Are you not at all bothered about going this morning?" For some reason she had to know.

"Not for myself," Alex told her simply.

His real thoughts, thoughts of protecting her no matter what, stayed quiet within him. He knew that if anyone so much as looked at her cross-eyed, he'd champion her like a mother with a hurting child.

Alex rose from the table to start breakfast, all the time wondering if anyone in town knew what a sacrifice she'd made. She had been threatened, humiliated, frightened, rejected, and nearly forced into marriage so she could stay in town, teach the children, and possibly tell someone of Christ's love.

Alex didn't for one instant fault her motives or feel used. In fact, he agreed with her and praised God that she consented to marry him. But part of him wanted people to praise her, to understand her commitment and love for the children, and to put her on a pedestal because of it.

Then Alex's thoughts went to Jesus Christ and His life on earth. No man was more misunderstood, no man had suffered more humiliation and rejection than He had. The "pedestal" He was put upon was a cross, to die for sins He could not possibly have committed.

Alex glanced back at the table to where Marcail still sat. She'd retrieved her Bible and sat reading quietly. He might be able to share his thoughts with her someday, but for now, he prayed. He knew God would show her in His special way that she'd done the right thing, and that He was going to honor her obedience.

By the time church was over, Marcail was convinced that rejection would have been easier to take than everyone's self-satisfied looks over their belief that she was no longer a "fallen woman." It was enough to make Marcail's blood boil, and she tried hard to keep her emotions in check.

They were eating lunch at Austins when Kay noticed Marcail was about to explode. Intending to give Marcail and Alex some time alone, she sent the girls on an errand after the meal.

"Talk to me, Marcail," Alex said as soon as he'd shut the parlor door.

"Two women I don't even know actually offered to have the party at their house when our baby is born!"

Alex was not at all surprised. He'd tried to keep her at his side as much as possible, but it seemed the people at church were determined to separate them.

"Honestly!" Marcail continued. "It was almost easier to take the cold shoulders I received last week than those ridiculous, speculative glances on the faces of certain people."

He was silent as he watched her flushed face. Marcail stood shaking in the middle of the room, her arms crossed over her chest and one small-booted foot tapping an angry tattoo on the rug.

A few minutes of silence followed, and then Alex watched as Marcail's shoulders slumped. She moved to the sofa and sat down heavily. Her body was still now, her hands limp in her lap, her foot motionless. Alex joined her on the sofa. She turned her head slightly away from him, but not before he'd seen the tears gathering in her eyes. He waited for her to bury her face in her hands and sob loudly, as his first wife had done so many times, but it was not to happen.

Alex watched her profile in fascination as silent tears streamed down her cheek. Marcail turned back to look at him, the tears still flowing. Not even when she spoke did she sound like she was crying, just slightly out of breath. It was the most heartbreaking thing Alex had ever witnessed.

"I know it's my pride, Alex; that's all it is. But I feel so hurt, so wounded that everyone believes the worst of me."

Alex put his arms around her, and Marcail allowed herself to be pulled against his chest. An occasional shudder ran over her frame, but other than the hot tears seeping through the fabric of his shirt, he'd have never known she was crying.

"Can you hear me?" he said softly after some minutes. Marcail nodded against his chest, but did not lift her head.

"It's going to take some time, but everyone will soon be used to our being married, and no one will think any more of it. I'm sure some of the older women in town think this is all very romantic. In their own clumsy way, they're trying to show you support."

Marcail raised her head to look at him. Alex, still one arm around her, gently wiped the tears from her face with his free hand. The action made Marcail feel cherished. He looked down at her with tender eyes, and Marcail found herself wanting to cling to him.

"You're not embarrassed about our marriage, are you, Alex?" The thought had just occurred to her, and her voice held a hint of wonder.

"What a silly question," Alex spoke softly and pressed a kiss to her forehead.

I like you, Alex, Marcail thought to herself. *I like you a lot.*

"Are you going to be all right?" Alex spoke into her thoughts, his voice warm and caring.

"Yes," Marcail answered, thinking his arms felt wonderful. "Thanks to you, I think I'm going to be fine."

Her words gave Alex a very satisfied feeling, although neither one spoke again for some time. The girls eventually came back, and the Montgomery family was joined by Dean, Kay, and the girls. The remainder of the afternoon was spent in good fellowship and fun.

Thirty

MARCAIL STOOD ACROSS the kitchen from her husband, her entire being radiating frustration. It was Friday morning, and they were leaving for Fort Bragg in just an hour. They were also having their first verbal disagreement.

It had started ten minutes earlier while they were still getting ready to go. Alex noticed Marcail was putting up her hair. He questioned her, and the argument ensued.

"Marcail, I don't think you should put your hair up for the train ride."

"I admit it would be more comfortable down, but I don't really have a choice."

"I disagree. If you just put your coat on, and keep your hair inside, it will never be noticed."

Marcail stared at him in amazement.

"Or," he continued, "you could put your hair up now and take it down as soon as the train leaves town."

"I will not take my hair down on the train." Marcail's voice was adamant.

Alex figured as much, but at this point he was willing to try anything to save her from a headache, including the risk of angering her.

"Well, I will not have you suffering with a headache all day," Alex told her without force. "Now I could ask you, and then leave the choice to you, but I'm not going to do that. I *do not* want you to wear your hair up today."

Marcail opened her mouth and closed it again. He had not raised his voice an octave or made her feel at all threatened, but she suddenly knew that every one of Dr. Montgomery's patients took their medicine when they were told. Still, everything inside of Marcail balked at the idea. Her chin rose a notch.

"And if I put my hair up anyway?"

"I'll take the pins out on the ride into town," Alex stated quietly, feeling pain for having to argue with her.

"Marcail." Alex's voice had not changed, but this time his words got through to her. "I have no desire to start our trip with an argument, nor do I wish to deceive anyone in town, but your headaches concern me. We *are* leaving town, so no one will be offended."

Alex had thought to have this discussion with her on Wednesday before Bible study. He knew she would want to keep her hair up even though they would be going to and from the Austins after dark. But Alex had been called out, and Marcail had stayed home.

"Did you figure I'd wear my hair down the entire weekend in Fort Bragg?"

"Yes, I did. I rather thought you'd enjoy the change."

I *would enjoy the change*, Marcail thought. *I'm just being stubborn because I don't like being ordered around.*

Marcail was on the verge of telling Alex her thoughts when he disappeared into the bedroom, giving her time alone. She stood for a moment in indecision, and then continued with her packing, leaving the pins behind. She figured she would have hours on the train to apologize and explain.

The scene from the train window on the way to Fort Bragg provided one surprise after another. The tracks wound their way west through hills and valleys, forests and plains. Alex and Marcail rode for the first hour in silence, just content to take in the scenery.

"Still mad at me?" Alex was the first to break the silence, and Marcail turned from the panorama to face him.

"I don't know if I was actually mad, but I was frustrated. There are times I don't like to be ordered around."

"I'm afraid I didn't handle it very well. Maybe it comes from being a doctor, but I can't stand to see suffering. We both know how miserable you'd be at the end of the line if your hair was up."

"I don't need to be so obstinate," Marcail admitted and then suddenly smiled, "but up to now, I believed that all the dictators were in other countries."

"Dictator?" Alex tried to sound outraged, but there was laughter in his voice.

Marcail laughed with him, and then watched his face turn serious. "I know this will seem like an abrupt change of subject, but there's been no opportunity for me to talk to you about my folks."

"Your folks?"

"Right. Their situation is a bit unusual, and I want to prepare you as much as I can." Alex searched his wife's face and then began his story. "My mother is completely bedridden. She has been since I was little more than a baby. I was too young to remember what happened, but they tell me she fell from a small ladder and injured her spine. My father found her almost immediately, but even though several specialists came to see her, they said nothing could be done. She has no use of her legs at all, and at times her arms grow numb and she can't move them."

"Does she ever get out of bed?" Marcail's face mirrored her compassion.

"No. She's propped against the headboard of the bed for most of the day, but she never gets up."

Alex fell silent for a moment, and Marcail's mind ran with images of a woman being bedridden for 30 years. "How does she do it?" Marcail finally whispered.

Alex smiled before answering. "She lets God use her right where she is. In fact, you won't be able to spend more than 30 minutes with her before she praises Him for her condition. She writes about ten letters a day, and she knows if she wasn't in that bed, she would never have been a letter writer."

"Letters to whom?"

"People all over the world who have heard about her or come to the house to meet her. She never talks about herself, but writes Scripture and words of encouragement to those who hurt or have not yet found the Lord."

"She sounds wonderful. How does your father handle all of this?"

"He tells people she's the light of his life," Alex told her with a tender gleam in his eye. "He teases her about never going dancing with him, but when we get there you'll see how well they manage. Their bedroom is on the first floor and set up with all the conveniences. Dad takes all his meals with Mother, and they sleep in the same bed every night."

"Is there someone who comes in to be with her during the day?"

"Yes, her name is Ida, and she's been coming for years. She cleans and prepares supper every afternoon."

"What about mornings?"

"Well, mother usually sleeps late, and she has Danny."

"One of your brothers?"

Alex chuckled at the thought. "No, Danny is a dog—a big dog. You'll meet him as soon as we get to the house. He's huge, but there isn't a vicious bone in his body, so don't let him scare you."

Alex fell silent once again and let Marcail have her thoughts. Alex's parents did indeed sound wonderful. It suddenly became clear why he was a thoughtful, caring person—he'd learned from godly people. Marcail's mind moved to his siblings.

"Tell me about the rest of your family."

"I think I told you I'm the youngest of five." Marcail nodded and Alex went on, "the oldest is my sister Dorothy, she's 39 and doesn't live in Fort Bragg. She's married to a man named Stan Crandall, and they live in Eureka with their four kids.

"My brother Skip is 37, and is actually named after my father, Samuel. He has three children, Amber, Jess, and Cole, and his wife is Judith."

"Do they live in Fort Bragg?"

"Yes, he shares the medical practice with my father."

Nodding, Marcail understood for the first time how her sister-in-law, Charlotte Donovan, felt when she was new to the family and trying to place everyone.

"Susan is in the middle at 36. Her husband is Jeremy Grey. They have four kids, Price, Nellie, Madeline, and Stuart. Jeremy's family owns and operates the bank, so he and Sue live right in town. My folks' house, which is also my dad's office, is at the edge of town."

"Who's next?" Marcail asked, hoping she could keep it all straight.

"Quinn, who just turned 34. His wife is Hannah, and their kids are Cindy and Derek."

"What does Quinn do for a living?"

"He's a logger."

"You didn't tell me the names of Dorothy's children."

"No, I didn't. You won't meet them this trip, and I figured you'd have enough to keep straight."

"That's true. What do I call your folks?"

"Well, they'd love to hear Mother and Dad, but something tells me you wouldn't be comfortable with that. Don't hesitate to call them Samuel and Helen; Judith always does."

"Is she the one who blushes?"

"No, that's my sister Sue." Alex chuckled at the thought.

"I can tell I'm going to spend the entire weekend lit up like a candle," Marcail commented without humor. Alex laughed, his eyes lit mischievously as he watched her.

In fact, he was still smiling impishly when Marcail reached into her bag for the lunch she'd packed. He sobered up when she threatened to eat his lunch. Marcail knew without a doubt that the weekend would be anything but boring.

Thirty-One

MARCAIL COULD SMELL the ocean even before she disembarked from the train. Her nose lifted as her feet hit the platform, and her eyes closed in bliss as she inhaled the smell of her childhood. A cold wind tugged at her coat and hair, but Marcail took no notice.

Alex came from behind and bumped her with the bags. The feel of the bags hitting the back of her legs and Alex's quick apology were enough to break the reverie. She turned to ask him the direction of his home, but she saw that his nose was raised, and he was sporting the same look of pleasure she'd just experienced.

Marcail watched him until he opened his eyes and noticed her scrutiny. He smiled without embarrassment, and Marcail grinned back at him.

"Is it good to be home?" she asked softly. "Immensely! Come on, Marc," Alex used her nickname for the first time. "I'll take you home to Mother."

The Montgomery house was a large structure that appeared to have been added to over the years. The central house was two stories, with wings on three of the four sides.

Alex walked directly in the front door without knocking, and Marcail followed. He moved with purpose through a spacious living room, set their bags by the long sofa, took Marcail's hand, and led her to a door at the end of the room.

Marcail had envisioned someone rather sickly, but the woman waiting in bed to meet her looked the picture of health with her sparkling blue eyes and warm smile.

No words were spoken as Marcail approached the bed. Helen, immediately noticing the hesitant smile of her new daughter-in-law, reached to hug her. Marcail couldn't help but respond to the love she saw there and went willingly into her embrace. When Helen released her, she patted the bed and Marcail sat down. Again the room was silent as Helen looked at the exquisite features of Marcail's face. She then turned to Alex.

"You didn't tell us that she has the face of an angel."

Alex's smile nearly stretched off his face as he saw Marcail blush. He leaned from the far side of the bed to kiss his mother's cheek.

"Hello, Mother."

"Hello, dear. Happy birthday, a few days early."

"Thank you," Alex replied with a twinkle in his eye. "And now if you'll permit me, I'll make the introductions. Mother, this is my wife, Marcail. Marcail, this is my mother, Helen Montgomery."

"Marcail." Helen spoke the name softly. "We've been mispronouncing it."

"With a soft *c*?" Alex wanted to know.

"Yes."

"I think that's the norm, especially if a person sees the name before they hear it."

Alex and his mother went on talking for the next few minutes. Marcail's attention began to wander around the room, and she found it as well equipped as Alex had described. The bed was spacious, with a lovely headboard and footboard. There was a small dining table with four chairs, and a small sofa, much like the one in Alex's living room. The room even boasted its own little pot-bellied stove.

Marcail's gaze moved past the stove and then shot back when she spotted a dog lying next to it. At least she thought it was a dog. It was big enough to be a small horse. Marcail was unaware of the way both Alex and Helen had stopped to watch her. Marcail's eyes were like dinner plates, and her mouth opened but no words came out.

"Come here, Danny," Helen finally spoke.

The enormous dog responded immediately, and as he slowly approached, Marcail moved back on the bed until she was against the footboard. Alex's arms seemed to come out of nowhere, and Marcail relaxed when she felt them.

"He won't hurt you," he said softly in her ear, and Marcail let her head fall back against his shoulder. She couldn't believe how good it felt to have him touch her. It wasn't that his family frightened her, but everything here was new and strange, and the feel of his arms was as secure as the feel of walking in the front door of her own home.

Danny came forward on Alex's command, and Marcail reached out to pet him. His entire back end moved in ecstacy over that attention, and Marcail knew in an instant that Danny was as gentle as Alex declared.

After a few moments Helen sent Danny to get Ida, something he'd been trained as a puppy to do. The housekeeper brought a light snack that was enjoyed by all, including Danny. Time seemed to race by, and Marcail was surprised when Alex said it was after 5:00 and he wanted to take her upstairs to get settled before going to meet his father and brother. Following Alex's lead, Marcail kissed Helen as they left the room. Alex reminded his mother they'd be back soon.

Alex and Marcail didn't see the smile that passed between Ida and Helen on their exit. Both women were thinking the same thought—their precious Alex had found a jewel.

Thirty-Two

ALEX AND MARCAIL had not reached the stairs before his father and oldest brother, Skip, came from their shared office to meet Marcail. Their smiles were warm and their hugs strong as they welcomed this "petite Montgomery," as Skip instantly called her.

Some moments went by before the Montgomery men turned their attention to Alex to congratulate him and wish him an early birthday greeting. Suddenly, and without hint of a noisy arrival, the house was converged upon by Montgomerys. In the space of a few seconds Marcail and Alex were separated, and Marcail was left alone to meet the rest of the family—one more brother, two sisters-in-law, one sister, one brother-in-law, and nine nieces and nephews.

Their welcome of her was exuberant, and Marcail was looking very pleased, if not slightly overwhelmed, when Alex finally made his way back to her side for the next 20 minutes.

All the families had brought food to eat, and a meal was in preparation when Alex led Marcail from the room. He headed her up the stairs, their bags once again in hand. In the hallway at the top of the stairs, Marcail finally spoke.

"I need to go down and help with supper."

Alex continued to usher her along. "They have all the hands they need. You haven't had a moment to yourself since we arrived. I think you should get settled in our room."

Marcail was escorted into a large, immaculate bedroom. The inviting room was tastefully decorated, but Marcail's attention was riveted to the wall opposite the door. The wall displayed the headboard of a solitary, full-sized bed. Marcail walked slowly into the room and stood at the footboard. She heard the door shut behind her, but she stood still, certain she could not face Alex just now.

"Look at me, Marc," Alex commanded softly.

Marcail hesitated before turning to find him in the room's only chair, the bags at his feet.

"If you're thinking this is a setup to get you to do something you're not ready for, you couldn't be more wrong."

Marcail swallowed audibly, but didn't reply.

"There are other beds up here, but I feel our marriage is a private matter. I'd just as soon we stay in the same room." His voice was very reasonable, and Marcail listened attentively. "We have three nights here. If you feel at all threatened after we sleep in the same bed tonight, and I do mean *sleep*, I'll move across the hall."

Marcail stared at her husband and then at the bed. *It's certainly wide enough,* was her first thought. *And he's proven to you repeatedly that he'll not hurt you. Aside from all that, he is your husband.*

"Marcail?"

Alex's soft calling of her name made her remember she hadn't answered him.

"All right, Alex," Marcail agreed, nothing that he didn't seem triumphant or even very pleased, just accepting of her decision.

The family had a bit of a surprise for Alex and Marcail when supper was over. They all gathered in Samuel and Helen's bedroom so each family could present them with a gift for their home. Marcail was so surprised she wasn't sure what so say. Samuel and Helen gave them six teacups with hand-painted flowers and matching saucers. A large mixing bowl came from Skip and his family. Jeremy and Susan presented them with embroidered pillow slips. Quinn and Hannah gave them ornate candlesticks and tall, tapered candles.

After the gifts were opened Marcail and Alex thanked everyone with grateful warmth. Marcail did so because the family had made her feel so accepted, and Alex because he'd so wanted his wife to see his family for the warm, generous people they were.

The celebration over, the children were served dessert and then stayed in Grandma's room for a story. The adults, all but Helen and Samuel, headed toward the large dining room table for pie and coffee.

As the family became acquainted with Marcail, and she with them, the dialogue took many twists and turns. Marcail was on her second cup of coffee when the conversation turned to a family, new to the area, that Quinn and Hannah were counseling. Alex asked how things were going, and Marcail had the distinct impression that the marriage was in trouble.

"How many kids do they have, Quinn?" Sue wanted to know.

"Four. All under the age of six."

"I spend a lot of time praying for those kids," Hannah interjected, "since their folks fight whenever the two of them are in the same room."

"It seems they don't even like each other," Quinn's voice was sad on this note.

Marcail, having just taken a sip of coffee, spoke without thought. "They must like each other a little if they have four kids."

The table grew abruptly quiet. Marcail, eyes still on her clean pie plate, became very still. She raised her head slowly to find every adult at the table grinning at her.

Marcail felt the blush begin on her chest and work its way upward to her throat and face. The smiles around the table grew wider, and before Marcail could guess what was about to happen, Skip grabbed the lantern and held it close to her face.

"Would you look at that face," he nearly whispered. "Lit up like a house-afire."

Marcail's face was so hot she thought it would flame. Turning her gaze to Alex, she found his look to be compassionate, but it also told her there was nothing he could do.

"Well, if there were any doubts in our minds about *why* Alex married Marcail, and there weren't," Quinn spoke now, "they're all put to rest. Montgomery men love a girl who blushes."

There was laughter around the table, and some of the attention was turned from Marcail. She was able to relax to a degree, but Alex had been right; they did tease her from time to time just to see her face flush.

Her deepest blush came when everyone decided it was bedtime, and they all left to go home for the night. What no one knew was that her blush this time had nothing whatsoever to do with her in-laws.

Marcail stood across the bedroom from Alex, not fully believing she'd agreed to share this room and bed. They'd just come in together, and Marcail watched as Alex sat on the bed and pulled of his shoes. His back was to her, but she told herself she'd sleep in her dress before she'd take her clothes off right then.

Marcail's thoughts were beginning to turn tortuous when Alex stood, went to the commode, and lifted the pitcher from the bowl.

"I'll go down and get some water for the morning," he said, as though he was simply mentioning the weather. Whereupon he strolled casually out the door.

Marcail stood frozen to her spot for a few seconds before, in her haste, she nearly tore the buttons from her dress. She didn't know how long she had, but she planned to be in her nightgown, under the covers, and sound asleep before her spouse returned.

Thirty-Three

Alex MADE HIS way slowly downstairs, and as he expected, found his father in the living room reading a newspaper. The elder Montgomery laid the news aside and smiled as Alex took a chair across from him.

"Is Marcail settled in?"

"I think so. She's getting ready for bed."

Something in his son's voice alerted Samuel. He was very close to all of his children, but Alex was the most like him. There was something on his mind, and Samuel knew if he stayed quiet, Alex would share.

"She's not like Linette," Alex commented softly.

"Yes, I'd noticed. Does that bother you?"

"Only for Linette's sake."

This remark might have confused someone else, but Samuel knew his son to be extremely loyal. He had loved his first wife and always wished she could have been happier.

"You were both very young when you started out, Al," his father reminded him. "And Linette never liked surprises, not even as a child."

"That's true, but I never should have assumed that she knew we wouldn't be in Fort Bragg forever. I mean, with you and Skippy already set up here, it just seemed so logical." Alex gave a helpless shrug. It seemed that all this should have been said years ago, but the truth was, they had never talked about it. He let his mind run, and in an instant all the pain returned.

He and Linette had grown up together. They had been nearly inseparable from the time they could walk, and as they grew older it just seemed a natural turn of events to be married. Within a year of their wedding Alex had gone away to medical school, and to keep things simple, Linette had moved back with her parents.

Alex came home as often as he was able, and at the time his absence didn't seem to affect their relationship. Near the end of his schooling, however, when Alex came home to say he'd found a nearby town that needed him, Linette changed instantaneously to a person he'd never known.

She raged at him over leaving Fort Bragg for Willits and threatened to stay behind. He told her that if she was so against their move they wouldn't go, but she began hiding her feelings at that point. They'd been living in Willits for nearly a year before Linette's true feelings came to the fore again.

Alex could do nothing right in Linette's eyes. He would be treated to days of silence for sins he couldn't remember committing. It didn't take long for Alex to see that Linette depended on him for her every happiness.

The marriage as a whole was not miserable, but Alex found himself starved for the sight of his wife's smile and a true helpmate to fill his days.

Linette was as much work, if not more, than many of his patients. Nevertheless, he loved her, and as he weathered each new storm he grew in the Lord. As head of the family, he tried to involve Linette in his study of the Word, but unless it made her happy, she would have nothing to do with it.

Alex had decided that they would have to return to Fort Bragg, but the very day he decided to give his wife her wish, she had the accident.

"I've lost you."

Alex came abruptly back to the present. "I guess you did. I was thinking about the changes in my life. First with Linette, then without her, and now with Marcail." It was obvious Alex had more to say, but he hesitated.

"It's all right to admit that Linette was not an easy woman to live with, Al," his father told him gently. "And it's also okay to tell me how much you love your new wife."

"I do love her, Dad, only I can't tell her."

Samuel was silent for a full ten seconds. Considering the fact that Alex had only mentioned the new school-teacher one time in a letter last fall, his words were no surprise. Then a week ago he'd written to say he was bringing his wife home for his birthday.

"Then you'll just have to show her," the older man finally said.

Alex nodded slowly and felt relief over his father's approval. Not that he doubted receiving it, but knowing that his father was in his corner did wonders for Alex's outlook.

Father and son sat up for the next two hours while Alex shared how he'd met Marcail and why they were married. Again, Alex felt no condemnation from his father. He listened carefully when Samuel told him how important it was that he get to know Marcail's family as soon as possible. Alex hadn't thought of it, but agreed wholeheartedly.

They parted company sometime before midnight, and as Alex expected, Marcail never stirred when he slipped beneath the covers beside her.

Thirty-Four

MARCAIL WOKE TO an empty bed. Stretching contentedly, she remembered where she was and quickly turned her head to see if someone was on the other pillow. Someone *had* been there, that much was obvious, but the sheets were cold and Marcail wondered what time it was.

She lay there a moment, feeling lazy, and had just decided to get out of bed when the door opened a crack. Alex's head came in next, and he looked toward the bed with raised brows.

"Good morning," Marcail called, and Alex took it as an invitation to enter.

"Good morning. How about a little coffee?"

"Ohhh, thank you." Marcail spoke with surprised pleasure and pushed herself against the headboard to receive the offered cup. Alex took the end of the bed, leaning against the footboard with his own cup.

"How did you sleep?" he asked solicitously after Marcail had taken a few sips.

"Like I always do, but I suspect you already know that."

"Meaning?"

"Meaning, I never heard you come or go, so I assume I slept as usual."

"You do sleep hard," Alex commented softly, his eyes on her disheveled appearance.

Marcail told herself she was not going to blush. She concentrated on her coffee cup in the silence that followed.

"How would you like to have breakfast at the beach?"

The cup paused halfway to Marcail's mouth.

"Who's going?"

"Just the two of us."

"What about your folks?"

"Dad's at the office, and I think I told you, Mother sleeps late. I'm sure my family will be around for the rest of the day, so I thought this might be my only time to show you Fort Bragg. Unless you're starved, I thought we'd take a basket and eat at the beach."

"I'd like that," Marcail said sincerely, seeing how much Alex wanted to leave the decision to her, but also how much he wanted to take her.

Alex stood and moved toward the door. Marcail noticed for the first time that he was dressed and ready for the day.

"I'll be ready anytime you get downstairs."

"All right. By the way, Alex, what time is it?"

"Almost 10:00."

Alex grinned at the shocked look on his wife's face before slipping out and shutting the door.

"This was my grandparent's house," Alex said as he pointed to a simple green house. "Quinn and Hannah live there now."

"What did you say Quinn did for a living?"

"He's a logger."

"Oh, that's right, and their kids are Amber, Jess, and Cole."

"No. Amber, Jess, and Cole belong to Skip and Judith. Quinn's kids are Cindy and Derek."

Marcail nodded but stayed silent. She hadn't needed more than a few days to know the name of every student in her class, but Alex's family was still beyond her.

Mentally placing everyone she'd met, Marcail realized that Alex had turned the horse and small buggy down the road toward the ocean. They moved closer to the view Marcail had seen from the Montgomery house, and in a matter of minutes they were pulling to a stop beside what appeared to be a private beach. Marcail sat transfixed as she watched and listened to the ocean beat on the shore. The sound was like music in her heart.

Alex, assuming it was her first view of such a majestic sight, stayed silent and let her look her fill. The quiet moment was broken when Marcail suddenly scrambled from the carriage. Alex watched in amazement as she sat in the sand, stripped off her shoes and stockings, and dug her toes in the sand. A moment passed before he heard her laugh with delight.

Alex stepped down from the buggy and went to sit on the sand beside his wife. She was still smiling, but there were tears standing in her eyes. He watched her, a questioning look on his face. Finally she noticed him.

A faint blush stained her cheeks before she spoke. "Don't mind me, Alex. It's just been so long."

"What has?"

"Since I've seen the ocean and felt the sand under my feet."

Again his look was questioning, almost baffled, and for the first time Marcail stopped to think how little he knew about her. After all they'd only been married for 13 days.

"I was born in Hawaii," Marcail told her husband softly.

"The Hawaiian Islands?"

Marcail smiled at his tone. "Right. I lived there until I was nearly nine. My parents were missionaries."

Alex could only stare, first at Marcail, and then out to sea. He had of course realized how little they knew of each other, but this! This was so surprising that Alex hardly knew what to say.

He turned his head back to look at Marcail and found her watching him. Seeing her sitting there with her hair down her back and her bare toes peeking out from beneath the hem of her dress made it easy to envision her as a girl running on the beach.

"Do you miss it?" he asked suddenly.

"Not anymore. When I was nine, I thought I would die of homesickness, but it's been 11 years, and I love my life here. I do miss my brother, Sean, and his family He's one of four pastors at the mission there, working with the village families."

Again Alex just stared at her.

"What are you thinking?" Marcail had to ask.

"That you're an awful lot of surprises for such a small package."

Marcail wasn't offended. She smiled and looked back out to sea. "Does my being small bother you?"

"No, should it?"

Marcail shrugged and then admitted, "I was never going to marry anyone who towered over me as much as you do."

"Why?"

The question brought Marcail's head around. "Because I didn't want my husband to view me as a child."

"Is that what you think, Marcail?" Alex's voice was suddenly intense. "That I think of you as a child?"

Marcail shrugged, realizing the conversation had taken an unexpected turn. She wasn't sure what to say next.

Alex didn't care for the shrug, but he was at a loss as to how to
tell Marcail what he really felt. To divulge that he found her lovely
and desirable at this moment, while they were having to share a
bedroom, could do irreparable damage. Frustration rose within him,
but he prayed for calm.

They sat in silence for a few moments, and Alex knew his first
premonition was right—he was going to have to let the subject
drop. As he moved to the buggy to retrieve the basket and quilt, he
told himself that someday his wife would know exactly how he
viewed her.

Thirty-Five

BY THE TIME they returned from the beach, some of Alex's family were at the house. Alex and Marcail were taken into the group without the slightest hesitation.

"Did you show Aunt Marcail where we live?" six-year-old Derek wanted to know when he found out they'd been on a drive.

"Yes, we went by your house."

"Then where did you go?" Jess, who was 11, piped up.

"To the beach."

"Wasn't it a little cold?" This came from Amber, who at 14 was taller than her new aunt.

Alex, who couldn't remember feeling cold at all, smilingly shook his head and glanced at Marcail's feet. Her shoes and stockings were back in place now, but he clearly remembered the way one foot had stuck out from under her dress while they were eating.

A single stroke of his finger had told him that his wife's feet were very ticklish. A fiendish glint over this newfound knowledge had entered Alex's eyes. Seeing that threat, Marcail had scurried for the far end of the quilt and tucked her feet protectively beneath her. She informed him, in her best teacher's voice, that he was *not* to tickle her feet. Alex continued to tease, but after some convincing arguments, she rung a promise out of him that he would not touch her feet while she was trying to eat.

Now, back in the living room, Alex raised his head to see that Marcail had been watching him. She knew the exact direction of his thoughts. Her look turned stern all over again, but all Alex could do was grin.

An hour or so after lunch, with nearly everyone present, news came that there had been a small fire at the hotel. The Montgomery doctors didn't hesitate a moment before going to assist. Alex gave Marcail his usual kiss on the corner of her mouth and went out with the others. Quinn also went along to help.

Susan took her four children home so that Stuart, her youngest, could get a nap. All were coming back for supper, so the children and women settled in various parts of the house for play or talk.

For the next two hours Marcail was in Helen's bedroom with Judith, Amber, and Hannah. Marcail loved the way they included her and would have sat all day, but Jess and Cole began to argue in the living room. When Judith arose, Marcail asked if she could go instead. Judith was more than happy to allow her, and within minutes Marcail had solved the argument by taking both boys outside for a game of catch.

Marcail held her own very nicely with her nephews. Jess had a good arm, and Marcail's hands stung on some of his harder throws. Jess was putting his all into one throw when Cole said something to Marcail and distracted her. The ball, hard as a rock, hit her on the side of the head.

Marcail's hand came to her temple and both boys froze. Marcail's eyes slid shut, knowing that any second her head would begin to throb. A few seconds passed, and Marcail opened her eyes. The boys had come up without her hearing, and Marcail tried to smile.

"I'm sorry," Jess said softly.

"Me too," Cole added.

She reached and hugged the boys, not wanting them to know how much her head hurt.

"Let's sit on the porch and talk awhile, shall we?"

Both boys nodded with relief, thinking their aunt was fine. It was wonderful to sit down, and Marcail was able to keep her pain private. Not knowing whether she was hurt badly or not, Marcail saw no need in alarming the family and upsetting these sweet little boys.

The three were still on the front porch when the men came back from town. Marcail, feeling a little disoriented, didn't notice them until the boys became very still.

Quinn and Samuel went into the house after saying hello, but both Skip and Alex stopped to talk with the three on the porch. Skip immediately noticed the guilty looks on his son's faces. Alex wondered at Marcail's strained smile, but thought he'd have to wait until they were alone to find out the cause.

"What's up, boys?" Skip spoke gently to his young sons.

"It was my fault," Cole began.

"But I was the one who hit her," Jess finished for him.

Skip said nothing for a moment. "You hit Aunt Marcail with the ball?" he guessed, since the offending object was still in Jess's hand. Alex's and Skip's eyes swung to Marcail simultaneously.

"I'm fine," Marcail nearly stuttered. "It was an accident." She hated the way they were looking at her, and when Skip suggested they step into the infirmary, Marcail came to her feet so fast she felt dizzy.

"There's no need really," she began to babble, her eyes wide with apparent panic. "I mean, accidents do happen and—"

Alex instantly measured up the situation and came to the rescue. He stepped forward and pulled her into his arms, effectively cutting off her flow of words. Skip saw immediately that he and the boys were not needed, so he ushered his family into the house.

Marcail, still not believing they were going to leave her alone, held herself stiffly in her husband's arms. His hands held her gently against his chest, but Marcail was not comforted. Alex, working at keeping the emotion from his voice, began to question Marcail.

"Where did the ball hit you?"

"In the head," Marcail answered after only a slight hesitation.

Alarm slammed through Alex, but again he hid his emotion. He moved gently until he was grasping Marcail by the upper arms in an attempt to look into her eyes.

"How long ago did this happen, Marcail?"

"I don't know," she said softly.

"Was it right after we left?"

"No, not that long."

"Show me where the ball hit."

Marcail reached for the spot above her left ear. Alex's hand followed hers and found a huge knot. His finger probed gently, but careful as he was, Marcail moved from his touch. Alex stood silent a moment, mentally debating his next move. Had this been any of his other loved ones, he would have ordered instead of asked, but with Marcail he chose to tread lightly.

"Are you going to panic if I suggest you lie down for a while?"

The thought sounded heavenly to Marcail, but she was worried about the boys' reaction. "I don't want to frighten Jess or Cole, or make them feel any worse than they already do."

"I'll handle the family." Alex was more relieved than his voice portrayed. "You stay right here, and I'll be back in a few minutes."

Marcail sank down on the porch steps as soon as he left and tried to pray. She'd put such store in this week-end; not just the break from teaching, but also the chance to get to know Alex and his family better.

Marcail's attempt at prayer was interrupted when Alex appeared beside her. He stooped, hooked an arm beneath her knees and one behind her back, and lifted her high against his chest.

"Oh, Alex," Marcail gasped. "That makes me dizzy."

"Just close your eyes," he told her calmly, and surprisingly Marcail complied, letting her head rest against his shoulder.

With her eyes closed, Marcail was unaware of the hands holding the door open for their entrance, or the compassionate, concerned adult eyes that watched as Alex bore his wife through the living room and up the stairs.

Marcail was not able to keep track of their progress as they moved though the house. She knew when Alex sat her on the edge of the bed, and that he was unbuttoning the back of her dress, but when her nightgown dropped over her head, she was taken totally off guard. Even so, that she was too tired to question or fight him.

She watched with eyes that hurt as he hung her dress on the back of the door. His hands were gentle as she was tucked beneath the covers, and the pillow felt as soft as a cloud to her throbbing head. She was going to thank him for something, but at the moment the thought eluded her as sleep swiftly crowded in.

Thirty-Six

MARCAIL WOKE TO the calling of her name. Her foggy brain told her someone was being very insistent. Since she didn't like the cold washcloth that was rudely calling her from slumber, she forced her eyes open and focused on Alex, who seemed to be engrossed with her face.

"I thought you were going to let me sleep for a few minutes?" Her voice was husky.

"I did." Alex's voice sounded hushed in the still room. "You've been asleep for nearly two hours."

Marcail was silent as she digested this. She heard sounds from downstairs, and at the same time her nose detected a wonderful smell.

"How does your head feel?"

"I'm hungry," Marcail told him.

"Well, that's a good sign. I'll bring you something."

"No. I'll come down."

Alex nodded after a brief hesitation. "All right." He rose from his place on the edge of the bed and retrieved Marcail's dress from the hook.

Marcail lay still as he placed it over the footboard. "I'll wait for you in the hall. Call if you need me."

Marcail thought it was a little silly of him to stand in the hall and wait for her, but that was before she threw the covers back and swung her legs over the side of the bed. The room took a moment to right itself, and Marcail wondered if her injury was more serious than she realized.

Then a sudden thought occurred to her, and she knew in an instant it was correct. Alex was far more worried than he was letting her know. For *her* sake he was down-playing his reaction. The idea moved her to the brink of tears. She had not expected anyone outside her own family to be so understanding about her fears, and especially not a doctor, but Alex was proving otherwise.

"Marcail?" Alex called from beyond the door, making her realize how much time she was taking.

"I'll be right out."

The door did open soon after that, but Marcail didn't come into the hall. She looked a bit hesitant, and then did something she never expected to do.

"Alex, will you button me?"

To his credit, Alex responded as though the question was as everyday as breathing.

"Oh, sure."

On these simple words he stepped behind her. Within seconds they were headed down the hall. At the top of the stairs, Marcail hesitated.

"I didn't brush my hair or put on my shoes."

"Your hair is lovely," Alex said as he took her hand. "And since we don't stand on ceremony around here, you don't need your shoes unless your feet are cold."

Marcail wondered at the lovely feeling that spiraled through her over his words, and the way his long fingers curled around her own.

Supper was another uproarious affair, and even though Marcail's head ached, she loved it. It reminded her of meals with Rigg's family. After the dishes had been cleared, the group converged on Helen's room for a game of Sticks.

Marcail was unfamiliar with the game, but she learned that it was something of a family tradition with the Montgomerys. She also learned the reason it was new to her: Helen had invented Sticks herself. The family had been playing it for years.

The game consisted of bodies draped all around the room, the more the better, a huge stack of cards with questions or commands printed on each, and dozens of small wooden sticks. Marcail was rather lost at first, until someone explained that the person with the most sticks at the end of the game was the winner.

Helen was in her element as she handled the cards. The questions ranged from easy for the children to outrageous for the adults. The cards that resulted in the most fun were those with commands. The players laughed until they cried when Skip had to stand on his head and say the pledge of allegiance, but everyone had to forfeit a stick when he did so without laughing. At times it seemed that Helen made up the rules as she went along, but she was always fair.

As the evening neared an end, Skip, Alex, and Hannah had the majority of the sticks. Marcail, whose head still ached a bit, was beginning to tire when Helen called her name as the next turn.

"All right, Marcail," Helen said with a determined look in her eye, "sing us a song in a foreign language."

"Oh, Mother," and "Oh, Grandma," were the sounds around the room. Marcail looked surprised at everyone's reaction until Susan spoke.

"That's mother's favorite question, Marcail. She's been asking it for years, and no one has ever done it."

Marcail's face was neither mischievous nor triumphant. The look she gave her mother-in-law was tender as she began to sing a Hawaiian lullaby she'd learned in the Islands. Her voice was high and pure and sweet, and the room was utterly still even after she was finished.

The room remained silent as Skip, Alex, and Hannah stood and gave *all* their sticks to the newest member of the family. Marcail's eyes filled with tears over such a lovely display of love and acceptance.

The room's silence was shattered as each family member erupted with questions. Alex found himself thanking God that he'd found out that morning where his wife had been born. He stayed quiet while the family questioned her and learned quite a bit about where she'd grown up. Some 20 minutes later Alex noticed her fatigue but wasn't sure how to get her out of the room without embarrassment. Thankfully his father noticed also.

"I think maybe the rest of these questions can wait until tomorrow at Al's party."

No one argued, since the next day was Sunday and all had yet to bathe their families. After everyone cleared out, Marcail thought how nice it would be to wash her hair, but she decided she was just too tired to make the effort.

"Want me to fix a bath for you?" Alex offered sweetly after they'd bid Samuel and Helen good night.

"It sounds wonderful, but I don't think I have the energy."

Alex nodded with understanding and silent agreement, thinking she could always bathe in the morning. He didn't mention that she could sleep late if she needed to, and probably would if he woke her in the night like he planned to do. It would be nice to see Pastor Cook and introduce her to his church family, but Marcail's health was more important.

As he waited in the hall, he realized his wife had admitted to him that she was tired. For her to admit even that spoke of how far they'd come in a few weeks. The fear was diminishing, and as Alex waited for his wife to ready for bed, he praised God for that.

Thirty-Seven

"IT'S DARK OUTSIDE, Alex! What time is it?" Marcail asked with sleepy dismay when her eyes finally adjusted to the light of the lantern.

"A little after midnight, I think."

"Why did you wake me?"

"Because I don't take chances with head injuries," he said as he pulled her into a sitting position on the side of the bed. It had been a chore to wake her from her nap the day before, but he found it nearly impossible in the middle of the night. Then he remembered the cool wash-cloth he'd used on her face earlier. It did the trick.

"I still don't understand why you woke me," Marcail scowled, swaying just a bit on the edge of the bed.

Alex put a hand out to steady her and explained, "People who get hit in the head as hard as you did have a tendency to go to sleep and not wake up. And since I'd like to do everything I can to have you around as long as the Lord wills, I woke you."

Marcail's brow lowered, and her tone was grumpy, "If I'd known what kind of a noisy roommate you were going to be, I'd have sent you across the hall on the first night!"

Alex smiled with amusement, but also relief. If she was feisty, she was going to be all right.

"I suppose," Marcail went on, her voice just as cross, "that you want to know my mother's maiden name or something equally as silly to see if I really know who I am. Well, I know exactly who I am! I'm a woman who's considering leaving her husband if he doesn't let her go back to sleep!"

Alex laughed outright at this, but he was also wise enough to listen to her. Within minutes she was tucked securely back beneath the covers and on her way to sleep.

Alex took a little longer to find his own rest. His mind dwelt on this unusual marriage in which he found himself. How did a man who'd been married for several years, widowed, and then married again, keep from touching his new wife? How did a man share a bed with his wife and manage to keep his distance, even though he found her desirable?

It had to be the Lord, Alex concluded. He knew himself to be a man like any other, with God-given desires. But God had also given him a wife who needed special nurturing at this time, and for that God's sustaining strength was proving to be more than sufficient.

As though the Lord spoke to him, Alex suddenly remembered Joseph from the New Testament, a man who'd married the woman he loved when she was carrying the Son of God. The angel had not told Joseph he could not touch Mary, but he chose to keep her a virgin until after the baby was born.

Alex was not trying to be blasphemous by comparing himself and Marcail to Joseph and Mary, but thinking of Joseph was an encouragement to him. Of course Joseph had known that the pregnancy would come to an end, whereas Alex had no such guarantee. Still, Joseph had been God's man for the job, and God had blessed him.

Alex rolled onto his side to see the woman lying next to him. The moonlight came through the window and illumined just a part of her face, but Alex didn't need the light to know how lovely she was.

"I love you, Marcail," he whispered, knowing she would not hear. "And I pray that someday you'll love me too." Alex slept then, but not before he asked God to let that day be soon.

When Alex woke again it was light outside. He'd intended to wake Marcail one more time before morning, but his body must have had other ideas.

Alex padded downstairs, barefoot and without a shirt, to find his father having breakfast in the kitchen. He knew his mother would still be sleeping. His father was ready for church, but had time before he needed to leave. Alex joined him.

"Good morning," Samuel greeted his youngest son.

"Morning," Alex returned as he poured himself a cup of coffee.

"Did I hear you up last night?"

"That you did. Sorry we disturbed you."

"No problem. I take it you woke Marcail to see if she was all right?"

"Right. She got hit pretty hard, and I wanted to be sure."

"How is she?"

"If feisty is any indication, she's in perfect health."

Samuel looked confused. "Marcail doesn't strike me as the feisty type."

"You've never woken her from a sound sleep. She all but told me if I didn't leave her alone, I could sleep across the hall."

Samuel laughed. "With as hard as you tell me she sleeps, I'm surprised you could rouse her."

"It wasn't easy, but at least it gave me peace of mind. I was going to wake her again before morning, but I slept through."

"I'm sure she's all right. She was pretty chipper last night until the end of the game, and then through the family's interrogation."

Alex smiled. "Have you noticed that when she's comfortable with you, she shows every emotion on her face?"

"Your mother and I find her as guileless as a child," Samuel commented.

"That she is."

"You know, Al," Samuel went on, "everytime we've talked this weekend, it's been about Marcail. Your mother and I both wonder how *you* are doing."

"I'm doing just fine," Alex assured his father. "Physically I'm in good shape, spiritually I'm learning to trust God in a brand new way, and emotionally, well, let's just say I'm getting there."

Samuel, who'd risen to retrieve the coffeepot, patted his son on the shoulder and thanked him for his assurance. "If you don't get a chance to talk with your mother alone before you go tomorrow, I'll tell her you're doing well. It will put her mind at ease."

"Have the two of you really been worried?"

Samuel smiled and then chuckled. "Not worried exactly, but try to realize, Al, that we've never seen you this way before. You and Linette were like brother and sister, and you didn't really have a courtship, just a wedding. But now, well now you have this look of delight on your face most of the time. If Marcail is in the room, you can't keep your eyes off her."

Samuel laughed at the dumbfounded look on his son's face. "I've got to get to church early today. If Marcail sleeps late enough, the two of you can breakfast with Mother."

Alex silently watched his dad leave. He realized that if his family could see his love for Marcail, then quite possibly it would be just a matter of time before Marcail could see it herself.

Thirty-Eight

"I CAN SEE you're feeling much better," Helen told her daughter-in-law as they breakfasted in her room.

"Yes," Marcail said with relief. "I feel like I'm back to my old self." It was 10:30, and Marcail had just had her bath. She was now having breakfast with Alex and his mother.

"Well, that's wonderful. I'm sorry you'll miss church, but your health is more important."

"If your pastor is anything like ours, I haven't missed a thing," Marcail said as she set her coffee cup down. Instantly she regretted her words. "I'm sorry," Marcail apologized. "That was completely uncalled for."

"That's all right, dear," Helen assured her. "Alex has talked with us about your church situation."

Wishing that Alex had talked with her, Marcail remained silent. The state of their church concerned her deeply, but she hadn't as yet been comfortable enough with anyone to bring up the matter.

"I take it you're accustomed to solid Bible teaching," Helen mused, beginning the conversation again.

"I guess I've been spoiled no matter where I've lived. In Santa Rosa, Pastor Keller never minced words over the fact that Jesus Christ is the Son of God and the Bible is the Word of God. Then in Visalia, my father was my pastor. He never leaves doubt in anyone's mind that Jesus alone can save us from our sins and give us a fulfilled life on this earth.

"Pastor Zimler doesn't even mention any of those truths. I fear for him, since the Bible speaks about how seriously God takes positions of leadership. He leads an entire church of people down a rosy path of lies week in and week out. He stands in the pulpit and tells us that if we try hard and do good, God will remember our good works when we die.

"Well, heaven is God's home," Marcail said, really in her element now. She sounded just like a teacher. "And He alone dictates how you come to that home—through His Son. Woe be to the man who preaches otherwise."

Alex and Helen couldn't have agreed with her more. They continued to discuss the Willits church for some time, until Alex made a comment that nearly brought Marcail out of her chair.

Alex stated sadly, "That's the way it is when the pastor of the only church in town sits in the pocket of the richest woman in residence."

"What did you say?" Marcail asked in shock.

Alex repeated himself, and Marcail gawked at him. Of course! It was all so clear now. The pastor was just preaching what he was told to preach!

"Alex," Marcail's voice was pained, "such a thing never occurred to me."

Alex's look was compassionate. "It's not very pretty, is it? But Marcail, we're going to keep praying, praying that more than three or four men will come forward and say they've had enough. I'd rather we go without a preacher than go on as we are now."

"Alex," Marcail suddenly wondered aloud, "how did the different families in town come to Christ in the first place?"

"Pastor Zimler has only been there for about three years," Alex explained. "Dick Peik, the man in the pulpit before him, was a man of God. Both on Sunday and Wednesday nights, he taught us how to know God and glorify Him in our lives. He was only in Willits for 18 months, but his effect can still be felt."

"That encourages me, Alex," Marcail said, soft determination in her voice. "God has not turned His back on Willits. Since I believe He's put me there and given me a love for the people, I also believe He will use me to further the news that His Son is the Light in this world."

Both Alex and Helen were so moved by Marcail's obvious burden that no one spoke for a time. Breakfast was finished in silence, each wrapped momentarily in his own thoughts.

"You mean, you don't include your mother in your birthday lunch?"

"It was her idea that we go to the beach," Alex defended himself. "She will be included in the gift-opening, which is always in her room. Honestly, Marcail, she doesn't feel excluded."

Marcail's fierce look softened. She'd quite simply fallen in love with her mother-in-law, and the emotions she felt were making her very protective.

The day was unseasonably warm, and Marcail had to admit that it was perfect for the beach. The cool temperatures from the day before had not kept her from enjoying herself when she went with Alex, but it was going to be nice to leave her coat behind.

Everyone brought quilts to sit on and food to eat. It looked like a feast to Marcail. Meat sandwiches, bread and butter, apples and cheese were passed to all waiting hands. Cups of water were dispersed to quench everyone's thirst.

After Jeremy said grace the talk was light and fun, and for some reason, Alex's family was bent on teasing him. It went on for some time before Skip accused Alex of killing off more patients than he cured. There were a few teaspoons of water left in Alex's cup, and without warning he tossed the contents at his oldest brother.

Skip ducked, and Marcail got it right in the face. There were cries of outrage from the women and laughter from the men, including Alex.

"I'm sorry, Marcail," he chuckled. "I was aiming for Skip."

Marcail was silent as Alex passed her his handkerchief. She wiped her face and then without taking her eyes from her husband, she sat swirling the water in her own cup, one that had just been filled.

"Now, Marcail," Alex began placatingly, immediately seeing her intent. "You have to admit it was an accident. I meant it for Skip, and it was only a few drops."

When all she did was grin mischievously, Alex resorted to a threat.

"I'll get you back if you do it, Marc."

"What will you do?"

"I just might throw you in the Pacific," Alex said, knowing he'd never do such a thing.

"You'd have to catch me first," Marcail said with sweet confidence, and the entire family erupted with laughter and catcalls.

When the noise died down, Alex's look was nothing short of condescending. "I don't think that would be a problem."

The narrowing of Marcail's eyes told him in an instant that he'd said the wrong thing, but his brain told him to move a moment too late. Before he could take a breath, Marcail had thrown the entire contents of the cup in his face. Staying on the blanket just long enough to enjoy the stunned look on his face, Marcail jumped to her feet and ran down the beach.

The shouts from the family told Marcail that Alex was after her, but she didn't look back as she made fast tracks away from her wet husband.

"Go, Marcail, go," came a woman's voice.

"She's not very submissive, Alex. You'd better do something about that when you catch her." This time it was Skip.

"Use every trick in the book, Marcail. Don't hesitate to bite him," Susan shouted as Marcail ran on.

The sounds of the family faded, and Marcail's feet pounded the sand. Alex, who was just beginning to wind, wondered why it wasn't a requirement that a man know all about his wife before he married her. Why were the vows said *before* he knew that she could sing in a foreign language or run like the wind down a sandy beach?

Marcail spotted a huge fallen tree and darted around the far side of it. She paused, ready to go again if Alex was still bent on pursuit, but as she hoped, he came up on the other side and stood, breathing hard and staring at her. A bit winded herself, Marcail knew she had more in her if needed.

"Where," Alex said on a gasp, "did you learn to run like that?"

"I'm not approaching the advanced age of 31, like a certain elderly husband I know."

Alex's eyes narrowed. "You're already in hot water, and now you're pushing your luck." Alex dropped to the sand and leaned his back against the huge log. Marcail stared for a moment at the back of his head before deciding the danger was over. She rounded the log and dropped to her knees beside her husband.

Her legs had no more hit the sand when Alex hauled her across his lap. Marcail's eyes showed her shock, but Alex only smiled triumphantly. He bent his head and wiped his wet cheek against her own.

"Oh, stop it, Alex!" Marcail laughingly wailed. "You're getting me all wet."

"That's the point." He spoke with amusement as he covered both sides of her face with the moisture from his own.

As swiftly as the laughter had come, it subsided. Marcail found Alex's mouth so close to her own she could feel his warm breath on her cheek. Alex hesitated a mere heartbeat before his lips touched down on her's.

It was the first time he'd kissed her squarely on the mouth, and it wasn't a brief kiss. In fact, Alex held Marcail tenderly and kissed her for several minutes. But he also succeeded in holding his emotions in check, causing her to feel cherished, not frightened.

Back at the quilts, both Jess and Cole asked if they could go find Uncle Alex and Aunt Marcail. Their father said no, and when asked why, he told them that someday they would understand.

Thirty-Nine

AFTER THE GIFTS were opened and the cake eaten, Alex's family hugged Alex and Marcail goodbye, telling them to come again soon. The day had been a wonderful celebration, but Marcail found it lovely to have a quiet supper with just Samuel and Helen. Since they would see only Samuel in the morning, they said their goodbyes to Helen before bed.

Marcail and Helen both felt as though they were losing a newfound friend.

"I'll write you," Helen assured her.

"And I'll write back."

"In His time, the Lord will bring us together again," the older woman assured her softly.

Marcail nodded, her throat closing with emotion. She knew she must be tired. It felt wonderful to climb into bed some minutes later. For the first time, Marcail wished that Alex had come to bed at the same time. She fell asleep thinking about the way his arms had felt as they held her close.

The next morning Samuel drove Alex and Marcail to the train station in his small buggy. He lingered while the train pulled away, and Marcail waved until the train rounded a curve and took them out of sight. She settled back in her seat for the long ride and felt Alex's eyes on her.

"Your family is wonderful," she said with sincerity.

"I think so. They were quite taken with you."

"The feeling is mutual."

"I'd like to get to know your family someday soon," Alex said, thinking of his father's words.

"I've thought about that. Maybe we could go to Santa Rosa when school lets out."

Alex nodded, wishing he could think of some way for it to be sooner, but no ideas came to mind. "We'll plan on it," he promised her.

They were fairly quiet on the way back to Willits, both thinking of the work awaiting them. Alex's mind wandered to two patients who were expecting, and Marcail's mind dwelt on Sydney. She prayed that he would come to understand how important he was to God, knowing that only God could change him.

Alex and Marcail fell back into their routine on Tuesday as though they'd never been away. There were letters waiting for Marcail when she checked her mail after school, but she could tell that they'd been written before her family received the news of her marriage.

After school on Tuesday, she told Alex she would see herself home. She wanted to go directly to Vesperman's and check to see if Alex's gift had arrived. It had, and she went away with a huge smile on her face and plans for the next day.

Marcail was up early on Wednesday morning. She moved quietly as she made fresh biscuits, scrambled eggs, and fried some of the bacon Alex had received from a patient just the day before. It didn't take long for the aromas from the kitchen to draw Alex from his bed. When the door opened, Marcail was standing by his chair, guarding a lumpy, wrapped parcel which sat next to his plate. She looked hesitant, and when she spoke she twisted her hands nervously before her.

"Happy birthday, Alex," Marcail said in a rush. "We have a tradition in the Donovan household of putting our birthday gifts next to our plates at supper. I realize I'm a few meals early, but I was rather excited about your gift and wanted you to have it now."

Marcail was thrilled over her plan when Alex's face broke into a broad smile. She stood back so he could sit down and then sat herself, watching with spellbound attention as he unwrapped his gift.

Alex was so surprised over the satchel he was speechless. It was the finest he'd ever seen. It was on the tip of his tongue to ask

Marcail how she could have afforded such a gift on the little he brought home when he remembered she was a paid teacher.

Suddenly Alex realized how well they had been eating since Marcail moved in; not just her cooking, but the food itself. Cookies with peanuts in them, more meat than usual, and muffins and other baked goods were just the start. Alex also realized in that instant that he'd never even mentioned their finances or offered her a dime of money.

"If you're not pleased, Alex, we can order something else." Marcail's soft, unsure voice cut into his thoughts, and Alex realized she'd misunderstood his silence. He immediately rose and came to stand next to her. He bent low, kissed her cheek, and then hunkered down before her.

"It's a wonderful bag, and I wouldn't trade it for any other. But I have to admit, I'd forgotten about your salary."

Marcail looked very confused, and then her face cleared. "Well, I did have to take some money from our savings account, but Mr. Flynn increased my salary because I'm not living in the house by the school. I wanted this to be special, and I know it will last you for years to come, and—"

Marcail rattled on, but all Alex heard was "our savings account." She must have combined their accounts and not mentioned it. It would be easy for his pride to rear its ugly head at this moment, resentful of the fact that his wife probably made more money than he did. In truth he was so touched by her actions that he wasn't the least bit upset. He silently thanked God for the generous wife he'd been given. When she was finished explaining, he kissed her again, thanked her, and then proceeded to load the supplies from his old bag into the new one.

Marcail watched him with tremendous satisfaction. He'd looked so hesitant for a moment that she thought he was going to refuse the gift. The gift and good breakfast were a fine start to the day, and when Alex finally left Marcail at the schoolhouse, she had the feeling that the entire day might be very special.

Her thoughts, however, were drastically altered long before noon. Sydney was at his worst, and Marcail had no choice but to keep him inside during the morning recess. He sat at his desk looking miserable, and after Marcail checked on the children outside, she sat down in the seat in front of him.

"What's wrong, Sydney? Aren't you glad I came back?"

"I guess so, but I still don't like you having to be married."

He'd said this to her in the past. She knew it was nothing personal against Alex, but since it was partially his grandmother's responsibility that she *was* married, she never knew how to answer him. Sydney spoke before she could reply.

"I hate my grandmother; I just hate her."

This statement was a first.

"Oh, Sydney," Marcail said softly. "You might be angry, but I don't think you hate her."

"I do. It's all her fault you had to get married and then go see the doctor's family."

Marcail hadn't realized Sydney understood Cordelia's part in the whole affair. "Why do you hate her because I went to Fort Bragg?"

"Because you're going to love them now and probably move away."

"I'm not going anywhere, Sydney." Marcail reached out and held his chin in her hand. "Don't you know that a teacher's love is like a mother's love. It doesn't divide, it multiplies."

Sydney stared at her, and Marcail wondered, not for the first time, what Sydney's parents were like.

"If a mother has more than one child, her love is not equally divided between the two, so it's 50-50. She loves each one, 100 percent. It's true that God has given me a distinct love for Dr. Montgomery's family, but the special love I feel for you hasn't changed in the least."

It took a moment for Sydney to nod. His face softened.

"*Now* Sydney, we've got to talk about why you're in here and not out playing with your friends." Again the boy nodded, and Marcail went on. "No matter what you're feeling, you *do not* have the right to pull the hair of the person in front of you or to kick the desks of those around you. Do I make myself clear?"

"Yes, Mrs. Montgomery. It won't happen again."

It was, of course, what he said every time. When, she asked herself on the way back to her desk, was he going to see that changes made on his own were never going to be anything but temporary? The thought plagued her until after lunch, but then something happened that made Marcail nearly forget about her class.

At about 2:00 Marcail was sitting at her desk and listening to the primary form read. Her profile was to the door, but she noticed that someone appeared to be moving around at the back of the schoolhouse. She wanted to give the offending student a chance to sit down without a reprimand, but whoever it was, he was causing the other students to become restless.

Marcail looked resignedly at Sydney's desk, but she was surprised to find him sitting quietly. Her gaze flew to the rear of the room and locked with the loving, concerned eyes of Patrick Donovan.

Forty

"PLEASE TAKE YOUR seats, Erin and Kathy," Marcail said to the two little girls at the front of the room. "You may join the rest of the class in silent reading at your desks.

After making this announcement, Marcail walked swiftly to the back. She turned at the doorway of the cloakroom for one more check on the children, and then stepped over the threshold straight into her father's arms. The feel of those strong limbs surrounding her caused tears to threaten.

"Hello, honey," Patrick whispered.

"Oh, Father, I'm so glad to see you."

"Well, you didn't have to make up a story about being married to get me to come." His tone was light, but his eyes begged her to tell him it had all been a tale.

"I'm sorry there was no warning."

Patrick felt as if his worst nightmares had come true. He'd missed so much of Marcail's life, and since he'd returned to the states, she'd become his last chance to share in the joys of courtship and marriage for at least one of his children. Patrick suddenly brought his thoughts up short; now was not the time to go into it. Marcail must have realized this also, since she was the first to speak.

"I dismiss the children in about an hour. I'd like to introduce you just before they go. Would you mind having a seat in the back?"

"Not at all," he answered, thinking that after all those hours on the train, it would feel good to sit on a chair that didn't vibrate or rock.

Patrick sat in a small wooden chair at the rear, and Marcail returned to the front.

"All eyes forward, please," she commanded softly. The children were swift to obey.

"You may put your readers away until tomorrow. Right now we're going to take a little time to look at our map of California." Marcail spread the map on her desk. "You may leave your desks quietly and come forward to gather around my desk."

The children complied, and in a moment they were having a discussion about various locations in the state. Marcail asked how many children had lived outside of Willits. Several raised their hands and were given a chance to show the class where they had lived. It was half past two when Marcail showed them the town of Visalia and told them she'd moved from there when she took the teaching job in Willits. They had all forgotten the stranger at the back of the room until Marcail instructed them to take their seats.

"We have a very special guest with us today. I'd like you to all be on your best behavior when you meet my father." The children looked surprised, and Marcail waited until her father had reached the front of the room.

"Children, this is my father, the Reverend Patrick Donovan."

The children greeted him cordially. Marcail let her father have the floor. The children were allowed to ask questions until they were released. Patrick fielded queries about where he lived, how long he was staying, his occupation, his family, and the train ride from Visalia to Willits.

Patrick was appropriately impressed with his daughter's class and the skillful, competent way she handled them. He was also impressed with the way the class responded to him. He loved their open expressions and genuine interest in their teacher's father. The half hour flew by, and Patrick walked with Marcail to the door to see the children off.

A moment of silence followed. Marcail wondered where to begin. Patrick sat down in the front when she returned to her desk and waited.

"I don't have any reservations about telling you the whole story, but Alex will be here in a few minutes to take me home, and I think we'll be more comfortable talking there."

"I didn't come here to wring some sort of confession out of you. Your letter covered a lot, but it didn't say if you were all right, and *that's* why I'm here."

Marcail nodded. "I'm glad you came. I am all right, but I want to tell you how it came about and have you meet Alex. We could just start walking home, but then Alex won't know where I am."

"I don't mind waiting," Patrick told her with a smile and then his eyes grew misty. "You're an excellent teacher, Marcail, just like your mother was. In fact, you look so much like her I—" Patrick stopped, not wanting to make her cry, but Marcail couldn't stop the teardrops that escaped her eyes.

"There isn't anything you could say to me that would mean more."

Alex chose that moment to enter the schoolhouse. He found a strange man sitting with his wife and the evidence of tears on her face. He wasted no time in coming to her side.

"Marc?" he questioned softly, his arm going around her as he knelt by her chair. When Marcail took a breath and didn't answer immediately, Alex rose and turned a speculative look at the stranger in the room.

Alex would never know that his protective manner with Marcail, as well as the use of her nickname, went a long way toward reassuring the older man that his daughter was in safe hands. He wasn't thrilled with the situation, but neither was he almost sick with worry as he had been a few times. In fact, as Patrick also came to his feet, his hand outstretched to shake Alex's, the thought occurred to him that he'd already seen all he needed to see.

Patrick's mind was not as easy some ten minutes later, when he was finally in his daughter's home and saw the very obvious evidence that Marcail slept apart from her husband. His eyes closed in prayer.

Oh, Father, it hurts me, he prayed silently, *to know that two of my children have not married for love. You in Your grace worked a miracle in Sean's and Charlotte's lives, but it's happened again with Marcail. All I can ask is that here too, You will intercede. Bring love to this home so Marcail and Alex can know the joy of children and have a loving earthly partner to see them through the years.*

Patrick would have prayed on but Marcail came in from saying goodbye to Alex, and he turned to greet her. He stepped forward swiftly when he saw her arms were loaded with wood.

"Oh, honey, why didn't you call me to help you?"

"I'm all right," she laughed. "Besides, you're our guest, and I don't want you to work."

Marcail stacked the wood by the stove. She dusted her hands together and looked at Patrick.

"You didn't really answer the children earlier, so tell me, how long can you stay?"

"As long as you need me."

Marcail smiled, but told him seriously, "I am really doing fine."

They were sitting across the kitchen table now, coffee brewing on the stove. Patrick looked at his daughter and marveled for the hundredth time at what a lovely young woman she'd become. It was far more than physical beauty; she was lovely on the inside as well.

"You were never really mad at me for going back to the mission field alone, I mean, like Katie and Sean, were you?" he asked suddenly.

Marcail thought for just a moment. "I don't think anger is the right word for what I felt—confusion maybe, but not anger. I was pretty young, and Katie, who's always been like a second mother anyway, was so constant for me. I just naturally clung to her."

Marcail had no idea of the pain her words caused Patrick. To think of his little nine-year-old daughter, confused and hurting as she watched him leave, was almost more than he could take.

"That was all a long time ago, Father," Marcail commented, seeing more than Patrick thought. "It was hard, but I watched Katie trust in God, and I learned to do the same thing. Believe me, I've used that knowledge more than once since I arrived here."

Marcail let a few moments of silence pass and then began to recount to her father the entire story. She spared few details. Patrick was as shocked as Marcail had been over the power Mrs. Duckworth wielded in town. She finished her story by telling him all about her weekend with Alex's family. He was thrilled at the loving way they had obviously welcomed her.

Marcail talked all through supper preparations, and with only a question here and there, Patrick listened. Alex was on time, and Marcail was very pleased at how easily the men conversed.

Marcail began to feel very selfish over talking nonstop about herself, so as the three sat down to supper, she asked Patrick about the people in Visalia. Marcail missed it, but Alex noticed the tender light in Patrick's eyes upon his daughter's question.

Forty-One

"EVERYTHING IN VISALIA is great. The folks who knew I was coming send you their love."

Marcail smiled as she thought of the people there who loved her. "How are Duncan and Lora?"

"Great."

"And Sadie?"

"Sadie is doing fine." Patrick said softly, but Marcail had turned to Alex to explain who all of these people were and missed her father's expression.

"My brother, Sean, met and married his wife, Charlotte, in Visalia. They lived there almost up to the time they went to minister in Hawaii. Their pastor was a bit older, and when he decided to leave the pulpit, God called Father to fill it. Duncan is the sheriff and his wife is Lora. They both attend Father's church. Sadie is Charlotte's aunt. She comes on Sunday morning, which is a tremendous answer to prayer, but we're still praying for her salvation."

"We don't need to pray for her salvation anymore." Patrick spoke softly, and Marcail turned to look at him. The look of utter serenity that crossed his features caused Marcail to jump to her feet and throw her arms around his neck.

"When?" Marcail laughed with delight. "When did this happen?"

"About a week ago. She's been coming to our midweek services off and on for several weeks. Last week she stayed late and talked with Lora. Lora told me the sound of longing she heard in Sadie's voice was heartbreaking. By the time they had finished talking, though, Sadie told Lora that all her fears were gone.

"Then Sadie and I talked the day before I received your letter. She told me that for the first time since her husband passed away, she is not afraid of death. She wakes up knowing that if today is her last day on earth, it will be her first day in heaven."

"Oh, Father," Marcail breathed, not needing to say more. Alex, too, was deeply moved. They continued to share, each about his own work and the people in their lives. When Alex mentioned Dean and Kay Austin, Marcail told her husband she'd completely forgotten about Bible study.

"I stopped to see Dean on my way home," Alex explained, putting her mind at ease. "I told him they might not see us."

"Please don't cancel your plans on my account," Patrick was swift to say. "If I can't accompany you, I'll find something—"

"Of course you can go with us," Marcail cut in. "The Austins would love it."

And thus it was settled. The dishes were done in record time, and the three set out for town. Marcail took the cake she'd baked for Alex, and they had a small celebration before the girls went to bed. As it turned out, they did not get to their Bible study.

Because Patrick had been a minister for many years and was a good deal older than the rest of the adults, Alex, Dean, and Kay went into detail about the situation with their present pastor and asked what they should do.

Patrick's first suggestion was to continue on in prayer, but for Cordelia Duckworth, and not just their pastor. He was convinced that she was the root of the problem and that was where they needed to concentrate their efforts.

Marcail was silent, but she'd believed that for a long time. She had no desire to see Sydney's grandmother crushed beneath the heels of the community, but someday, someone was going to have to say no to that woman. As always happened when Marcail's thoughts moved in that direction, she got the uncomfortable feeling that she would be that someone.

Patrick stayed until Friday morning. The Austins graciously opened their home to him, and he stayed both nights in their spare room. His days, on the other hand, were spent with Alex or Marcail. He joined Alex on his rounds, and even stayed in the examination room when Alex saw a few of his younger patients. He took in more of Marcail's expertise with her class and marveled repeatedly at her ease and ability to teach.

It was not easy to see Patrick go, but both Alex and Marcail were thankful for the brief time they had shared. Alex believed that God had given them these days to assure both himself and his new father-in-law that God's hand had been on their marriage.

They told Patrick of their plans to visit Santa Rosa when school let out. Patrick assured them that when he stopped off in Santa Rosa to see Katie and Rigg, he'd pass along the news.

Patrick left with a peaceful heart, believing that with Alex by her side, Marcail would come to no harm. What Patrick didn't know about was the extent of Sydney Duckworth's infatuation with his teacher, an infatuation that would drive him to do something he would regret for the rest of his life.

Forty-Two

"YOU LOOK A bit sleepy this morning," Alex commented over breakfast as he watched Marcail stare into her cup.

"I guess I am," Marcail said, covering a yawn. "I'm rather glad it's Friday, since Sydney's been weighing on my mind so heavily this week."

That, Alex thought to himself, *is an understatement.*

It had been two weeks since Patrick left, and Marcail, after hearing about Sadie's salvation, threw herself into the business of leading Sydney to the Lord. She found it to be exhausting work, and some days she believed they'd made no progress at all. Every night she fell asleep giving Sydney to God, but oftentimes, as the school day went on, she acted as if her efforts alone, and not those of a sovereign God, would save her young student.

Before Marcail knew it, it was time to leave for school. The puddles in the road had long ago dried up, but Alex enjoyed taking his wife to work, so he ignored her every time she suggested walking. She had walked home on a few occasions, but only when Alex could not get away.

The schoolhouse was quiet as Alex took Marcail's books to her desk. As always he kissed her, but after their kiss on the beach in Fort Bragg, his kisses were different. No longer did he hold her jaw and kiss the corner of her mouth, hitting more of her cheek than anything else. She now seemed very willing to accept his embrace and tender kiss, full on the mouth.

He didn't linger this morning as he was always tempted to do, but kissed her twice. His love for her grew daily, and he could never get enough of touching or talking to her. Marcail walked him to the door and smiled with contentment as he rode away.

She was at her desk, writing out a few notes, when she heard movement at the back of the room. It was a bit early for the children to be arriving, but Marcail looked up to see Sydney standing just outside the cloakroom door.

"Why, Sydney," she said with pleasure, "I didn't hear you arrive. How are you today?"

"Fine," the young boy answered, his sullen tone telling Marcail he was anything but. The young school teacher sighed mentally. On the days when Sydney was boisterous and unruly, Marcail knew where she stood. When he was withdrawn and uncommunicative, as he was now, he frightened her.

She knew there was no point questioning him when he behaved like this, so Marcail went back to the paper in front of her, thanking God the week was over and praying the day would be better than she hoped.

The morning progressed fairly smoothly, but Marcail's prayerful heart was never far from the unpredictable Sydney. The other children seemed to take their cue from him; they were quiet as well.

Marcail dropped into her chair at lunch as though she'd worked two days without a rest. She'd just reached for her lunch tin when Alex entered. It was a pleasant surprise. Marcail felt like she was seeing the first friendly face all day.

"Hi," Alex spoke as soon as he sat down. He thought she looked tired, which wasn't like her, and it concerned him. It also made the reason for his visit more difficult.

"Hello," Marcail smiled at him, unaware of the way her fatigue showed.

"I can't stay," he began, "but I wanted to let you know I won't be by after school. I've got to head out to the Castleton place, and I won't be back until evening."

"I don't mind the walk," Marcail told him honestly, thinking it would give her a chance to clear her head and time to pray.

"All right," Alex said, still hating the idea. "I'll see you as soon as I can."

Marcail walked him to the door and then went back to her lunch.

The afternoon was a waste of time. The children went from being obediently quiet to continuously talking out of turn, and Marcail let them go nearly 45 minutes early. It was cool but more than comfortable, and she felt that the students who normally had rides could use the exercise.

Marcail straightened the room and worked at her own desk for over an hour before gathering her books and slipping into her coat. Once outside, she closed the door behind her and moved unsuspectingly toward the steps. Her foot never reached the first step. It caught on a string that had been tightly drawn across the top.

Marcail's books flew through the air. Her hands went out to grasp for the railing and encountered only thin air. In an attempt to right herself, she turned partially with her back to the steps.

Her momentum was too great though, and the change in position didn't help. She ended up falling very hard, most of her weight going onto one side of her back. Marcail gasped for breath after the initial impact. Pain ran from the back of her head to the back of her right thigh. She lay still for long moments, breathing hard with pain and trying to determine if anything was broken.

Marcail didn't realize she was shaking all over until she tried to stand. For the first time since she'd moved to Willits, she wished the schoolhouse was more centrally located. After some effort, Marcail found herself on her hands and knees looking up at the steps above her, and to the thin string tied tautly across the top.

The ache inside of her was more painful than any of her bruises. This had been a deliberate and malicious act. Marcail was absolutely crushed. More from lack of will than from pain, Marcail collected her books with an effort and removed the string, slipping it into the pocket of her coat.

The walk home was accomplished without real thought to where she was going or how fast. She didn't touch the stove or start supper when she arrived, but slipped out of her coat and decided to lie down. She removed her shoes and lowered herself gingerly onto the sofa, careful of her bruises as she pulled a blanket over her.

She told herself she was just going to sleep for a few minutes, but even though her back throbbed, her body had other ideas. Sleep overcame her quickly, blissfully wiping away the steps, the string, and the troubled face of one little boy from her mind.

Forty-Three

MARCAIL WOKE TO a feeling of pressure on her hand. She focused slowly to find Alex kneeling down by the sofa, holding her hand. Her whole body ached like a bad tooth, but she didn't say a word.

"I know you like to sleep in on Saturday mornings," her husband's voice was soft, "but you were out so hard when I came home last night, I thought I should wake you and let you know I'm leaving for work."

"It's Saturday morning?"

"It sure is. You must have stretched out right here after you got home." Alex's voice was compassionate, and his fingers stroked down her cheek and then touched the collar of her dress.

Marcail wanted to sit up, but didn't think she could manage it. "I'm sorry I didn't get you any supper last night," she apologized, not really thinking clearly.

"I didn't wake you to make you feel bad. I'm fine, and I just hope you caught up on some of your rest." Alex stood then. "I'm off to work. I probably won't be home for lunch, but I should be done for the day around 2:00. There's hot coffee on the stove when you get that far."

Marcail said a soft goodbye that Alex attributed to sleepiness just before he kissed her. He didn't notice that she lay absolutely still as she watched him leave.

"Is it possible to feel worse today?" Marcail asked herself, as the door closed on her spouse. She had never taken a severe fall before and didn't know what to expect. Her skin had always bruised easily, but none of the bruises were ever the result of a serious accident.

As though her skin had turned into dried leather in the night, Marcail gingerly moved into a sitting position. She was careful to keep her back away from the sofa back, but the bruised side of her bottom and thigh were telling her to lie back down.

Marcail fought the urge. She pushed herself off the sofa and stood. It took some minutes to make herself move again, but Marcail knew that waiting any longer would not change a thing. Her first step forward told her it was going to be a long day.

Alex was thrilled to see his last patient leave at 1:30. He was tired and ready to go home. He cleaned up the examination area and readied his bag for emergencies. He was ready to leave when the door opened. Alex concealed his disappointment over being kept longer in town and went out to the waiting room. To his surprise he found Sydney Duckworth waiting for him.

"Hello, Sydney," Alex said carefully, looking past him once or twice to see if his grandmother was going to follow him through the door.

"Hello, Dr. Montgomery. Is Mrs. Montgomery here?"

Not until Sydney asked the question did Alex really look at the boy. His eyes were scared, his features even more pinched than usual.

"Is there something I can help you with, Sydney?" Alex offered kindly, thinking the boy seemed very upset.

"No, no," Sydney spoke as he backed toward the door. "I just thought maybe Mrs. Montgomery had come with you, and I would say hi."

"I'm sorry, Sydney," Alex smiled gently, knowing the boy was half in love with his wife. "I don't believe she planned to come into town today. Maybe you'll have a chance to talk with her at church tomorrow."

The words seemed to put the boy at ease, and Alex stood for a time after he'd left, trying to put his finger on what had been wrong. No answers came, and Alex, always ready to see his wife, put Sydney out of his mind and hurried toward the livery.

Wishing she'd gotten more done, Marcail looked despairingly around the house. The laundry was washed and hung out, but no baking had been done and supper wasn't even a thought in her mind. The day had passed in a painful fog, and Marcail had fought going back to bed every minute. She stared in surprise when Alex walked in the door, never dreaming it was that late in the day.

"Hello," he greeted her. "Did I startle you?"

"Not really," she admitted. "I just didn't realize the time." Marcail took a breath and kept talking, believing that she owed Alex an explanation.

"Alex, I'm sorry I didn't get much done today, but the truth is, I took a fall down the schoolhouse stairs yesterday, and it's made me kind of stiff and lazy."

"You fell down the stairs?" Alex's voice showed his concern, but since Marcail was so fearful of doctors, he told himself to move slowly and not press her. "Are you all right, Marcail?"

"I bruise easily, but I'm sure I'll be fine." Marcail's voice was as even as ever, and Alex, truly believing that by now she would be comfortable enough to tell him if she were really hurt, took her at her word. He took in her composed features and nodded with satisfaction. He also decided to put her mind at ease about the household chores, so he got out the bowl to mix bread dough.

"I really should be doing that," Marcail said from behind him.

"Not if you don't feel well," Alex said reasonably. "Anyway, I've always enjoyed baking. Oh, by the way, Sydney stopped in to say hello. I think he wanted to talk with you about something. I told him he'd probably see you tomorrow at church, and he seemed satisfied with that."

Alex had his back to Marcail and completely missed the look of misery that crossed his wife's face. Marcail did help Alex finish the baking, and if her movements were a little slower than normal, he didn't seem to notice.

Alex fixed supper after he'd done some odd jobs outside. They were just finishing when the bell rang, summoning the doctor's services in town. Alex, usually very pragmatic about his work, looked a bit let down. Marcail was secretly pleased because he was usually gone for at least two hours, and she'd been hoping for some privacy for her evening bath. She knew it was going to cost her to prepare the tub, but the soak was going to be worth it.

Ignoring the dishes, Marcail shuffled around preparing her bath the moment Kelsey galloped out of the yard. As Marcail had suspected, it took great effort to drag the tub out and fill it, but as she sank into the water, she had her first relief in 24 hours.

Sparing her right side as much as possible, Marcail soaped up and washed her hair. It was impossible to maneuver the rinse bucket with only one hand, and Marcail moaned as she was forced to lift her right arm above her head, taxing her bruised shoulder to the limits.

The job done, she sat back in the tub and tried to catch her breath. She found she was trembling all over again, but having her hair and body clean had been worth it.

It was a tremendous effort to leave the tub and dry off, but again Marcail moved slowly and got through it. She stood, nightgown in hand for some minutes, knowing that to lift it over her head was going to hurt. Holding the garment in front of her and feeling the cold of the room, she knew how warm she would be if she could just make the effort, but still she stood rooted.

Feeling weary in body and spirit, she would have continued to stand still, but the door opened quietly behind her. Marcail, wrapped in her own little world of pain and disillusionment, never heard the door's movement. As it was, only seconds passed before she heard Alex's horrified call. Forgetting for the moment the pain in her body, she turned to find him coming toward her, looking every inch the doctor she knew him to be.

Forty-Four

MARCAIL BACKED INTO the living room away from Alex until his hands on her upper arms brought her to a gentle stop. She was holding the nightgown to the front of her, as though it were a suit of armor.

Alex looked into her terrified eyes, knowing he had to do something that would probably destroy all the trust she'd come to have in him.

"Marcail," he spoke softly. "I have to check your back."

Marcail shook her head and opened her mouth, but no sound came out.

"I can tell," he went on in that same gentle voice, "even from across the room, that your bruises are serious. I *have* to check them."

"I told you I've always bruised easily," Marcail finally blurted out, sounding as breathless and terrified as she really was.

Alex's heart broke, but there was no way he was going to ignore the coal-black bruises and scrapes he'd seen on the back of her body.

With gentle insistency, his hands still holding her upper arms, he drew her back toward the kitchen where the lantern burned bright on the table. He turned her carefully toward the light, nearly changing his mind when he felt the violent trembling of her entire body.

Alex did not rush his examination, and had Marcail been capable of thinking clearly, she would have realized that his manner was completely professional. She felt his hand on her shoulder blade, the skin of her bottom, and the back of her thigh. It felt like forever, when in fact only a minute had passed before he was turning her so that her bare back was once again shielded from his eyes.

The light bounced off of the tears standing in her eyes, and Alex turned without leaving the room. He spoke over his shoulder.

"Put on your nightgown, Marcail." His voice sounded sad, but nothing registered with Marcail beyond her pain and humiliation.

She scrambled into the long, warm gown, and without a word, moved stiffly into the dark living room to sit on the sofa. Following with the lantern, Alex found her sitting sideways, protecting her back he was sure. She didn't change position to look at him as he placed the lantern on the table behind Marcail's turned back. He lowered himself to sit next to her.

Looking at his wife's stiff back covered by her still-wet hair, Alex was at a complete loss for words. Helplessly, he glanced around and spotted her hairbrush on the table where he'd set the lantern. He picked it up and began to draw it through her hair.

Moments passed in silence.

"You don't have to do that," Marcail said, her voice as flat and distant as when they'd first met.

"I realize that."

Again silence fell.

"You said you bruise easily." Alex spoke and let the sentence hang.

"Yes."

"Have *you* seen your back?" Alex wanted to know.

"No."

Alex digested these monosyllabic answers for a moment and then knew it was time for some gut-level honesty.

"I'm learning the hard way that I can't assume anything with you, Marcail. So I'm going to ask you some specific questions, and I expect honest answers." Alex paused a moment with her hair, but Marcail didn't reply.

"Does your back hurt?" The question had an obvious answer to his mind, but he needed to start somewhere.

"Yes."

"How much?"

Here Marcail hesitated. "Quite a bit," she finally returned.

"You say it happened at the school—was it on your way home?"

"Yes."

"Down the steps?"

"Yes."

"How did you fall?"

"I can't tell you that."

This answer was the last thing Alex expected, and he stopped brushing again.

"Why can't you tell me?"

"Because I'm too weary to fight you if you overreact."

Alex thought this statement was as cryptic as they came, but after a moment's thought, a horrifying idea came to mind.

"Marcail, did someone push you?"

"Not exactly."

Again Alex felt completely in the dark, and suddenly very discouraged. He'd begun to think that he knew this woman, that they were slowly becoming one, but she was as closed to him right now as she'd been before they wed.

Alex picked up the lantern and took it with him as he moved to the other side of the sofa. There was not as much room there, but Marcail shifted back slightly so Alex could sit in front of her.

The lantern light flickered across her eyes, eyes that had lost hope. Alex had never seen Marcail like this; it frightened him.

"Talk to me, Marcail," he pleaded with her softly. "Let me help you. I won't do anything you don't want me to do, but please don't shut me out when I care so much." Alex reached for one of her hands and held it between his own.

Marcail, in a fog of pain and anger, saw for the first time how difficult this must be for Alex. The look of concern she saw on his face was like a sudden lifeline. Prompted by his gentle touch and tender eyes, Marcail began to speak.

"I've gone over it and over it in my mind, and I can only figure that he saw us kissing."

"Who saw us kissing?"

"Sydney. He was at school so early yesterday morning. I didn't even hear him arrive. He's infatuated with me, you know, and it must have upset him to see you kiss me goodbye. He was quiet all day, and that always scares me, but I never dreamed he would—"

Marcail halted, and Alex urged her to go on. She pointed toward the string she had placed on the sofa table and Alex reached for it. Marcail spoke when it was in her hands.

"This was tied across the top step when I left the schoolhouse yesterday."

Alex could only stare at the heavy string, stunned beyond belief. He desperately wanted to hold her, but knew it would only give her pain.

"He's been my mission field since I arrived, Alex. I mean, I love the other children, but I felt so strongly that God wanted me to reach out to Sydney and that he needed me."

"Shhh," Alex spoke as he stroked her hand. "Don't try to understand it all now. We'll have plenty of time to pray and figure out what to do when you feel better."

"I don't think I could pray anyway. I want to, but the hurt—it's so bad . . ."

Alex quieted her again and helped her to stand. It didn't seem to register with her that he was taking her into the bedroom. He helped her carefully onto her good side in bed and covered her with the blankets. He'd lit the bedroom lantern and turned it low. Kneeling down, he found her staring sightlessly at his chest.

"I'm sorry, Alex," she said, her voice filled with utter defeat. "It seems that all you do lately is take care of me. What a disappointment I've turned out to be as a wife."

Alex didn't reply. Nothing could be further from the truth, but Marcail was in no shape to hear anything right now. He watched her eyes close and then flutter open again, this time in fear.

"Are you going somewhere, Alex?"

"No, I'll be right here," he assured her.

Marcail's small hand came out of the covers and touched his chest. He felt her grip the fabric of his shirt and say softly as her eyes closed in sleep, "I hope the bell doesn't ring again tonight."

Forty-Five

LONG AFTER MARCAIL slept, Alex sat in the kitchen struggling with his anger. The look on Sydney's face earlier that day was now easy to identify—it was guilt. Even at the very obvious evidence of his crime, Alex was not angry at Sydney but at his grandmother, and not just angry—livid.

He tended to be overprotective where Marcail was concerned, but this, this was an outrage! Because of the selfish, blind foolishness of an old woman, a little boy was being raised to think he could do anything that came into his head.

A sudden image from months ago, before he and Marcail were even friends, came to mind. He remembered one of the Austin girls telling him that Miss Donovan had not been feeling well so school had been dismissed early. Alex had stopped to check on her, wondering as he did about the scratch on her face. He now knew exactly who had caused that scratch.

The recollection did not help Alex's mood. He found his anger kindled anew at the very thought. However, just as suddenly as Alex's anger flamed back to life, it died. He sat very still when he realized he was being swept away by his emotions.

Alex reached for his Bible, always present on the kitchen table. He turned to a couple of verses he recalled, James 1:19,20, and read aloud in the still house. "Wherefore, my beloved brethren, let every man be swift to hear, slow to speak, slow to wrath; for the wrath of man worketh not the righteousness of God."

After he read, Alex began to pray. He started by confessing his wrath, and then gave the whole ugly affair to God. He thanked God that the ringing of the bell had been for a minor incident and he'd been able to come right home. As he prayed, Alex realized *he* was not the one who should be offended, but that sins had been committed against God.

He also realized that he was going to need to take his cue from Marcail. She had been afraid of how he would react, so he figured she must have some idea how she wanted things handled. It might take some time before she felt up to it, but as Alex climbed into bed beside his bruised wife, he determined to learn all he could from her concerning Sydney Duckworth.

Alex left the house first thing Sunday morning to see Stanley Flynn. He told him briefly that Marcail had suffered a fall and was not feeling well. He also told him not to expect her back at school for at least two days, possibly longer.

As he rode home he realized he might have made her furious with such a move, but unless he missed his guess, she was not going to want to do much of anything for the next 48 hours.

Marcail lay motionless in Alex's soft bed. Usually able to sleep through anything, the closing of the front door, along with the pain in her back, had startled her awake. She found herself silently imploring Alex to be coming in, and not heading out for the day. She rolled, ever so carefully, onto her back. A moment later Alex appeared in the doorway.

Marcail's fingers moved on the covers in a semblance of a wave, and Alex entered. He pulled the curtains back on both windows before retrieving a chair from the kitchen and placing it close to the bed. Not until he was seated and had taken a close look at Marcail's features did he speak.

"I have quite a few questions I'd like to ask you." Alex's mind was so set on the accident that he failed to ask Marcail how she felt.

"About my fall?"

"Not directly. I want to know about Sydney, and how he behaves in class."

Marcail nodded. "I'm still kind of sleepy, but I'll do my best."

"It doesn't have to be right now. I went to see Stan Flynn this morning. I told him you'd fallen, and he wouldn't be seeing you for at least two days."

Marcail's eyes widened at this, but Alex went on.

"I know you care about your class, Marc, but you can barely walk." Alex's voice was extremely reasonable. "You also have to teach for the next three months, and I don't think it's wise to tax yourself when you still have so many weeks before you're through for the summer."

"I may be through teaching long *after* the summer," Marcail said suddenly, and Alex stared at her. "I've decided to talk with Cordelia Duckworth, but I want to wait until school is out and I've had a few weeks off."

Alex could see this had been on her mind and wanted to show his support of her decision. "I'll go with you."

"You don't have to."

Alex's anger flared. Thinking she was still trying to keep him at arm's length, he retorted in a tight voice, "Whether you like it or not, Marcail, we *are* husband and wife."

Marcail blinked in surprise. "I never said I didn't like being your wife," she told him quietly.

"No, you haven't *said* anything, but you still think and *act* like a single woman. I'm sorry, Marcail," Alex rose wearily, thinking how tense all of this was making him. "I shouldn't have said that." He went on before Marcail could reply. "Would you like to sleep some more or have a little something to eat?"

"I'm not very hungry," Marcail told him.

Alex nodded. "I'll leave you to rest then."

Alex did leave her, closing the door on his way out. Marcail was still awake when he checked on her two hours later.

Forty-Six

"How about some soup?" Alex asked as soon as he saw that Marcail was awake.

"That sounds good. If you'll give me a few minutes, I'll come to the table."

It was on the tip of Alex's tongue to ask if she needed help, but he knew what her answer would be. He left and shut the door once again.

Marcail had prayed for most of the two hours that had passed, but the strain of her conversation with Alex was still present. She did not know what to do.

Maybe I do act like I'm single, she thought to herself defensively. *But it's hard to get close to someone you hardly know.* The moment the thought formed, Marcail saw it for the flimsy excuse that it was. Alex had showed her in countless ways that he wanted a real marriage, but Marcail had been hesitant. What she was waiting for, she didn't even know herself.

What a mess. Marcail muttered as she painstakingly climbed out of bed. Once on her feet, she realized she would have to go to the living room to get her robe. A glance at the kitchen table and the aromas filling the air told her Alex had been busy.

Marcail came back to the table feeling modestly covered and actually experiencing hunger pains. Alex prayed before they ate, and the meal progressed in near silence. As Alex cleared the table, Marcail spoke up.

"Did you want to hear about Sydney now?" Her voice was tentative, and Alex turned from his task at the basin.

"I would like to hear, but only if you're up to it."

"What exactly did you want to know?"

Alex rejoined her at the table. "I want to know if this is typical of Sydney. I mean, his behavior in your class— has he tried things before?"

Marcail nodded. "Sydney is unpredictable at best. He has trouble with his temper, not an unusual occurrence in any child, but he turns violent with little or no warning."

"Is this the first time the violence has been directed at you?"

"No. One day, very early in the year, he threw a rock and hit me in the face. I think he scared himself, because for a long time after that things were calm. Beyond that, he's pulled away from me when I have his arm, and shoved past me so strongly that I've had to take a step backward."

"What does he do to the other children?"

"Kicks their desks, pulls hair, that type of thing. I don't consider any of it harmless, and I always punish him. But since I can't go to Mrs. Duckworth, my hands are tied. I have used his love for me to get through to him at times. My telling him that I'm disappointed seems to carry more weight than anything else I say or do. By the way, how did he seem at your office?"

"I didn't recognize it at the time, but he looked guilty. At first I thought he was afraid of something, and then he seemed so relieved when I told him he'd see you at church."

They fell silent for a time, and then Marcail spoke. "At first I was too shocked to feel anything, and then I felt betrayed. Now I'm afraid. I'm afraid of Sydney, and I won't be able to let him out of my sight for the remainder of the year."

"Are you sure you should wait until summer to confront Mrs. Duckworth?" Fearing for her safety and halfway hoping she would lose her job, Alex wished he could order her to quit.

"Yes, of that I'm sure. I don't know why, except that I feel a definite peace about finishing the year. If I go to Mrs. Duckworth now, I'll lose my job as well as all touch with the children.

"Who knows," Marcail went on, her voice expressing a glimmer of hope. "Maybe God will use this accident in a mighty way—a way that would bring Him glory."

Alex didn't reply to this, and Marcail left the table moments later. She made up her bed in the living room, and Alex took that as a sign that she wanted to be left alone.

Alex's prediction about Marcail not wanting to work right away proved to be true. It was Tuesday afternoon before she put a dress on and began to even *start* feeling like her old self.

Things had continued on a strained note between husband and wife through this time, but Alex's care of Marcail could not be faulted. He was at home as much as his work allowed, leaving notes at his office to ring the bell for emergencies only. He had Marcail soaking in a warm bath both morning and evening, and even though Marcail hated it, Alex checked her bruises after each evening bath.

After supper Tuesday night, Marcail said she was desperate for some fresh air. Alex, knowing it could only do her good, helped her into her sweater. She planned to walk around the perimeter of the yard until he finished the dishes.

As it was, Alex had barely started the dishes when Marcail came back through the door. She tried to hide it, but Alex saw fear in her eyes.

"What's happened?"

"The Duckworth coach; it's coming up the road."

Alex's brows rose in surprise, but he spoke calmly. "It would seem, Marcail, that this incident is going to come to a head long before summer."

The young schoolteacher could only nod. Alex told her if she wanted to wait in the bedroom he would answer the door and then come for her. Marcail was tempted, but felt the problem was really hers and she should be present.

She took a place at the kitchen table, her hands clenching in her lap when the knock sounded. Alex answered the summons, and both were surprised to see Sydney standing alone on the step.

Marcail's heart broke at the sight of him, and she watched as he looked up at Alex and then peered tentatively past him to get a better view of her. His eyes were huge and questioning in his pale face, and Marcail wasn't sure what he expected to see. A moment later, he covered his face with his hands and burst into tears.

Forty-Seven

MARCAIL SAID NOTHING as Alex put a hand to Sydney's back and guided him to a kitchen chair. He pressed a clean handkerchief into the boy's hands and then sat down in the chair beside him.

Marcail, watching from her place across the table, was not sure what to say. She knew only that her heart was breaking with love for this little boy. She understood that to reject him right now would be devastating, but neither was she going to accept his standard line about it not happening again.

After some minutes, Sydney began to contain himself and look at the adults at the table.

"Sydney," Marcail spoke, sounding very much like a teacher. "Does your grandmother know you are here?"

"Yes, Mrs. Montgomery," he sniffed.

Marcail nodded. "She's not waiting out in the carriage, is she?"

"No, ma'am."

Again Marcail nodded. "Then why don't you tell us why you came."

This time it was Sydney's turn to nod, and suddenly he looked terrified all over again. His words were halting, but understandable.

"I came—to tell you—I'm sorry—" he stopped as though out of breath, and Marcail spoke.

"I forgive you, Sydney."

Sydney nodded again but didn't look at all relieved. "Can I ask you a question?" He paused, glancing between both adults, whose expressions were open and patient, before settling terrified eyes on his beloved teacher.

"Will I go to hell for what I've done?" he burst out, his face crumbling, tears barely held in check.

"Come here, Sydney," Marcail beckoned compassionately and shifted in her chair so she could take him in her arms. It was too much for the 11-year-old, and his tears came in a torrent. Another five minutes passed before he was able to breathe normally. Both Alex and Marcail took that time to pray silently.

Finally raising a tear-stained face, Sydney asked, "Will I, Mrs. Montgomery? Will I go to hell for what I've done?"

Marcail hugged him close once again. She stroked the hair from his damp little forehead and began to speak softly.

"What you did was very wrong, Sydney. I think you understand that."

Sydney's head came away from his teacher's shoulder. "It was a sin, a big sin?"

"Yes, you did sin. We all sin."

"Not you," Sydney spoke vehemently.

"Yes, I do, Sydney. The Bible says that *all* sin," she told him gently.

"So you're afraid of going to hell too?" Sydney's voice was full of wonder, and Marcail almost smiled.

"No, Sydney, I'm not," she continued with complete assurance. "You see, God has made a way for us to come to Him. Jesus Christ is the way. When we believe Jesus died to save us from sin, He comes to live inside of us. Then when we die, because of our belief in Him we'll go to heaven and live forever with God.

"So you see, Sydney, even though I sin, God has provided the gift of His Son to save me, and I've accepted that gift." Marcail hesitated, afraid that she might turn him away forever, but her next words had to be said.

"I don't think you've ever accepted God's gift of salvation, Sydney, and I'm afraid that without Jesus Christ, you'll never change. Each time something has happened, you've told me it will never happen again. But it does. God can change you, Sydney. He can help you control your temper and change the way you treat other people."

Marcail fell silent then, allowing her young student to absorb all she'd said. It seemed he wouldn't say anything, but he suddenly turned to Alex.

"I've hated you at times, and that's a sin, isn't it?"

"Yes, it is," Alex told him, his voice noncondemning. "But what Mrs. Montgomery was telling you is true—we all sin." Alex opened his Bible to the book of 1 John.

"You see right here in the first chapter, verse 8, it reads, 'If we say we have no sin, we deceive ourselves, and the truth is not in us.' But then if you turn back to the Gospel of John, chapter 3 verse 36," Alex held the Bible so Sydney could read along with him, "it says, 'He that believeth on the Son hath everlasting life; and he that believeth not the Son shall not see life, but the wrath of God abideth on him.'

"You can believe on the Lord Jesus Christ, and let Him make the needed changes in your life, as Mrs. Montgomery and I have. God is waiting for you to take the gift that He offers. Believe on Christ with your whole heart, and then learn to live God's way."

Alex's voice was kindness itself, and Sydney couldn't help but respond to the tenderness he saw there.

"And you think God would really want to give the gift to me, even though I've hated a lot of people?"

"Hate is a serious thing," Alex told him. "There is a man in the Bible named Saul who hated people so much that he had them killed. Then one day Saul learned that what he was doing was wrong, and he let Jesus Christ come into his heart. God changed his name to Paul and turned his life completely around."

"Would I have to change my name?"

"No," Marcail smiled as she answered. "But if you let Him, God can change your life."

"That's what I want," Sydney said after a moment, "but I'm not really certain—" He hesitated, and Marcail stepped in.

"I accepted God's gift when I was just a little girl. My father prayed with me, and I said something like this, 'Dear Father in heaven, I believe You sent Your Son to die for my sins, and right now I ask You to come into my life—take away my sins and live in me.' My father went on to explain that this didn't mean I would never sin again, but that God would never leave me, and when I did sin, all I needed to do was confess and turn away from those sins to be right with Him."

"Can I pray now?"

"You certainly can. If you want to pray out loud, I can help you, or you can pray silently in your heart."

Sydney opted for silent prayer, and both Marcail and Alex bowed their heads as he prayed. Sydney was done first, having told God he was sorry for his sin and that he wanted Jesus Christ to live in him. He then sat looking at his teacher until she raised her head.

He loved Mrs. Montgomery more than he had ever loved anyone else on the earth. When she'd first started talking about his need to believe in Christ, he thought he'd better do it in order to really prove to her how sorry he was for tripping her.

Then Dr. Montgomery had shown him the verses right out of the Bible, and Sydney had suddenly really wanted to know Christ. The verses he read gave him hope, more hope than he would have believed possible. And with this new hope burgeoning within him, it was very easy to sit quietly and wait for his teacher to open her eyes.

Marcail kept her head bent for some time, praying that Sydney's decision had been real, and not just something done to please her. She honestly saw no other way for him to become a sound, well-adjusted adult. Marcail trusted in God to change him, especially since his home life was so lacking in proper discipline. Sydney needed someone to answer to, and who more perfect than a loving heavenly Father.

Marcail asked God to become very real to Sydney in the weeks to come, so that even though he now had someone to answer to, he would understand that God was the most loving father any boy could want.

When Marcail finally raised her head, she found Sydney smiling at her. Marcail held her arms out once again, and this time there were no words of apology or regret, just genuine love between two of God's children.

Forty-Eight

I N THE DAYS and weeks that followed, Marcail saw that Sydney's conversion had been genuine. She learned in the first week that her speculation over why he had tripped her had been correct. But his remorse over the incident was sincere, and the changes in him proved it.

Marcail was not certain what he said to his grandmother, but nearly every afternoon the Duckworth carriage was late. He would stay after school to talk, ask questions about the Bible, or recite the latest verse he was memorizing.

Life in the classroom was not without its flaws, but Marcail was thrilled with the new Sydney. In fact, the entire class responded positively to the changes they saw in him. Marcail shared privately with the children she knew were praying for her and for Sydney. They continued their prayers, only this time they prayed that Sydney would grow in the Lord.

The weather was improving, and the class was now able to spend extra time out of doors, working on everything from nature projects to their spelling lessons. The end of the year was drawing to a close at an alarming rate. Even though Marcail was very pleased with the year, a dark shadow lay over her heart. It seemed the closer she and Sydney became, the further Alex and she moved apart.

He no longer took her home since the weather was so warm. In fact some mornings when Alex had to be out the door very early, she walked to school. This was really not a problem, but the most evident change in their relationship was the fact that he stopped touching her.

As they rode Kelsey, his touch was an impersonal one. He no longer kissed her goodbye or even walked her inside the schoolhouse once they arrived. At one time, Marcail would have said she preferred it this way, but she was discovering with heartrending clarity that she missed her husband's touch.

He was never rude or short-tempered with her, but along with his touch, the fun, light teasing he'd always lavished on her had also left their marriage. Much of the time he was busy at the office, but even when they did spend time together, it was like living with a polite stranger. Marcail would have been surprised to learn that Alex would have described her the same way.

Something had died inside of Alex when he found his wife so severely injured and knew that if it had been up to her she would never have told him. He had really believed they'd come a long way, but it seemed all feelings of love and trust had been on his part.

He tried to understand how shocked and upset she'd been after the fall, but her reserved attitude toward him continued even after Sydney had come to the Lord. At a time when he thought she would be walking on a cloud, she was as aloof and cold to him as when they'd talked months before on the road to the schoolhouse. Both husband and wife needed a good dose of togetherness, with no patient or student interruptions.

The last day of school was only two weeks away when Marcail decided she needed to remind Alex that she was going to Santa Rosa. If things had been warmer between them, she would also have reminded him that he had planned to accompany her. Now, however, her pride had come to the fore, and she told herself she wasn't going to beg him to do something he didn't want to do. It never once occurred to her *not* to go, or to wait until he brought the subject up.

They were having a rare evening alone when Marcail finally filled him in on her plans. Alex didn't say much from his place on a living room chair. He nodded quietly as she spoke, until she told him she wouldn't be back until the end of June.

"The *end* of June?"

"That's right." Marcail's chin raised slightly. "I haven't seen my family since Christmas, and with school out, there is really no reason for me to stay here all summer."

If she had slapped Alex in the face, she couldn't have hurt him more. Marcail hadn't meant it the way it sounded, and had it not been for the brief expression of pain she saw in his eyes, she wouldn't have said a word. But she *had* seen Alex's look of hurt, however brief, and decided to remind him that he'd planned to go.

"I thought maybe you'd come with me." Her voice was hesitant.

"I can't be gone an entire month," he told her softly.

"Then maybe you could come for half the time." Marcail wasn't sure why she said that after she'd told herself she wasn't going to beg.

"Are you sure you wouldn't mind my going along?" Alex was feeling too vulnerable to agree straight out-of-hand.

"I know my family wants to meet you." Marcail evaded the question neatly.

So that's why I'm going—to meet your family, Alex thought to himself. At the same time he knew someone was going to have to bend in this cold war in which they were now engaged. He was desperate enough at the moment to be that someone.

"All right; I'll stay for two weeks. When did you plan on leaving?"

"Saturday, a week from today. The day after school is out."

Alex nodded again and went back to the book in his lap. Marcail's eyes dropped to her school lesson, but she stared sightlessly at the page. The only thing she could see right then was her room at Kaitlin and Rigg's. It sat at the bottom of the stairs and sported *one* double bed.

Forty-Nine

I<small>T WAS A VERY</small> silent couple that boarded the train for Santa Rosa on Saturday, June 4. Kelsey had been delivered to the livery, and Alex had arranged to have the local veterinarian cover for him. It wasn't the same as having a doctor on call, but none of Alex's female patients were expecting, and having the elderly Dr. Crow on hand was better than nothing.

Marcail sat by the window, and Alex took the aisle seat. There was little conversation between them for the first 15 miles, until a sudden shifting of the car caused Marcail to fall into Alex's shoulder.

"I'm sorry," she said as she righted herself in the seat.

"I don't mind. I'm still getting used to the fact that you don't sleep on the train."

"I don't know what you mean."

"Linette never lasted more than two miles."

Marcail looked into his face as he spoke and suddenly realized how much she missed his talking with her.

"You never talk about her; is it very hard for you?"

"It was at first," Alex admitted, not understanding just yet that this was Marcail's way of trying to open the door that had been shut between them for so many weeks. "It's been four years, however, and time does heal."

"You grew up together, didn't you?" Marcail tried again when it seemed Alex would not go on.

411

"Yes. My folks have told me we were inseparable from the first time we laid eyes on each other. I don't know if we should have been married, but we were." Again Alex hesitated.

"Why do you say that?" Marcail was surprised.

"Oh, I didn't really mean it the way it sounded, but we were such good friends. As kids I'd always been her champion, and we could talk about anything, even argue, and still walk away as friends.

"But then later our friendship made our marriage difficult. I think I must have been more like a big brother to Linette than a husband. She always believed it was my job to make her happy. She came to depend on me so heavily that when she became miserable living in Willits it put quite a strain on our marriage."

"Why didn't she like Willits?" Marcail wasn't certain that any of this was her business, but Alex was really talking to her for the first time since she'd fallen down the schoolhouse steps, and she desperately wanted him to continue.

"It wasn't Willits specifically—that was the problem. Linette never wanted to live away from Fort Bragg. She couldn't seem to grasp that Fort Bragg already had two doctors and I needed to go elsewhere. I was thankful we were able to be as close as we were, but it wasn't good enough for her." Alex paused, his eyes staring out the window at nothing. Some of the pain flooded back to him.

"How did she die?" Marcail couldn't keep from asking.

"The actual cause of death was a head injury when she fell from a chair, but the fall, or rather the weakness that brought her off the chair, was caused by tuberculosis. In the mid to late stages of tuberculosis, patients run fevers in the afternoon and evenings, and Linette was trying to do too much when she wasn't up to it. I think she must have become a bit dizzy while on that chair, or possibly fainted."

Sharing absently about his past without really looking at his wife, Alex now turned to find that Marcail had gone very pale. She also looked tremendously grief-stricken, more grief-stricken than she should have been for a woman she didn't even know.

"What is it, Marcail? What did I say?"

"My mother died of tuberculosis," she admitted softly. "It's amazing what you can block out. I'd completely forgotten how ill she'd been every evening."

"How old were you when she died?"

"Nine."

Alex's heart broke just a little at the thought. A child is so young, and so much in need of a mother, when only nine years old.

Alex wanted to say something, but Marcail was ready to talk and there was no need.

"They kept her illness from us until we arrived in San Francisco. I'll never forget the first time I saw my aunt's house. It was huge. I'd never been away from Hawaii, and I didn't know they made houses like that. I was terrified of it. I remember holding onto my mother's hand with all my might as she led me inside. Her hand was so hot I thought she must be scared too.

"We had a few days of rest, but I could tell something was wrong. Katie and Sean were not as fun as they had been, and I thought maybe they were as sad about leaving Hawaii as I was. Then one night when Mother and Father put me to bed, Mother said the doctor had been to see her.

"I remember the peace I saw on her face even as she told me she was going to heaven very soon. I also remember thinking that the doctor was the most awful man on earth. I figured if he hadn't come, then Mother would still be well. Father tried to tell me otherwise, but my mind was made up. When I saw him at the funeral, I thought he didn't look like such a bad man, but my heart was convinced that he'd caused my mother's death."

"And you've been afraid of doctors ever since," Alex finished for her.

Marcail could only nod. She'd never intended to tell anyone that story, but found that a burden had been lifted from her heart. She also found the touch of Alex's arm as it slipped around her the most comforting thing she'd ever felt. Marcail snuggled unreservedly against his side, loving the clean smell of his shirt. Hope burgeoned within her that he might still care.

Neither one talked after that, which was fine with Marcail. She needed the quiet to gather her thoughts and pray about her family meeting Alex. A week ago there would have been grave doubt in her mind, but the train ride had restored her hope. Knowing that Rigg and Katie were going to love this man she had married left her feeling suddenly lighthearted.

Fifty

MARCAIL'S FEET HAD barely touched the platform before Rigg swept her into his arms. She laughed as he released her and turned to hug Kaitlin. After a brief hug Katie surprised Marcail by beginning to chatter in Hawaiian. Marcail, from long habit, answered her sister in kind. Marcail looked thin to Katie, a sure sign that the younger girl had been unhappy. Katie, momentarily forgetting all the wonderful things her father had said about Alex, presumed he was to blame.

Alex stood dumbfounded as Katie spoke swiftly and Marcail answered. He felt like a fool. For months he'd believed his wife knew a simple Hawaiian lullaby because she'd been born in the Islands. Now she stood speaking fluently in a language he had no hope of understanding.

It took a moment to gather his wits and drag his eyes from his wife, and when he did, he looked over to find Rigg grinning at him.

"You're doing better than I did. The first time I heard them go at it, my mouth nearly swung open." Rigg, still smiling, held out his hand to his new brother-in-law. "Welcome to Santa Rosa, Alex."

"Thank you," Alex spoke sincerely, and then glanced again at his wife. "They're not arguing, are they?"

"No," Rigg told him calmly.

"Then you understand them?"

Rigg shouted with laughter. "I don't understand a word of it, but believe me when I tell you, you'll *know* if the conversation turns angry."

Alex could only nod before glancing down beside Rigg and spotting a young girl struggling with a squirming toddler. Rigg noticed at the same time and rescued his daughter Gretchen from the terror of her little brother.

"Alex," Rigg spoke and smiled again, "I'd like you to meet my Gretchen. Gretchen, this is your Uncle Alex."

"Hello, Uncle Alex," Gretchen greeted him politely, and Alex studied the traces of Marcail he saw in her face. He greeted her and gave her his warmest smile.

"And this," Rigg went on, "is Donovan. Donovan, this is your Uncle Alex. Can you say hello?"

Donovan's answer was to shove his thumb a little further into his mouth, but Alex could see the beginnings of a smile. In fact, Donovan must have liked what he saw, because he abandoned his thumb long enough to hold out his arms, inviting Alex to take him. Alex didn't hesitate, and the youngest member of the Riggs family gave his father a cheeky grin as he settled on his new uncle's arm.

Rolling his eyes in amusement, Rigg attempted to draw his other daughter out to be introduced. Gretchen had been a picture of manners and grace. Molly, on the other hand, was not quite so amenable.

"Come on, Molly," Rigg coaxed gently as she hid behind his left leg.

Alex watched as she wrapped her little arms around her father's pant leg and peeked out, ever so carefully, to see him. A huge smile broke over Alex's face; it was like looking at a tiny version of his wife.

Rigg, knowing how Molly was going to appear to Alex, watched the younger man carefully. As he then called Katie over to be introduced, he found himself thinking that although their marriage might have started out as a convenience, without a doubt this man had fallen in love with his wife.

An hour later, Marcail and Alex stood across from each other in Marcail's room. Marcail told herself that she was not going to blush, but she had to tell Alex there was an alternative to sharing the bed. She watched as his eyes took in the one bed, the large dresser with mirror, the dressing screen in the corner, and the oak chest at the foot of the bed.

After he'd looked his fill, Alex's eyes settled on his wife. They were not hesitant or questioning, but steady, waiting for her to make the next move. She did not disappoint him.

"My sister is the soul of discretion, Alex, and if you want, I could ask her for a cot. Or," Marcail went on quietly, "we could share the bed like we did in Fort Bragg."

Alex knew this was not an invitation for intimacy, but that was fine with him at this point; he felt the place for such things was in their own home. He also understood that Marcail had no inkling of how tiring it had been for him in Fort Bragg.

"I have no problem sleeping beside you while we're here, Marcail." Alex stated this carefully, so his wife would know he had not missed her meaning. "However, I rose early and came to bed late in Fort Bragg so you would have privacy. I'd like to get a little more rest while I'm here, and that will probably mean less privacy for you. So you see, the choice is really yours."

Marcail nodded after just a moment's hesitation. "I don't think that will be a problem."

Alex, who'd been holding his bag, then placed it beside the bed. He slipped out of his coat and placed it over a chair. Marcail took her cue from him, and reached for her own bag. She put a few things in the top dresser drawer and then went to the closet in the corner.

A moment later she disappeared behind the dressing screen. Alex, more than a little curious about what she was up to, lounged back on the bed and waited. Less than five minutes passed, and Marcail appeared in a lovely white dress with a round neckline and puffy sleeves. Her hair was down, pulled back at her neck with a white ribbon.

Alex thought she looked like a breath of spring air. She also looked a little flustered over the way he stared, so she explained in halting tones why she had changed.

"It's warm here, and my other dresses are heavy, and well, I—"

"Don't explain, Marcail," Alex said smoothly. "I quite approve. It is hot here, and I hope your family won't mind my shirtsleeves."

Marcail shook her head. "I think you'll find we're pretty relaxed."

They continued to talk until they heard a commotion outside the door. It sounded as if Molly was squealing and Rigg was trying to quiet her. Alex's brows rose in question, but Marcail, as much in the dark as he, could only shrug.

Alex swung off the bed and opened the door so Marcail could precede him out of the room. They walked past the stairs and into the living room. When she saw Molly sitting on her brother's shoulders, Marcail halted abruptly. Alex nearly ran into her.

"Sean!" Marcail whispered, her mouth dropping open in a most unfeminine way.

Sean's smile was boyish as he caught sight of his sister. He swung Molly onto the sofa and crossed the room to hug her. Alex, quietly watching this reunion, had only one thought, *she had never planned on marrying anyone even as tall as I am, but all the men in her life are huge. I've never considered myself short, but Rigg and Sean dwarf me.*

"This is Alex," Alex heard Marcail say before Sean's hand took his own.

"Alex, this is my brother, Sean."

"It's good to meet you," Alex began. "I take it that Marcail knew nothing of this?"

"Right. We meant to be at the train station but didn't get away on time. Charlie?" Sean suddenly called over his shoulder. Alex watched as an adorable redhead approached.

"It's short for Charlotte," she said to her surprised brother-in-law.

Introductions were made all around. Alex met Ricky, who was a picture of Sean, and Callie, whose hair was the exact shade of her mother's. The entire family was gathered in the living room, and things were just settling down when Charlie announced that she was expecting once again. There was another round of mayhem as hugs and congratulations were shared. When the room was finally calm, Alex found himself next to Katie. His voice was very quiet and gentle when he spoke privately to her.

"Unless I miss my guess, you have an announcement of your own to make."

Katie could only stare at him for the space of several heartbeats. "How did you know?" Her voice as soft as his own.

"I'm not sure how I know; I've just always had this knack for sighting such things."

"I haven't even had a chance to tell Rigg."

Alex chuckled at her dry tone. "Then this is decidedly not a good time to reveal your news."

"Is it because you're a doctor?" Katie was still captivated by his perception.

"No, I don't think so. My father and brother are both doctors, but they've never been able to do it. I can't do it unless the woman herself knows, so you must give off some type of signal."

Katie nodded, looking deep in thought.

"I didn't want to intrude," Alex continued, still for Katie's ears alone. "But since you haven't decided whether or not you like me, I'd hoped to do or say something that would put your mind at ease concerning Marcail."

Again Katie could only stare. Had she not been so surprised, she would have blushed to the roots of her hair over being read so easily.

"It must be rather difficult to live with someone who can read your mind," Kaitlin spoke at last. "Poor Marcail, she's never been able to keep a single emotion from her face."

Alex frowned at Katie a moment as he thought of Marcail's reserve in the last weeks.

"You'd be surprised," was all he finally said.

Kaitlin, having had no idea what a sensitive subject this was, was a little taken aback at the look that had passed over Alex's face.

The subject was changed then, but Alex couldn't get his sister-in-law's words out of his head. He wondered if he knew his wife at all.

Fifty-One

THE NEXT DAY was Sunday, and Alex began seeing a Marcail he'd never met before. She was not the normally quiet and thoughtful person she seemed to be at home. She talked almost nonstop and laughed with an abandon he didn't know she possessed.

He continued to pray about their relationship, turning his emotions over to God. He was starting to feel desperate to know which Marcail was really his wife. Unfortunately the events of the morning church service would only cause that desperate feeling to intensify.

Alex met all of Rigg's family, and that was no small group. They were a cheerful, warm bunch, and Alex was grateful for their welcome. He also met many of Marcail's church family. Marcail had told him that Pastor Keller was an excellent Bible teacher, and Alex found himself looking forward to the sermon.

But before it began, Marcail, Kaitlin, and Sean all rose from their seats and moved to the front. Alex saw in an instant that they were going to sing. He knew Marcail had a nice voice, but he also knew how soft it was and wondered if they would even hear her at the back of the church.

They started with a Hawaiian hymn. It was beautiful, and the room was utterly still when Sean soloed. He was a perfect tenor, and Alex couldn't decide which he liked more, Sean's solo or the three voices blended together in perfect harmony. But this was before their second song, an English hymn, during which Alex heard his wife's true solo voice for the first time.

She soloed for two of the verses, and he discovered she had one of the purest, highest soprano voices he'd ever heard. The pews on which the congregation sat literally vibrated with her high notes. Alex was still taking it all in when Marcail returned to sit beside him.

In his confusion, Alex didn't enjoy the sermon nearly as much as he'd anticipated, or the lunch with the family at Rigg's parents' farm afterward. In fact, Alex spent the day under a painful cloud, which he tried to hide by smiling until his face hurt.

Marcail, who was having the time of her life now that she was home, didn't notice that the smile didn't reach Alex's eyes. Not until they returned to the house in the late afternoon and Alex told everyone he was going to take a walk did Marcail stop to think about how quiet he had been all day.

Rigg usually put the kids to bed, but tonight he and Marcail were alone in the kitchen. Katie felt it was best to leave them. Sensing the need for privacy as well, Sean and Charlie put the children to bed with their cousins and stayed in the living room with Katie.

The talk beyond the kitchen door began very lightly, but Rigg's heart was so burdened by what he'd seen on Alex's face during the morning service that he had determined to have a serious talk with his young sister-in-law.

"Was it good to have the school year end?" Rigg asked some minutes into the conversation.

"Yes and no. I'm ready for a break, but I can't think what I'll do to keep busy for the rest of the summer."

Rigg's brow lowered on Marcail's words. She noticed and had the good grace to looked ashamed.

"Tell me something, Marc," Rigg began again, "did Alex know you were going to sing this morning?"

Marcail gave a small, apologetic shrug. "I guess I didn't bother to mention it."

Again Rigg frowned. Things were worse than he first believed.

"Would you be mad at Katie if she hadn't told you?" Marcail asked, seeing his disapproval.

"Not mad, just hurt."

Marcail was not comfortable with that and tried to change the subject, but Rigg would not be swayed. Even though she was growing angry, he kept at her.

"Tell me something, Marcail, did you really get married?"

"What's that supposed to mean?"

"Only that nothing has changed. You still act like the single woman who left here over a year ago."

These words made Marcail furious, but Rigg believed someone had to tell her. "Has he ever seen your anger, Marc? Do you open your heart to him at all?"

"You don't know what you're talking about, Rigg," Marcail said to him, but knew it was a lie. Rigg had guessed perfectly how closed Marcail was to her husband.

"I do know what I'm talking about," Rigg stated emphatically. "Alex Montgomery is a man, with feelings and needs, not some toy for you to play with when your family isn't around."

Marcail jumped to her feet in one angry move.

"Sit down, Marcail!" Rigg commanded.

"Don't you order me around, Rigg. I'm a grown woman!"

"Then act like one." Rigg's voice turned so gentle on those words that it was almost Marcail's undoing. "I realize a person can't force feelings that aren't there, but I've been watching Alex. Marcail, he's in love with you."

Marcail slowly sat back in her chair and stared across the table. "You don't understand, Rigg. I've done something, and I don't know how to undo it."

"Talk to Alex about it," Rigg told her.

"I don't know how."

"Then I'll pray that you'll know, because you're selling him short, honey. I was impressed when I met him last year, and then when your father came back from Willits, he told us he thought Alex was as fine as they came, a real man of God. Give him a chance, Marc; in fact, give him your heart. I can see he would treasure it all the years of your life."

Marcail didn't know what to say, but then she didn't have to. Alex chose that moment to come in the back door.

"Am I interrupting anything?" He glanced at Rigg, but his eyes turned to his wife's strained features.

"Have a seat, Alex," Rigg invited.

It took a few moments for Rigg to bring Alex out, but they eventually began to talk about where Alex had been on his walk. This time it was Marcail who was quiet.

Fifty-Two

Alex, STILL HALF asleep, reached to wipe the hair from his face. It took a moment for it to register that it was not his own. Marcail's back was to him, but she must have just been asleep on his shoulder since his arm ached and her hair was spread across his face and chest like a fan.

Alex stretched, in no hurry to leave the warmth of the bed. It had taken only a few days for Alex to learn that Santa Rosa nights and mornings were cool. The heavy quilts on the bed made it a hard place to leave. That, and knowing that little Donovan was going to join them any minute.

Alex reached for his Bible. He was reading through the New Testament and just finishing the book of Mark. Not many minutes after he'd begun reading he heard the now-familiar thumping on the stairs outside the room. He knew what would come next as the bedroom door crashed back against the wall.

Donovan appeared beside the bed and grinned as soon as he saw Alex's face. Alex reached for him and put him on his chest. His big, dark eyes went to his Aunt Marcail's sleeping form and then back to Alex.

"Shhh," he said, one pudgy finger held carefully to his lips. Alex nodded in approval. Donovan had felt it was his job to wake Marcail the first two mornings they were there, but Alex had taught him that they must be quiet.

Katie came down the stairs and peeked around the corner to check on her small charge. When she left, Alex knew she would head to the kitchen and start breakfast.

Alex let Donovan sit on his chest and chatter softly to him until the smell of fresh coffee floated through the air. Alex rose, pulled on enough clothes to be decent, and went to the kitchen with his nephew.

No one was around, so Alex helped himself to the coffee. He kept an eye on Donovan to see that he didn't get hurt, but at 18 months old, the boy was bent on destruction. He had emptied two cupboards and was started on a third while Alex sipped his coffee.

Alex had just put everything back in the first two when Katie came out of the bedroom right off the kitchen. An experienced mother, she tapped two of the blocks together that sat on the floor near the table. Donovan took the bait. After he'd plopped down on his wellpadded seat, Katie helped Alex right the kitchen.

"I used to sleep as well as Marcail, but that was before children," Katie began conversationally.

"She scared me before I knew how hard she slept," Alex replied. "I checked her repeatedly, thinking she'd stopped breathing."

Katie laughed. "Before Rigg and I were married, he carried me from his parents' living room all the way upstairs. I didn't know about it for some time, but being such a sound sleeper can be very embarrassing."

"Marcail tells me that Sean held her upside down one time and she never woke."

Katie laughed again. "You know, I'd forgotten about that. Older siblings can be pretty awful."

"I never was," Rigg said as he came from the bedroom.

"Of course you weren't." Katie's voice was patronizing. "Tell us Rigg," she continued sweetly, "was it Jeff or Gilbert whom you lowered from the hayloft by the ankles and threatened to drop?"

"Oh that." Rigg was as calm as if it were an everyday occurrence. "It was Jeff, and he asked for it. If you don't believe me," Rigg said to Alex, "ask Bobbie—she has to live with him."

Alex grinned at the light banter. They were really a delightful couple. Alex had never had a marriage like they shared. Linette had been so serious and unhappy, and Marcail kept a carefully erected wall between them at all times. Alex had watched Rigg kiss his wife, hug her, tickle her, and even give her backside a playful smack when she walked by. None of this was offensive to him; it just caused him to yearn for the type of love they shared in his own marriage.

As he sat contemplating the mistakes he'd made in the past weeks, along with the indeterminable future before him, he was forced to ask himself whether Marcail was worth his efforts. Before the question could fully form in his mind, he knew the answer. As the Riggs' kitchen began to fill with people, Alex only half listened to what was going on around him: His heart was silently deciding to court his wife once again.

Marcail noticed the change in Alex even before breakfast was over. She was a little unsure of how to take this new Alex, with his attentive manner and gentle touch. He was acting as he had when they'd first wed, but Marcail, still a little bruised from the weeks of silence, was not sure how to respond.

She was sure of one thing, though. She did want to respond. Rigg had been correct about the way she hid her emotions, and Marcail knew that if she kept it up, it was going to be at her own expense. Right now she was looking forward to a time of new beginnings with her spouse.

Alex was spending the day at the mercantile with Rigg, and Marcail took advantage of the time to pray and ask God to help her love her husband unreservedly. Why she'd never prayed for this in the past was a mystery, but Marcail knew the time for waiting was over. She knew her feelings were not going to change overnight, but at least she was on the road and headed in the right direction.

The morning flew by, but a little before lunch, while Donovan was still taking a morning nap, Katie told Marcail that now was as good a time as any to cut her hair. Katie was wearing her hair a little differently these days, and Marcail wanted the same style.

"I meant to ask you to cut my hair when I was home for Christmas, but now I'm glad I forgot. I want you to take about ten inches off the back, Katie, and I want my bangs just like yours."

"You haven't said anything, so I wondered if you liked the way mine looked." Katie's hand went to the dark thatch of hair that covered her forehead, stopping just above her brows.

"They're darling. I want mine to be the exact length of yours."

Nodding her agreement, Katie knew how easy that would be. She combed and parted Marcail's hair in front, and for a time Marcail couldn't see through the fall of hair covering her eyes. The mirror was handy, however, and as soon as Katie was finished, Marcail checked her work.

"Oh, Katie," she exclaimed.

"Do you like it?"

"Yes!"

"I do too. I can get away with it because my face is round. And they're darling on you because they bring out your beautiful eyes."

Katie was behind Marcail now, brushing her hair straight. She was poised, scissors in hand and ready to cut, when Alex's incredulous voice broke through the air.

"What are you doing?"

Katie froze. Her gaze, along with Marcail's, flew to Alex. He stood in the doorway of the kitchen, his face clearly showing his displeasure. Rigg stood just behind him, and over Alex's shoulder he exchanged a look with his wife.

Just the night before Katie had been saying how she genuinely liked Alex, but she'd always believed Marcail needed someone with a firmer hand.

Rigg and Katie slipped quietly out of the room while Alex took a place at the kitchen table. He picked up a long strand of hair from Marcail's lap and fingered it for a moment. She was still behaving as though she were a single woman. At some point he had to make her understand that he cared enough to be included in every part of her life.

"Why were you cutting your hair?" Alex's question was simple, but it depicted just how complicated their relationship had become.

"Because of the headaches," Marcail explained, still watching his face. She'd never seen him this angry before.

Alex had completely forgotten about her headaches and said as much. "I wish you had talked to me," he added.

"I do too, *now.* But Katie knew I wanted it done and said she had time, so we just—" Marcail shrugged rather helplessly.

Alex reached and brushed his finger through her bangs. "I like the front."

"I'm sorry I didn't talk to you, Alex," Marcail said softly.

"And I'm sorry I was angry."

Alex reached for her face again, this time to brush his finger down her cheek.

"We'll just keep at it, Marcail, until we get it right."

The comment might have seemed cryptic to some, but Marcail caught his full meaning. She nodded ever so slightly, and for the first time in weeks Alex moved close and kissed her softly on the mouth.

Fifty-Three

THE REMAINDER OF the days in Santa Rosa were spent in idle pursuits. Marcail's family came to love Alex and approved of his tender care of Marcail. Sean and Charlotte had people they needed to visit, so some of their days were spent moving about, but Alex and Sean did get to have some time together, and got along famously.

The most memorable of their times together came on an afternoon when Alex and Sean ended up alone with the kids. All three of the women had gone shopping, and after the younger children were down for naps the men began to share. Alex was amazed to learn that Sean's marriage to Charlotte had been forced.

"I didn't even have the luxury of knowing her ahead of time. I saw her, and about ten minutes later, we were married."

Sean went on to explain the entire story about his run-in with the law, and Alex simply stared at him in amazement. When he was through, the room was silent as Alex digested all he had heard.

"But you have made a marriage of it," Alex finally commented, thinking how happy Sean and his wife seemed.

"Yes," Sean told him. "It was not without its pain, but God never gave up on either of us. I love my wife deeply, and I know she loves me. I hope that gives you hope, Alex."

"It does, Sean, thanks. I've made some mistakes, but it's never too late."

"You're right; it's not," he agreed. "I'll be praying for you both."

Alex thanked him just before the older children appeared, claiming to be hungry. The rest of the afternoon was spent playing with little ones and cleaning up their messes.

Marcail and Alex spent time alone together as well. They went for walks, took a boat out on the lagoon, and went out to supper a few times. Mostly, they talked. They cleared the air on many issues. Marcail explained that she had never meant to exclude Alex from her talk with Cordelia Duckworth. She also told him that it had been her lingering fear of doctors that had kept her from telling Alex of her bruises. She explained that her shock at the time had been so great, she had reacted without thought. She then admitted that, once better, the sin of pride reared its ugly head and kept her from approaching Alex sooner.

They talked about Marcail's fear of being herself with Alex, and even though talking about it didn't instantly right the situation, both husband and wife were relieved to have things out in the open. When Marcail asked Alex if he was working longer hours in order to avoid her, he confessed that he had been. For the first time a new understanding was growing between them.

The days flew, and both were surprised when it was time for Alex to leave for Willits. It seemed they had just arrived. Marcail was uncertain as to whether or not she should stay. As Alex packed she talked with him about it.

"Maybe I should come home with you."

Alex was very pleased by her offer, but now that they were once again talking with each other, he had no problem with her staying.

"You still have a few friends you didn't get to see," Alex said, adding, "School begins in less than two months, and then who knows when you'll get back here again."

"That's true," Marcail answered, trying to be as logical as her spouse.

Nothing more was said on the subject, and when Alex was ready, Marcail walked him to the train station. All the nieces and nephews had hugged him goodbye at the house, each one having come to love Uncle Alex. The adults were just as warm in their send-off, and Katie had fixed a huge lunch for him to enjoy on the train.

Once at the station, husband and wife sat quietly waiting for the train to arrive. For a time, both were content to sit and watch the train station activity.

"You will come home to me, won't you, Marc?"

Marcail turned her head as they sat on a bench by the ticket office and gave Alex a quizzical look. "Where else would I go?"

"You might not *go* anywhere. After I leave, you might find you like it better here and—"

"I'll come home," Marcail quietly cut him off. She'd never seen Alex look as hesitant before and found it rather heartbreaking.

"I think," Marcail added, hoping she was not being overly bold, "that the bed will be lonely without you."

Alex wished he could take her in his arms, and his eyes told her as much. "My bed at home is lonely without you too."

Marcail nodded, finding she was unembarrassed for the first time. Nothing more was said since the train was now coming into the station. Alex stood and pulled Marcail around to the quiet side of the ticket office. Without warning, he pulled her into his arms and kissed her as he'd done on the beach in Fort Bragg.

When Alex was finally on board, Marcail stood on the platform and watched the train as it eased out of sight. She found herself wishing she'd followed her heart. If she had, she would have been on the train with her husband.

Marcail closed the book she had been reading to Donovan; he was sound asleep. She knew she could carry him upstairs, but she rather enjoyed the feel of his warm little body snuggled against her own.

Rigg and Katie had gone out for the evening, and when his father had not been there to put him to bed, Donovan dissolved into tears. Both girls had gone to bed without a qualm, so Marcail took Donovan to the living room for a story.

Sean and Charlotte had left the day before for Visalia, to spend some time with Patrick, Duncan, Lora, Sadie, and the church family there. The house was very quiet. Marcail thought she could sit there for hours, holding her nephew and praying.

She ended her prayers by praying for Alex. Marcail couldn't believe how much she missed him. She was scheduled to leave in two days, and the idea of going early was tempting. Since two weeks was barely enough time to exchange mail, they had not tried to communicate, but he had been in her thoughts almost constantly.

After Alex left, Marcail thanked Rigg for his words to her. They had made her stop and think of all she was wasting by distancing herself from a man who obviously cared deeply for her. Marcail was not ready to go home and throw herself into Alex's embrace, but she *was* ready to go home and be herself.

Alex had proved that he was not going to reject her, and Marcail had finally figured out that this had been her deepest worry. There was nothing she had done to cause the death of her mother, or the way her father and then her brother had suddenly exited her life. After each departure, however, she had mentally prepared herself to be a very good girl so they would want to come back.

When Marcail was still a teen, she had done this with God, but her heavenly Father, in His perfect love, showed her that His acceptance was all-encompassing. That wasn't to say she could mindlessly sin and do as she pleased, but it did mean that full fellowship was just a prayer away. Marcail came to understand that God would never cast her aside. Now she was learning that neither would Alex.

It seemed for a time that he had decided she was not worth his effort, but all that was put aside. He had only been taking his cue from her, and Marcail realized she'd been as much to blame as he had.

Marcail hefted Donovan into her arms and took him to bed at last. She stood over his crib for a moment, her mind once again on Alex and what the future of their marriage might be and then on the adorable boy in the crib. She couldn't help but wonder if God would bless her marriage with love, and someday give them a little person like the one who'd fallen asleep in her arms tonight.

Fifty-Four

ALEX STARED AT the howling infant in his hands, still not fully believing he had just delivered a baby. Mother and son were doing fine, and the father was still lying exactly where he'd fallen in a dead faint some ten minutes earlier.

The morning was taking on a feeling of reality. At 5:30 Alex had awakened to the sound of the bell. He was just coming out of the barn with Kelsey when a wagon came tearing up the road. Frank Nelson was the man at the reins, and he had been too frantic to even wait for Alex to come to the office.

Frank breathlessly insisted that his wife was dying. Alex had swiftly tied Kelsey's reins to the back of the buckboard and climbed aboard. He held on while Frank drove to his farm, shouting the events of the past hours as they went.

It seemed his wife's stomach had started to hurt some six hours ago and had slowly worsened. Frank was not too keen on doctors, and since the pains came and went, he had held off coming into town. But about 30 minutes ago, his wife had started to bellow.

Frank shouted to Alex over the sound of the horse's hooves, telling him about the time he'd accidently driven a pickax right through her foot without her so much as making a sound. But after five minutes of her bellowing, he could take it no longer, certain that she was about to die.

It was fully light by the time they reached the house, but Alex would have had no trouble finding it in the dark. He'd have been led by the horrendous cries of the woman within.

Alex entered the house alone and followed the noise to the bedroom. On the bed he found an extremely overweight woman. She gasped for breath as he entered the room and tried to speak.

"I'm Dr. Montgomery, Mrs. Nelson. Can you tell me exactly what's wrong?"

Mrs. Nelson began to do so, crying about her stomach and the fact that she was dying—but before she could finish, she was suddenly gripped with another pain. Alex stood by the bed and watched as she cried out and writhed in agony. He then bent and placed his hand on her enormous stomach.

"Mrs. Nelson," Alex spoke when the worst of the pain had passed. "The pains you're having are not going to kill you. They're perfectly normal; you're having a baby."

A loud crash sounded behind Alex, and he turned to see that Mr. Nelson had come into the room behind him. The big man had hit the floor with an awful thud, but from a distance seemed unhurt. Alex would have checked on him, but Mrs. Nelson's next contraction hit.

"Would you like my assistance?" Alex shouted above her wailing. He went to work after witnessing the frenzied nodding of her head.

Ten minutes later he held a healthy baby boy up for his mother's inspection. Her cries this time were cries of joy, and after Alex had wrapped the baby in a shirt he found on a chair, he placed the tiny scrap of life into its mother's arms.

Mr. Nelson was coming around, and after Alex had a quick wash in the basin, he helped him onto a chair. The man seemed stunned, and Alex knew just how he felt. Some minutes passed before Mr. Nelson moved from his chair to sit on the edge of the bed. It became evident in the next few seconds that there was real love between this hardworking couple as they first stared at their tiny son and then at one another.

"Twenty-three years," Alex heard him say, his voice full of wonder. "Twenty-three years we go childless, and now in the space of a few minutes—" Frank suddenly chuckled. "I thought you were dying, Emmaline."

His wife laughed along. "I thought so too."

Mr. Nelson sobered suddenly. "Even if there hadn't been a baby, Em, I'm still glad you're here."

Alex exited the bedroom on this tender note. He waited in the kitchen for about five minutes, and then Frank called him back in. Alex was profoundly moved at the humble way they thanked him for the life of their son and then asked his fee for the delivery.

He left with the $5.00 in his pocket and a promise from them that they would bring the baby to his office in a week's time. Alex went back home to clean up and head to the office. Marcail was due in that very afternoon. Alex, anticipating her return, had believed the time would drag, but if it continued as it had begun, he had a feeling the day would fly.

Marcail stepped off the train and found a fair crowd of people milling about the platform. She stood still and waited for the throng to clear, and then spotted Alex leaning against the side of the ticket office. His stance was nonchalant, belying the thunderous beating of his heart at the mere sight of his wife. She had an extra suitcase with her, and Alex was pleased that she'd brought some extra dresses back as he'd asked.

Alex pushed away from the side of the building and met her halfway. Wanting to crush her in his arms, he immediately reached for her bags, thankful for something to do with his hands.

"Welcome home," he spoke sincerely.

"Thank you." Marcail smiled at him and bit her lip. He looked wonderful, and as she took in his white shirt, dark hair, and gorgeous blue eyes, Marcail wanted to hug and kiss him for the first time.

Alex led the way as they walked from the train station platform. Marcail looked for Kelsey as they moved, but didn't immediately spot him. She also missed the way Alex turned to watch her once she sighted the horse.

"Where did you get this?" Marcail questioned Alex when her surprised visage took in the small black buggy to which Kelsey was hitched.

"A patient who hasn't paid me in the last year gave it to us. When he saw me at church alone for two Sundays, he thought you'd grown tired of riding on the back of a horse and left me."

Marcail laughed with a mixture of astonishment and pleasure. "Maybe I should go away more often," she teased with exaggerated innocence, as Alex's hands took possession of her waist to swing her aboard the buggy.

"You're not going anywhere for a long time," he growled good-naturedly, with a hint of ownership.

Hearing that tone, Marcail's smile was one of pure contentment as she settled back against the well-padded buggy seat.

Marcail took the next few days to resettle. She cleaned the entire house and spent one day baking, all the while thoroughly loving the feel of being home.

Seth and Allie had eloped while Marcail was away, and this news was all over town. The newlyweds were living in a place near the train station, and Marcail went to see them on her fifth day home. Since her own marriage was becoming more precious every day, Marcail was no longer envious of the happiness she saw in her friend's eyes.

Alex had not pressed her to move from her sofa bed into the bedroom, but even though she'd only been home a few days, he was more attentive and their communication was stronger than it had ever been.

They fell easily back into their routine. Some mornings she was asleep when Alex left for work; others she was up and preparing breakfast. The Monday morning of her second week back was just such a morning. Marcail was up early and had breakfast started, but her face was pensive when Alex entered the kitchen.

Alex showed his pleasure at seeing her by planting a kiss on her cheek. She never stiffened at his touch now, and Alex always felt a bit lightheaded at the lovely smiles she gave him. This morning, however, her smile was somewhat preoccupied.

"I'd like to go see Cordelia Duckworth this morning. Is today good for you?"

"What were you thinking of, midmorning?"

Marcail nodded.

"That's fine. I'll head out pretty soon and then come back for you about 10:00."

"Thank you, Alex," Marcail was deeply moved by his willingness to accompany her.

Knowing that Mrs. Duckworth might refuse even to see her, Marcail spent the morning in prayer. If she refused to see her today, then Marcail would schedule another time. What Marcail had on her mind had to be said.

Fifty-Five

CORDELIA DUCKWORTH DISMISSED her maid with an angry word and turned back to the mirror. Her dress was so tight she could hardly breathe, and she blamed her son Richard for this fact. Richard and a few people from town. They were actually trying to gain control of matters that were lawfully hers to manage. It wasn't the first time the townspeople had tried something like this, and when they did, Cordelia ate.

She was a very big eater on a regular basis, but when upset, her appetite became enormous. Since Richard had been acting so strangely, she had been very upset indeed. Her eyes slid shut on her image as she remembered the argument they'd had a week ago.

"I'm thinking about moving back, Mother."

"Back where?" Cordelia had almost been afraid to ask.

"To Willits, of course. You could keep the west wing," he went on conversationally, "and Beverly, Sydney, and I would take the east wing."

"I will not live with that woman, Richard," Cordelia told him, her voice turning shrill.

"You forget whose house this is, Mother," Richard said coolly. It had taken years of living apart from his mother to finally put his own life together. He now saw Cordelia with new eyes. "I've let you run things for a long time, but lately I've been observing the situation a little more carefully. You've set yourself up as a queen in this town." His voice had turned scornful.

"Father would never have wanted that. Sydney has not been able to speak of it until lately, so I had no idea. What you're doing here is criminal, and it had better stop."

"I will not be talked to this way by my own son. How dare you come here and threaten me—"

Richard's laughter had cut her off. "Threats, Mother? No. Promises. Where Willits and Sydney are concerned, I *will* be more involved in the very near future."

"What do you mean?"

"I mean that if you want to see your grandson, you'll watch your step in this town."

He had never threatened her before, and she was so taken aback she was speechless. It was unfortunate that she chose to remember that scene on this particular morning, since it put her in a horrid mood. She nearly shouted when someone knocked on her bedroom door.

"What is it?"

"The door opened cautiously, and her personal maid tentatively stuck her head in. "Dr. and Mrs. Montgomery are here to see you, ma'am."

Cordelia's brow furrowed, and the maid steeled herself for a hairbrush or some other handy object to fly at the door.

"Tell them I'll be down shortly" was all the older woman said, and the maid, from years of experience, knew enough to close the door without a sound.

Alex and Marcail both looked around the huge living room with something akin to awe. Marcail, of course, had been in this house before, but at the time she had been too nervous to notice much of anything.

Alex commented that their entire house could fit in the living room, and Marcail nodded her agreement. Another five minutes passed, and Cordelia entered.

"Doctor," she greeted him with a regal nod of her head. "Mrs. Montgomery." Again the nod. "To what do I owe the pleasure of this visit?"

There was a bite to her voice, but the young school-teacher chose to ignore it.

"I'm here to discuss my position as Willits' school-teacher for the coming fall." Marcail's voice was quiet and respectful.

"Since you have a two-year contract, I don't believe there is anything to discuss," Cordelia told her simply. "You did break your contract by acting indiscreetly on one occasion," Cordelia went on in a judgmental voice, "but all of that's been forgiven." This last statement was made magnanimously.

"I do not feel I broke my contract," Marcail replied just as respectfully, "although I'm sure you would have preferred to find me frozen in the snow rather than safe and sound in the doctor's home. However I'm not here about that. I'm here about the fact that you and the school board broke *your* part of the contract."

"Well I *never*—" Cordelia was outraged.

"You *will* let me finish," Marcail used her sternest teaching voice. Mrs. Duckworth quieted instantly, and even Alex sat up a little straighter in his chair.

"The contract stated that I was to teach school, and yet you abused your power, and I had only six students in my room. In addition, as the teacher I have the authority to discipline the children, but your grandson was the exception to this condition and was on at least two occasions completely out of control."

Cordelia was livid, but this time was able to keep her voice calm. "Why have you waited so long to come to me?"

Marcail's voice was not accusing, but she spoke truthfully. "I was told quite plainly what your reaction would be if I approached you in any way. The consequences of my being caught in the white-out have proved the extent of your control. Unlike you, Mrs. Duckworth, I will not sacrifice the children's education for my own selfish motives."

Cordelia was now so angry she couldn't have spoken if she tried.

Marcail came to her feet, as did Alex, clearly showing her hostess that she was nearly through. Her voice was sad as she finished what she had come to say.

"Since it seems you cannot handle honest confrontation, I assume you'll now be searching for another teacher for this fall. Should you decide that you do in fact need my services for another term, I will teach on my own conditions. You have until the first day of August to inform me of your decision, and to discuss revisions on my contract."

Marcail turned toward the door but stopped at the sound of Alex's voice.

"There is one condition *I* will change on Marcail's contract should she return in August. She will dress and wear her hair in a manner pleasing to her husband and not the Willits school board."

Alex and Marcail exited then, leaving a silent Cordelia in their wake. Alex treated Marcail to lunch at the hotel before dropping her off at home and telling her he'd see her at supper.

Marcail prayed the afternoon away, knowing she'd done what was necessary, but feeling she may have burned her bridges behind her.

Fifty-Six

MARCAIL'S SPIRITS WERE a bit low in the days following her confrontation with Cordelia, but Alex proved to be a source of great encouragement. He felt she'd handled herself and the situation very well and told her so on several occasions.

They had talked in detail that evening and then prayed together about the future. Other than mealtime prayers, it was the first time they'd prayed as a couple. When they were finished, Marcail felt closer to Alex than ever before.

Marcail's new interest in Alex's work was also bringing them closer together. She found that she enjoyed accompanying him when he made housecalls, the first of which was to the Brents.

Mrs. Brent, Alex told her as they neared the house, was a woman in her sixties, whose frail, sickly body had never dulled her wit or the sharpness of her tongue. Marcail smiled at his description as she took in the neighborhood. The houses on this street were set farther apart than some, but were all quite small. Some of the homes were in disrepair, but most were well kept and welcoming.

The Brent home was one of the loveliest on the street. With yellow paint, white shutters, and a white picket fence along the front yard, the house was very well maintained. Alex held the gate for Marcail's entrance and then followed her up the path to the front door.

The door was opened by a woman in her mid-forties. Her name was Freda, and she was Mrs. Brent's spinster daughter. Freda looked very pleased at their arrival, and once inside she spoke in low tones to the doctor.

"How is she today?" Alex wanted to know.

"The same; certain that you're coming to cure her every ill. She—"

"*Freda!*" A strident voice cut into Freda's sentence. "Who are you talking to?"

Freda's features, already drawn and tired, seemed more so on the sound of that voice. Alex patted her shoulder when she would have answered her mother and then took himself off to the bedroom. Marcail stayed in the kitchen and had coffee with the younger Brent. They chatted easily, but Marcail prayed silently for Alex, since she was certain he was having to deal with an absolute shrew.

"I hope you've come to cure me" were Mrs. Brent's words the moment Alex stepped through the door. They both knew very well that she would never get out of her bed, and Alex had no trouble with the fact that she took her bad humor out on him.

"Well now," he spoke easily, "we'll see what we can do for you today."

Alex was bent over Mrs. Brent, listening to the sounds in her chest, when she noticed Marcail's and Freda's voices. He had just pulled the stethoscope from his ears when she bellowed with outrage and curiosity, "*Who is Freda talking with?*"

"My wife," Alex answered absently, his fingers searching for the pulse in her bony wrist.

"Well, bring her in here. I want to have a look at her." It was an order that Alex ignored. He found her condition just as usual, and regretted the scene he knew would follow when he told her she didn't need a change in medication. Mrs. Brent always took a change in medication as a good sign, but today she was too preoccupied with Marcail's presence to question the doctor's judgment.

"Are you going to bring her in here, or do I have to get out of this bed?"

Alex was putting his things away when she issued this final ultimatum. Still very much in control of the situation, he stepped to the door and called Marcail's name.

Mrs. Brent craned her neck to see around Alex's broad back as Marcail entered the room. Her eyes narrowed when Alex walked her to the side of the bed, her hand held within his own.

"Mrs. Brent, I'd like to present my wife. Marcail, this is Mrs. Brent."

"Hello, Mrs. Brent," Marcail said with a smile, only to have the old woman scowl at her.

"That brown dress is terrible on you," she finally said. "Do you take good care of this man?"

The change in subjects stunned Marcail for just a moment. Not that it really mattered. Mrs. Brent went on to talk of several things, giving Marcail no chance to speak. Neither she nor Alex said a word, and when Mrs. Brent had had her say, she informed the quiet young couple that they could leave now, since she was tired.

"It was nice meeting you, Mrs. Brent," Marcail told her and received a grunt in return.

"I'll see you in a few weeks," Alex added and moved to follow Marcail to the door.

"Doc."

Alex stopped, his hand on the door frame, and looked back to see Mrs. Brent sporting the most unselfish look he'd ever seen on her face.

"You take care of that little girl you've got there," she said seriously, "because you won't find a sweeter wife in all the county."

Alex grinned in her direction and took his leave. Once in the buggy, Marcail questioned Alex about what Mrs. Brent had wanted. Alex didn't give her a direct answer; he was too busy thinking that Mrs. Brent couldn't be more correct.

The month of July, although slow-paced for Marcail, was hectic for Alex. There were days when they barely caught sight of each other. It seemed the bell rang for Alex nearly every night, and if he spent too much time at home for lunch or left the office early on Saturday, the bell would again seek him out.

On the rare evenings they were not interrupted, Alex often fell asleep in his chair. Marcail never minded. It was a simple pleasure to sit and watch him. It was during one of those evenings that Marcail recognized the first stirring of true love for her husband.

The first of August came and went. Marcail had known deep in her heart that she would not be asked back for the fall term. But when the day actually passed with no word from Mrs. Duckworth, it was harder to take than she anticipated. She found herself praying for the teacher who would replace her. God blessed her willingness to trust Him for the future, and soon Marcail saw His hand when she received a surprise visit from Sydney.

It was August 4, and Marcail hadn't seen Sydney since she'd arrived home from Santa Rosa. She had missed him terribly and prayed daily that he would continue to yearn after God. He came directly to the house, and Marcail was a bit concerned when she noticed he had walked rather than been driven in the Duckworth coach.

"Hello, Sydney," she greeted him, joy filling her at the shy smile he bestowed upon her. "Did you walk all the way from home?"

"No, just from downtown."

"Does your grandmother know you're here?"

Sydney nodded, but some of the smile deserted his eyes.

Marcail didn't question his look until he was in the house and seated at the kitchen table.

"How are you getting along with your grandmother this summer?"

"We were doing all right until I found out about you."

Marcail had suspected this might be the reason for his visit. "She told you I wouldn't be teaching?"

"My father came yesterday, and before he left this morning, he and Grandmother had an argument. You could hear them through the whole house. Father was very angry to learn that Grandmother was looking for another teacher. Grandmother was very angry that Father was checking on her business affairs." Tears filled the 12-year-old's eyes. "I don't know what I'll do if you're not my teacher."

Marcail drew him into her embrace. She held him silently for long moments as she chose the right words. With his face cupped in her hands, she spoke.

"I know that you will have a wonderful school year—not because you like the teacher, because you may not, and not because the work will be easy for you, because it may not be, but because you're a new person in Christ. The old Sydney has passed away, and as you learn more about our Lord, He is changing you to be more like Him."

Sydney's young heart was lifted by her words. Marcail saw the relief in his face and pressed a tender kiss to his brow. They talked through the afternoon, the time getting away from them both. Marcail had to rush to get supper on before Alex came in the door, but she did have a meal ready when he arrived. During supper she told him all about the afternoon with Sydney.

"I'm just so thankful, Alex, that the door is still open between the two of us. I was afraid she'd never let him see me again."

"It's got to be our prayers," Alex told her fervently.

"Amen to that," Marcail agreed. She rose to get dessert, and Alex spoke again, having just remembered something.

"Mrs. Nelson paid with a chicken today. I left it in the barn."

"Why would you do that?" Marcail asked as she placed a piece of pie before Alex.

"Well, I didn't think you'd want it in here; it's just in a make-shift cage."

"It's alive?"

Since his mouth was full of food, Alex only nodded, completely missing his wife's horrified stare. Marcail gawked at her husband's bent head and then at her own pie. Her mind ran with things she wanted to say, but she stayed silent. "Maybe I can do it" was her last thought before turning her attention to her own dessert.

"I can't do it." Marcail spoke to the quiet barn as she looked into the dark, inquisitive eye of what was supposed to be dinner.

Nearly 48 hours had passed since Alex had calmly announced that a patient had paid her bill in the form of a live chicken. A determined Marcail had marched out the next day, knife in hand, to do her job. After seeing the chicken, her bravado lasted only a moment before she returned to the house and made vegetable soup.

Now she was back in the barn and wishing she could be any-where else. Katie had always done the butchering when they had been given an animal. Marcail knew that it was a way of life to kill animals for food, but she'd never been able to kill anything larger than an ant. To top it off, "dinner" was starting to look hungry. Marcail shook her head. It was no use. Even if she asked Alex to kill it, she'd never be able to eat it.

With a move born of desperation, Marcail lifted the cage. She carried it to the edge of the woods and opened the funny little door.

The moment the chicken was free, she began to peck around searching for food. Marcail, not wanting to think about how she would explain to Alex, turned and walked swiftly toward the house.

Fifty-Seven

ALEX STABLED KELSEY and immediately noticed the chicken was missing from the barn. He licked his lips in anticipation of what was sure to be a great supper. He knew from weeks of experience that Marcail was a good cook, and he entered the house, a smile on his face, ready for whatever she had prepared.

Unfortunately, one look at Marcail's stern profile told him something was wrong. Since she'd been back from Santa Rosa, he had seen the Marcail that Kaitlin had spoken of—the Marcail whose face showed every emotion. He wasn't exactly certain, but it appeared to him that her tight-lipped silence was from anger. To Alex's mind this made no sense; they'd parted on very good terms at lunch. Alex shrugged mentally and broke the silence with what was sure to be the perfect comment.

"I thought I would smell chicken when I came in the door tonight."

His voice was friendly, and he was totally unprepared for his wife's reaction. Marcail spun to face him so quickly that her hair flared around her back and shoulders.

"I *cannot*," she stated furiously, her eyes flashing with ominous fire, "look something in the eye and then have it on my plate. The next time a patient pays you with an animal, it had better be *dead!*"

Marcail turned away to finish cutting out the biscuits. Her hand was moving the cutter so hard against the breadboard it was leaving marks. Alex was relieved she'd turned her back because his whole body was shaking with silent laughter. He was not quite under control when Marcail turned to look at him and her eyes narrowed with suspicion.

Ten minutes later Marcail finished putting the bowls and plates on the table with unusual force, and they sat down to eat. Alex kept his prayer of thanks very brief. The meal was half over before he decided that Marcail was calm.

"What did you do with the chicken?" Alex asked conversationally.

"I let it go at the edge of the woods," she told him softly. "I just couldn't bring myself to kill it."

"She won't survive, you know," Alex told her, compassion filling his voice. "Some fox or another predator will make a meal of her."

"I hadn't thought of that."

"I'd have been glad to kill it if you'd asked me."

"I wouldn't have been able to pluck it, let alone eat it, once I'd seen it alive."

Alex suddenly began to chuckle again.

"Don't you laugh at me, Alex Montgomery!" Marcail tried to sound stern, but failed.

"Honestly, Marc, my mind raced to figure out what I'd done, and lo and behold I'm in the doghouse over a chicken."

Marcail finally saw the humor in the situation and began to laugh herself.

"I was all right until an hour ago, when I sat here trying to figure out how to tell you what I'd done. Suddenly it all seemed to be your fault, and I worked myself into a fine fury before you hit the door."

Alex was still laughing. "In the future, hang a dishcloth on the door so I'll have fair warning."

After the table was cleared and the dishes put away, husband and wife took a walk. Alex held Marcail's hand, and even though they talked some, most of the walk was spent in quiet reflection and the joy of each other's company. They stopped in a field and were watching the sun sink low in the sky when Marcail asked Alex a question that had been on her mind since they'd left the house.

"Are you upset with me over the way I acted before supper?"

"No."

"Are you sure?"

"I'm sure," Alex told her as he pulled her over to sit next to him on a huge boulder. "I realize it wasn't personal."

A peaceful smile passed over Marcail's face at his words of understanding.

"What does that look mean?" Alex wanted to know.

"I'm just pleased at how comfortable I am with you now."

"I'll admit it's very nice, just as long as you're not too comfortable."

Marcail looked at him with no comprehension whatever. "I don't know what you mean."

"I don't want you to view me as a brother, Marcail, or as a father figure."

Marcail was still not entirely sure what he meant. "Do I do that?"

"I don't think so, but I can't really be sure." Marcail was still looking at him strangely, and Alex knew it was time for some straightforward honesty.

"I'm in love with you, Marcail," he told her without apology, "and I'm not at all ashamed of the desire that love stirs within me. I am glad that you're comfortable with me, but I pray that at some point we'll have an intimate, passionate marriage. That's why I said what I did."

Marcail studied his face in the gathering dusk. "Are you afraid that I'm not a passionate person, Alex?"

Alex chucked softly and cupped her face in his hands. "After witnessing you in the kitchen an hour ago, not in the least."

Marcail smiled, and Alex bent his head. He pressed his lips to her forehead and the tip of her nose before finally claiming her lips. His kisses were tender, yet growing more insistent, and Marcail was taking longer to pull away every time he held her. But pull away she did, and much to his credit, Alex did not rebuke her or so much as frown in her direction.

He took her hand, and they walked back to the house in silence. They retired as usual to their separate beds, but even then Alex knew no frustration. That she was coming around was very evident in her response to his touch. Knowing this, and believing she was well worth the wait, Alex could bide his time.

Fifty-Eight

A WEEK LATER Marcail walked into town just before lunch, a picnic basket swinging from her arm. She still felt compelled to wear dark dresses and her hair up, so the walk was a warm one. Because she was no longer the schoolteacher, Alex had told her he preferred to see her dressed in lighter-colored clothing and with her hair down. In sensitivity to her feelings, however, he left it to her judgment as to when she would start dressing in greater comfort for her visits to town.

Alex's office was on Willits' main street, directly across from the bank and between a tiny dress shop and a lawyer's office. Her face was flushed by the time she arrived, but she knew the surprise she would be giving him would be reward enough for her effort.

Alex did not disappoint her. His eyes lit with delight, and since he had no patients, he took her into his arms and held her for long minutes. They were in the back room, and Alex would have been content to hold her for the next hour, but the outer door opened. He dropped a quick kiss on her upturned mouth and exited the room.

Marcail heard low voices, and then silence. A moment later Alex was calling to her. A man whom Marcail had never seen before stood beside Alex. He was obviously a businessman with his dark suit and shiny shoes. He held a top hat in one hand.

"Mr. Duckworth, this is my wife. This is Sydney's father, Richard Duckworth." Alex had turned to Marcail. "He'd like to speak with you," Alex added.

"It's a pleasure to meet you, Mr. Duckworth." Marcail's smile was pleasant, but her mind was abuzz with reasons why he might wish to see her.

"The pleasure is all mine," Richard told her, and meant it. Sydney had told him that his teacher was beautiful, but Richard, remembering his own hero worship of many of his teachers, had taken his son's words with a pinch of salt. He saw now that he should have heeded them; Marcail Montgomery was a beauty. She also seemed as sweet as she was lovely.

Well, no matter, Richard told himself. She could have the face of a horse, and I'd still think she was beautiful for the changes she's made in my Sydney.

"Why did you wish to see me?"

The sound of Marcail's voice made Richard realize he'd been staring at her like a man who'd taken leave of his senses. He cleared his throat and began.

"First, I'd like to thank you for the time and attention you've given Sydney. It's made a tremendous change in him, and his mother and I appreciate it."

"It really wasn't me, Mr. Duckworth. Hasn't Sydney shared with you—"

"Oh, you mean this God stuff," the older man interrupted. "It doesn't matter how it happened, Mrs. Montgomery, only that something *did* happen. Now," he went on before Marcail could correct him, "I understand that there has been some disagreement over your contract. I'm here to tell you that I want you as Sydney's teacher. Name your terms for this fall, and I'll have the contract typed up this afternoon."

"Is your mother feeling ill?" Marcail asked softly.

Richard stared at her, completely nonplussed. "No," he spoke, his voice filled with confusion. "I just left her, and she was fine."

Marcail nodded. "I do not wish to undermine your mother's authority. I've always dealt with Mr. Flynn or your mother; I can't say I'm very comfortable in doing something without them."

"Oh, well," Richard replied, thinking he understood,

"I'm taking over some of Mother's responsibilities, and since I want you as teacher, I'm here in her stead."

"With her approval?" Marcail went on serenely, and Alex had to fight a smile. He knew her well enough to know she was not as calm as she appeared.

Richard was tempted to lie in answering that question, but the direct, dark-eyed gaze of this diminutive teacher made him feel as though she could read his very thoughts.

"I can see my answer in your hesitation. Please do not think me rude, Mr. Duckworth, but unless your mother contacts me personally, I couldn't consider returning in the fall."

"But Sydney needs you." Richard hoped to appeal to the teacher within her.

"I love Sydney dearly, but I would say that what he needs most is to be living with his mother and father. Surely you've a competent teacher where you live."

"We're moving here," he told her simply, as if this solved everything.

Marcail was surprised, but it did not change her answer. "I'm sure Sydney will be very pleased about that, but as far as my teaching is concerned, I've given you my answer."

"I'm willing to pay you—"

"Please, Mr. Duckworth," Alex cut in, his voice not overly loud, but firm. "My wife has given you her answer."

Richard had nearly forgotten the other man's presence. He looked between the two and felt a little ashamed of how pushy he'd been. The doctor was very protective of his wife, and Richard was the first to know the feeling. His mother hated the mere sight of his Beverly.

"I apologize for my rudeness. I'll let my mother know what you've said, and hopefully I can persuade her to reconsider."

Goodbyes were said all around, and Richard went out the door. His shoes could be heard on the boardwalk for some moments.

Marcail turned to Alex, her eyes wide with disbelief. "Did that really happen, or did I dream it?"

Alex shook his head in wonder. "It happened all right, but I'm not sure when it will really sink in."

"What do we do?" Marcail wanted to know.

"We do what we've been doing all along; we just keep praying." Alex pulled her into his embrace and held her once again.

"For right now, however," he spoke after a moment, "I'd like us to forget about Mrs. Duckworth, her son, and the school long enough to see what my wife brought in her basket."

Marcail smiled and opened the top to reveal a splendid picnic lunch. Alex's brows rose in delight, and he eagerly put his "out to lunch" sign on the door. He then took his wife to a private, shady glen, where he could enjoy her company and her cooking for the next hour.

Cordelia Duckworth's entire body trembled with the emotions running through her. Richard had gone home that day and tried to persuade her to reconsider. Their argument lasted more than a week; it had been a nightmare. Cordelia had stood her ground, even amid threats of never seeing Sydney again.

On the last day, mother and son had had a huge row, whereupon Richard had stormed out of the house. Cordelia had looked up to see Sydney in the doorway. She really scrutinized his face for the first time in days, and knew that what was going on in his own house was tearing him apart.

Richard and Beverly had never visited much before, and Sydney's home with her had been a peaceful one. Now it was one fight after another, and the feud was over a woman Sydney loved with all of his heart.

At first Cordelia had been so jealous of Marcail that she could hardly see straight, but lately Sydney had begun to give more of himself to his grandmother than ever before. She knew it was time to put aside her pride and admit that Marcail Montgomery was the best teacher Willits had ever had, not to mention the best thing that ever happened to Sydney.

Now, because of her love for her grandson, she was in her carriage and headed for the Montgomery home. School was scheduled to resume in three days, and all Cordelia could do was hope that Marcail would reconsider.

Marcail heard the approach of the carriage and looked out, thrilled to know Sydney had been allowed to come for a visit. She took a moment to recover her poise when the black-garbed figure of Mrs. Duckworth emerged from the carriage.

"I'm sorry for coming without an appointment," Cordelia began, "but I hope you'll agree to see me anyway."

"Of course," Marcail told her warmly. "Please come in."

Marcail held the door open, and then followed Mrs. Duckworth inside. With the older woman's back turned, Marcail took a moment to wipe her damp palms together. She then realized with a start that she was wearing a pink calico dress and her hair was hanging down her back. Mrs. Duckworth was taking in the small house and didn't notice Marcail's look of chagrin.

"Please," the young hostess said, suddenly remembering her manners, "won't you have a seat in the living room?"

Marcail had to force her hands to her sides. The temptation to wring them and flutter about was nearly overwhelming. What did this woman want? A sudden thought came to her, and Marcail's heart thundered with concern.

"Mrs. Duckworth, is everything well with Sydney?"

Cordelia took in Marcail's suddenly pale features and felt the first stirrings of warmth for this woman. She also noticed the way the living room was set up like a bedroom and felt guilt—not a comfortable emotion. Into what had she forced this young couple?

"Sydney is very well, Mrs. Montgomery," Cordelia finally answered her. "I thank you for asking."

Marcail was so relieved she sat down in a chair. A moment later she was up again, mentally chastising herself for her breach of manners.

"May I get you some coffee, or something else to drink?"

"No, I won't be staying—" Cordelia stopped midsentence, realizing how thirsty she was. "Some water, please."

Marcail hurried to serve her. After she'd watched Mrs. Duckworth refresh herself, she sat once again and waited, this time in silence.

"I'm sure you must be curious as to the reason for my visit," Cordelia started, and Marcail determined to listen. "I realize we are many days past August 1, but I wondered if you might consider teaching again this fall."

Marcail bit her lip. This reason for the older woman's visit had passed through her mind, but she had dismissed it as impossible.

"Why?" was all Marcail could think to say.

Why Cordelia seemed taken aback.

"Yes. I mean, you must have looked for someone else, and I know you really don't want me as your teacher. Quite frankly, I don't think I could take another year like the last, another year of not having the whole town behind me. It was so hard to teach that way."

Cordelia looked ashamed. Richard was right; she had set herself up as a kind of queen in this town, and everyone hated her because of it.

"Last year is behind us, and I promise you it will not happen again. Richard is taking some of the properties off of my shoulders and—"

"Is that what you want?" Marcail knew she'd interrupted and been impertinent to boot, but suddenly this invincible figure was showing feet of clay, and Marcail was not as intimidated as she'd been before.

Cordelia sighed, seemingly not at all offended by the question. "It's taken some time, but, yes, it is what I want. I'm going to be traveling, and in truth, I'm tired of carrying the full weight on my own." The admission so surprised both women that they were silent for the space of a few heartbeats.

"I would love to come back and teach," Marcail said after some moments. "But it would have to be under the terms I mentioned to you previously, including my hair and dress."

Cordelia's eyes roved over Marcail's trim figure. "I'm sure that will be fine. I'll tell Stanley to work out the details with you. Neither Richard nor I will be on the school board, and I know that Stanley Flynn and the other men have only the town's best interests in mind."

Cordelia stood then, and Marcail followed suit. She moved toward the door, and Marcail thought she seemed defeated. At one time the thought might have pleased her, but not now.

"Thank you for coming, Mrs. Duckworth," Marcail said when it looked as though she would leave without a word.

"I don't suppose we'll be seeing much of each other in the weeks to come, but Sydney keeps me informed." The older woman paused and looked Marcail in the eye. "He thinks the world of you, did you know?"

"I realize that. I think quite of bit of him too."

"Yes, I can see that you do" was all the older woman said as she moved out the door, pulled herself into the carriage, and went on her way.

As the coach pulled away from the house, Cordelia contemplated the serene loveliness of Marcail Montgomery's face. Her home was small and a bit run down, but she seemed as content as a queen in a palace. Cordelia thought about her own home with its servants and beautiful furniture, and knew in an instant that it had never given her an ounce of happiness or peace.

"Her happiness comes from another source," Cordelia whispered as the coach moved along, and for the first time she forced herself to think about all Sydney had told her of his faith in Jesus Christ.

Fifty-Nine

"I'M WORRIED ABOUT this sudden depression you've fallen into," Alex teased Marcail as she nearly danced around the kitchen. It was the first day of school, and she was so excited she could hardly eat. In fact, she hadn't even sat down. She'd had a piece of bread in her hand at one point, but had laid it down and now couldn't find it.

With only three days to prepare, she kept thinking of new items she wanted to take back to school. Alex hadn't seen her standing still since he arrived home after Cordelia Duckworth's visit.

"Is my dress too low?" Marcail asked suddenly, her huge eyes watching her husband's face with concern.

"Simply scandalous," Alex answered with a mock shake of his head. The fabric of the lavender dress was nearly to her throat. "You really should try to eat."

"I will," Marcail called as she darted back into the living room for yet another missing schoolbook. Alex decided to sit back and let her run.

Marcail insisted they leave an hour early so none of the students would arrive and find her not in attendance. She had thoroughly cleaned the room two days earlier, but the first thing she did upon arriving was reach for the broom. Alex sat at her desk and watched her, a myriad of emotions running through him.

452

He was nothing less than thrilled that she had regained her teaching position, but they had been growing so close, and this was one more thing to take her mind from her husband.

Lord, he prayed silently, *I really believe she loves me, but the time hasn't been right for her to say the words. Please help her. Please help her to see that I would never reject her.*

This continued to be Alex's prayer that day and in the days to follow. As before, he did not know the Lord's timing, but as Alex continued to surrender his will and trust in Him, he found God to be sufficient.

The end of the second week of school was upon her, and Marcail waved the children off before straightening up her room for the weekend. Class was going very well, and Marcail couldn't have been more pleased. The students, all but Sydney, were still staring at her hair and clothing, but she knew they would eventually grow accustomed to the different dresses and hairstyle.

Each morning Alex drove the buggy as far as the school, and then left it at the side of the building until he returned for Marcail. For some reason, he was late this day. Marcail didn't mind since it gave her some time to sit and pray.

She poured her heart out to the Lord over her spouse. She now knew she was in love with Alex, but she didn't have the faintest notion as to how to tell him. She knew he would welcome the words, but they simply would not leave her mouth.

She also knew that when she told him, Alex would make her his wife in every way. There was no fear within her at the thought, just a little breathless anticipation. Marcail was finally in a position to heed her sister's words of long ago: "Marc, when the man you marry takes you in his arms, you won't feel fear. You'll desire him as much as he desires you. That's the way God meant it to be."

Marcail now understood those words, but she also knew she was the person who would have to initiate something, and here she drew a blank. She prayed until Alex came for her, but was no closer to a decision than before.

Alex saw that she was very quiet when he picked her up, and assumed she was tired. She was as sweet as ever through the evening, and he even found her watching him on several occasions. When he questioned her, she only shook her head. Alex wished she would share what was in her heart.

Once in bed for the night, Marcail found herself with the same wish. She knew she'd had several opportunities to tell him, but she had stayed silent. Now she wondered how she would feel if he was called away and something happened and he never came back? She would never have had the joy of telling him of her love.

Her tortuous thoughts did not lead to a good night's rest. Within two hours of falling asleep, Marcail awakened in the midst of a vivid nightmare. For the first time in their marriage, Alex woke to find her moving about the house in the middle of the night.

"Marcail?" he called softly to her as he came to the bedroom door. He found her standing before the window, hugging her arms around herself.

"Marcail, are you all right?"

"I'm sorry I woke you."

She sounded breathless, and Alex realized she was crying. He came forward and put his arms around her. She let her back fall against his chest.

"Bad dream?"

"Yes." Her voice was little more than a whisper.

"Want to talk about it?"

Marcail turned in his arms, "I wouldn't have let you fall," she told him, the light from the full moon catching the tears on her face.

"In your dream I was falling?"

"Yes," she said, her voice catching. "You were falling from a cliff, and I was at the top. You kept begging me to catch you. You said if I loved you I would catch you, but I couldn't reach you. I wouldn't have let you fall, Alex—I wouldn't have!"

"Shhh." Alex pulled her against his chest. "It was only a dream. Of course you wouldn't let me fall."

"You don't understand." Marcail pulled away from him, feeling desperate to make him understand. "What if you really did die, and I never told you I loved you. I couldn't stand it, Alex; I just couldn't stand it! I do love you, Alex, more than I can say. I wanted to tell you all evening, but I couldn't find the words."

Alex continued to hold her and spoke softly. "I'm sorry you had the dream, but I'm not sorry about what you told me."

"You don't seem very surprised," Marcail whispered to him and hiccuped.

"I've known for some time that you were in love with me."

"Why didn't you say anything?" This question accompanied yet another hiccup.

Alex chuckled and admitted. "There are some things a man likes to hear voluntarily."

The word "voluntarily" hung between them. Alex's greatest desire was to lift Marcail in his arms and carry her to the bedroom.

But just as he had waited for her admission of love, he also needed to give her time to desire their physical union. In his own mind, the two went hand in hand, but he realized that Marcail probably did not feel that way. He knew he'd done the right thing when Marcail stepped from his arms.

"Better now?" he asked softly.

"Yes, Alex. Thanks."

They moved of one accord then, back to their own beds. Marcail settled in quickly on the sofa, but sleep was miles away.

What did I do wrong? Did he not understand? Marcail didn't know when she'd experienced such confusion. *I think he's taking his cue from me as usual, but I don't know how to do this.*

An image rose in Marcail's mind of Alex taking her in his arms, and she knew real fear that swiftly turned to anger. After turning over uncomfortably on the sofa, she scolded herself.

You're such a coward, Marcail. Afraid of everything including your own husband. When are you going to grow up? Marcail carried on in this vein for the better part of an hour without a single thought of sleep. She remembered much later than she should have that she needed to pray. She had barely said ten words to the Lord, when she realized she *had* to talk with Alex about the way she was feeling.

You know he'll listen, she told herself as she rose from the bed. *However, he might wish you had waited until morning.* Marcail sat up on the edge of the sofa in a moment of indecision. When she finally moved soundlessly through the living room, she had decided on a plan.

The house was very dark, but Marcail moved with purpose toward the bedroom. The door was open, and she stopped on the threshold. Very softly, Marcail called Alex's name, knowing that if he was already asleep her voice wouldn't disturb him.

To Marcail's surprise he stirred instantly. She peered through the darkness as he rustled around and lit the lamp on the bedstand. When the room was illumined in soft light, Marcail saw that Alex had come up to rest on one elbow to watch her in her simple, sleeveless nightgown with its deep V-neck and buttons down the front. Her own eyes went to Alex's bare chest above the sheet and then back to his eyes. After taking a deep breath, she spoke.

"Katie told me a long time ago that when a man and woman are in love, there is nothing to fear. I seem to be struggling with believing her right now. I know I must seem like a child to you, but really I am afraid."

Alex's look was more tender than Marcail had ever seen. She watched him draw the covers back from one side of the bed in invitation. Of their own volition, Marcail's feet propelled her forward. She crawled onto the bed and knelt just a few inches from her husband.

"Katie is right." Alex's soft voice was deep, and Marcail felt a chill down her spine. "There is nothing to fear because we do love each other. I've never thought of you as a child. If you were a child, you wouldn't be ready to be my wife—and you've proved that you are by joining me tonight."

Marcail took great comfort in his words and found that all cowardice had melted away. She leaned forward until her lips found Alex's. She kissed him tenderly and when that wasn't enough, she reached to hold his face in her small hands and kiss him some more, hardly aware of the way Alex's strong arms had come up to hold her.

Alex's own heart threatened to thunder from his chest at her touch as well as the softly spoken words of love she whispered again and again. He knew this was a beginning for them, even as he knew she would spend this night and every night in his arms. Again Alex found himself asking if she had been worth the wait, and without a doubt, he knew that she had.

$\mathscr{S}ixty$

ALEX ARRIVED AT the schoolhouse a little early, so he stood and watched his wife play with the children in the schoolyard. It was a beautiful spring day, and the entire class had joined hands and was moving in a circle. A sweet song rose in the air, and Alex was content to stand and listen.

Alex watched his tiny wife from 15 yards away. Her skirt was dark, but her blouse was snow white, accentuating the dark color of her hair and eyes. He heard her laughter drift through the air and smiled. She was such a delight.

They had been married over a year, and Alex could say in all honesty that it had been the most joy-filled year of his life. The start had not been altogether easy, but now they were as close as a husband and wife could be, and Alex believed that with God as the head of their home, the future would hold many more years of love and joy.

The group broke up some minutes later, and the children greeted Alex as they filed past him up the steps to retrieve books and sweaters. Marcail did not follow them inside, but stood opposite Alex at the bottom of the schoolhouse steps. One little boy, on his way up the stairs, stopped to speak with Alex before going inside. When the child was gone and Alex finally looked up, it was to find Marcail's eyes on him.

"What are you thinking?" he questioned her softly.

"That I love you." Her voice was equally soft.

Very aware that the children would be reappearing at any moment, Alex pointed a finger at her. "That's not fair, Mrs. Montgomery. You're not allowed to say that when I can't kiss you."

Marcail's smile was impish, and Alex's look told her he'd collect that kiss another time. The children did appear just seconds later, and both Marcail and Alex talked with each one as they saw them off for the weekend.

"Mr. Flynn came to see me today," Marcail told him as soon as they were alone.

"About?"

Marcail hesitated. "He wanted me to sign another two-year contract."

Alex's brow rose. "I take it you didn't tell him about the baby."

Marcail frowned, and Alex laughed incredulously.

"Marcail," he said, laughter still filling his voice. "I'm your husband and a doctor. When are you going to believe me?"

"But I don't *feel* pregnant," she protested.

"I assure you, darling, all the signs are there. If it would make you feel better," his voice became very dry, "write Katie and describe your symptoms to her. Having four children makes her the expert."

Now it was Marcail's turn to laugh. She moved close and put her arms around his waist. "I do believe, Dr. Montgomery, that your feelings are hurt."

"No, but when you start to rival Kelsey for size, I'll just say I told you so." Alex hugged her back, and dropped a kiss on her head. "It's certainly a compliment that the board wants you for two more years, but now you have a decision to make."

Marcail leaned back in her husband's embrace, allowing her to see his face.

"Do you really think I'm expecting?"

"Absolutely."

Marcail smiled at the surety in his voice.

"Well, then," she spoke as a smile of pure contentment came over her face, "I believe the decision is already made."

Epilogue

Visalia, California— May 18, 1884

PASTOR SEAN DONOVAN stood at the front of the church and watched as his father came in from the side door, Rigg just behind him. He smiled down into those eyes that were so like his own until he let his gaze travel out over the congregation. He reflected for a moment on how much he liked having a wedding immediately following the sermon on Sunday. It had been Sadie's idea, and an excellent one at that.

Minutes passed and the organ played, allowing Sean to look out at his family and friends. Kaitlin stood with her four—Gretchen, already so tall, Donovan, a sturdy four-year-old and next to him, Molly, still a picture of her Aunt Marcail. Katie held 18-month-old Zachary in her arms.

Charlotte also stood with their own four rascals. Ricky was showing signs of being tall, and Callie was as ladylike as they came. Little Sadie, now three, was such a combination of both of them that Sean smiled at the sight of her. His youngest, Micah, in his mother's arms, was working on his thumb as if he no longer had need of it.

Alex and Marcail stood together, and resting contentedly on Alex's arm was their Megan. She was an adorable dark-haired toddler, and a sign to the family that their beloved Marcail and Alex had found a love to carry them through the years.

Precious friend, Lora Duncan, was in a front pew, alone for the moment. A change in the music drew Sean's attention back down the aisle. Lucas Duncan had entered the back of the church. On Lucas' left arm was Charlotte's aunt, Sadie Cox.

Sadie was dressed in cream-colored linen. Standing poised and serene, she looked straight into the eyes of the man she loved. Sean felt an unexpected rush of emotion when Sadie came to the front, and he saw the look of profound love that covered his father's face for the woman who stood beside him.

They'd both been alone for so very long, and now God had seen fit to bring them together. Sean watched as Duncan kissed the bride's cheek and took his seat next to Lora. Patrick and Sadie joined hands and turned to face him.

"We are gathered today . . ." Sean began the service, his voice confident, yet tender with emotion. Rigg was on hand to provide the rings and sign as official witness. The room cheered at the end of the service when Patrick kissed his wife. Family and friends alike filed out behind the bride and groom for a reception to be held at Duncan and Lora's.

As Sean came down the aisle, he plucked his niece Megan from Alex's arms and carried her outside. Alex and Marcail were the last to leave the building. Once alone, Marcail looked up at her husband, her eyes shining with happiness.

"That was beautiful, wasn't it?"

"Yes, it was," Alex agreed. "But then I've noticed that beauty tends to run in your family."

Marcail grinned at the compliment, and Alex bent to give her a long, loving kiss.

"Hey, you two," Rigg's voice broke in, teasing them from the door. "Break it up. The wagon won't wait all day."

Marcail laughingly jumped out of her husband's arms, pulling her most innocent face to the fore. Alex grinned at his brother-in-law, but pulled Marcail back into his embrace.

"It was a hard wait before I had this woman in my arms, Rigg. You go ahead with the wagon, it'll be worth having to walk."

Rigg stayed on the scene only long enough to see that Alex was kissing Marcail once again. *Yes, I imagine you would say it was worth having to walk,* Rigg thought as he climbed into the wagon next to Kaitlin. He leaned to kiss her and then slapped the reins, putting the vehicle in motion.

"What was that for?" asked a pleasantly surprised Katie.

Rigg smiled, but didn't answer. *Yes indeed,* he repeated to himself. *Worth the walk, and a whole lot more.*